Shadows Beneath the Stars

T.B. Lane

Cover by Meridith J. Albert

This is a work of historical fiction. While the narrative is set against the backdrop of actual events from World War II and features some historical figures, many characters, incidents, and dialogues are products of the author's imagination. Any resemblance to real persons (apart from those clearly identified as historical figures), living or dead, or to actual events is purely coincidental. For dramatic purposes, specific events, timelines, and characters have been altered or invented. The author has strived for historical accuracy, but has taken liberties to serve the story.

Prologue

THE WORLD IN JANUARY 1943 was a place of restless nights and distant thunder.

The Nazi war machine marched through Poland, France, and Belgium, destroying everything in its path; black and red banners with swastikas replaced national flags. American soldiers and sailors were now fighting enemies on two fronts: the Germans in Europe, and the Japanese in the Pacific.

The Holocaust gathered momentum in Europe. Millions of Jews faced an uncertain future, and places like Auschwitz and Treblinka would soon become synonymous with fear and dismay.

Across oceans and continents, the war reached into every home, including small towns across America, towns like Hanford, California.

At Hanford's only hardware store, Weisbaum's, Luke Pierce adjusted the volume of the Emerson radio sitting atop the store counter. Perhaps today would bring news of hope, yet he braced for another sober call to duty. The baritone voice sliced through the quiet afternoon stillness with the day's war update, each word momentous.

"Attention, patriots! In North Africa, the Allies launched Operation Torch. British and American forces have stormed Morocco and Algeria, clashing with Axis defenders under the merciless desert sun. Reports indicate fierce resistance but steady Allied advances across the coastal regions..."

Outside, the world was at war, but inside Luke's battle was silent and unseen. Boys not much older than him, classmates from last year, neighbors from down the street, were out there now, consumed by the war's insatiable demand for fresh bodies. At seventeen, his eighteenth birthday less than nine months away, the war felt close, an approaching storm that grew with each passing day, threatening to consume his future.

"...*This bold invasion seeks to seize control of the Mediterranean, prying open a southern front against the Nazis. General Eisenhower himself has declared the operation vital to Allied strategy in breaking the Axis stranglehold on Europe...*"

Luke switched the radio off. The words pressed in on him, heavy like the damp winter sky. All around him, classmates talked of joining, of duty, and glory. Posters in the Hanford post office and the school hallways showed smiling soldiers waving flags. Even the radio, his link to the broader world beyond Hanford, seemed to speak to him: *Do your part. Be brave. Join the fight.*

His father, Frank Pierce, a veteran of World War I, saw only one way forward for his son: enlistment. But Luke had dreams of a different path. He wanted to learn, to understand, to write. College was a promise that was both inviting and just out of reach; a future that was both incredible and impossible, as the world burned.

Outside, the wind rattled the windows. In the distance, a train whistle sounded, lonely and far away. America was at war, and the way ahead was uncertain, full of shadows and choices. He asked himself the same question he heard everywhere: *Will you go? Will you fight?*

His questions met with silence, but in the quiet, he felt something stir; a stubborn spark that refused to be extinguished.

One

Luke's fingers skimmed the walnut finish of the RCA Model 143, the radio's curves gleaming under his gentle touch. The wood was warm, almost alive, its grain polished to a sheen with Old English Red Oil Polish, applied with a soft cotton cloth. Luke was grateful that his boss, Moses Weisbaum, had given him the priciest polish Weisbaum's sold.

As he continued polishing the prized possession, he brought the fabric close enough to catch a faint whiff of the cedar blended mineral oil, breathing in the pleasant aroma. Finished, he lifted the RCA from the kitchen table, walked into the living room, and placed it carefully on the unpainted wobbly three-legged stool, salvaged just for this purpose.

Surrounded by faded drapes and nicked furnishings, the RCA radio, known as the Tombstone for its resemblance to a graveyard marker, stood like a trophy among castoffs. Sure that the radio was secure on the stool, Luke turned the knob, clicking the radio to life, a dim light emanating from within the cabinet as the tubes warmed. Static confirmed that it was ready. He rotated the dial, finding the familiar broadcaster's voice, then increased the volume.

"...American forces are facing fierce opposition in Guadalcanal, while Russians fight to preserve Stalingrad from advancing German troops..."

The news crackled, sharp and relentless, painting a world unraveling beyond Hanford, the tranquil Central California town. Luke adjusted the dial, coaxing the signal clearer. He loved the radio's precision, the way a twist of a knob could pull voices from all over the country, or across the ocean. It was an object of stability in a house that was volatile and unpredictable.

"Damn Japs," Luke's father muttered from the sagging armchair, his voice thick with malice. "Sneaky yellow devils, bombing us at Pearl Harbor. Now, these islands no one has ever heard of." He waved a hand at the radio, as if the war news was his son's fault.

Luke's jaw tightened, but he kept his eyes on the RCA. His father's slurs were as familiar as the creak of the floorboards at night; *Japs, Krauts, Jews,* whoever he blamed today for food and gas rations, the mill's long hours, or the war's expanding shadow. Luke had learned not to respond to the insults, tuning them out like the radio's static.

Katie, Luke's sister, sat on the couch, hands folded in her lap. Her blue eyes were soft and gentle, accentuated by auburn shoulder-length hair, styled in soft waves. At nineteen, she was the steady one, the one who ironed shirts, cooked supper, and held the house together when their father drank too much. She glanced at her father, her eyes soft but worried, then back to Luke. "Maybe turn it down," she whispered. "It's Sunday."

He hesitated, his fingers hovering over the knob. The radio was his refuge, its voices revealing a world beyond his father's anger. But Katie's voice carried weight. Always had. He nudged the volume lower as the broadcaster's tone shifted.

"*...President Roosevelt pledges more troops to Europe, as Nazi forces tighten their grip...*"

"Jews," Frank spat, leaning forward, face flushed. "They're the ones dragging us into this mess. Those Shylocks in New York, stirring up trouble so they can line their pockets. Always the same. That's why you'll never catch me shopping at Weisbaum's."

Luke's stomach twisted. The word 'Jew' hung in the air, ugly and sharp. He'd heard it before, from boys at Hanford High echoing their parents, or from customers at Weisbaum's when they thought Moses' prices too high. But here, it was heavier, like a millstone weighing their home down. He glanced at Katie, expecting silence.

"Dad, don't," she said, low but firm. "Mom wouldn't have liked you talking like that."

The room froze. Time stopped. Katie never mentioned their mother, not in a way that would have challenged their father. Luke and Katie's mother had died when Luke was eighteen months old, a ghost in their lives, her face a blurred memory they struggled to recall. Frank's eyes narrowed, his hand tightening around the neck of his beer bottle.

"What did you say?" he snarled, his voice threatening.

Katie lifted her chin, though her hands trembled. "I said Mom wouldn't have wanted you hating like that. She was kind. She..."

Frank surged to his feet, the half-empty bottle slamming the table. The force rattled the RCA, and before Luke could react, Frank's arm swung wide, glancing the radio's cabinet. The set tipped, its elegant frame crashing to the floor with a sickening thud. Glass shattered. The broadcast cut to a low hum, then silence.

"No!" Luke lunged forward, blood rushing to his face as he dropped to his knees beside the radio. The walnut case was scratched, the tuning dial bent, and shards of broken vacuum tubes lay scattered on the hardwood floor. His hands shook as he touched the scarred wood, the warmth gone cold. This was his radio—the one thing in this house that wasn't damaged ...until now.

"Get up, boy," Frank snapped, towering over him. "You treat that thing like it's your girlfriend. It's a damn radio."

Luke gulped, but he didn't look up. He cradled the radio's frame, his fingers tracing the destruction. He could fix it, maybe—solder loose connections, replace shattered tubes, sand out scratches—but the thought of it now broken pained him deeply. He wanted to shout, to shove his father back, but the words, the actions, wouldn't come. They never did.

Katie stood, her face pale. "Dad, that was Luke's. You know how much it means to him."

Frank glared at her; his eyes wild. "Don't you talk back to me, Kathrine. You think you can bring up Martha, your mother, like that? Like you know what she'd want?" His voice cracked, not just with anger but something deeper, something raw. *Pain?* "She's gone, don't use her against me."

Luke stiffened, his hands still on the radio. His father never talked about their mother. The agony in his voice was new, a wound he didn't understand. *Why did mentioning her make his father so angry? Why did everything—Jews, the war, even Luke—serve as kindling, fueling his rage?*

Katie stepped closer, her eyes locked on her father. "I'm not using her," she said softly. "I just want us to be a family again. For her sake."

Frank's face twisted, and for a moment, Luke thought he might strike her. But he turned away, grabbing his coat from the hook by the door. "I'll be back," he muttered. "Clean up this mess."

The door slammed behind him, the sound echoing off the walls of the modest room. Luke's pulse raced, his fingers still clutching the radio's frame. His father's chaos was gone, replaced by a mix of fear and questions he couldn't voice. *What did she mean about their mother? Why did Frank hate so fiercely?*

Katie knelt beside him, her hand gentle on his shoulder. "I'm sorry," she whispered. "I shouldn't have said anything. Not yet."

"Not yet?" Luke's voice was gruff, not his own. He looked at her, searching her face for answers. Her warm, expressive eyes were wet, but there was something else there: resolve, maybe, or a secret she wasn't ready to share.

"We'll fix it," she said, nodding at the radio. "You and me. Like always."

Luke nodded. He lifted the prized RCA, its weight heavier, as if it carried Frank's anger and Katie's words. In the silence, he recalled the broadcaster's voice, low but urgent, speaking of troops and battles, a war he couldn't fully grasp. He thought of Stanton's, the mill where his father worked, and Hanford High, the school where boys his age were signing up weekly to join the battle. And he thought of his mother, an elusive shadow he could never reach or hold.

Fighting back tears of rage, he held the broken pieces of the RCA and walked to his bedroom. He sat on the edge of his bed, the disassembled remains of the Tombstone now scattered across the worn quilt like wounded soldiers. Gazing at the broken radio, Luke mused that Tombstone was now the perfect name. Near his leg, Tippy, his faithful miniature collie, whined softly, nudging Luke's hand with his wet nose. The dog's brown eyes, usually bright with playful energy, now held a worried concern, mirroring the turmoil in Luke. Luke remained impassive, his attention fixed on the shattered radio.

Tears that threatened to form were blinked back. He'd taken worse verbal beatings from his father. A damaged radio was fixable or replaceable. But the chasm that had opened between him and his father seemed irreparable, a jagged wound that no amount of sanding or solder could mend. And what did Katie mean by "not yet?" What truth lay hidden beneath the strained silence? His gut twisted with a knot of confusion and a growing dread. He picked up the radio's walnut casing, running his thumb over the smooth wood, now marred with several deep gouges. The radio was more than wires, resistors, and tubes; it was a connection to the world beyond Hanford, to voices that muted his father's never-ending rage. It was an escape, a source of solace in a home desperately in need of an armistice.

Tippy whimpered again, licking Luke's hand insistently. Luke acknowledged the dog's presence, a small comfort in the suffocating weight of his thoughts. He reached down, stroking Tippy's head, the simple act a grounding force in the swirling chaos. The dog leaned into his touch, a low rumble vibrating in his chest.

As he petted the dog's head, he stared at the disassembled radio, the intricate workings now exposed and vulnerable. He could probably fix it, he thought, with enough time and patience. Mr. Weisbaum had taught him some basic electronics. But what about the other broken things—the fractured relationships and the unanswered questions that haunted their house like restless spirits?

Two

THE BELL ABOVE THE store's door jingled as Luke entered, the pleasing, familiar scent of sawdust and linseed oil welcoming him in. Weisbaum's Hardware was a maze of organized shelves; nails in metal tins were sorted by size, hammers were hung by type, and rolls of twine were stacked beside buckets of paint. In the year since Pearl Harbor, the store had grown quieter, customers less frequent as the limits of ration cards curbed purchases. For Luke, Weisbaum's Hardware was a sanctuary, a place where the world made sense, where tools had purpose and broken things could be fixed.

He found the worn wooden broom and began sweeping the floor as he'd done for over a year now. The work was simple: stock shelves, reorganize the nuts, bolts, and screws, and sweep the endless sawdust. It gave him purpose and structure, and the seven dollars a week helped Katie keep the pantry stocked with essentials. Today, though, his mind wandered far from the task at hand. The RCA Model 143 sat in pieces at home, its once-gleaming walnut case now scuffed and cracked, its delicate tubes shattered from his father's violent outburst two weeks earlier. Luke had tried to fix it, but the wire and soldered connections were beyond fixing with his limited tools. Each glance at its broken frame a fresh betrayal.

The cherished radio had been his window to a world beyond Hanford, one that lay outside his father's rage and the suffocating smallness of their home. He'd enjoyed listening to the sounds of Chicago blues, baseball games from New York, and episodes of The Lone Ranger and Superman, often imagining himself far away from the Central Valley heat and dust, a connection now severed.

Moses Weisbaum emerged from the back room, a leather-bound ledger tucked under his arm, wire-rimmed glasses balanced near the end of his nose. At fifty-two, he was paunchy but strong, with salt-and-pepper hair and a face creased with wrinkles, evidence of years of hard, honest work, first as a tailor's son in the crowded streets of Brooklyn, then as a respected shopkeeper in California's heartland. His eyes, sharp but gentle, caught Luke's haphazard sweeping pattern across the wooden floorboards. "You're leaving dust trails everywhere," he said, a placid smile tugging at the corners of his lips. "Something weighing on you?"

Luke paused mid-sweep, holding the broom handle like a humorless dance partner. He liked Mr. Weisbaum's voice, steady and warm, never biting like his father's. "Just thinking about the radio," he admitted, his cheeks flushing with embarrassment over such a trivial concern. "The one at home. It's busted. Beyond repair, I think."

Moses raised a bushy eyebrow, setting the worn ledger on the counter. His fingers lingered on the leather cover, tracing the embossed year, 1943. "Busted how? You're handy with those things. I've seen you tinker with the shop's old Emerson when it acts up."

Luke tensed. He hadn't told anyone about his father's explosive tantrum, the careless wave that had sent the RCA crashing. The memory stung fresh; his father's slurs echoed in the small living room, and the sickening, heart-stopping crash of the radio hitting the hardwood floor. "It was an accident," he said, the lie bitter on his tongue. "Fell off the table during cleaning. Tubes shattered, connections broken, and the case got pretty banged up, too."

Moses nodded slowly, his penetrating gaze lingering on Luke's face, as if he sensed the half-truth. "A shame indeed. That RCA was quite a beauty, from what you've told me. Walnut finish, five bands, right?"

"Six," Luke corrected automatically, a trace of pride cutting through the gloom. "Could pull in stations from Chicago on a good night, Detroit if the weather was just right. I once heard a live Benny Goodman concert from Minneapolis. Clear as a bell."

"Six, then." Weisbaum chuckled, his eyes softening with understanding. "Sounds like it meant a great deal to you."

Luke shrugged, turning back to the broom, sweeping with focused intent, but the words spilled out before he could stop them. "It was the only thing in the house that wasn't... used up or broken down. Made me feel like I could hear the whole world, you know? Not just Dad's..." He stopped abruptly, catching himself mid-confession. Not just his father's drunken rants, he'd almost said. Not just the hatred and bitterness that filled their home like venom, poisoning every corner.

Moses didn't press, but gestured toward the cluttered back room. "Come with me a moment. I've got something I'd like to show you."

Luke hesitated, glancing at the dusty floor, then propped the broom against a nearby shelf and followed Moses. The back room was a treasure trove of organized bedlam; crates of surplus tools stacked to the ceiling, a cracked mirror, a typewriter missing half its keys. Projects in different stages of completion occupied every available surface. Weisbaum knelt beside a wooden crate in the corner, its lid coated in a blanket of dust, and pried it open with a well-worn screwdriver. Inside, wrapped in burlap, was a radio. Not elegant or refined like the RCA, but sturdy and practical. It had a chipped cocoa-colored Bakelite case and a cracked control knob. A Zenith, Luke guessed, maybe from the late 1930s, its speaker frayed at the edges, but otherwise intact.

"It's no RCA Model 143," Weisbaum said, lifting it with careful hands from its makeshift nest. "Found it in a pawn shop in Fresno a few years back, thought I'd fix it up for the backroom, have some company during inventory. Never quite got around to it with everything else. Tubes should still be good. I checked when I bought it, and the wiring appears to be solid from what I can see. Needs a new volume knob and some serious elbow grease to clean it up, but it's essentially sound."

Luke blew out a long breath. He reached out toward the radio, then pulled back, unsure if he understood, afraid to hope. "You're... giving it to me? Just like that?"

Moses' smile was quiet, "Call it a loan, if you like. You fix it up, it's yours to keep. A young man with your knack for radios shouldn't be without one. Not these days, with the war news changing on the hour."

Luke's throat tightened, a lump forming that he couldn't swallow down. He touched the Zenith's case, its chipped surface rough under his fingertips. It wasn't elegant or expensive, not like the RCA with its polished walnut cabinet and gleaming brass dials. But it was solid, real, substantial, a second chance in a house where second chances were scarce. He thought of his father, his rants about Jews ruining the country, and the war being their fault. And here was Weisbaum, a Jew, offering him this gift, not out of pity, but genuine faith in Luke.

"Why...? Why give it to me?"

Moses set the radio on a nearby crate, one of the few with nothing else stacked on it, dusting his hands on his canvas apron. "My father, back in our tiny apartment in Brooklyn, he used to say, 'A man's got to have something to hold onto, something that's truly his own.' For him, it was his Wertheim sewing machine, which he brought from Poland. For you, it seems to be radios and the worlds they contain." He paused, his eyes slits, distant with memory. "I see you in here, Luke, working hard, keeping your head down, doing more than asked. You're a good kid with a sharp mind, but you carry a weight on your shoulders. I don't know exactly what it is, don't need to. I know that having a radio might lighten that burden a little."

Luke swallowed, wanting to tell Moses everything about his father; about the racial slurs that peppered every conversation, and the way innocent mentions of their mother's name turned family meals to mayhem. But the words remained trapped, not yet ready to reveal themselves. He thought of the stories Weisbaum had shared over the months: his parents fleeing violent pogroms in Poland with nothing but their skills, building a life from scratch in America, teaching their son to value hard work, education, and to extend kindness to others. Moses embodied everything Frank Pierce wasn't: steady, generous, patient, a man who built things up instead of tearing them down.

"Thanks, Mr. Weisbaum... er, Moses," Luke said, his voice thick with emotion he fought to control. "I'll fix it. I'll make it work again. I promise you."

"I know you will." Moses clapped a hand on his shoulder, the touch light but reassuring. "And when you do get it working, tune in to something uplifting. Not just war news and casualty reports. Maybe some Artie Shaw or Glen Miller, that's my personal favorite, I prefer swing to classical, but please don't tell anyone from the synagogue." His eyes twinkled with mischief. "Good music keeps the world from feeling too dark in times like these."

Luke managed a smile, the first in days. He lifted the Zenith and carried it to the counter. As Moses returned to his ledger work, Luke's mind raced with possibilities. He'd strip the case entirely, check and replace any questionable tubes, maybe carve a new volume knob from some scrap maple behind the store. It wouldn't be the gleaming RCA, but it would be his creation, a piece of himself that he would keep out of his father's destructive reach.

Outside, the winter light faded to a streaked purple dusk. Luke carried the Zenith radio, thinking of what waited at home: Katie in the kitchen preparing dinner, Frank dozing beneath the Hanford Sentinel, and the broken RCA, sitting in pieces in his closet. He didn't understand why his father was filled with hatred, or what terrible secret lay buried with their mother, that even mentioning her name could trigger outbursts of violence. Glancing at the Zenith, Luke felt a fresh resolve to decide his destiny, not dictated by others, certainly not his father.

Moses Weisbaum, a man whose faith and nationality Frank would curse without hesitation, believed in him. Maybe that belief was enough to start rebuilding what his father had torn down over the last fifteen years.

Journal Entry: *January 12, 1943 – The radio I loved lies broken in the closet. Moses Weisbaum gave me a replacement, plain but functional. I want to strike back and break something of Dad's. Moses urges restraint and says vengeance belongs to God. I wish I understood his faith.*

Three

HUNCHED OVER THE KITCHEN table, Luke chewed absently on his pencil, evaluating the math problem. The evening sunlight filtered through the gingham curtains, casting shadows across his notebook. He'd been working on the question for almost twenty minutes, determined to solve it before dinner. Near the range, Katie hummed a gentle tune as she slowly stirred the bubbling stew, the rich aroma of beef, carrots, and potatoes filling the room. Her apron, once white but now faded, was tied loosely around her slender waist.

The back door banged open with such force that Katie's framed graduation picture nearly fell off the wall. Frank stamped in, the day's Sentinel clutched in his fist, face flushed red with anger, the smell of grain dust and sweat clinging to his clothes. His work boots left small clumps of mud on the linoleum that she had scrubbed earlier.

"They're coming here," he announced, slapping the newspaper down on the table, just missing Luke's homework.

Luke's pencil froze mid-calculation. Katie's wooden spoon still: the only sound, the stew's bubbling.

"What are you talking about?" She asked, turning from the stove, concern etching lines around her otherwise radiant eyes.

"Those damn Japs, that's who," Frank replied, jabbing his calloused index finger at the bold headline: 'JAPANESE INTERNMENT CAMP

TO BE BUILT NEAR HANFORD.' His fingernail, stained with grease and soot from the granary, indented the newsprint.

"The government's setting up one of them camps just outside town. Bringing in hundreds of the enemy right into our backyard." Frank's voice rose with each word, carotid arteries bulging in his neck. "After what these sneaky bastards did last year at Pearl Harbor! All those boys killed!"

Luke dragged the newspaper closer, skimming the article while keeping one eye on his father's agitated movements. The camp, according to the paper, would house Japanese-American families relocated from the coast under Executive Order 9066. Construction would begin next month on farmland ten miles east of Hanford.

"But it says they are citizens," Luke said calmly. "Not soldiers. Families with children and grandparents."

Frank's open hand slammed the table with such force that Luke's pencil rolled off the edge and clattered to the floor. "Don't matter! They have yellow skin and slanted eyes. They're all the same. Spies, the lot of them. Can't trust a single one. Probably sending secrets to Tokyo right now!"

Katie wiped her hands on her apron, leaving damp streaks across the faded fabric. "Dad, please." Her voice held a familiar soothing tone she'd perfected over the years, mediating Frank's outbursts.

"Please, what? You want them here? Living next door? Plotting against us? Planning another attack?" Frank's face grew redder with each question, spittle gathering, then spraying from the corner of his mouth.

Luke thought of Akio Watanabe from his math class, who'd disappeared last month without saying goodbye. His family owned a small grocery store in Lemoore, a few miles west. Akio, second baseman on the Hanford High baseball team, was nicknamed Aki-Joe because he could quote every Joe DiMaggio stat from memory.

"Akio's family is American," Luke said, surprising himself with his courage. "They were born here. His grandfather fought in the last war. For us."

Frank's eyes narrowed, his nostrils flaring. "You defending them now? Weisbaum filling your head with that brotherhood garbage? That old Jew's feeding you ideas above your rank." He spat the word 'Jew' as if it were a foul taste in his mouth.

"It's not garbage to recognize people as people," Luke said, his voice stronger than he expected, emboldened by the memory of Akio's friendship.

"Didn't your family come from Europe? ...and Mom's?" He felt the heat rising in his cheeks.

Katie glanced at Luke, then at Frank, her hand clinching the wooden spoon, anticipating the angry response that was sure to follow Luke's forbidden line of questioning.

"You watch yourself, boy. This town's about to change. And they ain't gonna like it. You'd better figure out which side you're on." Frank jabbed a finger toward Luke. "And leave her out of this, we're talking about Japs! Your mother has nothing to do with this conversation."

Luke held his gaze, something shifting inside him —a surge of courage bursting through the years of accumulated fear. "I know exactly which side I'm on ...and I'll never stop thinking or talking about her! She wasn't only your wife, she was our mother, too."

For almost a minute, there were no words between them. Finally, Frank looked down, snatched the newspaper from the table, and stormed into the living room, slumping into the tattered armchair. The chair groaned under his weight as he snapped the paper open to its full width, creating a physical barrier that isolated him from his children.

Luke glanced at Katie, who gave him a slight shake of her head, a silent warning not to push further, her eyes communicating both pride and fear. But something had awakened in him, a courage he didn't recognize, fueled perhaps by Mrs. Dugan's encouragement to question, to think on his own.

"Dad," Luke said, rising from his chair, the wooden legs scraping against the muddied linoleum. "Those families didn't attack Pearl Harbor. They're Americans who own businesses, go to school, pay taxes..."

"Americans?" Frank lowered the newspaper just enough to peer over the top, his eyes cold and hard as marble. "You think having a piece of paper makes them one of us? They'll never be real Americans. Not with those faces, that language, those customs. Bloodline matters."

"Like the Jews will never be real Americans?" Luke asked, the words escaping before he could restrain them.

The room went still.

"What did you say?" Frank's voice dropped, a thundercloud ahead of the strike.

"I hear how you talk about Moses Weisbaum, and I see the disrespect you show to the Greenbergs. You apply the same slurs to them that you use for the Japanese. You call Moses 'that Jew' behind his back, but you shook his hand when he extended you credit."

Frank stood, newspaper falling to the floor in a cascade of crumpled pages. "You comparing me to something? You calling your father a phony in his own house?"

"I'm saying hate is hate," Luke said, his voice steadier than his legs. "And it doesn't make sense. Not when you look at actual people instead of stereotypes."

Frank's face reddened to a dangerous shade, the vein in his temple throbbing. "You think you know better than me? You think your fancy schoolwork makes you smarter than me, than what I've experienced in my forty-eight years?"

"No, I think books teach us to question. To look beyond what we're told to accept. To see with new eyes."

Frank rose and stepped forward, closing the distance between them. "Well, I think you've been poisoned against your own kind. Made you forget what side your bread's buttered on."

"Moses Weisbaum has helped me to see people as people. And Mrs. Dugan has taught me to stand for my own ideals; that everyone is not an enemy because of where they come from or what they look like."

Frank's laugh was harsh, "People? That's what you call them? Our boys die overseas fighting these animals? American blood soaking foreign soil?"

Katie moved between them, her body a fragile barrier against the mounting tension. "Stew's ready. Let's eat before it gets cold. I made those biscuits you both like." Her voice was light, seeking to diffuse the situation, her recurrent role.

Frank pushed past her, his shoulder roughly bumping hers as he grabbed his coat from the hook by the door.

"Dad, please..." she started, reaching out.

"I'm going out," he growled, yanking the door open. "Can't stand disloyalty in my own house. My son, defending the enemy!"

The door slammed behind him. Luke stood immobile, adrenaline draining from his body, leaving him empty and exhausted.

Katie touched his arm, her fingers warm and reassuring against his skin. "That was brave... stupid, but brave." Her eyes held his, her face a mixture of concern and respect. "He'll cool down. He always does."

Journal Entry: *January 19, 1943 - Dad hates me. No reason. He hates everyone. Does he hate himself? If I say nothing, I'm safe. But it seems like*

I'm betraying who I am. Who am I? What am I if I don't speak up? I wish my mother were here.

The next morning, at school and away from the turmoil at home, Luke entered Mrs. Dugan's English Composition class, the room thick with the lingering pungent odor of the bleach used to mop the floors each night. The wooden desks, worn smooth by generations of students, were arranged in neat rows facing forward. The morning light filtered through the faded yellow shades, casting a shadow across Mrs. Dugan's desk.

Ruth Greenberg stood at the front; her hands clasped behind her. Her dark curls were tied with a simple ribbon, revealing a face set with determination despite the tremor in her lower lip. The chalkboard at her back displayed a jumble of fractions and a crudely drawn map of Europe, the countries' boundaries blurred and faint, mirroring the escalating war. Headlines from yesterday's Hanford Sentinel about Allied advances in North Africa were posted on the bulletin board, a daily reminder of the conflict consuming the world.

Twenty pairs of eyes stalked Ruth, some curious, some hostile, all waiting with an intensity that made the air feel clotted. Above the doorway, the clock ticked, marking each second of the uncomfortable silence. Mrs. Dugan stood by her desk, her graying hair pulled into a bun, her eyes soft but anxious. The creases around her mouth had deepened over the past year. She'd seen the taunts, heard the whispers, and her quiet sympathy for Ruth served as a buffer against the growing storm that seemed to follow the Jewish girl everywhere she went.

"Ruth," Mrs. Dugan said gently, adjusting the collar of her blouse, "please explain the meaning of Yom Kippur to the class." Her voice was kind, but there was a tremor in it, a plea for Ruth to stand tall in a room seeking to crush her. Her fingers tapped the edge of her desk, confirming her awareness of the tension filling the classroom.

Ruth knew why the phrase had been chosen. Yom Kippur, the Day of Atonement, wasn't just a word; it was a spark in a room full of tinder. Many of the other students had been fed lies by their parents, words like *Kike* and *Heeb* spewed with accusation and disgust. Ruth had seen the hate scrawled on her locker only the day before, crude Stars of David that the janitor had partially scrubbed away, leaving blurred shadows behind. She had experienced it in the shoves in the hallway, the seats that emptied when she sat down in the cafeteria, and the invitations she never received. Now, it was a lesson, and every eye was on her, some narrowed with uncomfortable suspicion, others wide with curiosity.

She swallowed; her voice steady but muted. "*Yom Kippur* is the holiest day for Jews. It means 'Day of Atonement.' We fast and pray for twenty-four hours, asking God to forgive our sins. It's about reflecting on what we've done wrong and how to make it right, about cleansing our souls and starting fresh with God and with each other." Her fingers twisted the fabric of her skirt, but she remained calm, dignified, despite the weight of the stares.

A snicker cut through the air like a knife. Johnny White, his blond hair combed back in a duck-tail, popular among the boys, leaned forward in his seat, his voice sharp and cutting. The sunlight caught the gleam of his teeth as his lips curled into a sneer. "Sins? Like causing the war? My father says you Jews are why we're fighting, that you've got your hands in everything, making a profit from both sides. Why don't you atone for that? Maybe fast while our brave soldiers are dying."

The room buzzed with giggles, murmurs, and a few gasps from those shocked by his boldness. Someone in the back whispered something that made others nearby laugh. Ruth's face burned crimson, her eyes looking down at the floor, her shoulders tensing as if bracing for a slap. In the second row, Luke stiffened, his jaw tight, pencil gripped so hard it threatened to snap. He hated Johnny's sneer, despised the way the room fed on Ruth's pain like vultures. Most of all, he hated how it echoed his father's rants, which filled their house with venom. He had tried to explain to his father the previous night, without success, that the classroom should be a place where students look beyond what others have told them to think, discovering the truth and developing understanding.

"John, that's enough," Mrs. Dugan snapped, her voice firm, her eyes flashing with rare anger as she straightened to her full height. She rose and walked to Ruth, placing a hand on her shoulder in a steady, reassuring gesture. Her fingers jittered, but her stance was protective, maternal. "We're here to learn, not to repeat gossip or hate. This is a classroom, not a political rally. Please continue." Luke nodded in support, catching Ruth's eye for a moment, trying to convey solidarity without drawing attention to himself.

She lifted her chin, her demeanor still calm. She thought of her father, his haunted eyes scanning headlines about Europe every evening, the way his hands shook when letters arrived from relatives in Poland. She thought of her mother whispering prayers in the dark, lighting candles on Friday evenings with tears glistening in her eyes. Yom Kippur was more than a day; it was a belief in redemption when the world offered only hate, a tradition that connected her to thousands of years of survival against all odds.

"It matters," Ruth said, her voice growing bolder with each word, filling the suddenly quiet room, "because it's about hope. It's about believing you can be better, even when people..." her eyes centered on Johnny, then away, a flash of defiance in their dark depths, "tell you you're worthless.

It's about not being invited to the autumn dance because of my faith. It's about forgiving those who ignore you or ridicule you. It's about looking inside yourself and finding the courage to change, to admit when you're wrong." Her hands had stopped trembling now, and she stood straighter, her shadow stretching across the floor toward her tormentors.

Johnny shifted, his smirk gone, replaced by an uncomfortable scowl as he stared at his desk. A girl near the front, Ellen, fidgeted with her pencil, her eyes down, a flush of guilt coloring her cheeks. Luke clenched his desk, his chest tight with something he couldn't name; anger, shame, maybe both, as Ruth's words resonated with something deep inside him. Mrs. Dugan's hand squeezed Ruth's shoulder, a silent "well done," her eyes shining with pride.

Ruth's voice softened, but in the silence, everyone could hear her. "Yom Kippur is about carrying on, even when the world hates you for who you are. It reminds us that we're all human, all flawed, and all capable of becoming better than we were yesterday." The morning light caught her face, illuminating the quiet dignity in her expression and the unwavering certainty in her heritage, a certainty that Luke envied.

Mrs. Dugan nodded, her eyes bright, blinking away tears. "Thank you, Ruth. That was beautifully said. You've given us all something important to think about." She squeezed Ruth's shoulder once more. "You may sit."

Ruth returned to her seat, three rows over from Luke, the stares following her like prison searchlights, but Mrs. Dugan's warmth lingered, acting as a shield. Some students looked away, uneasy, while others found a new level of respect.

Luke watched her, his mind racing. He didn't know why her words hit so hard, why they were personal. Something deep within him suggested that he and Ruth shared more than dark curly hair and a love of writing. All he knew was that something in him was changing, a crack in the wall his father had built with years of hate and forbidden questions about his mother. Ruth sat down, her hands still trembling as she opened her textbook, but her spine straight, unbroken by the weight placed upon her young shoulders.

Journal Entry: *January 20, 1943 – Ruth was at home alone while others danced. Does courage come from faith, or faith from courage? I'll ask Moses tomorrow. I envy those who wear their identity with honor. Why can't I?*

Four

Luke stared at the ceiling, Tippy's warm body pressed against his side. The dog's steady breathing was the only sound in the room besides the occasional creak of the old house settling. Outside his window, the January night had turned cold, with fog filling the night sky and a thin layer of frost forming on the glass.

His mind kept returning to Ruth standing in class, her voice gaining strength as she spoke about forgiveness and carrying on despite the undeserved hatred directed toward her. There was something in her words that resonated deep within him, connecting him with her though he hardly knew her. She was attractive, a subtle, natural beauty, but it was not her appearance that drew Luke in. It was something much deeper —a gentle impudence, vulnerable yet unbroken. Yet, most of the students avoided her like she had leprosy.

The Zenith radio sat next to him on the bed, now fully restored. He'd spent hours working on it after school, finding comfort in the logical connections of wires and tubes. Moses had been right; it was something to hold onto, something that was his. Unlike the RCA with its polished walnut cabinet, this radio was scarred but resilient, something he wished for himself.

His fingers stroked Tippy's head as he thought about the patterns emerging around him: his father's hatred, Johnny's disdain, Moses' kindness, Ruth's courage. Different, they were all connected somehow, anomalous pieces of a puzzle he couldn't link.

Tippy shifted, looking up at Luke with longing eyes. The dog didn't care about wars, or religions, or the color of a person's skin; his loyalty was a picture of unconditional love. Luke scratched the collie's neck and sensed the dog's body relax, offering a faint sigh. Pushing his face into the resting dog's furry neck, Luke wished the world could be that gentle, that simple.

The floorboards creaked outside Luke's door. He tensed, recognizing Frank's heavy steps. Tippy's ears perked up, reflecting Luke's sudden anxiety.

Without warning, the door flung open. Frank appeared in the doorway; his shoulder supported by the doorframe. His reddened eyes scanned the radio next to Luke.

"Still tinkering with that junk?" Frank's voice rasped.

Luke's hands stilled over the Zenith's chassis. "It's not junk. Mr. Weisbaum gave it to me."

Frank's face darkened at the mention of the name. "Weisbaum," he spat. "That old Jew has you wrapped around his finger."

The familiar knot formed in Luke's stomach. He'd heard this before, his father's hatred flowing like a river fouled by poison. But tonight, something shifted in Luke. Ruth's courage in class, Moses's quiet dignity stood with him now, invisible allies against Frank's rage.

"He's a good man, and he's not old, probably only five or six years older than you," he said, his voice low but steady. "And he treats people with respect."

Frank stepped into the room, looming over the bed. "What's that supposed to mean?"

"Nothing." Luke focused on the radio, refusing to meet his father's gaze. "Just saying he's decent to folks."

"Unlike me? That what you're getting at?" Frank's fist clenched at his side. "You think I don't know what's decent? You think I don't know what's right?"

The question hung between them. Luke thought of his mother, the ghost whose name could trigger Frank's fury. He thought of Katie saying, "Not yet," and the secrets that haunted their house.

"I don't know what you know, Dad," he said, looking up. "You never talk to me. Not really."

Frank's face contorted, a muscle twitching in his jaw. For a moment, he looked confused, as if Luke's words had struck something unexpected within him.

"Talk to you?" His voice dropped to a treacherous growl. "What's there to talk about? I see you judging me with those eyes, Martha's eyes."

Luke stiffened. His father rarely mentioned his mother—and never and never like this—connecting her to Luke. The comparison seemed to agitate Frank further, his breathing growing heavier.

"You don't know anything," he continued, swaying in the doorway. "Not about life, not about war, not about what it means to lose everything."

"Then tell me," Luke challenged, Tippy pressing closer for comfort, for protection. "Tell me about Mom. Tell me why you hate everyone so much."

Frank's eyes widened, then narrowed to slits. He took a step forward, and Luke instinctively shrank back against the headboard.

"Your mother," Frank started, then stopped, his voice catching. Something flashed across his face. *Pain? Or maybe a memory he couldn't suppress.* "She was..."

The front door slammed, and Katie called out, "I'm home! Mrs. Donovan needed extra help with the twins."

Frank's mouth snapped shut. Whatever vulnerability had appeared vanished just as quickly, replaced by the familiar mask of displeasure. He scowled at Luke, then at the radio.

"Get some sleep," he muttered, turning away. "And keep that damn thing quiet."

He turned and walked out, leaving Luke alone with the unfinished sentence hanging in the air. *What had his father been about to say about his mother?* In that moment, he had glimpsed something beneath his father's rage, something raw, something wounded.

Luke stroked Tippy's back, questions filling his mind. Whatever secret his father carried about his mother, it was entwined with his hatred. Moses was right, hate poisoned from within. And his father had been poisoned for as long as Luke could remember.

He lay awake long after Frank had gone, the radio beside him forgotten in the skirmish. Tippy had fallen asleep, his warm body curled against Luke's leg. The confrontation with his father kept replaying in his mind; not Frank's usual anger, but that moment of hesitation, that unfinished sentence about his mother.

“Your mother, she was...”

What? What was she? Kind, as Katie had suggested? Someone who wouldn't have tolerated Frank's hatred? Or something entirely different?

He'd never known his mother. All he had were fragments; Katie's occasional whispered stories, and Frank's explosive reactions whenever her name was mentioned.

The floorboards in the hallway creaked. Luke tensed, thinking Frank might be returning, but the footsteps were lighter. The door eased open, and Katie's silhouette appeared.

"You awake?" she asked.

"Yeah."

She slipped inside, softly closing the door behind her. In the dim light, Luke could see that her face was teeming with worry. She sat on the edge of his bed, careful not to disturb Tippy.

"I heard Dad in here earlier," she said. "Was he... was he talking about Mom?"

Luke nodded, sitting up. "I think he was about to reveal something about her. Then you came home."

Her shoulders slumped. "I'm sorry. I didn't know."

"Katie," he said, leaning forward, "what did you mean yesterday when you said 'not yet'?"

She looked down at her hands, folding and unfolding them in her lap. "I've been thinking maybe it's time you knew the truth. About Mom, about... everything."

Luke's heart quickened. "What truth?"

Katie hesitated, then lowered her voice to a whisper, glancing toward the door as if worried Frank might be listening. "It's complicated, Luke. And Dad, he doesn't want you to know. He thinks he's protecting you."

"Protecting me from what?" He demanded, irritation creeping into his tone.

"From who you are," Katie murmured. "From who we are."

"Yes, that's exactly what I want to know: who are we?" Luke's gaze fixed on Katie's.

"Well, I'm not sure, but I believe it's connected to Mom's past, her family. I caught Dad talking with Bill next door, and he mentioned Austria. He might have been referring to someone else, but I sensed he was talking about our mother. It's not much information, but it's all I've gathered, more of a gut feeling."

"Protecting? Protection shouldn't involve yelling and overreacting to every reference to her," Luke responded, trying to recall the last time his father had shared anything meaningful. He didn't even know how many years his parents had been married, or whether they were, another of the endless details their father had omitted. Why wasn't there a single picture or any evidence of her existence? It seemed his father had purposely tried to erase her from his life completely, but she was their mother as well, and they had a right to know her, regardless of his father's unrelenting effort to forget.

"I've got a plan, said Katie, "but you'll need to trust me. Try not to bring up the name Martha for the next few days. I'm going to do my best to crack this mystery, with or without Dad."

"Alright. You know I have more faith in you than anyone. I hope you're successful. Something strange is happening; it goes way beyond Dad and this house. I sense it at school, at Weisbaum's. It's like a con..."

"Confluence?" Katie suggested.

"Exactly, like a web of individuals, locations, and events. Somehow, they all bind together. And, it involves you and me."

"I understand," replied Katie, not sure she did. "Tomorrow I'll see if we can't connect some dots."

She stood up from the bed and pressed her lips to Luke's forehead. He felt at ease, sensing his mother would have made the same gesture.

"Thanks, Katie," he said, wishing to express more, but her smile convinced him that his sanction of her plan was sufficient.

Two Lesser goldfinches chirped outside Katie's window, greeting the dawn. She lay still, ears straining to confirm the front door's thump, a signal her father had left for work. Her plan, hatched in whispers with Luke last night, now ready to unfold. She waited a few minutes, then got up, straightened the comforter, and walked down the hall.

She paused at her father's bedroom door, heart pounding. The adventure of uncovering his secret warred with the fear of being caught. She'd tidied his room many times, but today's intrusion felt iniquitous. The knob turned with a faint creak, her hand shaking. She flinched, then stepped into the shadowed space where answers ...or trouble ...lay waiting.

The room was stark: a solitary single bed with a coverlet stretched over the mattress, a walnut-stained dresser with a half dozen drawers opposite the closet, and a small nightstand. A lamp, its shade faded to a murky amber from years of cigarette smoke, and an empty porcelain ashtray were the only adornments.

Katie bypassed the dresser and looked under the bed, then walked to the closet, its neat work shirts, pants, and boots a silent rebuke to her intrusion. On the shelf above were several boxes and a thin photo album. She glanced through the album, which mainly contained pictures of her father from his youth. She returned it and found a worn metal box. As she reached for the box, it slipped, crashing to the floor and scattering its contents. She dropped to her knees, reaching for the spilled items in the dim light.

Propped against a work boot was a silver pendant, triangular in shape, tarnished with age. Katie picked it up and examined it. It bore a gold border and a muted green character or letter she didn't recognize at the center. Inside the border, there were three gold stars, one in each corner, also dulled by time. It had a loop at the top, which she guessed had been connected to a necklace, no longer present. She slipped it into her pocket, heart racing. Close by, she uncovered a photo that showed a couple in their thirties with a girl, six or seven years old, her smile bright, her dark curls framing her young, innocent face. She tilted it toward the light to get a better view; *Martha, our mother?*

In the corner, she sighted a wrinkled envelope, worn from its journey. The canceled stamp read "*Österreich, 20 Groschen, Salzburg 1927.*" It was addressed to Matya Pierce. *Austria*, thought Katie, recalling her father's conversation with the neighbor. She eased the envelope open, revealing a letter, its block letters painstakingly formed:

October 1, 1927

Dearest Matya,

How we miss you. We pray you are well. Here, it isn't easy. Salzburg's gentle days have faded, and so has the kindness of our neighbors. The bakery is quiet; people turn away, whispering "Juden" as we pass, as if we have become strangers in our city. We remember your farewell, the way you clung to Franz and Jenta, your favorite doll in hand. Sending you away was so hard, but it was the only way to keep you safe.

We think of your children, Katherine and Lucas, and wish they could know the laughter that once filled our home. Please, if you can, tell them of us and of the love that endures across oceans.

Write if you are able.

Your loving parents,

Hyman and Vetta

Tears formed as Katie reread the names Katherine and Lucas. Matya, their mother, was Jewish, her heritage buried by their father, even as the radio exposed the certainty of atrocious Jewish ghettos and hateful abuse.

She spotted another photo, face down, which she lifted and turned over. It showed a young woman, sixteen or seventeen, with Luke's wavy hair, brown eyes, and narrow jaw. She pressed it to her chest, sobbing. "Mama," she whispered, the word raw, unspoken for over fifteen years.

The questions came rushing in waves: *Why had her father changed Matya's name and hidden her faith? Shame, fear, something worse? Why had he hidden the letter and the pictures from his children?* She suddenly recalled her father singing lullabies, a distant memory, his voice soft and gentle. *Could that man return? Luke deserved the truth, but could he face it, admit it, and embrace it?*

Tippy barked excitedly, signaling Luke was back. Katie secured the letter and photo in her light cotton robe, vowing to uncover why their father had kept this truth secret and how it mattered, especially with the war closing in on the Pierce home.

Five

THE NUMBER OF PEOPLE at Hanford Station swelled under the April sun, bodies pressed together in anticipation. Luke stood with Katie near the back, his collar damp with sweat, watching as the passenger train from San Francisco crawled to a stop, belching thick clouds of steam across the platform. The locomotive's wheels screeched against the tracks, metal on metal, the sound piercing the murmur of those eagerly waiting.

"There he is," someone shouted, triggering a ripple through the crowd.

Willie Jensen appeared in the doorway of the third car, his Army dress uniform pressed, the olive-green fabric highlighting the Purple Heart affixed to his chest. A white-capped nurse with a stern expression and deliberate movements guided him down the steps, her hand supporting his elbow. His aluminum crutches clicked as he navigated the treacherous gap between train and platform, each movement careful and deliberate, distinct from the athletic confidence he'd once possessed. Where his right leg should have been, the pant was folded and pinned just below the knee, a void that pulled everyone's gaze, despite their efforts to look elsewhere.

The crowd fell silent, the only sounds the distant whistle of another train and the fluttering of the large American flag above the station house.

This wasn't the same young man who'd left Hanford sixteen months earlier, armed with a cocky grin and dreams of glory. That Willie Jensen had sprinted across football fields, his cleats hardly touching the grass as he dodged tacklers. That college-bound athlete had carried Betsy Lawton on his shoulders at the county fair without complaint, laughing and joking as if her weight was nothing. That favored son of Hanford had grinned when they'd waved goodbye and cheered, "Give those Japs what they deserve."

This Willie Jensen's face was aged, with creases beneath his eyes, older by years, not months. His skin was now sallow and gray despite the California sunshine. His once bright eyes, now sunken and shadowed, scanned the crowd, as if viewing strangers in a foreign land rather than neighbors he'd known his whole life. His hands, strong enough to throw a football fifty yards with pinpoint accuracy, now quivered against aluminum supports that held him upright.

Coach Daniels stepped forward first, breaking the paralysis that had gripped the onlookers, clasping Willie's free hand between both of his palms. "Welcome home, son," he said, his voice husky with emotion usually reserved for championship victories, his eyes squinting beneath the Hanford High baseball cap.

The spell broken, the crowd surged, a massive wave of handshakes and back slaps, voices joined in a harmony of gratitude. Willie nodded, smiling without warmth, his eyes blurred and his mind distracted, as if he was seeing beyond those assembled to something distant and terrible. His mother pushed through the throng, her cotton dress wrinkled from the long wait, its blue fabric darkened with swatches of sweat. She wrapped her trembling arms around her son, sobbing into his chest, her fingers clutching his uniform, afraid he might disappear.

"Give the boy room," his father barked, his own eyes damp, his calloused farmer's hand holding his son's elbow. "Can't you see he's tired? For God's sake, let him breathe."

Luke couldn't look away, transfixed by the change, a stark reminder of war's actual cost. Two years ago, he'd watched from the splintered wooden bleachers as Willie scored the winning touchdown against Visalia. The whole town had erupted in a frenzy of community pride. They'd carried him off the field that day, too, but in triumph, not necessity, his face flushed with victory, not the pallid exhaustion it now displayed. Luke remembered envying him then, wondering what it was like to be the center of such adulation. Now, watching Willie's discomfort beneath the town's attention, that envy morphed to sympathy.

Mayor Dickson, seizing the moment with political instinct, spoke about sacrifice and heroism, his voice booming across the platform, as he chose words to evoke patriotism, benevolence, and votes in the upcoming election. Willie stared at a point beyond the crowd, somewhere past one of Stanton's grain elevators that dotted Hanford's skyline. When the mayor handed him a gleaming brass key to the city, Willie's hand trembled so violently that his father had to wrap his thick fingers around his son's wrist to steady it.

"Speech!" someone called from the back, oblivious to the nervous tension in the air.

Willie's eyes focused, hardening as they swept across the sea of expectant faces, neighbors and friends suddenly transformed into an audience he'd never wanted. His jaw tightened, and when he spoke, he had the rasp of someone who had screamed himself hoarse in pain and distress, never fully recovering.

"You want to know what it's like?" His voice cracked, rusty from limited use. "It's not like the newsreels. It's not all glory. It's watching your buddy step on a mine and disappear in a red mist. And it's the smell." He swallowed hard, "You never forget the stench of burning flesh and jungle rot, the way blood turns black in the sun, or the sound a man makes when he's dying and can do nothing to stop it."

His mother touched his arm, fingers quivering against the wool of his uniform. "Willie, honey..." Her voice broke at his name, pleading without words.

"No, Ma. They want to know." His gaze found Luke in the crowd, eyeing him with unexpected intensity, recognition flaring for the first time. "You thinking of signing up, Pierce? You and Brock got big plans?"

Luke's throat dried, words evaporating before they could form, shame and confusion warring in his chest. "I..." The single syllable hung between them, inadequate and incomplete.

"Don't let them fool you, there's no heroes over there. Just scared kids trying not to die in mud so deep you can't see your boots. Nightmares that follow you." His voice dropped to a near whisper that somehow carried across the hushed platform, intimate as a confession. "They don't tell you about the rats that feed on the dead, or how the guys pray for a million-dollar wound, anything to get them out of there. You looking for heroes? Check the caskets."

His father murmured something inaudible, his large hand gentle on his son's back, guiding him toward their waiting Buick, which had been polished specially for the occasion. Mrs. Jensen hovered beside them, dabbing at her eyes with a handkerchief embroidered with Willie's initials.

"The scholarship's gone," Willie called over his shoulder, voice suddenly stronger. "Fresno State's not recruiting one-legged running backs this year. Funny how that works. They say they're sorry, but they're proud of my service." His laugh was sharp, bitter. "Not sorry enough to honor what they promised."

The crowd dispersed in uncomfortable silence, conversations muted, heads bent, averting one another's gaze, as if ashamed to have witnessed such raw truth. Katie squeezed Luke's hand, her fingers cold despite the warm day, her youthful face pale.

"That could be you," she whispered, "If you go, that could be you, wounded, or maybe not coming home at all."

Luke watched the Jensen's car pull away, Willie's profile rigid in the back seat, staring straight ahead as his mother fussed with a blanket for his lap, an unnecessary gesture in the April heat but one of care she couldn't suppress. The boy who'd left Hanford was gone forever, replaced by a man carrying wounds deeper than the missing leg, invisible injuries that no Purple Heart could compensate for, that no welcoming crowd or brass key could restore.

"I've gotta go," he said, pulling away from Katie's grasp, needing space to process what he'd witnessed, to reconcile the recruiting posters' promises of triumph with Willie's shattered reality.

"Where?" Her fingers reluctantly releasing his. "Dad's expecting us for dinner soon."

"To write. To think." *To try and make sense of a world that could transform Willie Jensen from hometown hero to broken stranger in sixteen months. To wrestle with the growing sense that he must face the same crucible.*

He walked home alone, cutting across the park where he and Willie, Brock, and Stevie had played baseball as kids. Willie was always the first one chosen, partly because he was the oldest, but more so because of his athletic prowess, which had been honed by the time he was ten. The image of Willie's empty pant leg burned in his mind, accusatory and prophetic. Not quite the adventure Brock described when coaxing Luke to enlist with Stevie and him. Not the noble cause depicted in the recruitment posters plastered all over town, with their bold calls for duty. Boys returning broken, if they returned at all, carrying scars that would never heal.

When he reached home, he went directly to his room. He pulled out his journal, the leather cover beginning to wear from daily handling, Mrs. Dugan's encouragement resonating in his mind. He opened to the first blank page and started writing about Willie Jensen, about choices that weren't choices at all, not when survival stood in opposition, when staying meant shame and going meant possible destruction.

Journal Entry: *April 15, 1943 - Katie seems troubled. Dad's comments? Hanford wants heroes. Willie's leg, the price of admission. My fate? Not many heroes among farmers or one-legged athletes. The world is destroying itself...one leg at a time.*

Six

KATIE SAT ON HER bed, holding the family relics she had uncovered. The secret she'd kept for two days was ready to be revealed. She heard Luke's footsteps in the hallway, heavy, bogged down with others' expectations that he become a soldier, disregarding his goal of attending college after graduation, only a month away.

"Luke?" she called, soft but urgent. "Can you come here?"

He appeared in the doorway, shoulders slouched. "What's wrong, Katie?" His voice mirrored a fatigue that had settled over him in the past few weeks.

She patted the bed beside her. "I need to show you something."

Luke sank onto the mattress, the worn springs offering little resistance. "You look serious."

Katie's fingers tightened around the recently uncovered treasures. "I found something in Dad's room. It's about our family, things he's kept secret from us."

His brow furrowed. "What kind of things?"

"You have to promise not to tell Dad," she whispered, though they were alone in the house.

"Why can't I tell him?" Luke's tone sharpened, concern overcoming his weariness.

"Just promise, or I won't tell you."

He studied her, then nodded. "Alright. I promise. What is it?"

Katie exhaled, her trembling hand uncurling to reveal the faded photograph and the silver pendant, shining faintly. "These belonged to Mom. From 1927."

Luke's eyes locked on the charm; its meaning unclear. He reached for the photo; his fingers hesitant. The teenage girl in the image gazed back, her dark eyes, curly hair, and high cheekbones standing out. His breath caught. "She looks just... like me."

"She's our mother," Katie whispered. "Her name wasn't Martha. It was Matya. We're Jewish. You and me."

"We're Jewish?" He asked, his voice filled with trepidation. "How do you know? Is Dad...?"

"No, not Dad. Mom. Her parents, our grandparents, Hyman and Vetta Spielmann, they're Jewish. They're in Austria, or at least they were sixteen years ago."

Luke's gaze alternated between the photograph and Katie, his mind racing. "Where did you get this? You went through Dad's room?"

Her shoulders sagged, wilting under the weight of the revelation. "I'm sorry I didn't tell you sooner because I wasn't sure how. Remember last week, when I asked Dad what Mom would've thought about his outbursts? He got so upset. Not just anger. It was like I'd touched a nerve ending, something painful, something he didn't want us to know."

Luke's jaw tightened, "He's always like that when it comes to Mom. Shuts down or blows up. But what does that have to do with this?"

"I couldn't let it go," Katie said, her voice still low. "He's different with you. He looks at me like I'm some treasure, something valuable, but with you... It's like you remind him of something he can't shake. I've seen it for years. It's not fair. You're not a disappointment, but I know he makes you feel like one. I had to know why."

Luke gulped, his eyes glistening. "You think he's ashamed of me?"

"No," she said. "It's not you. That's why I searched his room. I felt like a thief, but I kept going. I found a box in his closet and knocked it off the shelf. A letter, the pendant, the photograph... they were inside."

Luke's fingers traced the pendant's triangular edges. "You said there was a letter?"

"It's from our grandparents. They wrote about Austria, how their neighbors, people they knew and trusted, turned on them because they were Jewish. They sent Mom here with some family members when she was young. That's all I know." Katie rose, her movements slow. She crossed the room, pulled open a drawer, and retrieved the letter. Returning, she handed it to Luke. "Read it."

He gently unfolded the fragile paper, his eyes scanning the faded ink. The words were a window into a world of fear; pleas for Matya to stay safe, anguish at what was consuming their homeland. Luke's hands shook as he looked up. "Why would Dad hide this? Does he... hate that they are Jews? Does he hate us?"

Katie sighed. "I don't know. But it's not just Dad. There's enough hatred for Jews to cover the globe. Think about the report we heard on the radio last week about the Jewish ghettos in Poland and the Soviet Union."

Luke's mind spun, everything coming into focus: muted slurs in hallways, insults eliciting laughter in classrooms, crude words written on lockers. Jews blamed for the war, for rationing, for all that's wrong in the world, suddenly personal. His classmates' jeers at Ruth Greenberg as she described her faith took on a darker edge. His father's relentless pressure for him to enlist, to prove himself, shoving him toward the very same battlefield that might reject him if they knew who he was. For him, being Jewish wasn't just a secret; it was a target.

"What do we do?" Katie asked. "If people find out... especially you, if you have to join the army..."

"I don't know," Luke admitted. "I just know I'm done living in the dark. I'm going to find out why Dad hid this, why he's ashamed of Mom... and me. And I'm going to figure out what's behind all this hate."

Katie reached for his hand, her grip intense. "I believe you will. But be careful. The truth might hurt more than the secrets."

He nodded, the letter still in his hand, its weight pulling him toward a course of events he couldn't yet see. It was no longer about pleasing his father. It was about who he was, and who he'd have to become to face an uncertain world; a world that had a new reason to despise him.

Journal Entry: *April 16, 1943 – My father's anger is a storm I cannot escape. I'm always in its path. His hatred makes me question if he hates himself. Hate doesn't care who you are; it just destroys. Katie found the letter and pendant that explained part of the secret of our mother. I know there's more, and I'm going to find out what it is.*

Luke rose earlier than usual, studied the photograph once more, and dressed, placing the pendant in his front pocket. He arrived at Weisbaum's Hardware, hoping Moses was there. He pushed past the rows of hammers, saws, and nails to the back storeroom.

Moses looked up from behind the workbench where he was organizing a shipment of screws into small metal cases.

"Good morning. You're early today."

Luke nodded, his hand rubbing the concealed pendant. He'd been rehearsing what to say on the walk over, but now that the moment was here, his prepared words would not come.

"Everything all right?" Moses asked, noticing Luke's hesitation.

Luke took a deep breath. "Mr. Weisbaum, I was wondering if you might help me with something. Well, not me exactly. A friend of mine."

Moses set down the handful of brass screws and gave Luke his full attention. "What sort of help do you... Does your friend need?"

"He found something. A pendant, I think. It has some writing on it, and since I work for you, he asked me to show it to you. He thinks it might be Jewish." Luke pulled the treasure from his pocket, the silver triangle catching the light as it dangled from his fingers. "He's curious about what it means."

Moses extended his hand, and Luke placed the object in his palm. The older man's expression shifted as he examined the piece, turning it over with stubby fingers that knew the value of delicate things.

"This is quite old," Moses said, his voice softer than before. He adjusted his glasses and held the object closer to the light. "The tarnish speaks to its age, and it's worn, but the craftsmanship is evident."

Luke scrutinized Moses's face, searching for any sign that his boss suspected the truth.

"The letter in the center is *Shin*," Moses continued, tracing the faded green character with his fingertip. "It's the twenty-first letter of the Hebrew alphabet. It's a very significant symbol in our tradition."

"Significant how?" Luke asked, his brow furrowed, curious.

Moses smiled, the corners of his eyes crinkling. "In many ways. *Shin* is often associated with *Shaddai*, meaning 'Almighty.' It appears on *mezuzahs*."

“What are those?”

"*Mezuzahs* are small cases containing scripture that we affix to doorposts. It's a form of protection, a reminder of God's presence." He paused, studying the pendant again. "This particular style, with the three Stars of David in the corners, and triangular shape, was common among Austrian Jews last century. It's a beautiful piece with a rich history."

Luke's heartbeat quickened. *Austrian Jews.* The connection to his mother's letter was undeniable.

"The triangle represents the spiritual bond linking the divine, the Jewish people, and the sacred teachings," Moses continued, his voice taking on the tone of a teacher. "The Stars are actually composed of two interlocking triangles, one pointing up and one pointing down, and symbolize the relationship of God's protection and the Jewish people's identity. Whoever owned this cherished it. It wasn't merely for decoration; it was a link to their heritage."

Moses looked up at Luke, his eyes gentle but knowing. "Your friend found something very special indeed. And quite valuable, I might add."

Luke swallowed hard. "From what you say, it seems he has."

"And this friend," Moses said, the slight emphasis on 'friend' barely perceptible, "did he tell you how such a rare item came into his possession?"

"He... he didn't tell me," Luke replied, the half-truth suspended between them.

Moses nodded slowly, as if coming to a decision. He didn't press further but continued his explanation. "Itch shows signs of being worn regularly. See how the loop at the top is more tarnished? Someone wore this close to their heart for many years."

Luke thought of his mother, the woman in the photograph whose face he barely remembered. *Had she worn this? Had it rested against her skin as she nursed him as a baby?*

"There's an inscription on the back," Moses said, turning the pendant over. "It's worn, but I believe it says *Mazel*, which means 'luck' or 'fortune.' It's a blessing for the wearer."

Moses handed it back to Luke. "Your friend is fortunate to have found such a meaningful piece. As I said, it carries not just history, but identity."

Luke closed his fingers around the charm, feeling its light weight. "I don't know if I understand everything you said, but if being a Jew means being kind like you, Mr. Weisbaum, I see why people would want to be Jewish... even with all the hatred."

The words came out before Luke could catch them, honest and unfiltered. Moses's eyes widened, then softened with emotion.

"That's very kind of you to say." Moses cleared his throat and adjusted his glasses. "Being Jewish isn't about being any particular way; it's about a connection to something larger than yourself. It's a story that began long before you or me, and will continue long after."

He gestured toward the pendant in Luke's open hand. "Objects like that remind us who we are when the world tries to make us forget."

A hush settled between them, filled with unspoken understanding. Moses broke the silence with a warm smile.

"Well, I believe we have some actual hardware business to attend to. Those shelves won't stock themselves." He picked up his clipboard. "And tell your friend if he has any more questions about his find, or the Jewish faith, I'm always here."

Luke nodded, tucking the pendant back into his pocket. "I'll tell him. Thank you."

As he moved toward the work closet to fetch his apron, Luke weighed his mentor's words. It was no longer just a mysterious object, but a key, the key to a door that had been locked for as long as he could remember. Moses Weisbaum had just helped him understand how to unlock it.

Under the soft glow of his bedside lamp, Luke settled into the quiet sanctuary of his bedroom. The smooth, soulful notes of Benny Goodman's clarinet drifted from the Zenith radio, filling the room with a mellow warmth that calmed his mind. He reached for his journal; its leather cover was supple against his fingers. Flipping past pages filled with hopes, fears, and fleeting dreams, he found a blank page. The world outside faded as he began writing, the words on the paper harmonizing with Goodman's lilting melody.

Journal Entry: *April 17, 1943 - Katie's secret is now mine. I learned that our mother was Jewish. Her name was Matya, not Martha. Moses is wise and has real courage. But I'm not him. Do I get a college degree or an army uniform? Doesn't feel like it's my choice.*

Seven

THE HALLWAY BUZZED WITH the customary confusion of changing classes. Luke spotted Brock and Stevie leaning against the lockers, deep in conversation. He approached them, clutching his textbooks.

"Hey, Pierce!" Brock's face lit up. "Just talking about you."

Luke forced a smile. "Should I be worried?"

Stevie punched his arm. "Nah, just graduation plans. Can you believe it's less than a month away?"

Brock straightened up; chest expanded with pride. "My Pa's got the paperwork ready. Day after graduation, I'm headed to the recruitment office."

"Same here," Stevie added.

They both looked at Luke expectantly. The silence stretched before he cleared his throat.

"I'm still leaning toward college, Cal Poly or USC. It's not certain, both are currently focused on military training, specifically Navy cadets."

"College? Seriously?" Brock's eyebrows shot up. "With a war on?"

Luke shifted his weight. "It's what I want to do. You sound just like my dad, right now. After all these years, where's the encouragement for a friend?" His voice trailed. "...for a son?"

Stevie recovered first. "That's different. You're on the beam. Someone's gotta design the ships and planes."

Brock put his arm around Luke's shoulders. "Think about it, though. The three of us in uniform? We'd be unstoppable."

"If they let us stick together," Stevie added. "My cousin says they do that sometimes."

Luke stepped out from under Brock's grip, needing space. "Can I ask you guys something?"

Both friends stared at Luke, curious about what was to follow.

"What do you think about Ruth Greenberg and Sarah Weiss?"

Their confused expressions told him the question caught them entirely off guard.

"The Jewish girls?" Brock asked.

"Yeah. I see a lot of people picking on them. Why? Because they're Jewish? I don't get it."

Stevie studied the floor. Brock scratched the back of his neck.

"I don't know," Stevie mumbled. "Never really thought about it."

"You've joined in the jeering and the laughter before," Luke pressed. "I've seen it."

Brock's face flushed. "Maybe once or twice. Just going along with everyone else."

"But why? What have they done to deserve it?" Luke asked, his eyes locked on Brock's.

The hallway seemed to be quiet around them, though students still rushed past, eager to beat the bell for the next class.

Brock attempted a grin. "Well, they are Jews, and you know what they say about Jews."

The words hit Luke like a punch to the gut. The same blind prejudice his father spewed now flowed from his friend's mouth.

"You sound just like my dad." Luke's voice turned cold. "And that's no compliment."

"Hey, I was just making a joke."

"Was it funny?"

"I didn't mean anything by it. Anyway, my Pa says they're trouble."

Luke turned to Stevie, who had remained silent. "And you? Why don't you ever stand up for them?"

Stevie shifted uncomfortably. "What am I supposed to do? It's not like I started it."

"Saying nothing is just as bad as joining in. Maybe worse, because you know better, Stevie."

The warning bell rang, sending the few remaining students scurrying toward classrooms.

Luke pulled his books against his chest. "I need to get to class. But think about it. Ruth dared to stand before everyone and endure baseless ridicule. Do you know that she tutors younger kids struggling with math? These same kids' parents call her terrible names behind her back. What's she done to deserve that?"

He didn't wait for an answer, pushing past them. A week ago, he might have laughed at Brock's jesting or let it slide. Now, with the knowledge of his heritage burning inside, every slur, every joke, was personal.

As he slid into the seat at his next class, Luke wondered if Ruth and Sarah felt this alone all the time. He glanced across the room where Ruth sat, her dark curls falling forward as she bent over her notebook. Their features, he understood, came from a shared heritage. It now seemed so obvious. *How had he not noticed before?*

Mr. Belcher began lecturing about European history, but Luke's thoughts remained fixed on the confrontation in the hallway with his best friends. For the first time, he'd spoken up against the casual hatred that permeated his world. He didn't yet understand, but something had shifted inside him. A line had been drawn, and he couldn't retreat.

Journal Entry: *April 19, 1943 - Today, Brock and Stevie laughed about people I now consider family. They don't see the damage. Neither did I until a few days ago. I usually remain silent. So, am I any different from them? Will silence always be my shield?*

A day later, while Luke was squatting with his back to the door, an assortment of nuts and bolts spread out on the hardwood floor, a sudden burst of air brushed against his back, alerting him that a customer had entered Weisbaum's. He looked up from the inventory ledger, his pencil pausing the count.

The man was older, perhaps sixty, with graying hair, a stooped posture, and a tan fedora tipped low over his brow. His coat was patched at the elbows, and he carried a small canvas sack slung over one shoulder, the type often used by couriers. He didn't recognize him, not a regular. *Probably someone passing through town, maybe a peddler or a supplier.* The man's eyes, sharp despite the craggy lines around them, scanned the store before landing on Luke.

"Afternoon," Luke said, his voice polite but clipped, the way Moses taught him to greet customers. "Need help finding something?"

The man dropped the bag, landing with a soft thump. He leaned against the counter, studying Luke like he was calculating the threads on a bolt. "Maybe," he said, his speech thick, an accent Luke couldn't identify. "You the boy who runs this place for Weisbaum?"

"I just work here, sir," Luke smiled, "Mr. Weisbaum's my boss. He's the owner," He glanced toward the back room, where Moses would usually be busy counting or sorting inventory. "He's gone to the bus station to pick something up, and should be back in a few minutes."

"That's okay. You can help me. I need some wire, sixteen gauge, and a half-pound of three-inch ten penny nails."

Luke walked to the back, grateful for the opportunity to give his eyes a break from inventorying. Wire spools hung along the wall, grouped by gauge, an array of white, red, and black. He measured out the length with skillful ease. The stranger followed, his leather boots scuffing the store's floorboards. Luke felt the man's gaze on him, steady, unnerving.

"I'm guessing you're seventeen or eighteen. You enlisting soon?" the stranger asked, his tone casual but probing. "War's gobbling up lads your age."

Luke's hands stilled on the wire cutter. It was as if the stranger could see into his soul. He'd been thinking about the army continually; part of him longing to prove himself, another part of him wanting to escape, to leave Hanford. Perhaps he'd find peace and purpose on the Cal Poly or USC campus, thus avoiding the war altogether. The idea of war—real war, not the radio broadcasts—made his stomach twist. "I'm hoping to enroll in college," he said, realizing the dream was fading. "But if I do enlist, I'll probably wait until after my eighteenth birthday, in August."

The stranger grunted, as if he'd expected the answer. "*Der veg iz finster, ober di shtern shaynen*. The path is dark, but the stars shine."

Luke frowned, snipping the wire with more force than necessary. "What's that mean?" The stranger's words sounded like something Mrs. Dugan would quote from an archaic novel; poetic, but with little contemporary value. He wasn't in the mood for riddles, not with his head full of secrets and mysteries.

The man shrugged, picking up a nail from a nearby bin and rolling it between his fingers. "It's Yiddish. It means life's hard, but there's always something to guide you, even when you can't see it. Like stars in the night."

Luke sighed, wrapping the wire into a small coil. "Sounds like something my English teacher would say. No offense, mister, but right now, I don't need poetry. I'll manage." He turned to fetch the nails; his cheeks flushed with irritation. The man didn't know him, didn't know about the letter, or Frank's hatred, or the way he tensed every time he saw Ruth or Sarah. Stars? *What good were stars when you spent your life hiding in shadows?*

The stranger didn't seem offended. He just smiled; a knowing curve shaping his pursed lips. "You'll see. Keep it in mind when the dark comes."

Luke ignored him, scooping the requested nails into a paper bag. He rang up the order on the clunky cash register, the loud *ka-ching* bouncing off the walls. "That'll be two dollars and eighty cents."

The man handed over a few crumpled bills, his fingers stained with ink. "Keep the change," he said, hefting his sack. "And good luck, son, whatever you decide. Please tell Moe I said hello."

At that moment, the door opened, and Moses stepped in, a thin corrugated box under his arm. "Ezra, how are you, my friend?" he beamed.

The stranger reached his hand toward Moses, then drew it back, allowing him time to set the box down. Foregoing a polite handshake, they hugged fully; the kind of embrace reserved for a special few, if you're lucky.

"Luke, this is my friend, actually my rabbi, Ezra Cohen."

"We've met," Luke replied, sounding much colder than he intended.

"This is a fine young man you've hired, Moe. He's going places, even if the path is dark sometimes," said Ezra, giving Luke a wink.

"Well, I hope he isn't going anywhere for a while. You're right, he is a good young man. I'm lucky I found him."

"Well, nice to meet you, Luke, and I'll see you at synagogue soon, Moe?"

“Wish you weren’t so far away,” Moses said. “Fresno’s not exactly next door.”

Ezra smiled, then excused himself and went out the door.

Shaking his head, Luke watched him go, the bell jingling again as the door swung shut.

Moses clapped Luke’s shoulder, his grip firm. “You’re a good kid, Luke. Don’t let the old guys scare you, least of all the rabbis.” He headed back to the storeroom, humming again, leaving Luke alone with his thoughts.

Dark paths. Shining stars. The phrase was nonsense, the kind of thing elders said to young men to sound wise. He had bigger problems: keeping his mother’s secret, surviving his father’s rage, and figuring out how to face the army without losing himself. *I’m not looking for stars; I’m looking for answers.*

Luke knocked on the massive metal door at the back of Stanton’s Milling main office, carrying a brown paper bag containing his father’s forgotten lunch. Frank had stormed out that morning following a tirade about the war, all that Roosevelt was doing wrong. Luke had been eating his breakfast in silence, avoiding being drawn in as his father cursed the radio announcer reporting the day’s casualties.

Marty Jenkins, the security guard, struggled to open the bulky door. His weathered face crinkled into a half-smile. "Hey there, Luke. Your old man's in the break room with the others. Better hurry. Lunch’s almost over."

Inside, the massive machinery hummed and clanked with a steady cadence. The air was filled with flour particles that clung to everything. Luke's shoes left distinct footprints in the fine powder as he maneuvered between the towering equipment, toward the break area, just a corner of the mill floor partitioned off with stacks of empty grain sacks, a large metal table, and some folding chairs.

As Luke approached, he heard raised voices cutting through the granary's noise. He slowed his steps, the lunch bag clutched tightly.

"Nobody should be locked up for how they look or where their parents came from," said Rodrigo Fernandez, his passionate Hispanic accent thick. "My father saw the same thing happen in Mexico. First, the government takes people's rights; then it takes the people themselves. Puts them in camps, calling them threats. It always starts small."

Luke paused just outside the makeshift break room, standing behind a tall stack of flour sacks.

"They're Japs, Rodrigo," Frank replied, his voice carrying that sharp edge Luke knew well. "Enemy aliens. You want spies running loose all over California? Taking pictures of our shipyards and our factories?"

"They're Americans. Born here, raised here. Just like my children," Rodrigo countered, his gentle tone hardening. "My Emilio was born in the same hospital as your Luke."

"Not the same thing," Frank dismissed.

Luke edged forward enough to see into the break area. Five men sat around the largest table, thermoses and lunch pails scattered between them. His father stood with his back to Luke, neck and ears flushed red with anger, while Rodrigo, directly across from him, jabbed his thick index finger against the tabletop to emphasize his points.

"In Mexico, the government decides who is worthy to be Mexican," Rodrigo continued, his dark eyes intense. "One day you have rights, the next day you don't. You think this is different? Today they take the Japanese, tomorrow who? Mexicans? Chinese?

Frank slammed his palm on the table, making the coffee cups jump. "This is war, dammit! These people look exactly like the enemy that bombed Pearl Harbor. They've got family back in Tokyo fighting for Japan!"

"My son wears an American uniform right now in the Pacific. He writes how his sergeant calls him 'Taco' and is harder on him than others. Should I be in a camp too because my skin is brown and I speak with an accent?"

"Your boy's fighting for America. That's different. Japs, they're..."

"Americans," Rodrigo finished. "Just like him. Just like me. Just like you, Frank."

Another worker spotted Luke hovering at the edge of the break area and nudged another man. Frank turned, surprise and annoyance crossing his face. "What are you doing here? Shouldn't you be in school?"

"Katie sent your lunch," Luke said, holding out the paper bag. "You left in such a hurry this morning."

Frank crossed over and snatched the sack without meeting Luke's eyes. "Fine. Thanks."

Rodrigo smiled sadly at Luke from his seat. "You've gotta good kid, Frank. Thoughtful."

"He's got his studies to worry about, not politics and war talk," Frank muttered, turning away.

"This isn't about politics," Rodrigo said, his gaze moving between father and son. "This is about people. Families. Children."

Outside in the bright afternoon sun, Luke brushed the fine coating of mill dust from his clothes and hair. His mind was processing what he'd witnessed. Someone besides him had challenged his father's harsh views about people who were different. And for once, Frank hadn't been able to storm out and slam a door to end the conversation.

Eight

Mrs. Dugan's English Composition classroom was more frenzied than usual, students forming teams of two for the day's writing assignment. Luke looked up from his desk to see Ruth Greenberg standing in front of him.

"Looks like we're partners," she said, her voice matter-of-fact.

Luke nodded, shifting his books to make room as she pulled a chair to his desk. Mrs. Dugan caught his eye from across the room and gave him a furtive nod, confirming she had paired them deliberately.

"I've got the magazine article here," Ruth said, unfolding the *Life Magazine* dated February 1, 1943, to the article titled: "*Hollywood Takes on Hitler: 'Hitler's Children' and 'Education for Death' Expose Nazi Indoctrination.*"

The two bent their heads over the publication, shoulders almost touching. Luke was drawn into Ruth's presence; the sound of her shallow breathing and the fragrance of her hair shampoo, similar to Katie's. His thoughts turned to their shared heritage, and he wished he could tell her. He cleared his thoughts and turned his full attention back to the magazine splayed on his desk.

"These films sound terrifying," Luke said after they'd read through the piece. "Imagine turning fairy tales into Nazi propaganda."

Ruth nodded. "It says the movie shows German children being taught from infancy. Nazi lullabies, Hitler worship, hatred of Jews. Always, hatred of Jews. At the age of ten, they must join the Hitler Youth. It's the law in Germany."

"The part about racial purity is what gets me," Luke said, pointing to a paragraph. "How they measure skull sizes and check eye color. As if that determines a person's worth. Teaching little kids to treat Jews as worthless pigs. It's pounded into their heads over and over."

Ruth looked at him, calculating how much she should share. "It's not just in films. My uncle's family lives near Warsaw. We haven't heard from them in eight months."

Luke's throat tightened. "Maybe the mail's just delayed because of the war."

Ruth shook her head, "My father got word through connections in Switzerland. They're taking Jews to death camps. Thousands at a time."

The classroom chatter around them seemed to fade away. Luke stared at Ruth, the reality of what she was saying sinking in.

"Death camps?" he asked, eyebrows raised.

"Concentration encampments where they work people to death or just kill them outright." Ruth's eyes were dry, but her voice trembled. "That's what happens when you let hate go unchallenged. When you force it onto your children."

Luke thought of his father's rants, the casual slurs heard around town, and the mockery among the students.

"How do you do it?" he asked. "Come here every day, knowing what people say about Jews, what Johnny said to you in class that day?"

Ruth's mouth curved in a humorless smile. "You mean when he called me a Christ-killer? Or when he said we started the war and profit from both sides?"

"All of it," Luke said.

She looked toward the window, sunlight accenting her shapely figure. "I remember what my grandmother told me. In Poland, they'd be shooting me in the street. In Germany, they'd put me on a train to one of those camps. Here?" She gestured around the classroom. "Here, they just call me names and laugh."

Luke felt shame burn through him, convicted by his silence.

"The article talks about the contrast between Nazi totalitarianism and democratic values," Ruth continued, tapping the magazine. "That's what's at stake. Not just for Jews, but for everyone. If Hitler wins, if his crazy ideas win, we all lose."

Luke nodded slowly. "The films show how they indoctrinate children in Hitler Youth to become what they want: soldiers, fighters, and worst, Jew haters, even Jew killers. They're raising them to believe we're not human." He immediately realized what he had just revealed using the word "we," but made no effort to correct himself.

"That's why this matters," Ruth said, her eyes meeting his. "Words matter. Ideas matter. While we sit here in classrooms learning to read and write, play sports, and go to dances... if we're invited, teens in Germany are putting on brown shirts, being taught to hate, to torment, to kill."

In that moment, Luke saw Ruth, not as the "Jewish girl," but as someone facing unimaginable fears with remarkable courage.

"Ruth, would you like to go to the senior prom... with me?" Luke whispered, leaning back, immediately fearing he had gone beyond the boundaries of their assignment.

"Yes," she replied with a full-faced smile.

Journal Entry: *April 22, 1943 – They'd never guess I'm Jewish, but she does. She sees through me. Exposes my secrets. I want her to know. How can you see something every day and yet not see it at all? Ruth Greenberg is beautiful, inside and out. I need to learn how to dance.*

Bitterly cold for April in Hamburg, Germany, the damp air stung the teen's lungs as he stood at attention, surrounded by a throng of other boys, all in identical jet-black uniforms that proclaimed a unified creed.

The knife's hilt was snug in his grip as he executed the motion with precision. The polished wood pressed against his palm, an extension of his arm. He had performed this ritual hundreds of times, but today was different. Today, he was the leader. The weight of responsibility was intense, but he welcomed it.

"Blut und Ehre!" The words tore from his throat again as he swept the blade in a skillful arc, feeling the collective power of hundreds behind him. His voice reverberated across the square, bouncing off the buildings that had survived recent Allied bombing raids. The ceremonial HJ-Dolch dagger reflected intermittent sunlight, filtered through Hamburg's cloudy gray skies.

His unit captain observed from the sidelines, arms crossed, face impassive, occasionally nodding in approval. The man's uniform was pristine despite the drizzle, his posture rigid, a perfect reflection of the Nazi ideology he represented.

Last week, the leader had pulled the teen aside after drills, in secret, as if he were sharing sacred knowledge. "The *Führer* needs strong men like you, Zobel, men who understand what must be done." The words had been spoken with such conviction that they seemed to pulsate, resonating deep in the teen's psyche. Dietrich 'Dieter' Zobel had nodded, his body tall and straight, absorbing the honor.

"Your file shows exceptional aptitude, Zobel. The SS will welcome you next year, when you have celebrated your eighteenth birthday." To Dieter, the pact was more precious than gold or silver, more binding than any oath he'd sworn to the Reich. The black uniform of the SS materialized as he had closed his eyes and imagined the future.

The promise fueled him now as he barked commands, his voice cutting through the misty air like a knife. The younger boys, aged thirteen or fourteen, watched him with admiration, their eyes wide and hungry for his approval. Their brown shirts, most of which were too large for their growing frames, hung loosely on their narrow shoulders. They wanted to be him. They dreamed of being where he was, leading with the same confidence. The thought filled him with a fresh wave of satisfaction, seeing himself reflected in their eager faces.

Seven years ago, at ten, he'd joined the Jungvolk, the Hitler Youth's preparatory level. Unlike the boys standing before him, his uniform had stretched to fit his physique, his muscles more developed than those of others his age. His mother had pinned his first badge with trembling hands, her eyes bright with pride, "My strong German boy," she'd exclaimed. The memory of her fingers, rough from work yet gentle against the fabric, still buoyed him in the rare moments of doubt.

When he made claims about Jews being inferior to Aryan "pure bloods," his father had given a dismissive, "Nazi nonsense," earning the boy's scorn. His father reminded Dieter that when his mother was gravely ill and they had no money, it was Herr Goldmann, the Jewish pharmacy owner, who had provided vital drugs without charge. Dieter had tilted his head, struggling to bring the memory into focus. He had nodded in agreement, then dismissed the incident with a wave of his hand.

"I'm not weak like you," the boy had responded, his voice high, but firm, shaped by the *Jungvolk's* promises. His father had turned away, frustrated that he could no longer guide his son. The chasm widened, a conflict of opposing ideologies; one poignant, one proud.

A year later, at eleven, he'd taken the iron from his mother's hands as she prepared to press his uniform. "I am Aryan. I can take care of myself." Her hesitant but approving nod helped to seal his path. It had been heavy in his hand, but he refused to show weakness. He'd pressed his uniform that day, and every time since, the creases as sharp as the Nazi doctrine razing his young mind.

Under Adolph Hitler's control, the *Jungvolk* had been his underpinning. He wore the Boy Scout-like badges for camping, marksmanship, and navigation, as examples of his Aryan supremacy. He'd earned them with fervor, collecting them like tokens exhibiting his superiority. His fingers had traced their outlines at night, each one a step toward becoming an ideal Nazi.

He remembered how the *Gruppenführer* had mocked the American Boy Scouts as "Yankee cowards," describing them as soft, their campfires for marshmallows, not conflict. "They learn to tie knots while you learn to overcome the enemy," the officer had joked. The boys had laughed along, their young faces transformed in the campfire's shadows; their innocence sculpted into hate.

At fifteen, he had graduated to the *Hitlerjugend*, whose sole purpose was to prepare him for war. The transition had been marked with blood, his own, from a knife wound sustained during the ceremony. The scar on his palm remained, a permanent reminder of his covenant with the Fatherland.

There were now over eight million youngsters marching under the Hitler Youth banner, all bound by "Blood and Honor!" Dieter Zobel felt it in his bones. This was not a club; it was a forge, hammering him into a soldier, a weapon for the Reich.

The *Hitlerjugend* was now his family. "He who owns the youth, gains the future," the *Gruppenführer* had quoted Hitler, his voice reverent as if reciting holy scripture. Dieter believed it, pronouncing with fervor, "I am yours, my *Führer!*" While he had hesitated to say the words the first time, they now flowed as naturally as his breath. Parents were subordinate, their voices blunted by physical drills and Nazi dogma. Even his mother, stitching swastikas for the Reich, was secondary to the state. Her fingers, formerly quick and sure with needle and thread, now trembled when news of casualties reached their neighborhood. He pretended not to notice how she recoiled at the sound of bombers overhead, how she whispered prayers when she thought no one could hear.

Der Stürmer posters screamed *"Juden raus!"* (Jews out!) on every corner, caricatured faces leering from lampposts and walls. Garish illustrations of giant hook-nosed men that had once frightened him as a small child now reinforced his sense of superiority. The detestable posters peeled in the rain, but new ones always appeared, a constant reminder of the Nazi commitment to hatred. Dieter had been wholly indoctrinated. He hated all Jews, even the ones who had helped his family. He had vowed to punish, torment, and kill if necessary, any Jew he met.

On the rally ground, the mud obscured the shine from his highly polished boots. The *Gruppenführer* pinned the thick silver badge to Dieter's tunic: "For exceptional service to the Fatherland!" The metal felt heavy against his chest even through the fabric, a weight he bore with honor. His ninth award marked his elite rank. His uniform, adorned with symbols of his rising status, distinguished him from the boys around him.

The *Hitlerjugend* had taught him that weakness was *Volksfeind*, an enemy of the people; Jews were the rot eating away at German greatness. "The

Jew is our misfortune," they chanted weekly, daggers slashing straw targets, each imagining a Jew's heart beneath the burlap. At twelve, he'd taunted a Jewish baker's son in an alley, shouting *"Juden raus!"* as the boy flinched, his hands clutching a torn cap, eyes downcast in a fear that had thrilled young Zobel. The yellow star on the boy's coat had been like a beacon, drawing Dieter's hatred like a moth to flame.

He remembered the way the lad's shoulders had hunched, trying to make himself smaller, less visible, a response that had fueled Dieter's aggression. The intoxicating satisfaction of power had surged through him as he hit, then kicked, the boy repeatedly, leaving him in a heap.

Hate was his strength, fear his power. He had learned to channel both, to transform them into the rigid discipline that now defined his muscular frame. His body had been shaped by years of physical training, his mind by endless propaganda, until, at seventeen, Dieter Zobel exemplified the perfect Hitler Youth.

And by this time next year, he would be part of the *Schutzstaffel*, the German SS, the most feared agency in the world. Soon, all, Jews and Germans alike, would fear him; his life's goal now fixed.

Nine

May brought promises of graduation, but Luke's mind was tangled in an uncertain future. He sat on the school auditorium steps with Brock, whose pleas for Luke to enlist with Stevie and him had been relentless since he had turned eighteen in April. Luke had resisted, still hoping to hear from Cal Poly and USC.

"You can't hide behind books forever," Brock cajoled, flipping the cigarette butt onto the grassy patio area. "Every day we wait, more of our guys die while we sit safe in classrooms."

“Neither of the colleges has replied yet to my request for admission. I don’t want to make any commitments until I get responses from them," Luke countered.

"College will still be there after," said Brock, leaning closer, "The *Sentinel* says that the army is forming a new division, the 106th Infantry. It could be the best division the army has ever produced. The three of us could join; you, me, and Stevie, hopefully train together."

Before he could answer, shouts erupted from the courtyard. Sarah Weiss, all four foot ten of her, was standing toe-to-toe with Jack Thompson, her small frame dwarfed by his athletic bulk.

"Take it back," she demanded, her voice strident.

"Why should I? Everyone knows the Jews are the reason we're in this mess," Jack sneered.

"My cousin is a Jew and he died fighting at Midway," Sarah fired back. "He wasn't fighting for just one kind of American. He died protecting all of us, including ignorant bullies."

Luke viewed the contest as a boxer's sparring partner would, cheering from the front row. Sarah's comments landed on the much larger opponent with the weight of a fierce counter-puncher. Jack's crimson face was clear evidence that Sarah was winning.

"That's the problem with Hanford," she continued, "Lots of talk, little sacrifice. When Willie Jensen came home, his right leg decaying in some jungle in the Pacific, where was all the brave talk? I was there. All you aspiring warriors walked away without saying a word. You guys have to have someone to blame. Today the bankers, tomorrow the shopkeepers, next day... spare me."

For the first time Luke could remember, Jack was speechless, his lips quivering as he struggled to form a response. Lacking words, he glared at Sarah with clenched fists, wishing she were a boy. Red-faced and silent, he turned and sulked away, muttering under his breath.

Sarah did not move, her figure a statue of courage and strength. Luke looked at Brock, then back at Sarah. "Now, there's someone I would follow into war," Luke mused. Brock nodded, heartened that he had chosen a military example to make his point.

"I think I'll run over to Weisbaum's. Need some electrical wire," Luke lied. He rose from the step and went to where Sarah was. She stared at him, her gaze suspicious. Smiling, Luke reached for her hand, then lifted it. "Congratulations, Sarah, you won all ten rounds on the judge's scorecards." Sarah laughed. The few students nearby looked on, uncertain how to respond. "You're one tough cookie," he said, hoping she would see it as a compliment. "Thanks," she said, the single word ample. Smiling, she turned and walked away, precisely as she had arrived... alone.

Luke walked in the opposite direction, covering the six blocks to Weisbaum's, lost in thought, hoping Moses could unravel his growing web of questions, now shrouded in four females: Ruth, Sarah, Katie, and Matya.

"Back again?' Moses asked, polishing a wrench.

"Yeah, I needed to put some space between me and Brock. He never gives up."

"He still on you about enlisting?"

Luke slumped on the metal chair beneath the porcelain enamel sugar ration sign. "He's eighteen, got papers, wants my dad to sign a waiver for me. Thinks the three of us can win the war; him, Stevie, and me." He paused; his voice subdued. "Moses, what's it like being Jewish? I mean, how do you put up with... with all the hate."

Moses's hand stilled, "Why so curious? Still thinking about Ruth?

"Yeah, that and more. Today, another student, Sarah Weiss, faced down one of the toughest boys at school. He was blaming the Jews for starting the war. He sounded just like my dad, but she showed real courage. She stood up to him. Even called him a stupid bully right to his face."

He wanted to mention Matya, but hesitated. That could wait. "I know several women who are Jewish, and they're all courageous, strong. But when I hear about what's happening in Europe, that all goes out the window."

"How so?" quizzed Weisbaum.

"Well, they're saying that the Jews in Germany do whatever the Nazis, the Hitler Youth, tell them. They don't refuse them. They go along. Same thing in France. Some radio reports say that thousands of Jews have been killed for no reason. Why don't they fight back?" Luke paused, studying Moses' reaction to his question. "But these women I know, they stand up. They fight back and don't let the slurs and insults crush their spirits."

"You said several females, Luke."

Luke blushed, wishing he had not included Katie and Matya in his thoughts. "Just other girls I know," he lied. "Anyway, why don't the Jews in Europe fight back? Makes no sense."

Moses set the wrench down, observing Luke in the dim light from the incandescent bulb hanging from the ceiling. "It's 1943, and you're asking about the Jews in Europe, why they don't fight back. Well, they are. You've heard of Warsaw?

"Yes, isn't that where they forced the Jews to go when the Germans invaded Poland?"

"Yes," Moses confirmed. "Well, just a few months back, the Jews in the Warsaw ghetto took on the Nazis. Starving and with few weapons, they fought for weeks, holding off several Panzer tanks with homemade bombs. The Germans had to burn the ghetto down to stop them. That's not giving up."

He leaned against the counter; his voice steady. "But it's not just Warsaw. Over there, Jews are resisting however they can; hiding, smuggling, staying alive when the Germans want them dead. Here, Ruth is fasting on *Yom Kippur,* and Sarah is standing up to a bully. That's fighting, too. Same strength; different battlefield. And those other girls, I'll bet they've got some fight in them too."

Moses paused, his eyes softening. "Maybe you'll be heading off to war soon, Luke, and I know you're wrestling with something; who you are, or what kind of man you'll be. We have the same questions. Being Jewish today isn't easy; it's about enduring, standing tall. Four years ago, right here at Weisbaum's, the front window was smashed. They broke in and scrawled 'Jew' on the wall, and painted a swastika on the front door. I had to close the store for several weeks. I learned that being Jewish means being a target, even in Hanford. In Europe, it's worse; Nazi soldiers don't spare Jews."

Moses' words validated Luke's fears. Matya's blood meant he and Katie were Jewish. If this secret were leaked, he'd be just another minority in California, but an actual target in the war.

"What if... what if someone didn't know they were Jewish? Found out by accident?"

Moses' eyes narrowed, gentle but probing. "They'd face a choice: hide it or claim it. Both come at a price. But know this: truth never stays hidden, not even in the darkest places. You talking about you?"

Luke's breath caught, his secret craving to be released. "I..." He pictured how classmates would shun him, how the war would mark him. He swallowed. "No, I was just wondering. Thank you. That helped. I appreciate it."

He longed to hug the kind-hearted mentor who always seemed to have the right words, always at the right time. To embrace him, draw from his strength, and then release everything that was pent up inside him—tears formed in his eyes, the name Matya on his lips. There was so much more he wanted to say, but he could only muster an awkward handshake.

Moses, sensing Luke's anxiety, took his hand and looked into his eyes. "You're a good boy... I mean, young man. Wait here, I have something I want to show you."

Moses retrieved a small, brown book from his desk drawer, labeled *Jewish Holy Scriptures*, and handed it to Luke.

"What's this?" Luke asked, ruffling the pages.

"It's the *Tanakh*."

"Ta... naw," he attempted.

"Close enough," Moses chuckled. "It's a pocket Bible for Jewish service members. Rabbi Cohen's synagogue in Fresno gives them to enlistees."

"I must have sounded pretty stupid earlier, huh?"

"Not at all. You asked because you have compassion. Don't change. We can face the future with hope," Moses said, taking the book back and locating a familiar passage. "Read this, the first verse of Psalm 91."

Luke read, "*He who dwells in the shelter of the Most High shall abide under the shadow of the Almighty.*"

"Do you know what that's called?"

Luke shook his head.

"It's 'The Soldier's Psalm.' When things seem dark, you're always safe in the shadow of the Almighty."

"Shadows don't sound particularly safe."

"People hear 'shadow' and they think of darkness, of hiding. But in our tradition, a shadow is also a place of protection. The shadow of God is a place where you are safe, hidden from harm, where you can always find shelter.

"It's not just about safety. You don't always know what's in the shadow, what's coming. Sometimes you need to hide, but you're never alone. Our rabbis teach that even in death's shadow, we're never alone. Psalm 23."

"That's a lot to consider," Luke said, handing the book to Moses.

"No, it's yours," Moses insisted.

"Thanks," Luke said, checking the clock. "I should go. Katie will wonder what happened." Moses nodded knowingly.

Luke slumped in the chair, etching the mashed potatoes on his plate with a fork, while his father grunted between bites. The clinking of silverware against plates punctuated the otherwise silent kitchen, its walls dulled by years of cooking grease and cigarette smoke. The late afternoon sun cast long shadows through the dusty curtains, bathing everything in a golden-orange glow that belied the tension in the room.

"Saw the recruitment office was busy today," Frank said, eyeing Luke with a look that spoke disappointment. His calloused fingers gripped his fork as he stabbed another piece of meat. "Your friend Brock signed up yet?"

"No, but he mentions it every day," Luke replied, not lifting his head. He continued tracing patterns in the mashed potatoes, creating little hills and valleys.

Frank snorted, a harsh sound that rattled in his chest. "Figures. The boy's got spine. Not like some who'd rather hide in textbooks." He swallowed a mouthful of water, eyes never leaving Luke's downturned face.

"It's not hiding," Luke countered, the words escaping before he could stop them. "Cal Poly..."

"Cal Poly," Frank mocked, his voice rising. Bits of Salisbury steak covered in gravy flew from his mouth as he spoke. "What's a piece of paper going to do against Hitler? You think notebooks and journals can defeat bullets; that fancy education gonna make you a man while real men are bleeding on foreign beaches?"

Katie placed her hand on Luke's arm, her touch gentle but firm, a silent plea for peace. Her fingers were warm on his skin, an anchor in the storm of their father's latest diatribe. But Luke felt something shift inside him, as if a gear had finally engaged.

"I could design ships or planes," he said, meeting his father's gaze for the first time that evening. "Or work on radios. There's more than one way to fight. It could be my way to help us kill some Germans, some Japs, or best of all, some Jews."

Frank's face flushed, veins bulging from his neck and forehead. "What does that mean? We're not at war with the Jews." His voice had dropped low, the way it always did just before an explosion.

"We're not?" Luke responded, emboldened by his recklessness. "You're always talking about how bad the Jews are and how they started the war. Maybe I'll design a bomber that targets just Jews. A pilot, navigator, and a bombardier, all we need to get rid of them, once and for all?"

"You're a smart ass, Luke. I see through you." Frank's eyes narrowed, his breath coming in short bursts. "You can fool that old Jew, Weisbaum, and your schoolmarm, Mrs. Duncan, or whatever her name is, but they don't know you like I do."

"You know me, Dad?" Luke questioned, leaning forward. "What about Mom's part of me? What do you know about that?"

Frank's fist hit the table with a thunderous crash, sending the salt shaker flying. Lid freed, its contents spilling over the small room. Katie winced, drawing her hand back. Ignoring the granules scattered across the worn tablecloth, Frank glared at Luke without speaking, then waved his hand dismissively. "What can I tell you? You already know everything."

The word Matya formed in Luke's throat, heavy and insistent, but he held back. *Not yet.* The time wasn't right, the wound still too raw. He pushed away from the table, the chair legs scraping against the linoleum. Glancing one last time in the direction of his father, whose face had settled into stony silence, Luke retreated to his room from the salt-covered battlefield.

Katie found the broom and the dustpan and began sweeping up the wreckage, glad it was salt and not sugar, which was in short supply. She swept around her father's feet as he sat motionless, his head in his hands. As she moved from the table, she heard him whisper, “I failed her.”

Later in his room, Luke stared at the blank page of the journal, the soft yellow glow of his bedside lamp casting an ominous shadow across the bed where he sat, knees drawn to his chest. His father's latest explosion, Sarah standing bravely, and Brock's relentless prodding, melded into an image he couldn't bring into focus. Sarah was right, lots of people talked tough, but few did the things that mattered.

He recognized his own need for action, yet every choice seemed flawed, filled with consequence.

Journal Entry: *May 8, 1943 - Courage is found in the weak, not the strong. Ruth, Sarah, and Moses act with courage. His store was desecrated. But he didn't quit. Hate is real. Dad hid Mom's photo, hiding hope. Brock's convinced three soldiers can win a war. I doubt I'd make a difference. My secret wants out. It's choking me, but sharing isn't safe.*

Ten

THE KITCHEN WAS FILLED with the scent of Katie's bran muffins, a pleasant blend of toasted grains and sweet molasses, with hints of cinnamon and nutmeg. The pleasing aroma clashed with the scent of bitter steam rising from the coffee substitute she poured into her mug. Katie sighed as she stirred the dark, grainy liquid, thinking of the ration book in her purse. Coffee was a luxury, a memory of better days. *I'd trade a week's ration of sugar for one cup of the real thing.* The war had stripped away so much: sugar, silk, nylons... peace of mind.

Frank's work shirt hung over a chair, its sweat-stained collar a testament to yesterday's early summer heat, while Luke sat at the table, his textbook opened but untouched.

Outside, the dawn was a muted gray, another scorcher. In June 1943, the world teetered between hope and dread, uncertain where it would land. The Zenith tabletop radio offered little solace, its voice a steady drumbeat of war updates: victories in North Africa, defeats in the Pacific, and never-ending pleas to buy more bonds.

The screen door creaked as Brock and Stevie let themselves in. Brock, large and confident, dropped his cap on the counter with a flick. Stevie, diffident, hovered near the counter, his eyes drifting to Katie as she worked at the sink.

"Morning, Katie," Stevie said, soft and sincere. He managed a shy smile before looking away, feigning concern over a chipped cup. She caught his glance and smiled back, then returned to her dishes.

Brock turned to Luke; his voice raised above the din of the radio. "Tomorrow's the day, Luke. Recruitment office. The three of us, like we talked about. You in?"

Luke set his pencil down and looked at Brock, then Stevie, his answer steady. "For the hundredth time, I'm waiting to hear from Cal Poly and USC. If I get in, I'm going to college."

Brock's shoulders dropped, disappointed by the familiar answer. "I get it, Luke. You said you wanted to be an engineer or a journalist. I just figured we'd all go together, you know? You can do that other stuff later."

Frank stepped into the room, wiping a dab of shaving cream from his chin. His face was set, eyes hard. "You should listen to your friends. You think sitting in a classroom is real life? You'll be eighteen in three months. You don't have to wait. I'll sign the papers now. Time to decide what matters."

Luke looked in the direction of his father, "I know it matters, but not everyone serves with a rifle. Some build, some teach, and some make sure there'll be something to come home to when the fighting's over."

Brock nodded, not quite smiling. "We know you're not ducking out, Luke. You've always had our backs. If you don't get in, though..."

"If I don't get in," Luke interrupted, "Then I'll go with you, but I need to know first. That's all I'm asking. If you wait for me, you won't be enlisting tomorrow. Are you sure you can wait? It could be another few weeks, maybe a month."

Stevie answered, his voice quiet but confident. "We can wait. We said we'd do this together, and that's what we'll do.

Brock looked at both of them, then nodded. “Yeah. We wait. We go together, one way or another.”

Frank’s expression softened, just a little. He didn’t say more as the tension in the room eased.

Katie glanced at Stevie, then at Luke. “That gets my vote as well.”

For a moment, the only sound was the radio and the clinking of dishes. Luke felt the pressure to conform from every direction, with no escape from its clutches.

A week later, a letter arrived marked California Polytechnic College. Luke held the envelope, hesitant to open it, the contents crucial in determining his future. Katie watched from nearby, her hands clasped together in nervous anticipation as he scanned, then mouthed the indelible words:

We regret to inform you that California Polytechnic College is not accepting civilian admissions for the upcoming academic year. Resources are currently directed toward military training programs. We encourage you to apply after the conclusion of the current global hostilities.

The paper shuddered in his hands. He'd known this was possible, probable even, but seeing it in black and white was like a door slamming shut.

"What does it say?" Katie asked, her tone suggesting she already knew.

Luke handed her the letter and slumped back in his chair. "No civilians. Military training only."

Katie's eyes darted across the page before she set it down. She rested her hand on his shoulder, her touch gentle. "I'm sorry, I know how much you wanted this."

"There's still USC," he said, the words echoing hollow.

She nodded, a faint smile on her pursed lips, "Maybe."

That night, Luke lay awake staring at the ceiling, Tippy curled against his side. The dog's rhythmic breathing offered little comfort as his mind churned through possibilities. Maybe he could find work at the *Sentinel.* Perhaps the war would end sooner than expected.

But in his gut, he knew better.

Three days later, Katie found him in the backyard, throwing a ball to his loyal pal.

"This came," she said, holding out another envelope.

Luke wiped his hands on the front of his pants, then took the envelope, tearing it open with less care than the first. The message, worded differently, delivered the same fatal blow.

...regrettably suspending regular civilian enrollment... contributing to the war effort through specialized military training... welcome your application when regular academic operations resume.

Luke folded the letter and tucked it into his pocket, emotionless.

"Both the same?" Katie asked.

"Yeah, guess the country needs soldiers more than students right now."

"What will you do?"

He stared at the ground where Tippy lay panting, the ball forgotten. "What everyone expects me to do, I guess, what Willie Jensen did. What Brock and Stevie are doing."

"But..."

"It's okay, Katie." He forced a smile. "Maybe it's how it's supposed to be. Everyone's making sacrifices." *He wished he believed his own words.*

The recruitment office sat wedged between Blumenthal's Five & Dime and Murphy's Barbershop, its fresh coat of navy-blue paint and a shiny white awning standing out among the sun-bleached storefronts of Hanford's main street. A massive poster dominated the window, Uncle Sam's stern face exhorting Luke to submit, to enter the space where there was no turning back.

Brock pushed through the door with the confidence of a man who'd just won the heavyweight title. Stevie followed, shoulders squared, jaw set, eyes set with purpose. Luke hesitated at the threshold, his hand gripping the doorframe, resisting the cool air inside that beckoned—a relief from the summer heat.

"You coming, Luke?" Stevie called over his shoulder.

Luke looked back, then stepped inside, letting the door swing shut with a click that signaled the finality of his decision.

The office was smaller than he'd expected; just a desk, a few wooden chairs, and walls plastered with recruitment posters and maps. Behind the desk, a man in his forties, one sleeve hanging loose where an arm should have been. His otherwise hardened face broke into a broad smile at the sight of the three teens.

"Well now, looks like some of Hanford's finest decided to pay me a visit," he said, rising to shake hands with his remaining hand. "Sergeant Miller. You boys here to join the fight?"

"Yes, sir," Brock replied, standing at attention. "All three of us, ready to give Hitler what for."

Miller nodded, gesturing to the chairs. "At ease, fellas. Let's get you squared away. Let me see your papers," he said, glancing over each enlistment form. "Looks to be in order. Three friends enlisting at the same time. That's the kind of spirit that'll win this war."

"We want to serve together," Stevie said, "Same unit and everything."

"The 106th Infantry Division," Brock added. "Read they're forming up."

Miller's pen paused mid-stroke. "I'll put in the request, but I can't make promises. The Army has its way of sorting things out." He glanced at Luke, "Having second thoughts, son?"

"No, sir," he lied, forcing a smile.

"'The Hanford Boys', signing up together. Makes a man proud." Miller leaned back, his good arm gesturing. "I'll do what I can to keep you from being separated. You're right, the 106th is still taking men, but it's filling fast. There's a chance you'll all end up there if the paperwork moves quickly."

Luke's pen hovered over the signature line, a bead of sweat forming on his temple. This wasn't Cal Poly or USC. It was not the future he'd imagined. This was rifles, trenches, and orders. This was the path of least resistance, what his father wanted, and what Hanford expected.

He signed his name, the ink bleeding lightly into the paper. He'd traded one future for another, and there was no going back.

The Zenith crackled with static as Luke adjusted the dial, searching for a clear signal. Evening news reports filtered through: *Allied bombing campaigns over Germany, Japanese resistance in the Pacific, casualty counts rising.* Each announcement hammered home the reality waiting across the ocean. He moved to one end of the sofa, his canvas bag packed, resting by the door, ready for tomorrow's departure.

"They hit Hamburg again," Luke said, as Katie settled beside him. "Fifteen hundred tons of bombs. The city's engulfed in flame."

The radio continued its grim narration: *American forces continue to face fierce resistance in the Solomon Islands, with heavy fighting reported on New Georgia...*

Katie reached over and turned the Zenith off. "That's all the war news for tonight."

Luke stared at the now silent radio. "I need to know what I'm heading into."

"You'll know soon enough." Her voice caught.

Outside, crickets chirped in the gathering dusk. Through the window, Luke could see his father smoking his after-dinner cigarette, a ritual as predictable as the next racial slur. Since Luke had enlisted, Frank's rage had subsided to a low simmer, not quite peace, but something less than hostile. In an odd twist, war had provided a fragile truce in the Pierce home.

"I have something for you," Luke said, handing her the slim volume. "It's my journal. The one Mrs. Dugan had me start last year."

Katie's eyes widened. "I can't..."

"I want you to have it. Besides, I have a new one, a gift from Moe."

"Luke, I think that's the first time I ever heard you call him Moe. It was always Moses or Mr. Weisbaum."

"He's been a great boss, a solid mentor, and a good friend. Wish that could have been me and Dad. Anyway, everything's in there: about Matya, my hopes, my dreams, my disappointments. Probably best not to let Dad see it." He pressed it into her hands. "If something happens to me..."

"Don't talk like that."

"If something happens," he continued, "at least you will know what I was thinking. Who I was."

She clutched the journal to her chest, then hid it in the folded sweater beside her. "I'll keep it safe. And I'll write to you every week, twice a week."

"Tell me you'll be careful around Dad," He said, "Now that I won't be here to draw his fire."

"I've managed nineteen years with Frank Pierce," she said with a sad smile. "I'll manage a few more until you come home."

The door creaked as Frank entered, bringing with him a waft of tobacco and night air. He paused, regarding his children with an impassive look.

"Early start tomorrow," he said. "Best get some sleep."

Luke nodded, rising to his feet. "Yes, sir."

Frank hesitated, then added, "You've grown up, son. I can see it." The words were the closest thing to approval Luke could remember. He swallowed hard. "Thank you."

Frank lingered, as if wrestling with something unspoken. For a moment, Luke thought he might mention Matya; might finally explain why her Jewish heritage had been buried, why her name was forbidden, why Luke's resemblance to her wounded him. But the opportunity passed uncashed.

"Well," Frank said, turning toward his bedroom. "Goodnight then."

After he left, Katie squeezed Luke's hand. "He's trying, in his way."

"Too little, too late," he murmured.

Later, in his bedroom, Luke stood at the window watching the stars emerge. The moonless night seemed to multiply them. The very same stars would light European battlefields where he'd face men who would kill him without hesitation, men who would kill him twice over if they knew he was Jewish.

Journal Entry: *July 6, 1943 – Dad couldn't shake my hand. But he wants me to make him proud. What about the last seventeen years? I wonder if it would be easier without secrets. Katie is my anchor. Hanford is my proving ground. Soon, they will all know what I'm made of. More, so will I.*

Eleven

The Greyhound, a weathered relic with peeling green paint and a chrome grille pitted by years of travel up and down US Highway 99, shuddered to a stop at Hanford's sunbaked depot. Its engine coughed out a cloud of diesel smoke that swirled, consumed by the July heat. The windows, dimmed by dust, revealed a worn interior of faded blue seats, steeped in the stale scents of tobacco, sweat, and spilled soda. Luke shifted his canvas bag. Katie's parting kiss lingered on his cheek, her soft "Come back" reverberant in his mind. He scanned the familiar streets one last time: Weisbaum's Hardware with its crooked awning, the diner where they'd laughed over milkshakes, and the barbershop he'd skipped, knowing the army's clippers awaited.

"Alright, fellas!" Brock's voice boomed over the hum of goodbyes, his meaty hand clapping Luke's shoulder hard enough to jolt him forward. "Time to carve our names into the history books!"

"History's in Europe, Brock," Stevie shot back, his grin not quite masking his nerves, as he nodded toward the bus. "We're only going as far as Paso Robles."

The driver, a pudgy man with a sun-creased face and cigarette-stained fingers, grabbed their tickets with a curt nod. "Camp Roberts boys? Please go to the back. We'll have others joining us along the way."

They walked down the narrow aisle, shoes scuffing the creaky floor, the overhead racks sagging under lumpy canvas bags. The air was thick and warm, filled with the breath of anxious recruits. Luke snagged a window seat, pressing his temple to the smudged glass as the bus lurched forward. Hanford faded into memory. As they passed Weisbaum's Hardware, Moses was standing in the doorway, hand raised in a solemn farewell. Luke returned the gesture, a silent promise to return. *Would he*?

Brock sprawled across the aisle, his broad frame filling the seat, dark hair bouncing as he settled in. "I'm betting I drop ten Nazis by Thanksgiving," he bragged, his voice rising over the engine's growl. "My Pa says Germans crack like eggs when you push 'em."

"Your pa fought in the First World War," Stevie said, slouching beside Luke. "These Germans have been building military equipment since the twenties; tanks, bombers, rockets, and Lugers."

"Won't matter, American grit trumps all. Watch and learn."

Luke stayed quiet, eyes fixed on the cotton and the alfalfa fields zipping by the window. Growing up, those fields had defined his world. Now they receded into his past as they pushed toward a future he couldn't predict. His fingers brushed the Jewish pendant in his pocket, his only link to the mother he couldn't remember.

The bus rumbled south through the Central Valley, its shocks jarring over the pitted asphalt, stopping every half hour or so to pick up more recruits. Each town added more bodies, the bus becoming a rolling collection of teenagers; hair unruly, voices filled with bravado to mask their fears, swapping fables of female conquests, arguing over baseball stats, and sharing concocted images of battle victories, ignoring the fact that not one of them had ever faced a bullet. Brock led the charge, his bold predictions drawing an even split of chuckles and eye-rolls.

"First day at Roberts, I'm owning the rifle range," he declared, aiming an imaginary gun. "Bang, bang, two Nazis dead."

Stevie snorted. "You'll miss the target and cry for your ma. Drill sergeants'll eat you alive."

"They'll be saluting me," he said with a wink. "Tim Brockman, future legend."

Luke allowed a brief smile; his fresh new journal open on his lap. The coastal hills loomed beyond the window, rugged and unfamiliar, mirroring his unease.

Journal Entry: *July 7, 1943 - Somewhere near King City. The hills are different, strange. Brock's all medals and glory. Treats war like a sport. Stevie jabs back, but his eyes show fear. Did Matya feel this way leaving Austria? These boys talk of killing men they have never met. I think of the stories I want to tell. Less exaggeration. More truth.*

The journey was short—several hours—but the heat, frequent stops, and cramped seats made it feel much longer. The driver made a brief stop at a roadside fruit stand in McFarland, where a vendor handed out free apples, calling them "fuel for heroes." The recruits devoured them, their chatter filling the bus. After picking up ten boys in Bakersfield, the landscape shifted to rolling hills dotted with oaks, every seat now full as it neared its destination.

Camp Roberts, sprawling across San Luis Obispo and Monterey counties, was a hive of activity. Established in 1941, it was one of the largest training centers in the United States, its forty-two thousand acres warm and humid under the coastal sun. The camp's long, rectangular two-story wooden barracks, built from high-quality timber painted a drab olive, stretched in orderly rows.

The camp was at its peak, churning out infantry replacements for both the European and Pacific theaters; its fifteen-week boot camp was grueling, with endless marches through the parched hills, live-fire exercises, and obstacle courses designed to break the weak. The summer heat, often spiking past ninety degrees, would test their endurance.

As they rolled through the camp's gates, a sign beckoned: "*Camp Roberts: Through These Portals Pass the Best Soldiers in the World.*" Brock nudged Stevie, "That's us. You ready to prove it?"

Stevie glanced at Luke; his grin unsteady. "You good?"

"Not really, but I'm here."

The bus stopped, and the driver barked, "Out! Welcome to Roberts!" The recruits spilled onto the dusty ground, their voices hushed as drill sergeants emerged; hard-eyed NCOs shouting commands, men responsible for converting boys into soldiers, killing machines, and they only had seventeen weeks to complete the transformation.

By evening, the camp was a conclave of exhaustion, the air thick with the sweat and stale breath of bone-tired boys. Luke lay on the narrow bed, glad he got the lower bed on one of the metal-framed double bunk beds, placed in rows along the barracks' length. He chose a bunk near the door so he didn't have to walk so far; his body and mind were wearied from the first day's indoctrination: forms, shots, drills, and lectures. The thin, lumpy mattress offered little comfort from the rigid metal frame beneath.

His mind refused to rest. Enlisting with Brock and Stevie had seemed virtuous, even if it was not his first choice, a way to prove something to his father, to himself. But now, under the thin gray wool blanket that scratched his skin, doubt returned, denying him the sleep he desperately needed. The wall clock's hands glowed in the dark: 3:00 a.m., still time to get a little more rest.

Just then, all hell broke loose.

Clang! Clang! Clang! The sound was a violent assault of a baton banging a drab-green corrugated metal garbage can; each bang louder than the last, reverberating through the wooden floorboards and up through Luke's spine. Drill Sergeant Keith Lowry shouted, his voice filling the entire barracks, "Up! Up! Get your sorry asses out of those bunks!" His voice was a thunderclap, raw and unrelenting, the words sharp as knives. "You think this is a vacation? Move it!"

Luke shot up, forgot he was in a bottom bunk, and banged his head against the metal frame of the bed above his. Stars exploded behind his eyelids, and he bit back a curse. The room erupted into chaos; boys tumbling from their bunks, blankets tangling around legs, curses muffled by sleep-thick tongues. A cacophony of thumps, groans, and panicked breathing filled the air. Stevie, jumping from an upper bunk, tripped and sprawled across the floor. Brock, usually confident and unshakable, groped for his trousers, "What in God's name?"

"Five minutes!" Lowry roared, pacing like a caged beast. "Dressed and outside, or I'll drag you out myself!" His posture remained threatening, a predator among fresh prey. The gleam of his polished boots caught what little light there was as he strode between the rows of bunks, occasionally jerking a recruit out of his bunk if he wasn't moving as fast as the drill sergeant wanted.

Luke fumbled with his uniform, the stiff fabric scraping his skin. His hands shook as he tied his laces, each knot a small victory over the confusion. Around him, the others scrambled, their faces pale and drawn, eyes wide with shock and dismay. He caught Stevie's eye and offered a reassuring nod. No words, just a moment of solidarity. In that instant,

Hanford seemed a lifetime away, the peaceful mornings of his childhood replaced by a brutal awakening to military life.

Camp Roberts' barbershop hummed with the steady drone of clippers; the air was sharp with the scent of army-issue tonic. Luke sat erect, his fingers digging into the armrests as the barber, a man with thick, rough hands, snapped a white sheet over his shoulders. It settled cool against his neck. He kept his eyes forward, avoiding the mirror's reflection.

"Chin up," the barber muttered, nudging Luke's head. The clippers whirred to life, and with their first sweep, a jolt buzzed against his scalp. Dark curls, his mother's curls, cascaded onto the floor. He'd never had his hair cut this short, stripped down to nothing, each pass stealing more.

He wished he could remember Matya's voice or the tenderness of her touch. All he had was the photograph, yellow through age. She'd been young, seventeen or eighteen, her smile gentle, her eyes dark, her hair a tumble of curls just like his. He saw himself in her; the nose, the full mouth, the unmistakable stamp of their Jewish blood, a secret he carried, unspoken. It bothered him, this silence, this need to hide who he was, to become who they wanted.

The clippers grazed his temple, and he winced, shutting his eyes. Her face flashed, curls framing her smile, the mother he'd never known. "Be yourself, Luke," he imagined her saying. *How could he?* Here, in this chair, he was losing more than hair. He was losing her, and the thought of not sharing her Jewish heritage, now his, felt like betrayal.

"Almost there," the barber said, his tone abrupt, not harsh. Luke opened his eyes, catching his reflection. His head was a stranger's; shorn to stubble, raw and exposed. He looked older. But his eyes, her eyes, stared back, dark and restless. The barber swept the soft bristles across Luke's neck, applied a small amount of lotion with his palms, then yanked the sheet away. "Next!"

Luke rose, legs shaky, and brushed a hand over his scalp. It felt alien, vulnerable. Around him, other recruits sat in identical chairs, their transformations unfolding in silence or bursts of nervous laughter.

Outside, the sun baked his bare head, the air thick with engine fumes. Camp sounds swelled; shouted orders, synchronized boots hitting the asphalt, the crack of gunfire in the distance. He inhaled. He was one of them now, his individuality shorn. But beneath the surface, he held his mother's memory. He would succeed. He would do it for her.

Journal Entry: *July 8, 1943 – Cut my hair. None of Mom's curls are left. It was like losing a part of myself. But they'll come back. Until then, I will carry her strength inside me. One day, I will tell the world who she was. For now, I must learn to conform. Not easy.*

Twelve

The early California morning was already warm, the sun not yet risen above the La Panza mountain range to the east. The boys lined up, breath coming in short, hot puffs as they waited in the pre-dawn gloom. Their bodies formed uneven rows, shoulders hunched against the damp air, feet shifting on the dew-soaked ground. Camp Roberts stretched out around them, a sprawl of barracks and training fields, occasional calls of night guards breaking the stillness. The faint scent of wet grass and gasoline reminded them where they were.

Sergeant Lowry stood before them, his scarred face lit by the glow of a cigarette, the ember brightening with each deep drag he took. The scar on his cheek, a souvenir of a previous conflict, twisted his perpetual scowl into something even more fearsome. His eyes, intense and unyielding, swept over the group, sizing them up with a mix of disdain and expectation.

"Five miles," he said, his voice low and menacing. "You'll walk it, you'll hate it, and you'll thank me later. Fall out!"

The company of recruits lurched forward, boots squishing the damp earth. Some boys stumbled, unused to the heavy footwear, earning sharp rebukes from Lowry. The pace was merciless, a forced march through the morning darkness. Luke's legs were weak, each step a struggle, his breath coming in labored gasps as sweat formed on his forehead.

Beside him, Stevie wheezed, unsteady, his face flushed. "I'm gonna die out here," he gasped, half-serious, his usual sarcasm muted by his suffering. His body wasn't prepared for this kind of punishment, and every move sapped more of his energy.

"Keep moving," Luke encouraged, his voice hoarse from the lack of water. *Was he motivating Stevie or himself?* The line between the two blurred with each painful step. His legs ached, his calves tightening with every stride, but he couldn't let himself falter, not in front of the others, not with Lowry watching.

Brock trudged ahead; his shoulders hunched against the oppressive heat. "This is insane," he said, loud enough for the group to hear, but low enough to avoid Lowry's earshot. "My old man said the Army builds character. But he didn't tell me what it would cost." Despite his comments, there was pride in Brock's bearing, as if this hardship were the initiation rite he'd been waiting for—the first step toward fulfilling his family's military legacy. His father had served, and his father before him had served as well. Now it was his turn; sweat, pain, and all.

A few of the recruits chuckled weakly at Brock's lament, their snickers swallowed by the chirping of crickets and the rustling of leaves in the warm coastal breeze. The path twisted through the camp, past rows of tents and wooden barracks, the silhouettes of war machines lurking in the shadows: tanks and trucks.

Luke's attention narrowed to the rhythm of his steps; left, right, left, right, each step a battle against exhaustion. The warm air made the march seem more difficult, as if the air itself was pushing against him. By the third mile, his calves screamed, and sweat stung his eyes, trickling down his forehead and dripping off his chin. He wiped his face with the back of his hand, but it did little to help. The salt from his pores burned the minor cuts on his face, remnants of the previous day's mandatory shaving of nonexistent facial hair.

Stevie stumbled beside him, nearly tripping over a root hidden in the darkness. Luke grabbed his arm, steadying him before he could fall. "Thanks," he muttered, his voice weak.

"Don't worry about it," Luke replied, his strength waning. He could feel the weight of the march in every muscle, the relentless pace sapping his energy. But there was no stopping, not with the Drill Sergeant at their heels, not with the knowledge that this was only the beginning.

As they passed a cluster of supply sheds, he caught a glimpse of the camp's vastness. Barracks stretched into the distance; their outlines just visible in the dim light. Beyond them, the training fields lay silent, waiting for the day's drills. The air was filled with the sweet, earthy smell of gun oil, a reminder of the weapons they would soon be handling. Somewhere nearby, a dog barked, its call sharp and sudden, cutting through the night. He had a fleeting thought of Tippy, probably curled up asleep on his empty bed back in Hanford. *Lucky dog.*

Brock glanced back at Luke, his face glistening with sweat. "How you holding up?" he asked, his tone affable.

Luke nodded, though his legs felt like they might give out at any moment. "Yeah. Just... hot."

"Tell me about it," Brock said, wiping his brow. "It's like we're marching through a Louisiana swamp."

Stevie let out a weak laugh. "At least it's not snowing. I heard some guys talking about winter training, now that sounds like hell." He chuckled, "Imagine, hell covered in snow."

"Better than this," Luke muttered, though he wasn't sure. The heat was relentless, even in the early morning.

The group fell silent, conserving their breath. The only noise was the rhythmic thud of boots, an occasional cough or grunt, and the constant hum of the camp. Luke's mind wandered, drifting back to Hanford, to the life he'd left behind. It seemed like a distant world, one that was slipping further away with each step. He wondered if he'd ever see it again.

When they staggered back to the starting point, the sky was beginning to lighten, the first hints of dawn painting the horizon with streaks of pink and gold. The air was still heavy, but a light breeze had begun to blow as the sun crept higher. Lowry waited, arms crossed, his expression unreadable beneath his cap. His cigarette was gone, but the scowl remained, etched into his features like a permanent fixture.

"Pathetic," he spat, surveying the gasping, sweat-soaked recruits with undisguised contempt. "But it looks like you're all standing. Breakfast. Fifteen minutes. Go." He checked his wristwatch, making it clear that this deadline, like all the others, was set in stone.

The recruits stumbled toward the mess hall, their legs wobbly, but there was a sense of accomplishment, however small. They had survived the march. Luke glanced at Stevie, who was still breathing hard, but managed a weak grin. Brock clapped them both on the back, his usual bravado returning now that the worst was over and food was being served.

"We did it," Brock said, his voice triumphant. "First of many, I bet."

Luke nodded, too tired to speak. His body ached, his clothes were soaked through, but like Drill Sergeant Lowry said, he was still standing.

The mess hall roared with life, a symphony of clattering metal trays, the scrape of boots on concrete, and the low rumble of exhausted voices merging into a dull drone. The air filled with the bitter stench of burnt coffee, made worse by the leathery taste of undercooked bacon. Steam billowed, clouds of vapor drifting upward from the serving line. Luke slid onto a wooden bench, his hands trembling as he gripped a dented tin mug, the metal hot against his palm.

The meal was a bleak offering: half-fried bacon, gray oatmeal that clung to the spoon like wet cement, stale bread that crumbled into dust when he grasped it, and weak, bitter coffee, made bearable by adding plenty of sugar and cream. It wasn't gourmet, but he shoveled it in, too tired to care, forcing it down, his body craving fuel. His stomach churned, hunger battling with nausea, but he ate anyway; months of training loomed ahead, and beyond that, the war itself. He would need every bit of energy he could muster to face it all.

Across the hall, the recruits were a mixture of weariness and defiance. Some hunched over their trays, wolfing down rations with the urgency of men who'd experienced the depression, while others stared blankly into space, pale and shell-shocked, forks dangling, forgotten in their hands. The clink of a metal cup against a tray rang out sharp and sudden, followed by a curse as a recruit stumbled, spilling his coffee. Laughter, coarse and crude, erupted nearby, bringing a moment of relief from the fatigue.

Luke's gaze drifted from his friends to the unfamiliar faces around him. Stevie, seated across the table, poked at his oatmeal with a grimace, his body slouched in defeat. "This ain't food. This is punishment," his voice nearly lost in the din.

Luke managed a faint grin, the effort tugging at the corners of his mouth. "Eat it anyway, buddy. You'll need the strength to cry later."

A tired chuckle rippled between them. Luke's attention shifted as a shadow fell over the table. A stocky recruit with a farmer's tan slid onto the bench beside him, balancing a tray that wobbled under the weight of his untouched meal.

"Mind if I sit?" the newcomer asked, his voice warm, tinged with a slight drawl.

"Go ahead," Luke said, nodding. "Luke Pierce. Central California."

"Dean Olson," he replied, offering a calloused hand. "Iowa. You make it through the hike alright?"

"Yeah," Luke admitted, shaking his hand, "but my legs feel like they're still out there marching."

Olson grunted, a sound halfway between amusement and exhaustion. "Tell me about it. Thought I'd die when we hit that last hill. Never walked so far uphill in my life. At least at home the ground's flat."

"First time for everything," Luke responded, his eyes drifting to the window where the morning sun now shone bright.

"You see that drawing over there?" The Iowan nodded toward a map of Camp Roberts, its edges curling, pinned to the wall. "They've got a rifle range that stretches half a mile. Heard we're headed there tomorrow."

Luke followed his gaze, "Great. More marching."

"And shooting," Olson added, a trace of excitement breaking through the fatigue. "My old man taught me to hunt back home. You ever shoot?"

"Not much," Luke said, "More of a fisherman than a hunter."

Olson grinned, revealing a chipped front tooth. "You'll learn quickly here."

Another voice cut in from Luke's left, a skinny boy with dark hair and nervous eyes. "If the food don't kill us first." He slid his tray closer, extending a hand. "Isaac Epstein. New York City. Most people call me Eppy."

"Luke," he replied, shaking Epstein's hand, noting the faint tremble in his grip. "How are you holding up?"

Epstein shrugged; his smile tight. "Hike was hell. City legs ain't made for this."

"None of us are made for this," Luke said, his voice low, the weight of his doubts pressing in. He sized up the New Yorker. His appearance, combined with his name, led him to guess that he was Jewish, but he was hesitant to probe further.

"You think we'll make it through?" Eppy asked, his tone casual, but his eyes searching.

Luke hesitated, the question mirroring the concern he'd harbored since they had arrived. He wanted to say yes, but all he could manage was a shrug. "Guess we'll find out."

Eppy nodded, poking at his oatmeal with a sigh. "Yeah. Guess so. Man, I could sure use a bagel right now. There was this great little shop near the synagogue. Sorry, guess I'm a little homesick."

Luke longed to continue the conversation. He admired the way Epstein carried his faith without apology.

The clatter of a tray hitting the floor broke the moment, a recruit had tripped, scattering his breakfast across the concrete, and the room once again erupted in nervous laughter. Luke winced with sympathy as the boy scrambled to clean up the mess, his face red with shame. They were all on edge, all teetering on the brink.

Epstein grinned, "At least he didn't puke like some of the guys."

Luke pushed his tray aside, the stale bread untouched. Months, he thought again, the words a steady drumbeat in his skull. Months to become a soldier, or to break trying.

As the recruits began to file out, Luke stood, his legs protesting, and glanced at Olson and Epstein. "See you out there," he said, offering a nod.

"Good luck," Olson replied, walking to the door. Epstein paused, looked at Luke for a moment, then placed the middle three fingers of his right hand into his left palm, extending his thumb and pinky. Luke's expression conveyed his confusion.

"Oh, I thought you were Jewish," Epstein said, smiling. "That sign is the *Kemitzah.* The Jewish priests used it as a sign of blessing. It comes from the *Tanakh...*"

"Ta-naw," Luke interrupted, "I know what that is. It's the Jewish Holy Book. My old boss, who's Jewish, gave me one just before I left home. It's hidden in my footlocker."

Epstein paused, concerned by the word "hidden," but let it pass. "That's great, *Kemitzah* is from the story of Esther. She was a beautiful Jewish queen who rescued her people from an evil man, Haman, who wanted to kill all of the Jews. You should read it. Haman was today's Hitler. Anyway, we use the *Kemitzah* to say to one another, 'God bless you.' I'm sorry if I offended you."

"No, no offense at all," Luke blurted, eager to sop up more of Epstein's courage. "It was a pleasure to meet you, Eppy. God bless you."

Epstein smiled and extended his hand for a more traditional handshake, which Luke cheerfully accepted. "See you around," he said as he turned, hurrying to catch up to some other recruits he recognized from his barracks.

Luke remained motionless, gauging what had just occurred. Another person, a stranger, had mistaken him for being Jewish, which was no mistake at all. In that moment, he held an image of being naked in an open field, fully exposed, his mere appearance signaling to the world... *I am a Jew.*

Suddenly, he realized he was the only recruit left in the mess hall. He forced the unsettling vision from his mind and sprinted to his barracks.

Three weeks into basic training, Luke walked between barracks, sweat soaking through his uniform. Camp Roberts still seemed alien. The massive training facility was approaching the size of Fresno, with almost fifty thousand recruits. He paused, looking out over the dry Salinas River bed that cut through the camp. In the distance, the Santa Lucia Mountains rose against the darkening sky. The air carried the familiar scents of dust, gunpowder, and the faint aroma of tonight's dinner being prepared in the mess hall.

"Move it, maggots!" A drill sergeant barked at a group of recruits stumbling through marching exercises nearby. "The Krauts won't wait for you to get in step!"

Luke ducked his head and kept walking. His muscles ached from the day's training, which had included eight hours of crawling under barbed wire, scaling wooden walls, and running obstacle courses in the punishing heat. His hands were blistered from rifle drills, and his throat raw from shouting "Yes, sir!" at every command.

He reached Barracks Four and pushed through the door. Inside, the space hummed with tired conversation, others lost in thought, writing letters home. Brock sat on his bunk, polishing his boots with fierce concentration. His beefy features had already begun hardening in the few weeks since they'd arrived, his face tanned and lean. In an upper bunk, Stevie lay flat on his back, staring at the ceiling, a letter clutched in one hand.

"Thought you got lost," Brock said without looking up. "Or maybe you were hiding out in the latrine again with your journal."

Luke ignored the jab and collapsed onto his bed. "Just needed some air."

"Air's the same everywhere in this dustbowl," Stevie said, folding his letter and tucking it under his pillow. "Ma says it's been over a hundred degrees in Hanford for nine days straight."

"Hanford in July," said Luke. "Glad we're here where it's a little cooler."

"At least we're not at Fort Ord," Brock said. "My cousin said the fog there is so thick you can't see five feet in front of you during morning drills."

Luke pulled off his boots, wincing as the fabric scraped against his raw heels. Camp Roberts had been built for efficiency, not comfort.

"Mail call!" The barracks door swung open as Private Jenkins entered, waving a stack of envelopes. The room perked up, men sitting straighter, conversations halting mid-sentence.

"Landers... Billings... Johnson..." Jenkins called out names, tossing letters to the eager men.

Luke suppressed the hope rising in his chest. He hadn't received any mail since arriving, relying on Brock and Stevie for the latest news from Hanford.

"Pierce!" Jenkins shouted, flipping the envelope in Luke's direction when he saw Luke's head snap up.

Luke caught the envelope, recognizing Katie's neat handwriting. He tucked it away. He'd read it later, when the barracks were quiet and not so full of chatter. For now, he closed his eyes, unable to neglect the persistent throbbing in his feet, knowing tomorrow would bring more of the same.

Outside, the bugler sounded taps as the flag was lowered for the day. The mournful notes drifted through the open windows, bringing a moment of unexpected beauty to the harsh military routine. Even after three weeks, the notes, clear and mournful, slow and deliberate, moved him with emotions he couldn't name; pride, solemnity, resignation, and determination melded together.

When night fell and the barracks quieted, he pulled his sister's letter from beneath his pillow. He angled the pages toward the dim bulb hanging from the ceiling, the only light remaining after lights-out. Around him, men snored and shifted in their narrow beds, some muttering in their sleep.

Dear Luke,

How are you doing? Tippy spends most of his time by the front door, waiting. Breaks my heart to see him there, head on his paws, perking up at the slightest sound that might be you. He hardly touches his food. I've taken to hand-feeding him bits of meat to keep him going.

He swallowed hard, picturing his loyal companion watching the door.

Dad's gone quiet. Hardly says a word at dinner. He ran into Mr. Jensen, Willie's dad, at Peterson's Grocery, and they talked about Willie for half an hour. I think seeing what happened to Willie made something click inside Dad. He might regret pushing you to enlist, though he'd die before he would admit it.

The paper slipped from Luke's hand. He quickly retrieved it from the floor, glancing around to see if anyone noticed.

I've kept our secret safe, and Dad hasn't said anything. Sometimes I wonder if we should tell Moses. He would understand better than anyone. What do you think?

Luke lowered the letter, considering. The thought of sharing their Jewish heritage with Moses had often crossed his mind, coming close on several occasions. Reading Katie's words, he wished he had.

Tell Brock and Stevie I'm thinking of them. Let Stevie know, I'll bake a whole batch of those muffins he loves when you boys come home. I still remember how many he ate last Christmas!

Stay safe,

Katie

Luke looked across the darkened room where Stevie slept, mouth open slightly, one arm dangling off his bed. A strange thought formed as he re-folded Katie's letter: Katie and Stevie would be good together. She deserved someone tender and thoughtful, who could make her laugh. Stevie had always looked at her with quiet admiration. The nine-month difference in their ages didn't seem so great here, unlike when they were in high school. When he got back to his bunk, he tucked the letter under his pillow, comforted by the small connection to home, even as his body ached, tomorrow's demands already casting dark shadows.

Thirteen

The perpetual haze of Camp Roberts transformed every day into an endurance challenge for the three companions who had climbed onto the bus together six weeks earlier. Reveille jolted them awake at dawn, and drills pounded their bodies until dusk. Everyday comforts had faded into distant memories, replaced by the relentless rhythm of shouted orders and marching through mud, sticky, wet dirt that clung to their boots and made every step a contest.

The mess hall offered little comfort; just rushed meals wolfed down amid the clatter of metal trays and the constant threat of drill sergeants who would decide if the recruits were eating too slowly. Letters from home became lifelines, read and reread until the paper began to fray. Luke had taken to jotting quick notes in his journal whenever he found a quiet moment, determined to keep the connection to his old life, even as Mrs. Dugan, Katie, and Hanford itself faded into the background.

For Luke, military training was a test of his resilience; though he stumbled through specific physical tasks and still wrestled with self-doubt at times, he'd developed a resolve that kept him moving forward. His arms, once sturdy from stocking shelves at Weisbaum's Hardware, now bore new muscle, earned through rifle drills and climbing exercises that left his hands calloused and strong. The change wasn't just physical; his mind had sharpened, learning to cut through fatigue and chaos, to find clarity amid shouted commands and the crack of gunfire. He welcomed the ache in his limbs each night, proof he was tougher than the night before, someone who might survive whatever waited across the ocean.

Brock was an unstoppable force, barreling through the training as if he'd been preparing for it his whole life. He tackled every challenge with unfiltered enthusiasm, his voice booming over the clatter of rifles, rallying weaker recruits when their spirits wilted under the relentless pace. His broad frame, often covered in mud, seemed immune to exhaustion as he powered through obstacle courses that left others, even the instructors, gasping for breath. While on nighttime maneuvers, when darkness hid the field and recruits stumbled blindly, he moved with uncanny confidence, his military lineage evident in every task he undertook. His energy was contagious, sparking a fire in the weary men around him, pushing them to match his tenacious drive when their resolve faltered.

"This is what we signed up for, boys!" he'd shout during the most challenging drills, his grin undimmed by the sergeants' efforts to break them.

Stevie navigated the grind of military life with a different sort of strength. Of average build and quick with a gag, he handled the drudgery with a smile and a knack for defusing tension. When the sergeants barked orders, Stevie was ready with a clever retort, usually under his breath, just shy of insubordination, but sufficient to draw laughter from those near enough to hear. He tried to keep pace with the marches, sometimes lagging, at other times leading, but always managing to turn a stumble into a joke or a misstep into a punchline.

When he slipped, instead of getting frustrated, he'd flash a wry smile and say, "I'm just making sure the mud's evenly distributed." When Drill Sergeant Lowry loomed close, face twisted in a scowl, Stevie would react with a steady calm and a glint of mischief. "Don't know about you, Sarge, I'm just here for the food."

Luke viewed Stevie with a mix of admiration and relief. Where others wilted under pressure, his humor was his shield, his coolness a mild anchor for the entire group. He handled weapon drills with a steady hand and a running commentary that kept his fellow recruits smiling, even when their muscles fatigued. At night, his bunk was often the center of whispered jokes and relaxed laughter, his wit a welcome relief against the day's bumps and bruises.

His resilience was different from Brock's raw energy or Luke's quiet determination, but it was no less vital. He didn't just endure, he helped others persist. In a place designed to break men down, his spirit was a reminder that sometimes, the most effective weapon was a well-timed joke and the courage to keep smiling, no matter how demanding the day had been.

As Luke considered his two lifelong friends, he was glad they had decided to enlist together. Camp Roberts would be much more difficult if they weren't the "Hanford Boys," as Sergeant Miller had dubbed them at the recruiting office.

Reveille tore through the barracks at 0500, a jarring clang that jerked the boys from their restless sleep. Luke rolled out of his bed, his muscles aching from the previous day's drills, moving on newly-gained military instinct. As usual, the stale odor of sweat and damp wool blankets filled the confined space.

"Move it, ladies!" Sergeant Lowry's voice boomed from the doorway. Luke pulled on his fatigues and laced up his boots with quick, precise tugs. Across the aisle, Stevie fumbled with his boots, his fingers not yet awake. Luke caught his eye and offered a curt nod, but Stevie missed it, working hard to double-knot the laces. Brock, two bunks down, was already dressed, cracking his knuckles, anxious to get the day underway.

Outside, Camp Roberts was waking. Luke's squad gathered on the parade ground, breath fogging in the crisp air. Sergeant Lowry stood like a statue, arms crossed over his broad chest, his scarred face fixed with a customary scowl. "You've been here two months, past the halfway point. You're almost soldiers now, not high school students," he snarled, his voice rough as sandpaper. "Prove it today, or go back home to your mommies and daddies."

The task was a mock assault on a hill held by another platoon. The squad crouched behind sandbags, rifles in hand, plotting their move. The mound rose directly in front, a scruffy mound of dirt and grass, but in this moment, it was a battlefield. Brock tapped his rifle butt against the ground, eyes glinting. "We rush 'em, no hesitation. Straight up the gut."

Luke frowned, scanning the terrain. "We should split, half go left, the others right, alter their focus, then take the ridge."

"Too fancy," Brock shot back. "Hit hard, one unit. Done."

Stevie, hunched beside Luke, was waiting for instruction. "You cover the left," Luke said, keeping his tone firm. "Stay low, watch their line."

"Got it," Stevie mumbled, his voice subdued, eyes fixed forward.

The whistle shrieked, and they charged, a ragged line of green surging forward. Brock led like a bull, head down, while Luke yelled, "Keep tight! Stay together!" Then it unraveled: one of the recruits, Charlie Howland, got his foot snagged on a root, crashing into the dirt as his rifle tumbled noisily out of reach. The enemy platoon pounced, their mock fire cutting through the squad's momentum. Luke's shouts couldn't keep them in unison. Confused, they scattered, retreating in a breathless mess.

Lowry was waiting, his glare intense. "Pierce, your squad's a damn disgrace!" His eyes locked onto Howland, who was busy brushing mud off his fatigues, his head bowed. "You maggot! You're the weak link. Shape up or ship out!"

Howland recoiled, shrinking smaller. "Sorry," he whispered, voice cracking.

Luke's fists clenched, frustration burning hot. "Just stick with us next time," he snapped, sharper than he meant. The squad trudged back to the barracks, Lowry's words a heavy shadow over them. Failure stung, but Howland's slip had made it personal, and he wasn't sure how long they could carry him.

Drill Sergeant Lowry watched without speaking, taking note of how Luke was performing as a leader, not confident that he recognized how far he had come in a few short weeks. *I think I've found my squad leader.*

That night, Luke lay in his bunk, staring at the ceiling. The day's failure played on repeat in his mind; the squad's disorganized charge, Howland's stumble, Lowry's harsh words. He closed his eyes, trying to erase the memory, but sleep refused to come.

A lament broke the barracks' quiet. Luke lifted his head, listening. The noise came again, a gasping sob from Howland's bunk across the room.

"Shut up, will ya?" someone hissed from the darkness.

The sobbing grew louder. Luke sat up, squinting through the dim light. Howland sat hunched on his bunk, face buried in his hands, shoulders heaving.

"I can't... I can't do it anymore," Howland choked out between sobs. "I'm not cut out for this."

Luke swung his legs over the side of his bed, unsure if he should approach. Before he could decide, Howland's voice rose to a shout.

"I want to go home! I don't belong here!" He slammed his fist against his bed frame, the metal clanging in the quiet barracks.

Brock sat up in his bunk. "Howland, get a grip."

"No! I'm done! I can't take another day of this hell!" Howland bent forward and forced open his footlocker, then flipped it over. An extra uniform, underwear, socks, and personal items were scattered across the floor. He kicked at them, his breathing ragged and wild.

The door banged open. Sergeant Lowry filled the doorway, his enraged silhouette backlit by the exterior lights.

"What in God's name is going on here?" he demanded, loud enough for everyone in the barracks to hear.

Howland turned to him, tears streaming down his face. "I want out, Sarge."

Lowry's face remained impassive as he studied Howland. The sergeant's eyes, usually hard as flint, held something else, resignation, possibly. He'd seen this before.

"Pierce," he barked. "Get your squad back in their bunks."

Luke jumped to his feet. "Yes, Sergeant."

Lowry stepped outside and returned with two Military Police officers. "These men will escort Private Howland to processing," he announced, his voice flat. "The rest of you, get back to sleep. Tomorrow comes early."

The MPs gathered the scattered belongings and stuffed them back into his footlocker. Howland stood, suddenly quiet, his face blank with exhaustion or relief, Luke couldn't tell which. As they led him away, Luke caught Howland's eye. Something passed between them, an apology, or the simple recognition that he wasn't built for battle. A few minutes later, a third MP came and removed Howland's footlocker.

Luke learned that Howland had been categorized as "Inapt," a recruit who did not possess the required degree of adaptability. It was an administrative discharge deemed an ELS (Entry-Level Separation) because it occurred within the first 180 days of service. He was pleased that the army recognized that not everyone was suited for military service.

The door closed. He returned to his bunk, the empty bunk bed across the room a stark reminder of how quickly things could change.

Following another week of intense drills, the men of Squad Four collapsed onto the weathered steps of their barracks. Charlie Howland was replaced in the squad by a capable recruit named Marty Burnette.

Luke leaned against the railing, his muscles sore but solid, a testament to the two months of grueling training he had endured. He was thankful that the three friends from Hanford were in the same squad. Brock stretched his broad frame with a groan. "Man, I'd trade my boots for a cold soda right now." There was a hint of weariness in his voice.

Stevie, slouched on the step below, perked up, buzzing with nervous energy. "Or a dance. My cousin wrote about one at Camp Atterbury, where he's training; girls, music, the works. Said it was like stepping back into the real world."

Luke chuckled, wiping the sweat from his eyes. "Yeah, well, that's a pipe dream until we're done here. Lowry's not handing out passes for another eight weeks."

"Eight weeks?" Brock groaned, throwing his head back. "I'll forget how to dance by then."

"As if you ever knew how," Stevie shot back, a grin cracking his tired face. "I've seen you try. You looked like a bear wrestling a broom."

Brock laughed, kicking Stevie lightly. "Watch it, runt, or I'll step on your toes on our first dance."

"The only way you two girls can dance is if Lowry lets us out," Luke said, his tone dry but warm. "Which he won't. Not 'til we're... how does he say it? Soldiers worth a damn."

As if summoned, Sergeant Lowry's low growl cut through the dusk. "Daydreaming, ladies? You fellas are not fit for a latrine pass, let alone a night on the town. Earn it first." His silhouette loomed against the fading light, his face stoic.

The boys snapped to attention, their fleeting vision of girls and dances evaporating like smoke. When Lowry stalked off, they lumbered inside, the barracks' rank air suffocating. The recruits settled into their evening routines: showering, polishing boots, checking rifles, movements honed by several months of discipline. Luke sat on his bunk, staring at the hardwood floor, his mind churning. Nine weeks had hardened more than just his body; his resolve was now honed. He'd led his squad through today's obstacle course, and the victory was a step toward something significant. Yet, the reality was that they were only at the halfway point. It would take another two months of intense training until the recruits would become soldiers.

Brock broke the silence, "You know, I'm starting to like this place. It's tough, but it's making us into men."

Stevie, across the aisle, piped up, "I don't know how you do it, Brock. There are days when I feel like I'm just hanging on."

"You're doing fine," Luke said, turning to face him. "That course today? You climbed every wall. Not everyone did."

Stevie's eyes sparkled with hope. "Still seems like I'm slowing us down."

"Nah," Brock said. "We're a team. We lift each other."

Luke nodded. "Nine weeks down, eight to go. Plenty of time to catch up."

But his words were hollow. He'd overheard two sergeants outside, their voices carrying through the open window. "Next month's brutal," one said. "Night ops, mock battles, live fire. They'll break or they'll make it." The other had chuckled darkly. "Gotta be ready for Europe. No room for weak links there."

Luke's gut tightened. He thought about Howland, then about Europe. Newsreels flashed through his mind; beaches torn apart, soldiers falling in the mud. The following month would push them harder, preparing them for the deadly reality of war. He glanced at Stevie, half-asleep, and Brock, snoring softly, glad he wasn't doing this alone.

Journal Entry: *August 26, 1943 – Howland crash-landed. Some days I feel like I'm on the same flight, losing altitude. Brock is solid, carved in granite. Stevie is malleable, sculpted in lead. Together, we've made it halfway, past the point of no return.*

Fourteen

Luke's shoulders tensed as Sergeant Lowry spread the map across the wooden table, the yellow beam from the flashlight highlighting the geographical lines.

"Fifteen miles, gentlemen." Lowry's finger traced a route through the training grounds. "Compass bearings and these stars are your guides tonight." He gestured upward to where stars punctured the darkness. "No flashlights except for emergencies. You'll navigate by starlight, just as you might have to in Europe."

Luke studied the map, committing key landmarks to memory: the ridge to the east, the dry creek bed, the oak grove. Beside him, Stevie shifted uneasily, while Brock stood, mentally conquering the terrain.

"Pierce, you're leading." Lowry's eyes locked with Luke's. "Don't disappoint me."

"Yes, Sergeant," Luke snapped.

The squad shouldered their packs and rifles, adjusting straps in the dim light. Marty Burnette mumbled something about snakes. Rafael Sanchez checked his canteen twice, typical of his attention to detail.

"Move out," Luke ordered, his voice steady.

They marched into darkness, the camp lights fading behind them. He led with a compass in hand, his mind calculating bearings and distances. The night enveloped them, a blanket of stars overhead, the only illumination. The soft dirt path muffled the thud of boots; the trail felt more than seen.

After three hours, fatigue set in. Luke's shoulders ached under his pack, sweat trickling down his back despite the cool night. He called a brief halt, allowing the men to grab a quick sip of water from their canteens.

"How much farther?" Stevie whispered, his face pale in the starlight.

"We're not yet halfway," Luke admitted. "But we're on track."

Or so he thought.

After another hour of marching, Luke began to face a growing concern. The ridge they should have passed remained elusive. He rechecked his compass, squinting at the dial.

"Something's wrong," Brock muttered, coming alongside. "We should have hit the creek bed by now."

Luke rechecked their position, a cold realization dawning. The compass needle was erratic enough to lead them off course. He'd been so focused on maintaining pace that he'd failed to verify their direction against the stars.

"We've drifted west," he admitted. "Too far."

A distant crack echoed through the night, not thunder, but gunfire. Then another. The team froze.

"Is that...?" Burnette's voice trembled.

"Live fire," Sanchez confirmed, his face tight. "Night exercises on the range."

Luke's stomach dropped. They'd wandered close to the live ammunition training grounds, a strictly off-limits area without proper authorization and supervision.

"My God," Stevie hissed. "We're dead if they catch us here."

As if confirming his fears, a red sign materialized in the gloom: "DANGER - LIVE FIRE RANGE - KEEP OUT."

Panic rippled through the squad. One of the recruits started rambling about court-martials, while Sanchez cursed in Spanish. Stevie's breath came in short, gasping breaths. "We need to turn back," he pleaded. "Right now, Luke."

Brock shook his head. "We can't just abandon the exercise. We push through, find our way back to the route."

"Through a firing range?" Stevie's voice cracked. "Are you crazy?"

"Around it," Brock insisted. "We can still complete the mission."

The squad looked to Luke, their faces etched with uncertainty in the dim starlight, the responsibility falling on him. One wrong decision could mean disaster.

He took a deep breath, then tilted his head skyward, finding the North Star, Polaris, constant and unwavering. He knew that Polaris represented true north, not magnetic north, which allowed them to correct their course.

"We're not going through the range, and we're not abandoning the mission," Luke said firmly. "We'll skirt the perimeter, head northeast until we intersect our original route."

He pulled out the map and spread it on the ground. The squad huddled close as Luke traced their new path with his finger. "It'll add two miles, but it keeps us safe and completes the objective."

Relief washed over their faces, all except Brock, who looked disappointed at the circuitous approach, but he nodded, accepting Luke's authority.

They moved out again, more cautiously now, with Luke checking both compass and stars frequently. The sound of gunfire grew louder, then faded as they curved around the range's boundary.

"Vehicle," Sanchez whispered suddenly, his keen ears picking up the distant rumble of an engine.

"Down," Luke ordered. The squad dropped to the ground, pressing themselves into the brush.

Headlights swept across the landscape as a jeep patrolled the perimeter. Luke held his breath as the vehicle neared their position. If they were discovered here, so close to the range, the consequences would be severe.

The jeep paused. A flashlight beam cut through the darkness, sweeping left, then right, missing them by less than ten feet. After an eternity compressed into seconds, the engine revved and then continued on its nightly beat.

"That was close," Stevie breathed once the vehicle disappeared.

Luke nodded, "Let's move out. Single file, five yards apart."

The night deepened around them as they pushed on. Luke's eyes burned with fatigue as his mind recalculated their position. The stars wheeled overhead, Polaris his constant focus.

Near midnight, they finally intersected their original planned route. Luke allowed himself a moment of relief before urging the squad forward. They still had miles to go.

The hours blurred together, endless steps in the darkness, the weight of the pack increasing with each passing hour. The eastern sky lightened imperceptibly, stars fading as dawn approached. His legs moved more by will than by strength.

They crested a final ridge as the sun breached the horizon, casting long shadows across the training grounds. Below, Camp Roberts sprawled, their barracks visible in the distance.

"We made it," Burnette said, weak with exhaustion.

Sergeant Lowry waited at the checkpoint, stopwatch in hand. His eyebrows raised as he checked the time.

"Cutting it close, Pierce," he said as the weary men trudged in. "But you're within parameters."

Luke stood at attention, fighting to keep his voice steady. "Squad completed night navigation exercise, Sergeant."

Lowry studied their faces, noting the weariness, the dirt, the relief. If he suspected their detour, he kept it to himself. "Acceptable performance," he said after a short pause. "Your endurance is improving. Get some chow, then clean your gear."

The squad dispersed toward the mess hall, their shoulders slumped with fatigue, but their spirits buoyed by the completion of their task. Luke lingered, double-checking his compass. The needle now moved freely, pointing to magnetic north.

"Small things make big differences out there," Lowry said, suddenly appearing at his shoulder. "A defective compass. A misread map. They can kill you... and your men."

He met his gaze. "Yes, Sergeant." A look passed between them, suggesting that Lowry provided the faulty compass.

"You found your way back. That's what matters." Lowry shook his hand, then walked away.

Later, as dusk fell, the squad gathered around a small campfire, a rare privilege granted after their march; the weary men mesmerized by the dancing red-hot orange and yellow flames.

"Thought we were goners when that jeep came by," Burnette admitted.

"I nearly pissed myself," Sanchez added with a weak laugh.

Stevie looked across the fire at Luke. "You got us through it. You knew exactly what to do."

"The North Star," Luke said. "It's always there, even when you can't see it."

"My friend's a natural leader," Brock mused. Luke stared into the flames, thinking of the responsibility he'd shouldered, the faith these men had in him. It was different from anything he'd known before. His father had always made him feel inferior, always accusing him of making wrong choices. But here, his fellow recruits, even Drill Sergeant Lowry, seemed to trust him completely. This level of trust was new, and it would take him some time to process the ramifications. "We made it together. That's what matters."

As the fire burned low, he thought about leadership, about guiding others through darkness. Perhaps this was why he was here, not just following his father's expectations or his country's call, but someone who could remain cool when others panicked, who could lead when others were lost. On cue, the stars made their evening appearance, Polaris shining through the dark, constant and steady.

Fifteen

THE OCTOBER SUN HUNG low, casting long shadows over Camp Roberts's sprawling grounds. The final week of boot camp stood before them, a test to seal the previous fourteen weeks of hard work into seven days that would complete the transition from recruits to soldiers. For Luke, Stevie, and Brock, it was more than finishing training; it was leaving behind the security of who they were for a future where nothing was certain.

The final phase began with a twenty-mile march, each soldier burdened with a fifty-pound field pack that included entrenching tools, canteens, and extra ammunition magazines, serving as serious reminders of what was to come. Their olive-drab fatigues clung to them, damp from the abnormal humidity, as M1 helmets, heavier with new hinged steel ear covers, were cinched tight. Combat boots that had been polished to a brilliant shine were now dull as they kicked up clouds of dust. Luke kept his eyes forward, counting strides for the first quarter mile until his tally was interrupted by thoughts of home. Sixteen weeks had reshaped him; his once-lanky arms now corded with muscle, his stride steady and sure, a far cry from the teen who'd fumbled his first rifle drill.

Brock marched beside him, his broad shoulders making light work of the load. "This is nothing," he said, flashing that same cocky grin he'd worn when they'd raced bicycles down Hanford's dirt roads, daring each other to go faster. "Give me another twenty miles. I'll still be singing."

Luke smiled. Brock had always been the strongest of them, the one who had hauled Luke and Stevie out of Lake Tulare when they'd capsized their makeshift raft.

Stevie, trailing a few steps behind, was red-faced but resolute, his back curved under the pack's weight. "Speak for yourself," he panted, adjusting the straps that bit into his shoulders. "It'd be easier to carry a cotton bale."

Luke stifled a laugh, remembering Stevie at fifteen, insisting he could wrestle Brock and win. That stubbornness was still there, etched in the set of his jaw, the way he refused to fall behind. He had always been the reflective one, the one who noticed things, like the time he'd spotted Katie crying behind the auditorium and stayed with her until she could talk. She did not know that he had a secret crush on her, hampered by the fact that she was nine months his senior. Now, as the march stretched on, Luke saw that same quiet resolve in Stevie's eyes, a determination to prove he belonged here.

The march was just the beginning. Over the following days, they faced a gauntlet of tests designed to forge them or break them. Marksmanship came first, the crack of M1 Garand rifles echoing across the range as they fired at targets from one hundred to three hundred yards away. Luke's hands, shaky in the early weeks, now held steady, his sharp eyes tracking each shot. He did well enough to earn the Sharpshooter badge, a small pin that he wore as a testament to his fortitude. Brock grinned proudly as he accepted the Marksman badge, the lowest of the three rifle badges. Luke saw the tinge of disappointment in his friend's eyes, the same look he'd had when his pa was forced to sell the family's repair shop to pay debts five years ago.

Stevie, to everyone's surprise, excelled. He stood steady as he aimed, hitting twenty-six of thirty targets, a score that placed him among the top three recruits in a platoon of forty. When the instructor pinned the prestigious Expert badge to his chest, his face flushed, not with effort but with something more like disbelief. Luke caught his eye, and for a moment, they were back in Hanford, Stevie beaming after landing his first fish, too proud to admit he'd panicked at the thought of putting a wriggling worm on the hook. "Didn't think I had it in me," he admitted later, his voice humble as they sat on their bunks, the badge glinting in the dim light. Luke wanted to tell him he'd always known that Stevie's good nature and quiet strength had held them together more than he realized, but it remained unspoken. Instead, he nudged his shoulder, a silent reminder of their childhood, when words weren't necessary among true friends.

As the week wore on, the tests piled up: synchronized marching drills, obstacle courses, night maneuvers, but it was the moments between that secured them. Sharing a joke or a memory under the stars, their laughter a distraction from the ache of their bodies. Brock's stories of his Hanford High football heroics were exaggerated enough to make Stevie snort, and Luke confessed that he dreamed of his mother Matya's voice calling to him, referring to her as Martha, then hating himself for the betrayal.

Live ammunition drills followed, the boys lobbing grenades at wooden targets on the range. The explosions shook the ground, sharp and deafening. Luke's throw landed dead center, earning a nod from the instructor. Brock's grenade sailed far, veering off line. Stevie, gripping the grenade like a baseball, threw with unexpected force, hitting the target square. "Not bad, Cower," Sergeant Lowry grunted, a rare compliment.

Bayonet drills tested their close-combat skills. They charged straw dummies, thrusting and parrying with fixed bayonets. Brock moved like a force of nature; his strength overwhelming. Luke's movements were precise, his training evident in every strike. Stevie struggled but pushed through, his determination outweighing his lack of finesse.

The final test was a mock battle—a field exercise simulating a real battlefield. Luke was selected to lead the squad through a wooded area, directing them to dig foxholes and set up a .30-caliber machine gun. They conducted patrols, navigated obstacles, and engaged "enemy" forces in a simulated firefight. Luke's voice was calm, his orders clear. "Grayson, cover the left flank. Cower, survey the ridge." His team moved as one, the squad's trust in him unspoken but absolute. When finished, they stood muddy and exhausted but victorious.

Sergeant Lowry gathered them on the field. "You've done well," he said, his face softening slightly. "You're soldiers. Tomorrow, you graduate."

The company had started with 200 raw recruits, divided into five platoons of 40 each, and had completed the training, having lost less than 10. The details of their training, the miles marched, the targets hit, were just the framework. For Luke, Brock, and Stevie, the real story was in their shared experiences, the way they carried one another's doubts, and how they relished in each other's victories. Together, they were now soldiers, forged over fifteen grueling weeks.

The graduation ceremony unfolded on Camp Roberts's parade ground. The young men stood in formation, their uniforms crisp: field jackets buttoned, helmets gleaming under the morning sun, and boots polished to a mirror shine. A small pin on their lapels marked their achievement. They were now officially soldiers of the United States Army.

A military band played "God Bless America," the notes carrying across the grounds. Brigadier General Arthur W. Lane, Commanding Officer of the camp, took the stage, his chest weighted by medals earned over a stellar career. "Soldiers," he boomed, "you've completed one of the most rigorous training programs in the world here at Camp Roberts. Your efforts over the past four months have earned you the title of United States Army soldier. But this is only the beginning. Many of you will soon join the fight against a strong German military, born in tyranny, in France or some other European country. Carry the skills you've learned here, and never forget you serve a cause greater than yourselves."

Luke stood tall. Brock, beside him, grinned broadly, his confidence unshakable. Stevie's eyes shone with relief. At times, he had doubted himself, but here he was, a soldier. As General Lane finished, each platoon marched by the reviewing stand, saluting sharply.

That evening, the mess hall hosted a celebration. Tables creaked under trays of roast beef, mashed potatoes, and apple pie, a rare treat. The boys laughed, swapped stories of Lowry's tirades, and toasted with tin cups of weak coffee they'd come to love. For the first time in months, they felt human, no longer the drill sergeant's "useless maggots."

Following dinner, Luke strolled back to the barracks, the last night in the structure that had been his home for the past fifteen weeks. It was nothing fancy, but it was familiar and secure. Tomorrow, they would receive new assignments, not as recruits, but as soldiers.

Journal Entry: *October 20, 1943 - Graduation! Sergeant Lowry says I'm "sharp." Not sure I agree. Complimented my leadership. New direction starting now. I hope I'm ready.*

The next morning, Luke stood among hundreds of Camp Roberts graduates on the dusty parade ground. Beside him, Brock shifted his weight from one foot to the other, unable to contain his nervous energy. Stevie remained perfectly still; his usual jokes silenced by the enormity of the moment.

"Think they'll keep us together?" he muttered.

Luke kept his eyes forward. "We requested it. That's all we can do."

"Quiet in the ranks!" barked a passing sergeant.

Colonel Hodgkins approached the podium, a stack of papers in hand. The man's weathered face betrayed nothing as he adjusted the microphone.

"Men, you've completed basic training. You're not recruits playing soldiers. You are United States Army Infantrymen." His voice carried across the silent formation. "When I call your name, come up, receive your orders, and move to your designated area."

Luke's heart raced as the colonel began reading names. Each Duty Assignment separated friends who had sweated, trained, and bonded together during their time at Camp Roberts. Some faces lit up with relief, others fell with disappointment.

"Cower, Steven. 106th Infantry Division, Camp Atterbury, Indiana."

Stevie accepted his papers and moved to the assigned location without looking back. Luke exchanged a glance with Brock, both holding their breath. The Colonel read out the names of twenty assignments before he came to Brock's name.

"Brockman, Timothy. 106th Infantry Division, Camp Atterbury, Indiana."

Brock's shoulders relaxed as he took his orders and joined Stevie. Only Luke remained, his gut tense.

Names continued to be called, each one increasing his anxiety. *What if they split us up now, after all we've been through together?*

"Pierce, Lucas. 106th Infantry Division, Camp Atterbury, Indiana."

Relief flooded through him as he moved to the podium. Colonel Hodgkins handed him the papers, their eyes meeting. "Good luck, son."

Luke joined the other thirty soldiers assigned to the 106th. The three friends, now army soldiers, hugged each other. Stevie verbalized what all three were thinking, "The 'Hanford Boys' ride again."

The group threw their duffel bags near the designated bus, then traded congratulations and shared jokes while officers organized their departure.

"Indiana," Brock said, examining a map someone had produced. "That's a hell of a trip."

"Two thousand miles at least," Luke calculated. "Through half the country."

"Think we'll see anything interesting?" Stevie asked.

Sergeant Lowry appeared, clipboard in hand. "Listen up! You're heading to join the 106th Infantry Division, the Golden Lions. It's a new division, activated last March. You'll complete advanced training there before deployment." His eyes swept over them. "Get aboard. You're leaving in ten."

The bus rumbled to life, belching diesel fumes as the soldiers settled into worn seats. Luke claimed a window, watching Camp Roberts, their home for the past four months, disappear behind them. The California landscape unfolded, hills eventually giving way to desert as they crossed into Arizona.

"You think the 106th will ship out soon?" Brock asked, his voice uncharacteristically quiet.

"Depends where they send us," Luke replied. "Pacific or Europe."

"Europe," Stevie said. "They're building up for something big. My cousin in supply says so."

"Well, that makes it official," said Luke, breaking into a hearty laugh, Brock and Stevie joining in. The laughter continued until all three were crying, struggling to catch their breath. The three had not laughed so hard since the Senior Prom, when Luke had fallen on top of his date, Ruth Greenberg, while trying to do the Lindy Hop.

The bus rolled through small towns where children waved and women blew kisses to the soldiers. They stopped at roadside diners where waitresses served them extra portions, "for our boys," and refused tips from the servicemen.

Nights were spent at army bases along the route, sleeping on cots in temporary barracks. During the day, they saw America transform outside their windows: Arizona's red deserts, New Mexico's mesas, Texas's endless plains, Oklahoma's farmland, Missouri's rolling hills, and Illinois's prairies.

On the third day, as they crossed into Indiana, the landscape was green and lush. The afternoon sun illuminated farmhouses and silos as they approached Camp Atterbury.

“Man, this camp’s in the boondocks,” Brock observed.

"There it is," the driver called back, pointing out the bus’s front window, just as they turned onto a road lined with military police.

The massive military facility sprawled before them; rows of wooden barracks, training grounds, and administration buildings bustling with activity. Trucks loaded with supplies rumbled past, while formations of soldiers marched in perfect unison.

"Home sweet home," Stevie muttered.

"For now," Luke replied. Somewhere beyond those gates lay advanced training, deployment orders, and eventually the war itself. Uncertainty settled over them as the bus passed through the checkpoint.

Sixteen

The morning of Dieter Zobel's eighteenth birthday was gray and cold. Hamburg, Germany bore the scars of Operation Gomorrah, the Allied bombing raids that had reduced entire neighborhoods to rubble, killed thousands, and left a lingering stench of death and destruction. The Zobel family's apartment had survived, but its walls were cracked, its windows now reinforced with tape. The ceiling sagged in places where water damage had weakened the plaster. Inside, the air was stale, the furniture worn and faded from years of use, and the rationed breakfast of thin porridge and ersatz coffee did little to lift their mood.

Dieter sat at the small kitchen table, his broad shoulders hunched, his blond hair cropped close to his scalp in the military style he'd maintained since joining the Hitler Youth eight years earlier. His fingers, rough from years of drills and physical training, drummed impatiently against the wooden surface. His mother, her once-beautiful face now lined with fatigue and worry, placed a cake before him, adorned with a swastika, hand-drawn in black icing. "Eighteen," she said, her eyes shining with pride as she gazed at her son. "A man of the Reich. Werner would be proud." Her eyes, bright with tears, lingered on the medals pinned to Dieter's *Hitlerjugend* uniform; badges of achievement that represented years of dedicated service to the *Führer* and the Fatherland.

His father, slumped in a chair across the table, said nothing, his hands shaky as he sipped his coffee, the cup rattling against the saucer. The war had broken him; his speech was now laced with bitterness and defeat. His shoulders, once strong and square, bore the resemblance to those of a much older man. Dieter avoided his gaze, focusing instead on the cake, its swastika a beacon of hope. He had dreamed of this day for years, the threshold to manhood, to the *Wehrmacht*. But the path was not as straightforward as he'd imagined. Whispers among the Hitler Youth spoke of new requirements: tests of intellect, strategy, and language, in addition to physical strength and loyalty. Dieter's stomach churned with anxiety beneath his stoic expression. He was a warrior, built for action and combat, not a student poring over books. *What if, after all these years of training, he failed to meet the Reich's expectations?*

"Eat," his mother urged, cutting a thin slice of the cake, careful not to nick the swastika. "You'll need your strength today." She placed it before him, her fingers lingering on his shoulder.

Dieter nodded, forcing a smile. "For Germany," he said, his voice steady despite his concern. His father muttered something about Nazi gibberish, but he ignored him. He would prove himself, not just to his mother with her unwavering faith, but to his true father, the *Führer*, to the Reich that had shaped him from boyhood into the soldier he was about to become.

As he ate, savoring each bite of the rare treat, the Loewe-Opta 739GW radio on the table crackled to life, its static giving way to the triumphant, nasally voice of Joseph Goebbels. *"Fellow Germans, a great victory for the Reich! Last month, our brave SS-Hauptsturmführer Otto Skorzeny led a daring raid to rescue our ally, Benito Mussolini, from the traitors of Italy."* Dieter leaned closer, his pulse quickening with excitement, the cake forgotten. Goebbels described in vivid detail how Skorzeny's commandos had landed gliders on the treacherous Gran Sasso mountaintop, stormed the heavily guarded Hotel Campo Imperatore, and freed Mussolini without firing a single shot. *"A triumph of German courage and perfect execution!"* he declared, his voice rising with rehearsed theatrical fervor.

Dieter's eyes were bright with admiration. Skorzeny, tall and scarred, with his commanding presence and tactical brilliance, was the embodiment of the Aryan ideal; bold, cunning, loyal to the death. He imagined himself leading a mission, earning the *Führer's* commendation, his medals gleaming like Skorzeny's against the glossy black uniform of the *Wehrmacht*. But a hint of doubt crept in, cooling his enthusiasm. *Could he ever rise to such heights? Would his physical prowess be enough?*

Shaking off the thought with a determined frown, Dieter adjusted the radio dial, tuning into a shortwave frequency he'd discovered several months earlier. It was risky; the Reich had declared that all Germans were to have the *Volksempfänger* VE301 (the People's Radio) which lacked shortwave bands. Capable of receiving only medium- and long-wave broadcasts, Goebbels, the Reich Minister of Propaganda, was able to control what the people heard. Allied broadcasts were forbidden and punishable by imprisonment or worse, but Dieter justified keeping the Loewe-Opta to practice his English and to prepare for whatever the Reich might require.

A crisp American voice cut through the static, measured but dismissive: "*German forces, led by SS officer Otto Skorzeny, have rescued Benito Mussolini from captivity in Italy. The operation, a propaganda coup for Hitler, underscores the Nazis' desperation as the war turns against them on multiple fronts.*"

He frowned, irritated by the American's scornful tone and blatant lies. They didn't grasp the heroism, the sacrifice, the brilliance of German military strategy. Yet, he listened closely, his brow furrowed, noting phrases like "propaganda coup" and "desperation," repeating the words under his breath to mimic the smooth American accent. His English was improving, but the guttural edge of his German remained. He would need to be better, sharper, more convincing for whatever was planned.

His mother entered the kitchen again, her eyes bright. "Did you hear? Mussolini is free! Our boys did it! The *Führer* always keeps his promises." She clasped her hands together in prayer-like devotion.

"Yes, *Mutter*," he said, switching back to the local German station to avoid suspicion. "A true victory for the Reich and the Italians."

She placed a hand on his broad shoulder, squeezing it with maternal pride. "You'll do great things, too, my son. Like Skorzeny. I've always known it, from the day you first put on your *Jungvolk* uniform."

He nodded stiffly, but the weight of her expectations worried him. He had to prove he was more than just muscle and blind obedience. The Reich needed soldiers who could think and adapt to the changing tide of war.

Dieter walked to the Hitler Youth headquarters, whistling *"Es zittern die morschen knochen"* (The Rotten Bones Are Trembling), the official song of the Hitler Youth, which Dieter had learned when he was ten years old, years before Werner's death. The morning was brisk, but he didn't notice the chill, as he was caught up in the front-line training that would begin today. A sudden commotion snapped him back into the moment. A woman and a child, five or six years old, were being beaten by two SS officers. Dieter admired their black SS uniforms, but flinched at the force that the men used against the defenseless woman and child. He remembered when he was a younger and his father had lost his job. With no money, neighbors had turned on his family. He had responded with anger, pushing a boy about his age to the ground who had compared Dieter's family to Gypsies. Werner, Dieter's older brother, had pulled him off the boy. Now, watching the mother and her son lying on the ground, bleeding, he questioned the brutality of the Nazi training, but did not move to help them.

At the Hitler Youth headquarters, a squat concrete building spared from recent bombings, he stood among the sea of black uniforms, red swastika armbands wrapped around their biceps. The hall was filled with nervous anticipation. Boys his age, some even younger, awaited their assignments with a mixture of enthusiasm and dread. He was certain his path led to the *Wehrmacht*. The war was turning against Germany, with Soviet victories mounting on the Eastern Front, and Allied landings in Italy threatening the west. The Reich needed soldiers more than ever, but it was desperate for men who could outthink the enemy, not just outfight them.

"Zobel!" *Gruppenführer* Bauer's voice cut through the chatter. A coarse man with a prominent dueling scar across his left cheek, his mere presence commanded respect. "To my office. Now!"

Dieter saluted, his boots clicking sharply as he followed Bauer through a corridor lined with propaganda posters of the *Führer* and heroic German officers. Inside the office, Bauer sat behind a desk cluttered with papers and maps, his eyes assessing Dieter's imposing physique. "You've been recommended for advanced training," he said without preamble. "Your language skills caught someone's attention up the chain of command."

Dieter blinked, surprised by this unexpected turn. "English, sir?" he asked, forgetting the proper protocol of speaking only when addressed directly.

Bauer nodded, seemingly unperturbed by the breach of discipline. "The Reich has special plans for boys like you. Men who can speak the enemy's tongue, understand their ways, and infiltrate their thinking. It's not enough to fight anymore, Zobel. The war has changed. You must think as well as act. Report to the training center at nine o'clock tomorrow morning. Don't be late." His tone made it clear that failure would not be tolerated.

"Yes, sir," Dieter said, saluting again with perfect form, his arm extended at precisely the right angle. As he left the office, he experienced a complex mix of pride and apprehension. English had come easily to him, secretly learning phrases and cadences from prohibited radio broadcasts and captured propaganda leaflets. But this was different, far more serious. This was an official assignment—a test of his value to the Reich that he couldn't simply muscle through with brute strength or intimidation. *What if he failed? What if his skills weren't as refined as Gruppenführer Bauer believed?*

The training center was a converted schoolhouse on the outskirts of Hamburg, its brick walls pockmarked from shrapnel, its windows reinforced to prevent shattering during air raids. Inside, the classrooms had been stripped of childish decorations and filled with rows of military-style desks and charts of English grammar. Dieter joined a dozen other boys, ranging from thirteen to nineteen, all selected for their language aptitude or strategic potential. The instructor, Herr Schwein, was a middle-aged man with a pinched face and cold, calculating eyes, his wire-rimmed glasses reflecting the dim light as he surveyed his new students with skepticism. "You are here to learn the enemy's language," he announced, his voice sharp and precise. "Not just their words, but their culture, their patterns of thought, their weaknesses."

The lessons were relentless, grueling in their intensity. They studied English vocabulary and American slang for six hours a day. Dieter struggled with the nuances of pronunciation; phrases like "swell" and "buddy" were awkward and foreign on his tongue, but he realized he was as good, if not better, than most of his classmates.

One afternoon, Herr Schwein paired the boys for conversation practice, assigning them roles in mock scenarios. Dieter was assigned to work with Rolf, a scrawny fourteen-year-old with wide, fearful eyes and a trembling voice. His brown uniform was ill-fitting and awkwardly worn, and his hands shook visibly as he held the English dialogue script. "I can't do this," he whispered in German, his voice breaking with anxiety. "I don't understand half of this. They'll send me to the Eastern Front."

Dieter's first instinct was to snap at him. Weakness was unacceptable in the Hitler Youth, a lesson beaten into him years ago. But something in Rolf's terrified expression restrained Dieter from using harsh words. The boy reminded him of himself at ten, overwhelmed by the *Jungvolk's* demands, mocked and bullied by older boys until he'd grown taller and stronger and learned to fight back. "Look," Dieter said softly, glancing around to ensure no one overheard. "It's not as hard as it seems. Start with this simple phrase." He pointed to the first line of the script. "Say, 'What's your name?' Slow, like this: 'Wot's... yor... naym?'" He exaggerated the sounds, emphasizing each word.

Rolf hesitated, then tried, his voice shaky and uncertain. "Wot's... yor nime?"

"Better than I expected," Dieter said, nodding with approval. "Now I respond, 'My name is John.' You ask again, clearer this time."

Rolf repeated the phrase, his pronunciation clumsy, but improved with each attempt. A small, grateful smile broke across his thin face, and Dieter experienced an unexpected glint of pride that wasn't about medals or glory, or even the *Führer's* approval. "Keep practicing," he added. "You'll get it eventually. The Reich needs every one of us."

Herr Schwein, watching from the front of the classroom, nodded in Dieter's direction, an oblique acknowledgment. Dieter turned away, suddenly embarrassed by being caught in a moment of uncharacteristic kindness. He slapped Rolf on the back of the head, harder than necessary, sending the clear message to the instructor and anyone else that he wasn't soft. The boy winced but said nothing, accepting the blow as the price of Dieter's assistance.

The days blurred into a punishing routine of language drills and physical training. Dieter excelled in the latter: marching, climbing, marksmanship, his body responding to the familiar demands with ease. But the English classes tested him in ways he'd never experienced, forcing his mind to stretch and adapt.

At night, in the barracks, while others slept, he stayed awake, practicing English phrases, mimicking the precise intonations of the voices they'd heard on the radio. As he learned their language, forcing his German mouth to shape their softer words, he wondered what American soldiers were really like. Probably lax and pampered, he determined with contempt. They had never experienced bombing raids on their cities, never known genuine hardship. They were too busy playing baseball. *Weak, all of them, unworthy opponents for the hardened soldiers of the Reich.*

But self-doubt resurfaced when he overheard two schoolmates talking in hushed tones after class, unaware of his presence. "Zobel's just a brute," one said, "All muscle, no mind. They'll send him to the front to die in the snow, not to think or plan." The other laughed, a soft, superior sound. "He's strong, I'll give him that. Good for breaking things and intimidating younger boys. But the *Wehrmacht* needs brains, not just brawn. The

Russians are pushing back, and the Americans aren't as stupid as Goebbels claims."

Mouth closed, Dieter forced air through his nose, his face burning with humiliation and rage. He wanted to step around the corner and confront them, to prove them wrong with his fists. But he held back, forcing himself to breathe, recalling what *Gruppenführer* Bauer had said about thinking, not just acting. Instead of attacking, he listened, absorbing their criticism. He would show them all that Dieter Zobel was more than muscle and blind obedience. He would master English, strategy, or whatever the Reich required.

The ultimate test came in early October when a *Wehrmacht* officer, Captain Drechsler, arrived to evaluate the class's progress and potential. His uniform was immaculate, his Iron Cross gleaming, his monocle menacing as he surveyed the assembled students with cold calculation. "You are the future of Germany," he announced, his voice carrying the authority of one who had shed blood on the battlefield. "Today, you will prove whether you deserve that honor or not."

When Dieter's turn came, he stood at attention, his hands steady at his sides. He launched into a prepared dialogue about American culture, describing baseball games and radio shows he'd heard, weaving in details from the Skorzeny broadcast he'd practiced in secret. His accent was still noticeable, the hard edges of his German origins impossible to completely smooth away. When he finished, Drechsler nodded almost imperceptibly. "Well done, Zobel. You have potential. The Reich may have use for you beyond the infantry."

Dieter treasured the praise, but doubt lingered in the back of his mind. Potential wasn't enough. He needed to be exceptional, the absolute best. Nothing less would satisfy the demands of the Fatherland, or the expectations of his mother, who saw in him the future glory of Germany.

That evening, he walked home through Hamburg's ruined streets, passing hollow-eyed women queued for meager rations, thin children digging through rubble for anything edible. The once-proud city was a ghost of its former self, its magnificent harbor now clogged with sunken ships. He thought of his brother Werner, of his mother's silent tears when word of his death came, of Skorzeny's triumphant Italian rescue mission. The war was slipping away, despite what the propaganda broadcasts claimed. The English lessons, the officer's grudging praise, steps toward something bigger, something he couldn't yet comprehend. He imagined himself in the *Wehrmacht*, perhaps in intelligence or special operations, in a role that required cunning and language skills rather than just physical strength. *But what if he wasn't ready? What if, when the crucial moment came, he failed the Reich, or worse, his father, the Führer?*

He passed a group of *Jungvolk* boys chanting patriotic slogans on a street corner, their high-pitched voices fervent with rehearsed devotion. He remembered the day he had first joined the *Jungvolk*, standing proudly in his new uniform as he swore allegiance to Adolf Hitler. Almost a decade had passed since then, eight years of indoctrination and training, learning to hate the right enemies, especially Jews, and obeying the right leaders. He straightened his shoulders, pushing aside his doubts. He was Dieter Zobel, soldier of the Reich, forged by years of sacrifice and training. He would not falter or fail. Germany would triumph, and he would be part of that victory, whatever the assignment.

Seventeen

The barracks at Camp Atterbury were quiet as the first light of dawn slipped through the narrow windows. The air carried all the familiar scents of Camp Roberts: leather, gun oil, and sweat, odors that reminded Luke of the grueling weeks of basic training that had shaped him into a soldier, now part of the 106th Infantry Division. Today, just ten days after graduation, Luke sat on the edge of his bunk, his duffel bag packed and resting at his feet. He knew the moment had come to break the news.

He cleared his throat, the sound breaking the silence. Brock and Stevie stirred; their faces half-lit in the dimness. Brock, always quick to wake, sat up and stretched his arms. Stevie blinked leisurely, then propped himself up on an elbow.

"Hey," Luke began, his voice steady but soft. "I've got something to tell you both."

Brock grinned; his optimism unshakable even at this hour. "What's up? You get promoted to General?"

Stevie's brow creased with concern. "Yeah, what's going on?"

Luke took a deep breath, feeling the weight of the words he was about to say. "I'm leaving today. For Fort Monmouth."

"Fort Monmouth?" Brock's grin faded into confusion. "Where's that? What for?"

"New Jersey, Signal Corps training," Luke replied, keeping his tone even. "They're sending me to learn radio operation and repair. It's a six-month course."

Stevie sat up, his eyes narrowing. "Six months? Why so long? Will you be back before we deploy?"

"I hope so. I'll be learning everything about radios and communication. Sergeant Lowry assigned me to the training. The word is that the 106th will be preparing for a year before deployment to Europe. I should be back before then, probably in April. But, for now, it means I won't be here to train with you guys."

Brock leaned forward, his optimism rebounding. "Well, that's not so bad. Heck, you'll probably be the guy keeping us all talking when we're out there. Six months ain't forever. We'll still be here when you get back."

Stevie frowned. "But what if you don't make it back in time? Worse, what if they assign you somewhere else?"

Luke shook his head. "Hopefully, they won't. As of now, I'm still part of the 106th. This is just specialized training. I'm betting we ship out together."

Silence settled over them, heavy with the reality of their diverging paths. They had always imagined facing everything as a trio, but now Luke was stepping away.

Brock wrapped his arm around Luke's shoulder, "You better write. And don't go getting too smart on us with all that radio stuff."

"I'll try not to. And you two, don't slack off while I'm gone. I expect you to be in top shape when I get back."

Stevie nodded, but couldn't hide his unease. "Just don't forget how to shoot straight. It's still an infantry division."

They stood, the three of them, and for a moment, no words were needed. Brock pulled Luke into a quick, firm embrace, followed by Stevie's more hesitant and far less animated hug. Though brief, it carried the depth of their friendship.

“Take care of yourselves,” Luke said, choking back emotion.

“You too,” Brock replied. “And hey, maybe you’ll get to see the Atlantic Ocean while you’re out there.”

Luke chuckled. “Yeah, maybe.”

He hefted his duffel bag and headed for the door. Stepping outside, the crisp October air stung his face, thankful the summer’s heat had passed. He glanced back one last time. Brock and Stevie stood in the doorway of the barracks. He raised a hand in farewell, and they returned the gesture. Then, turning away, he walked toward the bus that would carry him to the train station and his new home for the next six months: Fort Monmouth, New Jersey.

The bus jolted along the dirt road, its diesel engine straining as it carried Luke and a handful of other soldiers away from Camp Atterbury. He pressed his forehead against the window, watching the Indiana countryside roll by: golden fields, scattered farmhouses, and the occasional cluster of trees shedding their autumn leaves.

At the train station, Luke boarded a troop train bound for the East Coast. The cars were packed with GIs, their voices a low whir over the clatter of the wheels. He found a seat and settled in, his duffel bag tucked beneath his feet. As the train lurched forward, he had a mix of apprehension and excitement. Fort Monmouth was uncharted territory; New Jersey, the Signal Corps, and six months of training.

The journey spanned two days, weaving through towns and cities, with layovers and transfers along the way. As the miles rolled on, Luke's thoughts drifted to Brock and Stevie, to the drills they'd be running without him, and to the letters he'd promised to send. He thought of his family back home, Katie's quiet strength, his father's unyielding temperament, and wondered how they'd take the news of his new assignment. *I should write Katie.*

Finally, as dusk settled on the second day, the train pulled into the station. He and a few others disembarked, boarding a rickety olive transport bus for the final leg to Fort Monmouth. Through the broken window, he caught his first glimpse of the base, a sprawling complex of barracks, classrooms, and laboratories stretching across more than seventeen hundred acres. The air vibrated with activity, soldiers moving with purpose, and the faint crackle of radios in the distance. It was unlike anything he'd ever seen, and as the bus rolled through the main gate, he felt the enormity of this new adventure.

He was directed to the processing center, where he and the other arrivals were checked in and assigned quarters. It was Block Ninety-Three, part of the Eastern Signal Corps Training Center. The building was stark; rows of bunk beds, metal lockers, and several small windows letting in the evening light. The sharp scent of disinfectant filled the air, reminiscent of the classrooms at Hanford High, a stark contrast to the lived-in smell of Camp Roberts and Camp Atterbury.

After stowing his gear, he joined the others in the mess hall. The meal was simple—meatloaf, mashed potatoes, and green beans—but it was warm and filling. Around him, conversations buzzed with speculation about the training.

"They say the first few weeks are brutal," one soldier muttered. "Morse code drills until your ears bleed."

Another laughed. "Better than running five miles in the mud."

He ate silently, listening and observing. He was eager to begin, counterpoised by the uncertainty of what lay ahead.

That evening, the new trainees gathered in the auditorium for orientation. The room was sizable, with rows of wooden seats facing a stage. A tall, stern officer stepped to the podium, his voice cutting through the murmurs.

"Welcome to Fort Monmouth," he said, his tone commanding. "You are now part of the United States Army Signal Corps, the lifeline of our military. It is our job to keep the forces linked, whether on the battlefield or across oceans. What you learn here will be crucial to the success of our operations."

He paused, his gaze sweeping the room. "Over the next six months, you will be trained in radio operation, repair, and maintenance. You will master Morse code, signal procedures, and troubleshooting gear under pressure. This is not easy work, but it is vital. Gentlemen, you are the voice of the army, or you will be when you complete your instruction."

Luke sat up straighter, the reality of what lay ahead hitting him squarely.

The officer outlined the daily routine: reveille at dawn, physical exercise, classroom instruction, hands-on practice, and evening study. It would be demanding, but Luke resolved to meet the challenge head-on.

Back at the barracks, he met his bunkmate, Joe Moore, a lanky Texan who smiled easily.

"You ever worked with radios before?" he asked as they unpacked.

Luke shook his head. "No, but I've owned a few and tinkered a bit, but I wouldn't say I've worked with them. Hopefully, I'll be a quick learner."

Joe chuckled. "Good. From what I hear, you'll need to be. You and me both."

Reveille sounded at exactly 0600, a sharp bugle blast that jolted Luke from a restless sleep. He dressed quickly in his fatigues and joined the others for physical training, which included calisthenics and a two-mile run around the base. The cool, moist air, much colder and damper than Indiana's, stung his lungs, but within a few minutes, he was alert and ready.

After breakfast, the trainees reported to their classrooms. Sergeant O'Malley, a bristly man with a thick Bostonian accent and a no-nonsense demeanor, led Luke's group.

"Alright, ladies," O'Malley barked, "today we start with the basics—radio fundamentals. You're gonna learn how these machines work, inside and out. Because when you're out there, and your equipment goes down, you're the one who's gotta fix it."

He pointed to a blackboard covered in diagrams: circuits, antennas, and waveforms. Luke listened as the sergeant explained the principles of radio transmission, the nuances of modulation, and the critical role of grounding. The morning passed in a haze of technical details.

After lunch, they moved to the workshop for hands-on practice. He was assigned an SCR-300, a backpack radio used for field communication. With O'Malley's guidance, he was shown how to assemble and disassemble it, check connections, and test the battery.

"It's not too difficult," Joe said from the workbench next to Luke's.

Luke nodded, his fingers tracing the components. He could see the importance of this skill; on the battlefield, a working radio could be the difference between life and death.

Late afternoon brought Morse code practice. O'Malley distributed training buzzers and code sheets. "Morse is the backbone of communication," he said. "You'll learn to send and receive faster than you can blink. We'll start with the basics; dits and dahs."

Luke tapped out "Hello," *dit dit dit dit—dit—dit dah dit dit—dit dah dit dit—dah dah dah*, his movements slow and deliberate. The buzzer's sharp tones thrilled him. This was a new language, but one that would take some time to become proficient in.

The second day mirrored the first: physical training took place at dawn, followed by classroom instruction. The focus was on signal procedures—call signs, message formats, and net operations—with O'Malley pushing the student soldiers with both precision and speed.

"In combat, every second counts," he said. "You don't have time for chit-chat. Get it across, get it right."

Luke took meticulous notes, determined to master the material. After the lecture, they practiced sending mock messages over training radios. It was tough, but he relished the challenge. In the workshop, they diagnosed an inoperable SCR-536, commonly known as a "Handie-Talkie." Luke and Joe identified a loose wire in the headset, earning a gruff, "Good job," from O'Malley.

As evening fell, a moonless night with many stars, Luke walked along the Avenue of Memories, a tree-lined path with monuments to fallen Signal Corps soldiers. The plaques spoke of courage and sacrifice, increasing his resolve. At the same time, he acknowledged the life-and-death risks associated with becoming an army radio operator.

Journal Entry: *October 27, 1943 – Radios were fun. Now they're work. But I enjoy it. Wish I had the RCA that Dad broke. Bet I could fix it. My new roommate, Joe Moore, is a nice guy, but he's not Brock or Stevie. I get the feeling something good is going to happen here. I haven't felt that way for a long time. Maybe never.*

Eighteen

The November chill seeped through the windows of the classroom, but Luke scarcely noticed as he hunched over an SCR-300 radio, its backpack frame resting on the workbench. The Signal Corps training had consumed his first three weeks at Fort Monmouth, each one a relentless cycle of reveille, physical drills, lectures, and hands-on practice. The SCR-300, a 32-pound beast with a whip antenna that could stretch over six feet, was his constant companion. He'd learned to assemble it blindfolded, to tune its frequencies with a flip of the wrist, and to troubleshoot its idiosyncrasies.

Sergeant O'Malley paced the training, his eyes sharp. "These radios are your lifeline," he barked, holding up a battered SCR-300 battery pack. "In the field, you're not just a soldier, you're the voice of your unit. If you fail, your unit's cut off. No artillery, no reinforcements, no tomorrow. You think the Krauts care if your battery's dead?"

Luke nodded, his fingers tracing the battery contacts. The sergeant had drilled into them the importance of maintenance: checking for corrosion, cleaning terminals with a wire brush, and always carrying a spare. "In a pinch, you might have to scavenge parts or jury-rig a fix. Get creative, but get it working." Luke practiced swapping batteries in under a minute, even in the dark, imagining a battlefield where every second counted.

The SCR-536, the "handie-talkie," was another focus. Smaller—just five pounds—it was designed for short-range communication, primarily within infantry platoons. He also learned its peculiarities: its limited quarter-mile reach in rough terrain, its vulnerability to moisture, and the need for precise antenna alignment. "These things are finicky," Joe muttered as they practiced. "One drop of water in the wrong place, and you're just flapping your jaws in the wind. Better to use two cans and a string."

Driven to prove himself, Luke excelled, but a darker undercurrent shadowed his days. Antisemitism, though not as blatant as in Hanford or Camp Roberts, simmered at Fort Monmouth.

One afternoon, during a break in the workshop, Luke overheard a conversation that pushed him to the edge. Two instructors, discussing promotions, mentioned a Jewish officer who'd been passed over. "He's good, but you know how it is," one said, shrugging. "They have strange beliefs, and they don't fit in." The other chuckled, and Luke's blood ran cold. If even officers faced such bias, what chance did he have? He fought the impulse to confront them, but stayed silent, the fear of exposure holding him in place.

Later that night, he lay in bed staring at the ceiling, his mother's face, gleaned from the photograph Katie had found, vivid in his mind: her dark eyes, her gentle smile, the mystery of her life in Austria before she came to America. Her legacy lived in him, a truth he couldn't share. *What would happen if they knew? Would I become the target of their jokes?*

The army wasn't a place for weakness, and revealing his heritage would expose a vulnerability. But not telling the truth was a constant betrayal of his mother.

He sat on his bed, his head in his hands. The antisemitism was eating away at him, a poison that threatened to unravel everything he'd worked for. He thought of Brock and Stevie, back at Camp Atterbury, and wished he could talk to them. But even they didn't know his secret. He felt like a man adrift, with nowhere to turn. *He didn't know that things were about to change for the better.*

On a rare Saturday pass, four weeks after arriving at Fort Monmouth, Luke took the bus to Asbury Park, seeking a break from the sameness of life on the base. The coastal town, subdued since the start of the war, still pulsed with vitality. The boardwalk stretched along the Atlantic, its planks groaning beneath his feet, the walkway lined with shuttered amusement stalls and scattered open diners. The air carried the intoxicating blend of salt and fried dough, a welcome respite from the disinfectant that permeated every corner of Fort Monmouth.

He wandered into *Adira's Seaside Grill*, a small diner with red vinyl stools and a jukebox where Sinatra's *"I'll Be Seeing You"* filled the space with melancholy promise. He sat on a counter stool and ordered coffee. The first sip flooded his senses; mild, not bitter, a taste that confirmed his temporary escape from the base.

The eye-catching waitress who took his order exuded a commanding presence. Young, perhaps seventeen or eighteen, with dark hair bound with a ribbon and alluring brown eyes that gleamed with unshakable confidence. "You from Monmouth?" she asked with a smile that suddenly awakened something deep within Luke, a place that had been untapped.

"Yeah," he replied, managing a nod. "Signal Corps."

"Must be tough work," she said, leaning on the counter, her gaze holding his. "I'm Shaina, Shaina Levine."

"Lucas Pierce, Luke," he said, taking her outstretched hand. Her grip was firm; her smile was genuine in a way that struck him to his core. Something about her evoked Katie's warmth and allure, but at a much more intimate level.

Their conversation flowed with unexpected ease, as they discussed the town, her family's history there since the 1920s, and her affection for the boardwalk. He found himself surrendering his caution and reluctance, drawn irresistibly to her gentle strength. When he called her Katie, the slip became a gateway to stories about his sister, omitting their father from the narrative. As she turned to serve another customer, a twinkle caught his eye—a small Star of David, reminiscent of Matya's pendant, gleaming on her neck.

"Are you Jewish?" The question slipped out, unstoppable, potentially catastrophic.

She touched the necklace, her expression cautious yet dignified. "Yes, I am. Shaina means 'pretty' or 'beautiful' in Hebrew. My father likes to call me his '*Shaina Madela*,' his "pretty girl." Why? Is my being Jewish a problem?"

"No, not ...at all," Luke rushed, words coming in spurts. "I... my mother ...was Jewish. Her name was Matya. She died ...when I was an infant. And your father's right, you are ...very pretty." Luke's face blazed with heat, surprised at the bluntness of his words.

Her expression transformed, softening as she leaned closer, creating an intimate space between them. "That must be hard, losing your mother as a baby. Do you know what *matya* means in Hebrew?"

Luke, burning with embarrassment yet unable to look away, was grateful she passed over his clumsy compliment.

"No, I only learned a few months ago that her name was Matya, from Austria. My sister and I thought her name was Martha."

"*Matya* means 'gift of God.' It reflects the belief that God is generous and provides blessings."

"Thank you," he whispered, tears welling, a dam breaking within him. "I believe she was a gift of God, even though I can't remember her."

"Glad I could help," Shaina replied, a smile playing at the corner of her mouth like a promise. "Is it hard for you to talk about your mother being Jewish?"

Luke nodded, months of silence crumbling. "It is. You're the first one I've told. I hear things; soldiers talking, awful conversations. I want to say something, but I'm at a loss for words. If they knew..."

Shaina's eyes captured his, their depths holding understanding that reached into his soul. "You're not alone. My family's heard it too, here, in town, even from some soldiers. But you don't have to hide who you are, not with me."

For the first time in months, perhaps years, he felt the crushing weight lift from his chest. Talking to Shaina was like discovering an oasis in a desert, and he drank her in without reservation. They spoke in snatched moments between her duties, until her shift ended and she invited him to walk the boardwalk. The ocean's distant roar became the background to a bond forming, a spark igniting something new and unfamiliar to him.

She shared her parents' journey as Polish immigrants who'd weathered America's hostility, and how she wore her necklace as an open act of defiance against prejudice. She said her mother's name was Adira, thus the name of their eatery. Luke confessed he knew very little about his mother and how he'd kept silent at times, wishing he had shown more courage. With Shaina, he glimpsed the possibility of finally being honest, free from the feelings of betrayal he experienced when he hid Matya's name or the fact that she was Jewish.

When it was time for him to head back to the base, she pressed a slip of paper into his palm. "If I'm not here at the diner, I'll probably be at this address; her words were an invitation.

He returned to Fort Monmouth with a renewed sense of purpose. The antisemitism still stung, but Shaina's presence gave him hope. He threw himself into his training, mastering the SCR-300's traits and the SCR-536's limitations, knowing these skills would be crucial to his success. In the back of his mind, he saw the frozen forests of the Ardennes, where radios would falter, and he vowed to be ready. And in his heart, he carried something new: Shaina's smile, a light to guide him through the unseen darkness ahead.

Journal Entry: *November 13, 1943 – I met a girl ...a woman. I've never felt like this before. It's a strange feeling, one I never want to lose. Her name is Shaina, Shaina Levine. Her courage to be herself lights a fire in me. I want to be that brave. I want to stop hiding and begin living the truth. I will start ...soon.*

Nineteen

The workshop reeked of heated flux and solder, alive with the sound of radios. Two months into his Signal Corps training, the SCR-300 and SCR-536 were no longer mysteries, but tools Luke employed with growing skill.

Sergeant O'Malley, his voice as brusque as ever, loomed over the trainees. "Month three, boys. You're not recruits anymore, you're soldiers. On the battlefield, you'll be under fire, in mud, in snow. Your radio goes down, your unit's as good as lost. Fix it fast, or you're done."

His hands were steady as he checked the SCR-300's vacuum tubes. The past eight weeks had been a challenging yet rewarding ordeal. In November, he'd mastered the basics: radio fundamentals, Morse code, and the mechanics of the SCR-300's frequency range. Now, in December, the training intensified, focusing on field operations and advanced troubleshooting skills that would prove critical in the chaos of war.

The Signal Corps manual, *The Radio Operator*, emphasized practical application. He learned to set up a field radio under simulated combat conditions, stringing antenna wire through trees to maximize range while avoiding detection. He practiced adjusting the SCR-300's antenna for optimal signal in dense terrain, a skill that would prove critical in the snow-choked Ardennes. He drilled on message encryption, using simple ciphers to secure communications, and learned to recognize German jamming techniques, bursts of static or false signals that could mislead a unit.

The SCR-536 posed different challenges. Its quarter-mile range was useless in hilly or forested areas unless the antenna was perfectly aligned. He practiced elevating the antenna on improvised poles, a trick that could extend range but exposed the operator to enemy fire. "You're a target out there," O'Malley warned. "Keep low, keep moving." Luke internalized the lesson, imagining a frozen forest where a dead radio could strand his platoon.

Battery maintenance remained critical. The BA-70, used to power the SCR-300, drained without warning in cold weather, and he learned how to insulate them against moisture. He practiced field repairs, replacing a cracked crystal oscillator with scavenged parts and soldering a loose connection under a tarp in the rain. These skills, O'Malley stressed, could mean the difference between calling in artillery or being overrun. Luke didn't know it, but within a year, the lessons learned in the classroom would be put to the challenge; batteries failing in the cold and radios rendered useless in the midst of battle.

Morse code drills consumed hours. He could now send and receive at fifteen words per minute, his pencil recording the correct letters with precision. The rhythmic dits and dahs; *dit dah* for the letter A, *dit dit dah dit* for the letter F, and so on, became a fluent language, a skill that would permit messages to travel longer distances. He also studied signal security, learning to authenticate messages with prearranged codes to avoid enemy deception—a tactic the Germans employed.

Yet even as he thrived, a battle raged within. His fear of being discovered compelled his silence, but he grew troubled by the hypocrisy; the very bigotry they were being drilled to combat in Europe was overlooked and accepted throughout military facilities in California, Indiana, and now, here in New Jersey.

The visit to Asbury Park had changed everything. Shaina Levine, the slender dark-haired waitress at Adira's Seaside Grill, had become a ray of sunshine in Luke's sometimes dark world. Her Star of David necklace, worn with quiet dignity, had inspired him, an amulet that openly displayed courage. On his second trip, after a week of internal debate and restless nights, he'd revealed more about Matya.

Shaina had reached across the counter, her hand resting on his. Her skin was warm, her touch gentle. "You don't have to hide anything with me. You're not alone." Her brown eyes, luminous, held no judgment, just an understanding that seemed to reach beyond her eighteen years.

For the first time since discovering the hidden letter and pendant a year ago, Luke felt relieved. The secret he'd carried when he left California, lighter now, shared between the two of them in the bustling diner. What he could not release on his own, she had drawn out of him with nothing more than her presence and quiet acceptance.

Shaina, gentle and comforting, reminded him of Katie. But this was deeper, a connection that touched his core, a new sensation he relished. The way she listened when he spoke about his fears and discoveries about his mother's past. The way she nodded when he described his father's silence on the matter, understanding the complexity without him having to relive the pain. Love? The word floated in his mind, both thrilling and terrifying. He'd never felt this way about anyone before, certainly not about the girls he'd dated at Hanford High.

Yet the fear lingered, casting shadows across this newfound light. Confiding in Shaina was a step toward accepting who he was and who his mother had been, but the prejudice surrounding him was a constant threat. He'd seen the sideways glances some patrons gave her when they noticed her necklace, and he'd overheard the whispered slurs when they thought no one was listening.

The war news from Europe grew darker by the day, with rumors of atrocities that turned Luke's stomach. He wondered if he'd ever be released from this fear, the need to hide part of himself, in a world where who your ancestors were could determine whether you lived or died. It was difficult, often unbearable, but Shaina Levine revealed a nobler world, one free of guilt and shame.

On a Saturday pass in early January, Luke returned to the diner. It was busy, the late afternoon air filled with the pleasing aroma of freshly brewed coffee and frying hamburgers. Shaina greeted him with a smile that warmed him against the winter chill. "Back so soon?" she teased, sliding a coffee his way.

"Can't stay away," Luke said, his grin wide. They talked easily, about her family, his training, and the boardwalk's quiet beauty, now covered in a blanket of fresh snow. Her eyes sparkled as she described her dream of studying literature after the war, and he found himself falling harder, drawn to her beauty, but captivated by her spirit.

Their conversation was interrupted by the jingle of the door. A soldier stumbled in, his uniform disheveled, his breath laced with alcohol. Luke tensed, the memory of his father drunk and obnoxious renewed. The soldier plopped onto a stool; his eyes bleary as he scanned the counter. His gaze landed on Shaina's necklace, the Star of David catching the light.

"Hey, Missy," he slurred, pointing. "What's that star mean? Saw a bunch of 'em at the cemetery instead of crosses."

Luke's jaw tightened, but Shaina remained composed. "It's a Star of David," she said politely. "It's a symbol of my Jewish faith."

The soldier squinted, unconvinced. She turned back to Luke, her expression calm but firm, clearly intent on ending the exchange. "So, you were saying about the radios?" she prompted.

He started to respond, but the soldier's voice cut through. "Hey, Jew girl, I'm talkin' to you!" he shouted, slamming his hand on the counter.

The words hit Luke. The volcano of anger he'd suppressed for months, years, erupted. He was off his stool in an instant, crossing the diner in three strides. "Shut your mouth!" he roared, grabbing the rude soldier's shoulder and yanking him off the stool and onto the floor. His fist connected with the man's jaw, once, twice, the impact jarring his knuckles. The soldier flailed, too drunk to fight back effectively.

"Luke, stop!" Shaina's voice broke through, urgent and pleading. "He's not worth it! You'll lose everything, your training, your stripes!"

Her words pierced his rage. He froze, fist raised, ready to deliver another blow, the soldier groaning beneath him. He looked at her, her eyes wide with fear, not for herself, but for him. She was right. A skirmish like this could end his time at Fort Monmouth and derail his role with the 106th. He let go, standing slowly, his chest heaving.

The defeated soldier staggered to his feet, wiping blood from his lip. He looked from Luke to Shaina and back to Luke, his eyes narrowing. "Think I'll find a better place to eat," he muttered, stumbling toward the door. "This place's too damn unfriendly."

The diner fell silent, patrons staring. Shaina rushed to Luke, her hand on his arm. “Are you okay?” she asked softly.

He nodded; his mind still engaged in the scuffle. “I’m sorry,” he said, his voice low. “I just... I couldn’t let him talk to you like that.”

“I know,” she said, her touch reassuring him. “But you don’t have to fight my battles. Or yours. You’re stronger than that.”

They sat for a while, but the mood had shifted. Luke paid for his coffee and promised to return soon. As he boarded the bus back to the base, his thoughts churned. The confrontation had cracked something open. His secret was spilling out, impossible to contain. *Was that a good thing, or a danger that could cost him everything?* He thought of Shaina’s courage and her unapologetic pride, and he experienced a moment of hope. But the fear revisited, just as it always did, a shadow he couldn’t outrun.

Back at Fort Monmouth, Luke threw himself into training, but the incident was never far from his mind. In the workshop, he practiced setting up a field net under simulated enemy fire, his hands steady despite his internal turmoil. The equipment was reassuring against his fingertips as he connected wires and adjusted frequencies with growing confidence. He repaired an SCR-536 with a damaged antenna mount, his soldering iron securing the delicate components, while O'Malley stood over him, stopwatch in hand.

"Good work, Pierce," the sergeant said, scribbling on his clipboard, a rare compliment from the gruff Bostonian, "Fastest time in the platoon." Luke nodded, feeling a momentary flash of pride. His technical skills were sharpening daily, becoming instinctive, but his heart, aroused and awakened by Shaina, remained a battlefield of conflicting emotions and unresolved questions.

The workshop hummed with activity around him, as other recruits cursed under their breath at stubborn equipment, and instructors barked corrections. He moved through it all with mechanical precision, his body present while his mind wandered miles away, to the small diner in Asbury Park.

As he lay in his bunk that night, he saw Shaina's face floating in his mind's eye, her dark eyes serious and knowing, her Star of David necklace defiant. He wondered if he could ever be as brave as she was, wearing her identity openly in a world that could be cruel and unforgiving. His secret was no longer a private burden. It had become an integral part of him, acknowledged by another person, and hiding it seemed cowardly.

He shifted on the thin mattress, creaking springs responding to his slightest movement. The future stretched before him, vast and uncertain, filled with the chance of combat and the possibility of death. But in the present moment, he clung to what he knew: the skills he was mastering day by day, the feel of radio dials in his fingers, and the hope that Shaina had sparked in him with her acceptance and understanding.

Twenty

THE LAST WEEK OF April hummed with restless anticipation at Fort Monmouth. The Signal Corps training program, an unrelenting six-month trial of radio repair, Morse code, and field operations, was nearing its end. For Luke, the base had transformed from an intimidating sprawl of red-brick barracks and towers into a second home. He'd arrived as a new soldier and was now poised to step into the war as a full-fledged radio operator. Graduation day loomed, a milestone marked with both triumph and trepidation.

The parade ground stretched wide under a pale spring sky, the air sharp with the scent of blooming dogwoods, their showy white leaves bursting forth. Rows of trainees stood perfectly straight, exactly one arm's length apart, their khaki uniforms crisp, boots gleaming. The American flag whipped above them, a vivid slash of red, white, and blue against the bright sunlight. Luke assumed the "at ease" posture, hands clasped behind his back, eyes locked on the wooden stage where Colonel James Haskell, the base commander, organized his notes.

The colonel's gravelly words cut through the morning stillness. "Gentlemen, today you join a brotherhood that holds our brave soldiers together. The Signal Corps isn't just about wires and radios; it's about lives. When the enemy cuts through our lines, when the fog of war blinds us, your signals will pierce the chaos. You'll call the shots that save platoons, guide bombers, and turn the tide of battle. Make no mistake: you are the army's eyes, ears, and most, its voice."

Luke's throat tightened. He stole a glance at Joe, his roommate for the past six months, whose easy-going manner yielded a familiar smile.

They were a patchwork crew: farmhands, students, sons of immigrants, all bound by the same grueling months of training. Luke remembered his first day, fumbling with a Morse key, tapping out "H-E-L-L-O," Sergeant O'Malley hovering over his shoulder, the dits and dahs a jumbled mess. Now, he could send and receive twenty words a minute, repair an SCR-300 under pressure, and set up a field net in the dark, all skills learned over the past six months.

The ceremony unfolded with the typical precision of a military operation. Names rang out, one by one, and when "Pierce, Lucas," boomed across the grounds, he marched forward. He saluted crisply, accepting his certificate from Lieutenant Harper, whose somber face softened with a nod of approval.

"Top marks, Pierce," the lieutenant offered, handing over the paper. "Ninety-six percent on the field test, best score with the SCR-300 this cycle. You've got the hands for it and the head. Don't lose either."

"Thank you, sir," Luke replied, his voice steady. The award bore the words "outstanding proficiency," a quiet testament to his growth.

After the formation dissolved, the trainees scattered, some to pack, others to share a smoke or scribble letters home. Luke lingered, drawn to the edge of the parade ground where the flag still danced in the breeze. He saw a group of recruits drilling in the distance, their movements clumsy, a reminder of his beginning. He had survived, more than that, he'd thrived. But leaving Fort Monmouth meant leaving more than the base. It meant leaving Shaina.

The bus to Asbury Park jolted along the coastal road, each bump tightening the knot in Luke's stomach. The worn leather seat beneath him offered little comfort, carrying him toward a goodbye he didn't want to think about. Shaina Levine had entered his life like a light, releasing affections that had been hidden deep within. Over the past five months, their bond had deepened into a love that secured him; fierce, tender, and unyielding. She knew him; his fears, his secrets, his Jewish heritage kept from him by years of silence, and the impact of his father's rage. With her, he wasn't Frank Pierce's disappointing son or a faceless soldier in an endless war. He was a man, now whole, with normal hopes and dreams.

The coastline blurred, the Atlantic stretching to his right. Other passengers chatted or dozed, oblivious to his building unease. He brushed the dust from his uniform, a reminder of what lay ahead. Signal Corps training had prepared his mind to face adversity on the battlefield, but nothing could prepare his heart.

Outside Adira's Seaside Grill, Shaina waited, her navy-blue coat cinched against the April wind that whipped strands of dark hair across her face. She stood perfectly still among the hurried pedestrians, scanning the street with an intensity that made his breath catch. When she spotted him, her smile broke through the gloom; radiant, fragile, penetrating his heart. The sight of her Star of David pendant sent a twinge through him, a reminder of all they shared.

Luke closed the distance, weaving through the crowded sidewalk, hardly noticing the shoulders he brushed. He wrapped her in his arms, lifting her feet off the ground, holding her tight against him, wishing he could freeze the moment forever. Her body fit against his perfectly, as though the same sculptor had carved them.

"I don't know how to say goodbye," he whispered into her hair, her scent a blend of lavender and sea salt, flooding his senses and etching itself into his memory.

"You don't have to know," she said, her voice trembling despite the strength in her eyes. "Just promise you'll come back. That's all I need to hear."

They wandered to the beach; hands entwined so tightly Luke could feel her pulse in his palm. The sand crunched beneath their shoes, wet from a light morning rain. The ocean churned before them, waves crashing against the shore with a steady rhythm that seemed to count down their remaining moments. The boardwalk behind them stood nearly empty, leaving them in a private world of wind, water, and words of parting.

They settled on a salt-worn bench, the wood cool and moist on their thighs. They sat in silence, watching gulls wheel overhead, their screeches carrying over the pounding of the surf. She broke the quiet, turning to face him, her gaze fierce and unwavering.

"Luke, you're stronger than you think. You've carried so much. This war, this distance, it won't break you. I won't let it. Not after everything you've already survived."

He blinked back tears, her faith penetrating more than his father's harshest words ever could. "You make me believe that. Before you, I was just... surviving. Moving through each day, writing in my journal, dreaming of escape. Now, with you, I've got something worth fighting for."

"Then fight," she said, her hands framing his face, thumbs brushing away moisture from beneath his eyes. "And don't stop. Not for a second. The world needs men like you to come home."

She reached into her coat pocket and removed a small object, which she placed in his palm: a silver locket, its surface etched with a delicate star, the points worn smooth from years of handling. "My grandmother's," she explained. "She wore it through hard times in the old country, through everything they did to her family. It protected her. Now you."

His fingers closed around it, the metal warm from her touch and the shelter of her pocket. "I'll keep it close," he said, voice thick with emotion. "Every day, every night."

Their kiss came then, a collision of longing and promise. Her mouth was soft, insistent, tasting faintly of the Boardwalk's sea air. Luke poured himself into it, knowing it might be the last for months, maybe years. When their lips parted, he rested his forehead against hers, breathing her in, etching her into his memory; the curve of her cheek, the flutter of her lashes, the small freckle near her nose.

"Write to me," she murmured, slipping a photograph into his hand, her smiling face captured in black and white, the diner's counter visible behind her.

"Every chance I get," he vowed, tucking the photo into his breast pocket, close to his heart. "You too?"

"Every day," she said, a shaky laugh escaping. "The customers are already tired of hearing about my soldier boy."

One last embrace, her warmth seeping into him like a salve against the chill that awaited, and then he turned away, forcing his feet to move. Each step toward the bus felt like wading through quicksand, his chest throbbing with mounting grief. The driver nodded as he boarded, a knowing look on his face, not the first time he'd seen this scene play out.

Onboard, he clutched the locket and photo, staring out the window as Shaina's figure dwindled to a speck, consumed by the shoreline. A piece of his soul remained attached to the windswept beach, to the girl who had shown him who he truly was, and the girl who promised to wait for his return. He smiled at the thought of their future reunion, then put his head in his hands, and wept.

The train back to Camp Atterbury clattered through the night, its rhythm a metronome reverberating through the dimly lit car. Luke sat by the window, his duffel bag stuffed with Signal Corps manuals resting at his feet, a faint yellow bulb swaying overhead, casting moving shadows across the worn leather seats. Outside, the miles rolled by in darkness; nameless towns, silent fields, and occasional rows of light off in the distance. He was returning to the 106th, to Brock and Stevie and the familiar bedlam of camp life, but he felt adrift. Shaina's absence was now a void in him, a persistent ache that deepened with each mile the train covered.

The memory of her on the boardwalk, the Star of David necklace against the soft skin of her throat, her dark eyes holding his until he was forced to pull away, played in his mind like a newsreel on a loop that he couldn't shut off.

He shifted in his seat and pulled out a notepad and pencil from his jacket pocket, needing to share his thoughts before they overwhelmed him completely. The letter was for his sister, his sole confidante since childhood, the one who'd always understood him when words failed and his feelings were too tangled to express.

Dear Katie,

I'm on the train back to Camp Atterbury, watching the miles blur past through a smudged window. I left my heart behind in New Jersey, tucked away in a small diner with checkered tablecloths and the best apple pie ever.

Training is done. I graduated near the top of my class, something I never would have imagined a year ago. The instructors say I have a gift for it. I can hear messages in static that others miss, and I have a certificate with gold lettering that says "Outstanding Proficiency" to prove it. But that's not what's keeping me awake tonight as the train rocks and everyone else around me sleeps.

He folded the letter and tucked it into his pocket. *His heart wouldn't let him write more... not yet.*

Twenty-One

As Luke stepped off the bus, his duffel bag heavy on his shoulder, he was struck by how much more Camp Atterbury smelled of combat than Fort Monmouth. The air was thick with diesel fumes, gun oil, and sweat, a pungent odor that signaled preparation for war. The 106th Infantry Division's home base buzzed with activity as soldiers marched in formation. Trucks rumbled past, and officers barked orders that resounded across the sprawling grounds. He had returned, but he wasn't the same person who'd departed; the months of specialized training had transformed him from a fresh recruit into something more —a soldier with purpose.

He spotted Brock and Stevie by the mess hall; their silhouettes unmistakable. Brock stood tall and broad with his characteristic military posture, while Stevie leaned against the wall, his blond hair catching the afternoon sun. When they noticed him, Brock's face split into a wide grin as he waved with enthusiasm. Stevie straightened up, his eyes lighting up with a genuine warmth that made Luke quicken his pace.

"You're back!" Brock called, jogging over, grabbing Luke's hand, and pulling him toward his bulky chest for a rough embrace that nearly knocked the wind out of him. "How's it feel to be a radio genius?"

Luke grinned, the fatigue of his journey easing in their presence. The long train ride and endless waiting were now worth it. "It's good, but I'm glad to be back with you knuckleheads. Fort Monmouth was all business, all the time."

Stevie stepped forward, the slight grin turning to a full-faced smile as he neared Luke. He clasped Luke's shoulder, then pulled him into a quick hug. "Missed you, brother. Camp's way too quiet without you."

They walked toward the barracks, the familiar scent of pine trees and dust enveloping them as Luke filled them in on his training. "It was intense, SCR-300s, SCR-536s, Morse code drills till my fingers felt like they would fall off. The instructors were relentless, rising before dawn to study until lights out. Learned to set up field nets, troubleshoot under pressure, and even repair equipment with minimal tools. Believe it or not, I got top marks."

Brock let out a low whistle, his eyebrows shooting up in exaggerated surprise. "Top marks? Look at you, the 'Scholar of Signals.' What'd you do, bring apples to the instructors?"

Luke patted his duffel bag, pride warming his chest despite his attempt to remain modest. "Got the proof right here. 'Outstanding Proficiency,' written in gold letters."

Stevie turned to face Luke, a teasing glint in his eye as they rounded the corner past the supply depot. "And what about that girl you met? Shaina, right? Don't tell us you spent all your time tuning radios. Your letters made her sound like some angel."

Luke's cheeks flushed, but he couldn't hide the smile that spread across his face at the mention of her name, the memory of her dark eyes, and the Star of David that always caught the light around her neck. "Yeah, Shaina. She's... she's something else. Smart, fearless, not afraid to speak her mind. Didn't think I'd find someone like her, not now, not there, with everything so uncertain."

Brock nudged him with his elbow, grinning. "Luke Pierce, the quiet kid who hardly dated in high school, is now head over heels for a waitress from Jersey. What's the world coming to? Next thing you know, Stevie here will start writing poetry."

Luke shook his head, still smiling as they approached their barracks building. The wooden structure looked exactly as he'd left it, somehow both foreign and familiar. "Guess I just needed to grow up a bit to figure out what love is. Shaina's it. It's real and profound, the kind of love that inspires you to be better. She causes me to think about things, about the war, about what we're fighting for."

Brock's expression softened, the teasing giving way to something more genuine. "That's good, Luke. I'm happy for you. We all need something to hold onto in this mess."

They ducked into the barracks, the familiar scent of perspiration, boot polish, and wool blankets greeting them like an old friend. As they sat on Stevie's bunk, the metal frame creaking under their weight, the conversation shifted to what Luke's friends had been up to during his absence.

Brock stretched out, hands behind his head, staring at the ceiling. "We got sent to Tennessee for maneuvers, three months, in the middle of winter. Grueling stuff, let me tell you. Steep mountain hikes with full packs, camp set-ups in the rain and mud, and mock battles till we dropped. Sergeants are pushing us past breaking points. Like the real thing, at least what I think the real thing will be."

Stevie nodded, sitting cross-legged, his voice steady. "Yeah, and they picked me for sniper training after I qualified expert. Weeks of special instruction, learning to read wind, calculate distance, and stay hidden for hours. Guess all those hours at the range paid off."

Luke's eyes widened, genuinely impressed. "A sniper? That's huge. You've come a long way from that kid who didn't own a BB gun. Your dad must be proud."

Stevie shrugged, a mixture of pride and discomfort crossing his face. "Thanks. It's a lot of pressure, but I'm ready. Funny how things work out, huh?"

Brock grinned, sitting up and leaning forward. "And I led our squad up a hill during one of those Tennessee exercises. Since you weren't here to lead with your fancy strategies, someone had to step up. Colonel even mentioned it in the debriefing, said I showed 'natural command presence.'"

They burst into laughter, the sound bouncing off the wooden walls. For a moment, it was just the three of them, back in Hanford, joking over milkshakes at the diner after school. The war, the training, and the uncertainty of their futures; for a few minutes, it all faded into the background.

But things were about to change.

The calendar read 6 June 1944. All day, the barracks hummed with rumors, whispers of something big across the Atlantic. By evening, a crowd had gathered around the scruffy table radio in the mess hall, its Bakelite case scuffed and worn from years of use. The soldiers sat on benches, leaned against walls, or crouched on the floor, their eyes all fixed on the glowing dial.

The familiar commanding voice of Edward R. Murrow resonated through the static. "*This is CBS London. D-Day has come. Early this morning, the Allies began the invasion of Nazi occupied Europe. Assault troops have landed on the northern coast of France.*"

A roar erupted, the men cheering and clapping each other on the back. Luke's heart raced, a mix of admiration and adrenaline. This was it; the turning point they'd been waiting for.

Fixated on the radio, the men gathered could see Morrow, his matter-of-fact delivery, his trademark cigarette, his worried expression. He continued, "*Paratroopers have been dropped behind enemy lines, and naval forces are bombarding the beaches. The invasion is underway.*"

Morrow then read General Eisenhower's order to the troops. The men gathered around the radio cheered at the General's decree, "*We will accept nothing less than full victory.*"

Brock punched the air, his grin wide. "Yes! We're finally taking it to the Krauts! The war'll be over by Christmas!"

Stevie nodded. "Hope it holds."

There were many more reports, all painting a vivid picture: landings at Utah, Omaha, Gold, Juno, and Sword beaches; waves crashing against landing craft; soldiers wading through gunfire. A BBC correspondent, Howard Marshall, described riding a command barge that struck a mine, his voice cut off mid-sentence. Luke imagined the chaos; young men his age—18 and 19-year-olds—storming the French coast.

One report stuck with him: "*The Allies have secured a foothold on the beaches. Despite heavy casualties, the invasion is progressing as planned.*"

Luke thought of those soldiers, their courage, their losses. He glanced at Brock, who was still cheering, and Stevie, whose eyes remained fixed on the radio, his jaw tight. The room pulsed with hope, but Luke was anxious, discerning that this was only the beginning.

As the broadcast continued, others echoed Brock's enthusiasm: "Fighting will be over by Christmas! Maybe the 106th won't even see action. Just mop up the leftovers."

Brock leaned in, "Think they're right? Could we miss the fight?"

Luke shook his head. "Doubt it. This is big, but it's far from over. We'll be needed."

Stevie nodded. "Yeah. I think a lot more GIs have to die before the Germans wave the white flag."

Despite Stevie's forewarning, the optimism was infectious, hugs and laughter drowning out the radio's small cloth-covered speaker. For a moment, victory felt close, but Luke couldn't shake his premonition of what lay ahead: frozen forests, failing radios, and the moans of soldiers dying in the snow.

As summer moved into August, the 106th struggled. Normandy's toll had gradually gutted the division, as seasoned men were siphoned off and replaced by recruits who tripped over their boots and fumbled with equipment they didn't yet understand. The once-crisp drills turned sloppy, formations ragged. Men shuffled where those before them had marched sharply, their lines now wavering. One sweltering afternoon, Luke stood in a clearing flecked with patchy sunlight, an SCR-300 radio perched on a rickety wooden table that wobbled with every move. He was coaching Private Phillip Hartwell, a fresh-faced kid who looked like he should still be delivering newspapers, not training for war. His hands shook, wet with sweat that beaded on his forehead and dripped onto the disassembled components, as he wrestled with the unwieldy BA-70 battery.

"Smooth, Hartwell," Luke said, keeping his voice steady. "Like I showed you. Firm grip. It's government property; it can take it."

The battery slipped, crashing to the dirt with a sickening thud. A bright blue spark flared against the ground, acid hissing as it spilled across the dry ground. Luke lunged forward without hesitation, scooping up the damaged battery and tossing it into the nearby sandpit as Hartwell stammered, his face flushed. "Sorry, I... I don't know what happened. My hands just..."

"Yeah, that could've been bad," Luke cut in, his outward calm masking the frustration churning beneath. He wiped his hands on his fatigues. "In combat, that's not just equipment lost. That's people's lives. Your buddies. Maybe your own."

Later, Luke vented to Brock and Stevie in the mess hall, the air filled with the odor of overcooked cabbage and cigarette smoke as men shuffled through, their conversations a low, constant murmur. "Kid nearly sparked us up today. Dropped a battery like it was on fire. No instincts, no focus. Couldn't follow basic instructions."

Brock stabbed his fork into the soggy cabbage with unnecessary force, the tines scraping against the metal tray. "Half these guys can't even load a rifle properly. Some can't tell a grenade pin from a shoelace. We're a damn mess, is what we are."

Stevie leaned in, his voice dropping to a conspiratorial level, just over the clatter of trays and muted conversations. "Heard we lost nearly two thousand experienced men to replacements since June. They're shipping in fresh recruits with no more than six weeks of training. No grit, no experience, just warm bodies to fill the gaps."

Luke frowned, pushing the food around his tray without appetite. "You think the officers see it? See what we've become?"

"Yeah," Brock said, his eyes darting toward the officers' table across the room, where Captain Reynolds sat with his back straight, laughing at something another officer had said. "He calls us Golden Lions in briefings, talks about honor and tradition, but his eyes say something different. They're worried, all of them. You can see it when they think we're not looking."

The lion's roar that had once been their division's pride seemed more like a whimper now, drowned by the war's insatiable hunger for men and material. Luke sensed that the 106th Infantry Division was being fattened for slaughter. He couldn't shake the feeling that they were marching toward a destiny far worse than they imagined.

Journal Entry: *August 12, 1944 – We're not ready. It's like we're football players with no pads or helmets, or baseball players with no gloves. The officers smile, but their eyes say they're worried. I feel like lambs being led to the slaughter.*

Twenty-Two

Luke adjusted his helmet, the weight of the M1 Garand familiar in his hands, but the division's rhythm was off. The camp, once a model of disciplined marches and synchronized drills, now resonated with the clumsy steps of recruits. The metallic smell of military equipment, mixed with the earthy scent of the training grounds, had become as natural to Luke as the aroma of the Pierce kitchen back in Hanford.

He had returned from Fort Monmouth in April and rejoined the tight-knit unit, the 106th, a division forged over a year. However, the division began to change by late June, just weeks after the Allies stormed the beaches of Normandy. The toll was brutal, over ten thousand casualties as Allied forces pushed inland and engaged in fierce combat in the battles for Caen, Saint-Lô, and the Falaise Pocket. These names, once just dots on a map during strategy briefings, now represented hallowed ground soaked with American blood.

The 106th, now designated a lower-priority division, had become a well-spring for replacements, sending hundreds, then thousands, of its seasoned soldiers to replace the wounded and the fallen in Europe. In their place came raw recruits: boys just out of high school, dropouts from programs no longer supported by the military, and college students who'd lost their deferment. They stumbled through formations, marching in uneven lines, a far cry from the precision Luke remembered. The 106th, meant to be a cohesive unit, was fracturing. Every morning, Luke would wake to find familiar faces gone, shipped out overnight to combat units across the European theater.

As summer dragged on, news from Europe filtered in through radio broadcasts and the men's passing around newspaper articles in the barracks. The liberation of Cherbourg, France, in late June brought raucous cheers and impromptu celebrations, but subsequent reports of fierce fighting and mounting casualties along the Norman hedgerows tempered the enthusiasm. Luke gathered with others, listening to the latest updates, each man calculating his odds when it would be his turn to cross the Atlantic.

In the quiet of his bunk after lights out, he wrote to Shaina, a flashlight clinched between his knees providing the necessary illumination. He poured out his jumbled thoughts about D-Day and what might come next. His pencil moved quickly across the page, capturing his hopes and fears in cramped handwriting. *Everyone's hopeful about the invasion's success, but I sense in my gut it's far from over. The Germans won't give up easily, but enough about war. I miss you every day, more than I can express in words.*

Private Kenneth Baker rolled over in his bunk. "Writing to that girl from the diner again, Pierce?" he whispered, "You must've filled a book by now."

Luke smiled, not bothering to hide his letter. "Just trying to make sense of everything," he replied softly, careful not to wake the others. "Helps to put it down on paper."

The next afternoon, while watching a batch of fresh-faced recruits stumble through basic drills on the parade ground, he reflected on the distance he and his two childhood friends had traveled since they enlisted. The midday August sun was intense as a drill sergeant's voice carried across the field, barking the same commands he had once struggled to follow. Dust kicked up with every misstep, visible evidence of their inexperience.

"Remember when we were that green?" he said, wiping sweat from his forehead with his sleeve. "Tripping over our own feet and each other's? Drill Sergeant Lowry nearly had an aneurysm that time you dropped your rifle during inspection, Stevie."

Brock laughed, his eyes never leaving the confused formation of newcomers. "Seems like a lifetime ago. Hard to believe that was us a year ago." He squinted against the bright sun, his face now tanned and leaner than when they'd joined.

"We didn't even know how to lace our boots properly," Stevie added with a wry smile, leaning on a nearby tree for shade. He nodded toward the recruits. "We're not those naive kids anymore," he said, his finger writing "Katie" on the tree's bark, his usual sarcasm subdued.

The war that had once seemed distant was near, growing closer with each passing day. The officers spoke with increasing confidence about victory, about how they'd soon be mopping up a defeated enemy. Something in Luke's gut told him otherwise. He'd read enough history to know that when cornered, enemies fought the hardest, and the Germans had been cornered for a year or more. As he observed the recruits fumble through their drills, he wondered how many of them would not be returning home by the time the war was over. *Would he be returning?*

October brought a welcome chill to the air as the division braced to move. The smell of boot polish, sweat, and cigarette smoke, mixed with frantic activity and nervous energy, filled the cramped space. Equipment was sorted and resorted. Footlockers were filled, then slammed shut. Letters were scratched out, men hunched over blank sheets of paper, striving to capture what might be their final thoughts before heading overseas. Some wrote with furious speed, but most stared at empty pages for long minutes, struggling to find words that wouldn't worry their families back home.

Luke sat on his bunk, composing a brief letter to Shaina, his heart aching with each word. *The invasion is advancing across Europe, but the fight is far from over. I miss you more with each passing day. I wish I could see you one more time before we ship out.* He paused, remembering the way her dark eyes shone when she smiled, how she'd tucked stray hairs behind her ear while serving coffee at her parents' diner. As the weeks apart grew, he rehearsed the moments they had spent together, now etched deeply into his memory.

The last night at camp, they sat on wooden ammunition crates outside the barracks, passing around a dented canteen filled with bitter, lukewarm coffee. The liquid sloshed against the sides as it moved from hand to hand. Other clusters of soldiers huddled in similar formations, their voices interrupting the night's stillness.

Stevie joked that he relished army coffee, calling it an acquired taste. "Kind of like war," he added with a forced laugh, lightly shaking the canteen to determine how much remained. "Terrible at first, then you just get used to it." No one responded, but Luke winked, acknowledging his wit.

The stars pierced the darkness overhead, bright and distant. The cool air carried the scent of pine from the surrounding woods, mixed with the ever-present smell of diesel fuel and gunpowder.

Brock's usual bravado faltered as he stared into the night sky, his voice uncharacteristically soft. "You think we're prepared for what's coming? Most of these kids can't hit the target. Some of them look like they should still be in high school."

Stevie scuffed the dirt with the heel of his boot, creating small furrows in the ground, his face half-hidden as he took another swig of coffee. "We've got to be ready. No use dwelling on it. Better to focus on what's ahead, one day at a time." He wiped his mouth with the back of his hand, passing the canteen to Brock.

Luke's fingers found Shaina's silver locket, the metal cool against his hand. He rubbed his thumb over its surface, a ritual that had become as natural as breathing. The simple action steadied him, bringing her closer despite the miles between them. "We've got each other to lean on. That's enough to get through whatever's waiting for us over there." He spoke with greater confidence than he actually possessed, sensing his friends needed to hear the words.

Brock managed a faint grin, though it didn't quite reach his eyes. "That's assuming some jittery rookie doesn't blow us all to kingdom come first. Did you see Thompson on the field yesterday? Pulled the grenade pin and just stood there. If the soldier next to him hadn't wrestled it from him and heaved it, we'd be deploying three or four guys short." He shook his head, the memory still fresh.

Their laughter rose briefly before fading into the night, swallowed by the vastness of what lay ahead. The sound seemed out of place, irrelevant against the backdrop of their impending departure. A cool breeze rustled through the nearby trees, carrying with it the distant sound of a harmonica playing somewhere in the camp.

Luke tilted his head back, eyes tracing stars and familiar constellations; Polaris guiding true north, brilliant Sirius burning blue-white, Gemini's twins, Castor and Pollux, winking at them like distant guardians. The same stars would shine over Hanford tonight, over Shaina's diner in New Jersey, and over the Ardennes Forest where they would soon be fighting for their lives.

Moses Weisbaum's words drifted back: *When I survey the heavens, the moon and the stars, what are men that You, God, should care for them?* Moses had said that it was a Psalm about God's watchful care, even when things seem impossible. *Does God really care about us when we're going to war, to kill or be killed?*

Twenty-Three

THE AIR IN THE cramped office was stale, heavy with the scent of cigarette smoke and the faint aroma of fresh ink from the marked-up maps strewn across the desk. Dieter Zobel stood rigid, his boots planted firmly on the worn wooden floor. Before him sat *SS-Brigadeführer* Helmut Bischoff, the silver death's head insignia on his cap gleaming under the harsh overhead light. It was September, and the war had stretched the German military to its limits. The Reich's once-unstoppable momentum had faltered, and the failed assassination attempt on Adolf Hitler two months prior had only deepened the disorder within the high command. Dieter felt the mounting tension. Sweat trickled down his back, soaking into his uniform, but he dared not move to adjust his stance.

"Do you go by Dieter or Dietrich?" Bischoff asked. His eyes bored into Dieter's, unyielding and cold. A half-empty schnapps glass sat at his elbow, the amber liquid glossy in the light.

"Dieter, Sir," he replied, forcing his voice to remain steady. He fought the urge to clear his throat, knowing any sign of weakness would be judged.

The senior SS officer gave a curt nod. "Well, Dieter, how have you been doing with your English lessons these past few months?"

His mind scrambled for an answer. He knew this moment could determine whether he'd finally achieve his dream of joining the *Schutzstaffel,* the SS—a dream that had burned in him since he was twelve, when he'd seen a parade of black-clad soldiers marching through Hamburg, their presence commanding both awe and fear. The memory was seared into his psyche; the stiff legs with synchronized footfalls, the gleaming boots, and, most of all, the terror they commanded with a mere glance.

"I believe they've gone well, Sir," he said, squaring his shoulders as he spoke.

The officer's expression didn't shift, his face a mask of stern indifference, weathered by years of harsh decisions. "Why do you think we pulled you from patrolling the streets of Hamburg to sit in a classroom?" His fingers interlaced and joined beneath his chin, elbows resting on the desk, his eyes never leaving Dieter's face.

Dieter swallowed; his throat was dry. "I'm not certain, Sir. They told me it was because I had a knack for languages, something I picked up from my mother," remembering how she had taught him phrases in English and French before such instruction became suspicious.

The officer leaned back, his chair creaking under his weight, fingers still interlaced, now resting on his chest. "A knack for languages, yes. But the real reason, Zobel, is that we've been grooming you for a mission of utmost secrecy. Do you understand the significance of secrecy?" His voice dropped lower, forcing Dieter to lean in to catch every word.

"Yes, Sir," he answered. "It means something that cannot be shared with others." He thought of the oath he'd taken in the Hitler Youth, hand raised, pledging allegiance to the *Führer* above all else.

"Precisely," the officer said, his tone dropping to a grave whisper. "Not even your friends." The warning was clear in his steely gaze. The consequence of betrayal was death.

"I have no friends," he replied, the words spilling out before he could check them. It was the truth; his dedication to his duties left him little time to cultivate allies. He had always treated other Hitler Youth as competitors, not companions.

The officer's eyes narrowed, a hint of suspicion passing over his features. For a moment, he feared he'd overstepped, that Bischoff might probe further into his lonely existence, might see it as a flaw in his character. But the officer let it pass, his focus shifting back to the matter at hand, satisfied that a man without friends had fewer opportunities to reveal classified secrets.

"This mission is top secret," he continued, his voice hardening. "No one outside this room must know what we're planning. Not your comrades, not your superiors, not even your mother." Dieter balked at the mention of his mother, wondering how much the SS knew about his home life. "Tell me, do you know who Otto Skorzeny is?" The name was spoken with a mixture of respect and resentment.

He nodded, "Yes, Sir. He rescued Benito Mussolini, the Italian Prime Minister, from the Gran Sasso. Skorzeny's a German hero, a close friend of the *Führer*." The story had been plastered across every German newspaper, trumpeted in every radio broadcast. The daring rescuers had snatched the deposed dictator from his mountain prison without firing a shot. He had memorized every detail.

"True, that's the reputation he carries," the officer said with a faint edge of skepticism. "Skorzeny is more than a liberator. He's a master of deception, an actor who can slip into and out of any role. Some call him a magician for his abilities." The words carried a hint of bitterness, as if Bischoff had been overlooked while Skorzeny basked in Hitler's favor.

Dieter tensed. He'd heard the tales of Skorzeny's daring, how he'd led the glider-borne assault to free the Italian dictator, earning Hitler's favor and a legendary status among the ranks. The photographs showed a tall, imposing man with a dueling scar etched into his cheek. To be linked to such a man stirred something fierce in him, a fresh hunger for glory that had driven him since his first days in the Hitler Youth.

The officer leaned forward, his stare piercing through him. The desk lamp cast a harsh shadow across his face, deepening the lines around his mouth. "Do I have your word that not a single detail I'm about to share will leave this office?" His voice was slow, each word delivered with deadly seriousness.

"You have it, Sir," he vowed, his voice firm with conviction. "I'll speak to no one about this, whatever it is."

The officer's lips pressed into a thin line, "You'll be killed if you breathe a word of what I'm about to tell you. I will shoot you myself." His hand moved to his Luger, the motion slow and deliberate to ensure that Dieter understood the gravity of the mission. "I need you to grasp the enormity of this. The mission I've been tasked with overseeing is codenamed '*Unternehmen Greif*'" (Operation Grief).

Dieter sat upright, a chill running down his spine. The mere name of the operation sounded ominous.

"*Unternehmen Greif* is an operation designed to infiltrate the Americans occupying the Ardennes," the officer explained, tracing a line across one of the maps with his fingertip. "German soldiers, men like you, will don the enemy's uniforms, speak their language, and sow confusion behind their lines. We'll disrupt radio transmissions, alter road signs, issue false orders, and redirect their troops into traps. The goal is to stop their advance during the coming offensive. This mission was conceived under the *Führer's* direct command." The officer's eyes gleamed with a fanatical light that unnerved Dieter.

His mind reeled. The audacity of it—the sheer risk—was staggering. He pictured himself in an American uniform, mimicking their slang, slipping through their ranks like a wolf among sheep. The thought both thrilled and terrified him.

"This operation stems from the highest levels," the officer went on, reaching for his schnapps, gulping the balance. "You've heard of the attempt on the *Führer's* life in July, I assume?" His tone suggested that ignorance of this event would be unforgivable.

He nodded. The plot to kill the German leader was no secret. A group of disillusioned officers had planted a bomb at Hitler's Wolf's Lair headquarters, hoping to kill him and bring a negotiated end to the war. The explosion had torn through the room, killing four, but Hitler had emerged, shaken but alive. He remembered the rage he'd felt, the betrayal by Germany's officers, men who had sworn undying loyalty.

"The *Führer's* survival has only hardened his resolve," Bischoff said, "He's obsessed with striking back, proving the Reich's strength. But he's... unpredictable." He glanced at the closed door suspiciously. "The attempted assassination left scars on both his body and his mind. He rants for hours, changes plans on a whim, and trusts no one." This last admission was whispered, treasonous in its implications. *Unternehmen Greif* is his brainchild, a way to outwit the Allies and silence the doubters within our ranks. Skorzeny's been given the reins, and we've been tasked to make it happen, no matter the cost."

Dieter absorbed the words, the stakes crystallizing in his mind. This wasn't just about victory on the battlefield; it was about propping up a faltering regime, about proving loyalty to a leader teetering on the edge. The pressure was immense. This was his chance to get noticed, to rise above his peers, to fulfill the destiny his mother had always promised was his.

The officer stood, "You've been chosen for your toughness, your language skills, and your dedication. But understand this: the risks are colossal. If you're caught in an enemy uniform, the Allies won't hesitate to execute you on the spot as a spy. Are you prepared for that?"

He met the officer's gaze, his jaw tightening, recalling the tenets learned in his years in the Hitler Youth: strength, obedience, and unwavering loyalty to the Fatherland. "Yes, Sir. I'm ready to serve, whatever it takes."

The officer studied him for a long moment before nodding, apparently satisfied with what he saw in the young man's eyes. "Good. Your training begins tomorrow at 0500. You'll perfect your English, learn American mannerisms, and master the tasks you're assigned. You'll get to know their slang, their baseball terms, their popular songs, everything that might give you away. Skorzeny himself will oversee your preparation. Don't disappoint him, ...or me."

Dismissed with a sharp salute, Dieter stepped into the cool night air, his mind ablaze with all he'd just learned. Hamburg lay dark around him, buildings reduced to jagged silhouettes, the distant rumble of anti-aircraft guns a constant reminder of the war pressing in from all sides. Operation *Grief* was his chance to rise, to shed the Hitler Youth of his childhood and claim a place among the *Schutzstaffel*; the black uniform, the lightning bolts on the collar, the symbols of power he had long coveted.

But beneath the opportunity, a thread of fear existed. He must not fail. The Reich was counting on him, and failure meant not just dying, but disgrace for his family name. Yet, he could not deny that the war was not going well, confirmed by the BBC reports he caught while others slept.

As he walked through the darkened streets, he touched the Hitler Youth knife at his belt, a symbol of his devotion. He silently renewed the oath he'd taken almost a decade earlier: loyalty unto death.

Twenty-Four

The dawn broke over Camp Atterbury with a chill. The sprawling military base hummed with the urgency of impending departure. Soldiers of the 106th Infantry Division, including Luke's 423rd Regiment, were packing their gear, checking rifles, and preparing for the journey to an undisclosed location. Tomorrow, they would board trains, the first step toward the European Theater of conflict.

Luke stood outside his barracks; his breath visible in the crisp morning air. He pulled the small photograph of Shaina from his pocket, her dark eyes sparkling as she smiled at him from the diner in Asbury Park. Over stolen moments by the ocean, they had fallen in love, their connection sealed by weekly, sometimes daily, letters exchanged since he had returned to Camp Atterbury. Now, with deployment looming, he couldn't bear the thought of leaving without seeing her one last time.

"You look like you're carrying the weight of the world," Brock said, emerging from the barracks. His broad shoulders filled out his uniform, and his easy confidence was a stark contrast to Luke's quiet intensity. Beside him, Stevie, chipper and upbeat, adjusted his cap and nodded in agreement.

"I need to see Shaina. She's coming to Indianapolis today. I got authorization from Captain Newcastle."

Brock raised an eyebrow, his grin fading. "You got a pass? The day before we ship out? You're lucky he's got a soft spot for you."

"It's not luck," Luke replied, a faint smile tugging at his lips. "I told him she's my fiancée. He didn't ask too many questions."

Stevie let out a low whistle. "Fiancée? You didn't tell us you popped the question!"

"I haven't... yet. But I'm going to... today."

The three friends stood in silence for a moment, their uncertain future settling over them. The division had trained for a solid year, enduring long marches, live-fire exercises, and the muddy fields that earned the camp the nickname "Mudbury." Now, as they readied to leave, the rumors swirling were optimistic: the Germans were on the ropes, the war would probably be over by year's end. He clung to that hope, not just for himself, but for Shaina and their future together.

"Go get your girl," Brock said, wrapping his arm around Luke's shoulder.

"Yeah," Stevie added with a grin, "just don't miss the train tomorrow."

Luke nodded, grateful for their brotherhood. "Thanks, guys. You're real pals."

He tightened the drawstrings on his ditty bag and headed toward the camp's main gate, where a bus waited to take soldiers to the nearby town of Edinburgh. From there, he would catch a train to Indianapolis, a 40-mile trip that would take just under an hour. His pass was good until evening roll call, giving him a few precious hours with her. It wasn't much, but it would have to do.

Shaina Levine stepped off the train at Union Station, her legs stiff and aching from the fifteen-hour trek from Asbury Park. The station was a whirlwind of frenzied activity: soldiers in uniform hurrying to their destinations, civilians trying to match tickets to gates, and porters laboring to move heavy luggage. She adjusted her wool coat, which, despite its thickness, did little to ward off the chill. Her dark hair was pinned under a floral-patterned silk scarf, her deep brown eyes betraying her bone-deep exhaustion and nervous excitement. She had left her parents' bustling diner in Asbury Park on a whim, driven by Luke's letter urging her to come to Indiana before he shipped out.

I don't know when I'll see you again, or if I'll come back the same man, he had written, his words scrawled in the hurried hand of a soldier with too many thoughts and not much time. *But I need to see you, Shaina. I need to hold you one more time. Please come to Indianapolis on the 8th. I'll get a one-day pass, somehow.*

The journey had been daunting and exhausting, over seven hundred miles by train, with crowded transfers in Philadelphia and Pittsburgh, where she'd almost missed her connections. Her parents had protested, worried about the considerable cost of the tickets and the danger of a young Jewish woman traveling alone. Still, she had insisted with a firmness that had surprised even herself. Luke was worth it: every penny, every risk, every moment of discomfort. Their love, though young and tender, was honest and powerful, forged in stolen moments by the misty Jersey Shore and sustained by letters filled with ardent declarations, shared dreams, and promises of an extraordinary life after the war's end.

She checked her watch: 11:45 AM. He had promised to meet her at the station by noon. Finding a wooden bench near the main entrance, she sat down, her mind cluttered with concerns and uncertainty. What if he couldn't get away from his duties? What if the army had suddenly changed its plans and shipped him out early? What if this had all been for nothing? She pushed the troubling thoughts aside with determination, focusing instead on the vivid memory of his crooked smile, the way his eyes crinkled when he laughed, and the gentle way he had held her hand as they walked along the boardwalk under winter stars, which he knew by name.

At noon, as if materialized from her concerns, she saw him. He emerged from the surging crowd, his uniform neat and pressed despite what must have been a long and stressful morning, his eyes scanning the bustling station until they landed on her. Her breath paused, and she stood abruptly, her suitcase forgotten at her feet as she ran toward him, weaving between startled travelers.

"Luke!" she screamed, her voice breaking with a mixture of relief, joy, fear, and love.

He caught her in his strong arms, lifting her off the ground as they embraced, his face buried in her hair. For a precious moment, the commotion and noise of the crowded station faded to nothing, and it was just the two of them.

"I can't believe you're here," he whispered against her ear, his voice thick with emotion. "I've dreamed about this moment every night."

"I couldn't let you go without seeing you one more time," She replied, her face pressed against the rough fabric of his uniform, breathing in the forgotten scent that was uniquely him. "I had to come, no matter what anyone said."

They reluctantly pulled apart just enough to see each other's faces, and he took her hand in his, his thumb gently brushing over her knuckles as if memorizing the feel of her skin. The Star of David necklace glinted in the light as she looked up at him.

"Come on, let's get out of here," he said, glancing at the clock atop the depot, and then over his shoulder. "Let's put your suitcase in a locker. I don't have much time. I want to make every minute count."

They left the station and walked into downtown Indianapolis. Soldiers in uniform and civilians in work clothes mingled on the streets, a blend of movement and purpose. The air vibrated with the sounds of car horns, train whistles, and the constant chatter of conversation. Newspaper boys shouted headlines about Allied advances, while shop windows displayed patriotic posters urging citizens to buy war bonds. He led her to a small park near the Hotel Severin, where a cluster of ancient oak trees offered shade and some privacy amid the city bustle. They sat on a weathered wooden bench, their hands clasped tightly, fingers intertwined as if afraid the war might tear them apart if they dared let go.

"I got a pass from my CO," he said, his voice low and tinged with nervous excitement. He glanced around before continuing, "He wasn't supposed to give me one, but he did. Said I have to be back by evening roll call. No exceptions."

Her deep brown eyes widened, "You risked that for me? You could get into serious trouble."

"You're worth it," he said, his gaze steady. A gentle breeze ruffled his hair as he took both her hands in his. "I've been thinking about you every day since we've been apart. I know we haven't had much time together, but I love you." He paused, rose from the bench, then knelt before her. "And I want you to know that when I come back from overseas, I want to marry you... If you'll have me."

Her breath hitched, tears welling in her eyes. A tear escaped, tracking down her cheek. "Oh, Luke... of course I'll marry you. I knew you were the one since that day you defended me at the diner. I love you more than anything in this world."

They kissed, a desperate, tender kiss that held all their hopes and fears for the uncertain future, their lips conveying promises that words couldn't. They stared into one another's eyes, foreheads touching. He smiled, though his eyes were bright with surging tears he refused to let materialize. "The guys in my unit say the war's almost over. The newspapers, too. Sounds pretty optimistic, but they think we'll be home by the end of the year. We can start our life together then."

She nodded, clinging to the hope he was right. Her fingers reached up to touch his face, memorizing every contour. "I'll be waiting for you. No matter how long it takes."

They spent the afternoon talking beneath the sprawling oak trees, sharing memories and dreams. Pigeons pecked at crumbs nearby, and other couples strolled past, many in similar circumstances, stealing precious moments before inevitable separation.

They laughed over small things; the time he had spilled coffee on himself at the diner and tried to play it cool, and the way she had teased him about his clumsy dancing. Then, more seriously, the way he had pounced on the drunken soldier who had made antisemitic remarks to her, defending her honor without hesitation, despite being outweighed by thirty pounds.

"You were so brave," she said, touching his cheek. "That's when I knew."

As the sun began to dip toward the horizon, casting long shadows across the park, it brought with it the reality of their situation. He sighed, his shoulders slumping. "I have to go. If I'm not back by roll call, I'll be in deep trouble. Could lose my stripes, or worse."

"I know. ... hold me one more time. Hold me like you'll never let go."

He pulled her into his arms, enveloping her in a fierce embrace, holding her as if he could imprint the feel of her against him. "I love you, Shaina. I'll write to you every chance I get. And I'll come back. I promise you that. We'll celebrate New Year's Eve on the Boardwalk, just like we talked about."

"I love you too," she whispered, her voice breaking on the words. Her fingers clutched at his uniform jacket. "Be careful. Please be careful. Come back to me."

They stood there for a moment under an ancient oak, reluctant to break their connection, as if the strength of their embrace could somehow protect him from what lay ahead. Finally, he released her, pressing one last kiss to her forehead before starting toward the station with measured steps. He looked back several times and waved, his heart aching with each step that increased the distance from her. She remained under the oak, her hand raised in a small, trembling wave, her eyes locked on him until he disappeared into the crowd, taking a portion of her heart with him. *Please come back to me, my love.*

He slipped back into the barracks minutes before the evening roll call began. Brock and Stevie were waiting, their faces lighting up with relief when they saw him.

“You made it,” Brock said, “How’d it go?”

“It was perfect,” he said, his voice quiet but firm. “I asked her to marry me. She said yes.”

Stevie grinned. “Well, damn. You’re gonna have to survive this war now. You’ve got a wedding to attend. Just remember, you’ll have to choose between me and Brock, who's gonna be your best man." *He was wrong, but he had no way of knowing what was ahead.*

Luke managed a laugh, though his heart was heavy. He pulled Shaina's photograph from his pocket, tracing her face with his thumb. The barracks were filled with the sounds of soldiers preparing for the move. The 106th was pulling out, heading into war's teeth. *Were they ready?* He harbored a growing uneasiness, a gut feeling that too soon they would learn that time was not on their side, that fate had already written outcomes they couldn't change.

TWENTY-FIVE

THE TRAIN JOLTED ALONG the tracks. The men of the 423rd Regiment of the 106th Infantry Division sprawled across worn seats or leaned against the walls, their duffel bags shoved under benches or piled in the aisles. Luke sat by a window, his shoulders hunched as he stared out at the passing landscape. The flat fields of Indiana had given way to rolling hills, dotted with small towns he didn't recognize. His radio manual, dog-eared from his training at Fort Monmouth, rested on his lap, but his eyes weren't on the pages. They were fixed on the horizon, his thoughts drifting back to Shaina. He could still feel the press of her hand in his, the quiet promise they'd made before he left. *I'll come back.*

Brock's voice broke through his daydream, "Hey, Luke, you gonna tell us where we're headed, or you just gonna stare out that window all day?"

Luke glanced over, offering a faint smile. "If I knew, I'd tell you. But I'm guessing New York."

"New York!" Stevie piped up from the seat beside Brock. "That's what I heard, too. Big ships, troop carriers. Maybe the Queen Mary or Queen Elizabeth."

Brock snorted. "Yeah, or maybe they're sending us to Florida in dinghies to fight alligators. You believe every rumor you hear?"

"Not every rumor. Just the ones I like," Stevie offered with a grin.

The railcar buzzed with speculation. Some said New York, others Boston. The officers had given them nothing concrete, only orders to board the train and to be ready. Luke tuned out the chatter, his fingers brushing the edge of his manual. He wanted to be prepared, to master the radio skills that could keep him and his friends alive.

The transport screeched to a halt just after dawn, and the men spilled out onto the platform, blinking against the rising sun. Camp Myles Standish, a sprawling complex located near Taunton, Massachusetts, put an end to the speculation. Wooden buildings lined the grounds, flanked by mess halls, training fields, and a few scattered recreational buildings. It was a staging area, the final stop before deployment.

The officers wasted no time in assigning the 423rd Regiment to barracks. Briefings were short and vague, and security was tight, but the men were told they'd be there for a while, processing last-minute preparations. There would be equipment checks, medical inspections, and some light drills. Passes were available for those who wanted to venture into Taunton or Boston, provided at least half of the unit remained on the base.

Luke had no intention of leaving the camp. He set up in the barracks, his bunk neatly made, and pulled out his radio manual. The transient soldiers could investigate the local scene; he'd rather stay sharp.

Brock and Stevie had other plans.

"Come on, Pierce," Brock said that evening, leaning against Luke's bunk. "We don't know how many days we're gonna be here, and you're just gonna sit around with that book? Let's hit Boston, visit the USO, maybe cut a rug with some girls."

"Not my thing, Brock. You go ahead."

Stevie frowned, tossing a balled-up sock at Luke. "You're no fun, you know that? What's the point of a pass if you don't use it?"

"You can have my pass," he said, tossing the sock back. "I'd rather stay here, write to Shaina, keep my head on straight."

Brock's eyes lit up. "You serious? You're giving up your pass?"

"Take it," he said with a shrug. "Just don't do anything stupid."

Stevie winked. "No promises."

Two nights later, Brock and Stevie made their way through the heart of Boston. The downtown area was alive with music and activity. With their off-base passes in hand, they arrived at the Boston Buddies USO Club just off Boston Common. The lobby was humming with action: junior hostesses in snappy dresses, the sweet scent of fruit pies drifting from the kitchen, and the sounds of a swing band tuning up for the night's ballroom dance. A poster near the door read "Welcome, Servicemen!" under a hand-drawn flag, reminding the boys they were among friends.

Inside, the room sparkled under the Omega glitter ball, its 1,200 tiny mirrors reflecting the targeted beam of light in all directions.

Stevie's gaze swept the crowd, appreciative. "Some place, huh?"

"It's something, all right," Brock replied, flashing his easy grin to a passing hostess, who giggled and waved them over to the refreshments table.

They moved among the clusters of soldiers and hostesses, brightly colored paper streamers hanging overhead. Brock, ever the ladies' man, struck up a conversation with a striking hostess with lively eyes and an infectious laugh. She wore a pale green dress with a colorful floral pattern, which accentuated the freckles on either side of her nose. He reached for a doughnut.

"California, right?" she teased, pulling back the plate. "Didn't think we'd find anyone this far from the Pacific."

"Good guess, Ma'am. Thought I'd see what the Atlantic looks like," he quipped, leaning in just enough to let his confidence show, but not so close as to be offensive. He grabbed a doughnut, and the hostess laughed softly, as if only for him.

Stevie wandered over to a corner table piled high with letters and postcards. A group of volunteers was helping service members write home, and looking grateful, he picked up a pen. He wanted to write to his mother, but was struggling for the right words. A kindly hostess, noticing his hesitation, offered gentle advice on what to say. "Tell her about the music, the dancing... Or maybe about a friend you've made," she said, cheerful and vaguely suggestive. She then helped him write the letter. When they were finished, he told her it was the best letter he'd ever written, which evoked a broad smile from the helpful hostess.

He relaxed under her encouragement, glad they had decided to visit the USO club. He glanced up to see the band launch into Artie Shaw's "*Lady Day*," the clarinet soaring sweetly above the conversation and shuffling feet. Brock was at the edge of the dance floor, the hostess in green talking him into a quick lesson in the jitterbug.

"Ever danced this before?" she teased, as he followed her steps, clumsy but willing to laugh at himself. His bravado faded into easy laughter, revealing a side of him few knew: charm without pretense, genuine and warm.

Stevie watched from the sidelines, uncertain, until another young lady, full-figured and friendly, gave him a gentle nudge. "You look like you could use a spin around the floor." Self-conscious, he let himself be pulled onto the dance floor, his initial stumbles melting away in the friendly atmosphere. Soon he was smiling, even laughing, not robust laughter like Brock's, but every bit as genuine.

As the set ended, Brock rejoined Stevie at the punch table, cheeks flushed. "You, see? War's not so bad when you've got a dame and a good doughnut."

Stevie grinned, "You're the same whatever you do; head first, no fear. That's not me, but I admire it in you."

Brock shrugged, but there was a rare note of sincerity in his eyes. "You do all right yourself. Fact is, sometimes I'd be better if I asked for help before jumping in without thinking."

They looked out over the lively crowd—their fellow soldiers, the bustling hostesses, the lingering strains of music—and for the next few hours, the certainty of war faded from view.

Ten days at Camp Myles Standish passed in a blur of activity. The men inspected their rifles, went through medical checks, and packed, unpacked, and repacked their gear. Training drills sharpened their fighting skills, though the workouts were lighter than at Atterbury. Briefings hinted at deployment, but details were sparse. The camp's purpose was clear: get the men ready, then ship them out.

Luke spent most days in the barracks, poring over his manual or scribbling letters to Shaina. He wrote about the base, the boredom, and the way the leaves were turning red and gold. He didn't mention his concerns, the division's readiness, or the growing anxiety of what lay ahead. Instead, he told her he loved her, that he'd see her again.

On October 20, the division loaded onto trains again, the mood tense but electric. "New York," Stevie said, peering out the window as the train rolled out of Massachusetts. "Gotta be. Where else are there ships big enough for all of us? Queen Mary, Queen Elizabeth, something like that."

Luke thought about the trip ahead. He'd heard about both, massive liners turned troop carriers, ferrying thousands across the Atlantic. *If that was their ride, England was next, then the front.*

The train pulled into New York shortly after dusk, the city's lights dimmed for security. A cold rain fell, driven sideways by a biting wind that cut through their uniforms. The men shivered as they stepped onto the platform. The docks were cluttered with cranes and crates, the air thick with the acrid scent of saltwater and the stench of diesel fuel.

They were soon herded toward the wharf, where Red Cross volunteers greeted them with trays of cookies, milk, and coffee. The young ladies stood under makeshift awnings, smiles bright despite the weather. Brock made a beeline for a pretty blond, her smile warm. "Well, hello," he said, helping himself to a cookie. "You're the cutest thing I've seen all day."

She laughed as she handed him a coffee. "Flattery won't get you extra, but thank you."

Stevie, trailing behind, tried his luck with another volunteer. "Uh, you're pretty ...I mean, the cookies are pretty... I mean, the cookies are good."

The girl raised an eyebrow, amused. "Thanks, I think. Here, take two or three."

He blushed, clutching the cookies as Brock snickered. "You're about as slick as sandpaper, Stevie boy."

"Oh, yeah, how many cookies did you get?" Stevie asked, unable to stifle a smirk.

Luke hung back, sipping his milk and watching his friends. Their antics lightened the mood, if only for a moment. The rain drummed on the awnings, and the wind tugged at their coats. None of them knew, but it would be more than six months before they were again on American soil, and many would not return at all.

Officers directed the men toward the docks, where the *HMS Queen Elizabeth* towered over the water. It was a colossus, over a thousand feet long, with smokestacks rising several stories, its hull painted wartime gray. The pier was wet and slick, and several of the men slipped, packs and all. An icy wind whipped off the water, forcing the men to scrunch deeper into their coats. The ship formed a massive shadow against the stormy sky. Stripped of its peacetime luxury, it was now a troop carrier, built to haul fifteen thousand men across the ocean.

"Amazing," Stevie breathed, his voice muted in the wind. "That's the biggest boat I've ever seen."

Brock whistled. "Fifteen thousand of us on that? Better hope it floats."

"It'll float," Luke said, his voice steady. He couldn't tear his eyes away. The ship was a symbol; powerful, unyielding, ...their passage into war.

They lined up, bags slung over their shoulders, and began the slow climb up the gangplank. The deck vibrated with the whirr of engines, docks bustling with activity, crates being loaded, voices shouting. The rain pelted down, soaking their uniforms, but the men pressed on.

At the top, Luke paused, glancing back at New York's distant glow. The wind tugged at his cap, and he pulled it lower to fend off the cold. Brock and Stevie flanked him, their usual banter stilled.

"Eighteen months," Stevie said suddenly, his voice soft. "All those changes in the division, transfers, new guys, we're lucky the three of us are still together. I'll bet Sergeant Miller back at the recruiting office wouldn't believe it. We'll have to stop by and see him if we get back to, ...I mean, when we get back to Hanford."

Brock nodded, seriousness in his eyes. "Yep, damn lucky, if you ask me."

Luke looked at them, filled with gratitude for his valued friends. "Yeah. I'm glad it's us."

Ahead lay the Atlantic Ocean, the English Channel, and the battlefield, which would cost them significantly, ...far more than any of them realized.

Twenty-Six

Dieter stood at attention in Major Hartmann's confined office, his heart pounding with anticipation. The officer, a stern man with a neatly trimmed mustache, leafed through the personnel file, his eyes scanning the pages with a critical gaze. Since childhood, Dieter had dreamed of the day he would fight for the Fatherland. Now, in October 1944, that day had come.

"Dietrich Zobel," Hartmann began, his voice sharp, "your record is impressive. Top marks in physical training, good grades in English."

He hesitated, then answered with conviction. "Thank you, Sir. Since *SS-Brigadeführer* Bischoff requested that I participate in the mission that would require these skills, I have mentioned it to no one."

The major nodded, a thin smile softening his serious expression. "Smart assessment. You're right, *Unternehmen Greif* is highly classified." He then reiterated the mission specifics Bischoff had shared with Dieter a month earlier.

The opportunity to attack the Americans, to outmaneuver them, to demonstrate his value, and above all, to avenge Werner's death, burned within him. Operation Grief, a component of Hitler's daring *Die Wacht am Rhein* (The Watch on the Rhein) strategy to penetrate the Ardennes, was the type of assignment he had envisioned for the past two years.

"So, are you prepared, Zobel?"

"Sir!" he replied, "I'm ready to serve the *Führer* and the Fatherland."

"Good. You'll report to a training ground where you'll be under the command of *SS-Obersturmbannführer* Otto Skorzeny himself. He's assembling the men for this operation, and he has requested that you be a part of the team."

"I won't let you down, sir."

"Make sure you don't," Hartmann replied. "Dismissed."

"Heil Hitler," Dieter replied, his right arm extended, a determined expression covering his face. This was his chance to become a hero, to join the *Schutzstaffel*, the SS, and to make his father, his true father, the *Führer*, Adolph Hitler, proud. And most, he would punish the Jew who had killed Werner.

Two days later, Dieter arrived at a secluded facility deep in the German forest. The air was crisp, the earth damp from recent rain. The complex was bustling with activity, as young men, handpicked for their skills and loyalty, were being trained for a mission that could turn the tide of the war. Operation *Grief*, Hitler's brainchild, designed to infiltrate Allied lines, could determine the success of the *Wacht am Rhein* campaign.

The training was grueling but exhilarating. In language classes, he parroted English phrases, his voice hoarse from repeating, "What's the password? Where are you headed?" He was among the best, his fluency acknowledged by the instructors. Uniform fittings were next. He stood before a mirror, adjusting an American helmet; the olive-drab uniform felt strange against his skin. For a moment, he questioned the honor of wearing the enemy's clothes, but he dismissed the thought. The Allies were subhuman, as he had been taught, aggressors bent on Germany's destruction. Deceiving them and using whatever was necessary were the mission.

Physical training was where he shone. In everything corporeal, running through the muddy forests, climbing ropes, sparring in hand-to-hand combat, he dominated. His size and strength intimidated his peers, and he relished their respect... or their fear. He was determined to be the best, to earn his place in the elite German unit.

The day *SS-Obersturmbannführer* Otto Skorzeny arrived was electric. He stood in formation, his head lifted, trying to look as imposing as his six-foot frame allowed. When Skorzeny stepped from his car, he felt a jolt of awe. The man was taller than he'd imagined, his scarred face a testament to battles fought and won. His SS uniform gleamed with medals, his presence commanding instant respect.

Skorzeny's voice boomed across the courtyard. "Men, you are the spearhead of Operation Grief. You will infiltrate the enemy, wear their uniforms, speak their language, and sow chaos within their ranks. You are the best of the Reich, and I expect total dedication."

Dieter hung on every word of the German hero, his determination swelling. This was his moment.

After the speech, Skorzeny walked among the troops, inspecting them. When he reached Dieter, he stopped, his eyes piercing, "And you, soldier, what's your name?"

"Dietrich Zobel, sir!" he replied, standing even straighter.

"You look like you can handle yourself. Are you willing to serve the Reich, even to die for it?"

"Yes, sir!" he answered without hesitation. "I will give my life for the Fatherland. I'll crush the enemy, make them pay dearly for ever attacking us!"

Skorzeny nodded, a faint smile on his lips. "Good. We need committed soldiers like you."

He was pleased and relieved. He had impressed Skorzeny, the hero of the Reich. He was determined to prove himself.

Just then, the air raid sirens wailed. The trainees froze. Confusion erupted as Allied bombers roared overhead. "Take cover!" Skorzeny shouted.

Explosions shook the ground, sending dirt and debris flying into the air. Dieter ducked, covering his head as the heat from a nearby blast singed his skin.

"AN-M64 five-hundreds," said Skorzeny, describing the American general-purpose bombs, six feet long, and fourteen inches in diameter. "Bastards!" he shouted, shaking his massive fist at the air.

Through the smoke, Dieter saw it, an unexploded bomb, lying in the grass not far away. His mind raced. If he could remove the fuse, it would show his courage. He had learned during his training that the American bombs used the M158 chemical time-delayed fuse, which contained a glass vial of acetone that corroded celluloid disks to trigger detonation, sometimes immediately, sometimes minutes after impact. If he could remove the fuse, he would surely earn Skorzeny's admiration.

Ignoring the shouts to stay put, he sprinted toward the bomb. A sergeant yelled, "Zobel, get back! That's an order!"

But he ignored him. "I have to do this!" Another explosion drowned his reply.

He reached the bomb, finding it heavier than he expected, but with effort, he managed to rotate it slightly, straining under its weight. He wasn't a bomb disposal expert, but he was sure that if he could remove the fuse, he could prevent the bomb from detonating. He struggled, knowing at any moment it could ignite, but managed to loosen the fuse. He could not remove it, but assumed he had done enough to render the bomb a dud.

Satisfied, he started back to where Skorzeny and the others were watching. He had covered about half the distance when a faint click echoed in his ears, and time slowed. He felt the concussion at his back and realized, too late, that he had been unsuccessful in disarming the detonator.

The explosion was blinding. He was thrown forward, landing face-first on the ground. Pain seared through his leg, and the world went dark.

When he regained consciousness, he was on a stretcher, medics rushing him across the field. His leg was a mangled mess of blood and bone, the pain so intense he could scarcely breathe. He tried to scream, but his voice had vanished. Through the smoke, he saw Skorzeny standing nearby, his face etched with disappointment.

Shame washed over him. He had failed, not just himself, but Skorzeny, the Reich, ...and most, his brother's memory.

At the hospital, the doctors worked frantically to save his life. Hours later, he woke to find his leg bandaged, the pain a constant throb. A doctor approached, his expression grim. "You're the luckiest man in Germany, Dietrich Zobel. That blast should have killed you. The grass cushioned your fall and saved your life, but your leg is severely damaged. We were able to save it, and you'll walk again, ...with a limp, maybe need a cane. You won't be going to the front lines."

His world had collapsed. His dreams of glory, of joining the SS, of avenging Werner, all gone in an instant. He clenched his fists, tears of frustration burning his eyes, but he refused to let them escape. Even in disappointment and agony, weakness was not an option.

Anger surged within him at the Allies for bombing them and ruining his life. He thought of the *Führer*'s words, echoing from his Hitler Youth: "The Allies are the enemy of our people. They must be destroyed." He had believed it then. He resolved it now.

"I'll make them pay," he whispered, his voice trembling with rage. "I'll find a way."

A nurse approached, checking his chart. "How are you feeling, Dietrich?"

"Fine," he lied, his tone cold.

She offered a sympathetic smile. "You're young; you'll recover. There are many ways to serve the Reich."

His eyes narrowed. "Yeah, like what?"

"Well, with your injury, you can't fight, but you could be a guard at a prisoner-of-war camp. There is a prison in Muhlburg, Stalag IV-B, I believe. They always need guards to keep the prisoners in line."

"No!" he said, disgusted. "I was meant for greatness, not guarding prisoners! They use older men and boys for guards. Real soldiers are fighting the Yanks and the Tommies in the west, and the Soviets in the east. I will never be a guard." He turned his head away from the nurse, signaling his wish to be alone.

Alone in the hospital room, he closed his eyes and recalled that terrible October night in 1941, when he and Werner were at the Munich train yard, ordered there by their Hitler Youth leader. The Reich was deporting Jews to the East, and their unit's job was simple: keep filling the cattle cars; none were to escape. Werner was in charge, while he trailed behind, mimicking his brother's confidence. "They're animals," he had sneered, pointing at the shivering figures being prodded aboard. "Weak, cowardly lowlifes."

Then, the incident had erupted. A Jewish boy, no older than Dieter, with dark, wavy hair tumbling over his forehead and sharp, defiant, brown eyes, broke from the line. He darted toward the rusted train cars. "I'll get him!" Werner had called, sprinting after the boy with Dieter a short distance behind. The chase had ended at a stack of splintered crates, and the boy was cornered. "Nowhere to run, Jew?" Werner had taunted, cracking his knuckles.

Before he could strike the frightened boy, a woman, likely the boy's mother, burst from the darkness. With a desperate cry, she had shoved Werner hard, sending him stumbling. His foot had caught a loose rail, and he had fallen, his head hitting the iron tracks. The woman had hesitated, her face pale, then, grabbing the boy's hand, they had fled into the shadows. Dieter had rushed to his brother's side. He had knelt beside him, pleading, begging to know what he could do, but Werner had remained silent, eyes vacant. The escaping boy had stopped for a moment and glanced back, his eyes locking with Dieter's. That look, unyielding, almost daring, was seared into his mind. The boy's hand had tightened around his mother's, a small, protective grip. Then they had vanished.

The Hitler Youth leader had run to his aid when he heard Dieter yell. When he saw that there was nothing to be done for Werner, he had looked in the direction the boy had run, "Jewish filth. Murderers!" Dieter had stood, trembling with fury. His brother had just been doing his duty, and they'd killed him for it. The Hitler Youth had taught him to hate Jews, but now it was real, raw, and personal. He'd never forget that boy's face, those eyes, and that defiant clutch of his mother's hand.

A week later, he attempted to walk with crutches. He swung his legs over the bed, gripping the metal aids. His left leg, encased in a cast, was a dead weight. He took a step, but his good leg buckled, and he fell back onto the bed.

"Easy there," the nurse said, rushing over. "You need to take it slow."

"I can't be useless," he snapped, a scowl on his face.

"You're not useless," she said gently. "You'll find your place."

But he wasn't listening. He saw his reflection in a nearby window; pale, broken, nothing of the warrior he had been. The cast was a constant reminder of his failure. He thought of Werner, and the anger grew.

That night, as he lay in bed, he made a vow. He might not fight on the battlefield, but somehow, he would exact revenge on his enemy. He had been thinking more about the idea of being a guard and had softened from his first reaction to the idea. He imagined himself standing over Allied and Soviet prisoners, their faces etched with fear, forced to obey his every command. He could make them pay for his brother, his leg, and his shattered dreams.

"One day," he said, his voice low and venomous, "I'll make them all suffer."

He closed his eyes, a grim resolve settling over him. The path to glory was gone, but the path to revenge was just beginning.

Twenty-Seven

Every spare inch was being utilized as the men found their assigned quarters aboard the *Queen Elizabeth*. The term "quarters" was generous. Elegant sitting rooms from the ship's days as a passenger liner were now sleeping chambers, packed with three-tiered bunks that offered little breathing space. The ship's hull, stripped of all its ornate fixtures and rails, was painted gray for camouflage on the open sea. They replaced her royal name with a more appropriate nickname: "The Gray Ghost."

"Home for the next week," Brock lamented, securing a bottom bunk by throwing down his duffel. "At least I don't have to climb to get some sleep."

Luke chose the center bunk above him, while Stevie took a berth opposite the cramped passageway. Around them, soldiers vied for space, stowing gear and voicing grievances.

"A week in this sardine can?" someone moaned nearby. "I'll lose my mind before we reach England."

He eased onto his bunk, the thin mattress flattening under his weight. A week wasn't long, but in this overcrowded maze, he knew it would seem much longer.

The journey began with a lurch as the ship pulled away from the docks, its steam turbines rumbling to life. The first day was a whirlwind of drills and briefings, during which the Queen's crew drilled into them the realities of life at sea. German U-boats haunted the Atlantic, a silent threat beneath the surface. But the ship's speed, thirty knots, offered some reassurance. She was fast enough to outrun most submarines, though her captain took no chances, guiding the vessel in a zigzag pattern to throw off any lurking predators.

He felt the ship's motion, a subtle sway that grew more pronounced as they hit rougher seas. The weather had turned stormy by the second day, waves crashing against the hull, but the ship's size and weight held it steady. It sliced through the swells with quiet power, a fact that eased the men's minds inside.

Meals provided little comfort. The galley churned out standard military grub—canned meat, beans, and bread—served in shifts to accommodate the thousands being transported. The soldiers lined up with their mess kits, shuffling through the cramped dining areas, the complaints about the food a constant refrain.

"Better than field rations," Stevie said one evening, prodding a lump of stew with his spoon. "At least it's warm."

Brock eyed Stevie's bread covetously. "Could use more of that, though."

Luke tore off a chunk of his own and passed it over to him. "Here. Gotta keep the lion fed."

Brock accepted it with a grunt of thanks, and they ate in silence, surrounded by the non-stop drone of idle conversation.

With little to do beyond eating and sleeping, the men sought distractions. A few movies were shown in a converted lounge, the screen coming to life with old comedies and war reels. The seats were packed, soldiers squeezing in to escape the monotony. Luke took in only one, a film he vaguely remembered from home. Seeing the actresses, his thoughts drifted to the women in his life, Matya, Katie, and Shaina. It was Shaina that his mind settled on. *Just get out of this war alive, then I can spend the rest of my life content.*

Physical exercises filled the mornings, though the tight surroundings limited their activity. Officers led them through calisthenics, including jumping jacks, push-ups, and sit-ups, within the cramped quarters. The air grew thick with sweat as they worked out, the sergeants barking orders to keep them sharp. Luke pushed through the exercises, his muscles aching, but his mind grateful for the focus.

When they weren't training and the movies weren't running, card games took over. Poker, blackjack, and rummy sprang up in every corner. Some played for laughs, while others played for stakes: cigarettes, candy, or rounds of drinks when they docked. The games grew louder as the days wore on, and tempers flared easily.

Luke was perched on his bunk, half-listening to the chatter below, when Brock's voice rose above the general chatter. "Come on, fellas, don't snap your cap. It's just a game."

"You've been winning way too much," a soldier shot back, his voice rough with irritation. "You're a cheater."

Brock laughed, but it was a tight, forced sound. "Cheating? Nah, I'm just lucky. Always have been."

The soldier, broad-shouldered and serious, glared at Brock. "Lucky, huh? Or maybe you're one of those *kikes* who steal other people's money."

The word sliced through the air, sharp and ugly. Luke felt as if he'd personally been struck. The noise around them faded, the insult left hanging.

Brock's expression darkened. "What'd you say?"

"You heard me," the soldier sneered, standing now. "I know your type. You're just like them, always grabbing what ain't yours."

Brock rose to meet him, fists balled at his sides. "Say it again. Go ahead."

The tension swelled; a spark ready to ignite. Luke wanted to say something, but his tongue was tight, his body tense. He remained silent.

Stevie, an unlikely mediator, stepped in, "Cool it, both of you. We're all on the same team here."

The soldier glared at Brock, then Stevie, then, spitting a curse, he stalked off.

The group dispersed, the game abandoned, but the air remained tense. Brock stayed standing, his jaw clenched, while Stevie cracked a weak joke to break the silence. Luke walked away, finding a quieter corner near the deck railing.

The night was chilly, the sea a vast inky expanse beneath a starry sky. He gripped the rail, the metal cold against his palms, and let the question claw at him: *Why didn't I say something*?

That word *kike* was a dagger in his heart, one he'd experienced before. Growing up, he'd heard it from his father, always spoken with venom. It had stung then. It stung now. Something was menacing and violent in the word. Beyond that, it was now a slur against his mother, his sister, and his fiancée. He thought of New Jersey, the one time he'd acted, when the drunken soldier had been rude to Shaina, calling her a "Jew girl." He had stepped in, fists flying before he could think, defending her honor. Beyond that single incident, he remained reticent.

Here he was again, silent in the face of hate. A coward. He despised that word, hated how it fit him. He'd done well since enlisting, earned respect, but to admit he was Jewish, that was still a line he hadn't crossed. *Not yet. But when?* The slurs he overheard, the hatred, and the cruelty always left him repulsed. Worse, it shamed him that he never spoke up, never pushed back.

Even with the war raging and stories of what was happening to Jews in Europe, his silence still felt like a betrayal. *When would he find the courage to honor the women who knew his secret, to honor himself?*

The sea offered no reply, just the steady crash of waves against the hull. The ship churned onward, its turbines a constant whine, drawing them ever closer to the war front. All the soldiers sensed it, the battleground looming nearer by the hour, tension growing.

On the sixth morning, a cry rang out over the intercom: "Land ho!"

Luke, Brock, and Stevie joined the rush to the decks, the cold air biting as they craned for a glimpse of land. A faint line emerged on the horizon, sharpening into the coastline. The sky was overcast as the "Gray Ghost" safely navigated the harbor and moored at the dock in Liverpool.

"Finally," Brock said, rubbing his hands together, "we're done with this floating cage."

Stevie smirked. "What, no love for the Queen?"

"Next time, I'm walking," he shot back.

Luke smiled, but his mind was elsewhere. As the ship entered the harbor, he saw the docks bustling with activity and the outlines of buildings taking shape. They'd made it.

Soldiers lined up along the ship's rail. He scanned the faces around him, some eager, some grim, all bracing for what lay ahead. He questioned his courage, disappointed that he had not spoken up earlier. Maybe it would come in the battles ahead. Perhaps amid the turmoil, he'd find the strength to stand tall, to claim who he was. For now, he was simply a soldier, and duty called. *There was no turning back.* Inhaling deeply, he hoisted his pack and followed Brock and Stevie down the gangplank, ...stepping into the fight.

Journal Entry*: November 17, 1944 – We have arrived. England. Eighteen months of preparing suddenly seem inadequate. The war is not just out there; it's inside me. Every battle I fight is with fear, with the need to keep secrets. I have to overcome this fear. It's not the fear of battle. It's the fear of others finding out who I am.*

Twenty-Eight

The *HMS Queen Elizabeth* was safely docked, its decks no longer packed with soldiers from the 106th Infantry Division. The "Golden Lions" had crossed the Atlantic and were now embarking on a world far different from the training grounds of Camp Atterbury. Luke, recently turned nineteen, stood on the dock, his eyes taking in the unfamiliar coastline.

"Move it, maggots!" barked Sergeant Paul "Guns" Getty, a grizzled veteran with a slight limp from a shrapnel wound he'd received in Italy. "We ain't here for sightseeing."

Luke slung his duffel bag over his shoulder and began walking, nearly tripping over the soldier in front of him. Behind him, Lieutenant Donald Johnson, a recent graduate from Officer Candidates School (OCS) at Fort Benning, scanned the crowd, his face calm despite the stress of his new responsibilities. At twenty-four, he was scarcely older than his men. This was the state of the United States Army in late 1944: young men leading still younger men.

The division relocated from Liverpool to the Cotswolds, an area characterized by rolling hills and stone villages. The 423rd Infantry Regiment was stationed near Cheltenham, a town of elegant buildings and muddy fields. The weather was unwelcoming; cold, rain falling in sheets, turning the ground into a constant quagmire. Training began immediately, with combat tactics to prepare the green division for the battles to come.

A week later, the 423rd gathered in a drenched field outside Cheltenham for a night navigation exercise. The sky was moonless, the air thick with mist, and the temperature hovered just above freezing. Luke adjusted his helmet; his fingers numb as he checked his M1 Garand. He was eager to prove himself among the company's veterans.

"Listen up!" Sergeant Getty's voice boomed. "You're splitting into squads. Your job is to reach the checkpoint, a stone barn three miles east, by 0200. No lights, no noise. Use your compass to stay on track and avoid getting lost. Move out!"

Luke unfolded his map, the red filter on his flashlight casting a dim glow.

"Let's go, men. Stay close to the guy in front of you. Don't lag," barked Corporal Juan Diaz, who had a knack for keeping spirits high, even in the worst conditions. "This terrain's tricky, and the mud doesn't help. Pierce, you're on point with Smitty."

The squad moved into the forest, their boots sinking into the slimy muck. The sound of the group was muted, broken only by the occasional snap of a twig or the rustle of wet leaves. Luke's compass needle wobbled, and he struggled to keep his bearings.

Halfway through, a loud crack echoed through the trees. The squad froze, weapons raised.

"Halt!" Diaz whispered, his hand signaling a stop. "Who's there?"

"It's just me, Corporal," Brock replied, emerging from the shadows. "Had to relieve myself, and I stepped on a damn branch. This place is worse than a haunted forest."

Diaz exhaled, frustrated by Brock's indifference. "Stay together, men. We're not playing games."

They pressed on, the mud deeper. Luke's boot caught on a buried ration tin, and he fell face-first into the muck, his rifle clattering. Stevie, bringing up the rear, hauled him up with a chuckle. "You're a mess. You're proving war ain't clean."

They reached the barn, its sagging roof nearly invisible in the darkness. The squad collapsed against the stone walls, exhausted but triumphant. Corporal Diaz checked his watch.

"Good work, men. We made it with eight minutes to spare."

The successful maneuver convinced Luke that, although they were untested, they were as ready as the current schedule allowed.

At 0400 on 1 December 1944, I Company of the 423rd Infantry Regiment transferred from the troopship *Empire Javelin* to *LST-473*, one of over a thousand LSTs (Landing Ship, Tanks) produced for the war. The entire division was now boarding the small craft for the fifty-mile crossing of the English Channel to Le Havre, France. Each LST carried almost two hundred men. The process was grueling, soldiers climbing down rope nets, their heavy packs making each step precarious.

Luke hesitated at the top of the net, the LST's deck swaying below.

Brock shouted, already halfway down. "You got this, buddy."

He gripped the ropes, his palms sweaty despite the cold. He descended slowly, his foot slipping once, but he made it to the deck, where Lieutenant Johnson was organizing the men.

"You men go to the tank deck below. It has room for twenty Shermans, but we're transporting soldiers today, not tanks. Find a spot and stay put," Johnson ordered. "It's gonna be a long ride."

The LST's hold was a cramped entanglement of soldiers, vehicles, and supplies. As the ship pulled away from Southampton, the English Channel's notorious December weather took hold. Winds howled, and waves crashed against the hull, sending the boat pitching and rolling. Luke felt his stomach lurch, and he wasn't alone; men around him gagged, their faces green.

Hours into the crossing, the sea grew rougher, the LST groaning under the strain. Luke sat against a bulkhead, fighting the strong urge to vomit. When he could no longer resist, he retched into a bag, his face burning with embarrassment. Diaz offered a small packet of pills. "Seasickness meds. Swallow 'em quick. You'll feel better."

He nodded, grateful, but the relief came slowly. The compartment was a cacophony of groans, muttered curses, and the clatter of equipment. Soldiers tried to sleep or stared into space, grateful they had not enlisted in the Navy.

A sudden clang echoed through the hold, followed by shouts from above. Luke jumped. "What's that?" he asked, his voice tight.

Brock stood, hand on his pistol. "Probably a loose hatch. Stay calm."

Stevie climbed to the upper deck, returning minutes later, his face grim. "A jeep broke free. It nearly crushed two men. They're securing it now, but we need to check our gear."

The three helped to lash down crates and vehicles as the ship rocked. The task was exhausting, but it kept their minds, if not their stomachs, off the churning sea.

As dawn broke, the LST's engines slowed, and the French coast appeared through the mist. "We're here," Sergeant Getty announced. "France. Get ready to move."

The men climbed to the deck, the cold air a refreshing blast after the stifling hold. The LST beached itself, the bow door slowly lowering, enabling the regiment to disembark quickly as they stepped onto French soil. Luke's legs were shaky, but the firm earth filled him with renewed determination. They had crossed the Channel. *The war was here*.

The "Red Horse" staging area, a muddy field near Le Havre, was the temporary home for the 106th. Tents dotted the landscape, offering little protection from the freezing temperatures and light snow. The division reorganized, sorting men and equipment for the next phase. Luke and Brock were tasked with setting up I Company's mess tent, struggling against the frozen ground and biting wind.

Luke swung a mallet at a tent stake, his hands numb. The stake hardly budged, and he cursed under his breath. "Come on, Pierce, hit it like you mean it!" Brock teased, his efforts producing no greater results.

Stevie stood by an English Oak, half its limbs burnt or missing from previous assaults on La Havre by the Germans. "Guys, we need this done before dark. The cooks are already griping about the open air."

As he waited, a group of French civilians approached Stevie, led by an elderly farmer named Henri. The man's weathered face was creased with deep lines, his calloused hands clutching a small bundle. Several villagers stood with him, their clothes worn and patched, eyes filled with a mixture of hope and wariness. The farmer offered a gift—a bread loaf wrapped in a faded blue cloth, still warm from the oven—along with a wedge of pale-yellow cheese. His English came hard, but the emotion behind the words was unmistakable.

"You fight the *Boches*, yes? Good. We welcome you." Henri's voice quavered, his eyes darting east and west as if expecting German soldiers to materialize at any moment. Beside him, his wife nodded vigorously. "*Sous eux pendant quatre ans*," she said in French, which he perceived meant they had been under German rule for the past four years, not so much by her words, but by her passionate arm waving.

He accepted the gifts with an easy smile. He straightened his helmet and stood a little taller, looking every inch the American liberator the French people had been waiting for. His usual sarcasm was shelved as he replied with genuine warmth, "*Merci, monsieur*. We'll do our best." He took the bundle, treating it with the reverence of someone who understood that the gift had been given sacrificially.

That evening, around a small fire, Corporal Diaz spread out a map. "We're heading to Belgium soon. The 2nd Infantry Division is holding the line in the *Schnee Eifel*. It's quiet there. They're calling it a 'ghost front,' but let's not get complacent."

"Quiet sounds good to me," Luke sighed.

Brock shook his head in disagreement. "Quiet means the Germans are planning something."

He had no idea how accurate he was.

On 8 December, the 106th began its journey to Belgium along the "Red Ball Express" route. The fog was thick, the roads rough, and the icy chill suffused everything, man and vehicle alike. By 10 December, they crossed into Belgium, and on 11 December, they relieved the 2nd Infantry Division in the *Schnee Eifel*, a forested ridge near the German border.

Since the area was considered "safe" by military standards and unlikely to experience significant enemy action, it was decided that the 106th would replace the 2nd Division, "*man for man, gun for gun.*" The divisional brass had determined that this swap-out would be easy to accomplish. They would replace the experienced veterans of the 2nd Division with the untested troops of the 106th; foxhole by foxhole, weapon by weapon, a simple exchange.

The convoy stretched for miles, a line of trucks crawling through the frozen mud. Luke, Brock, and Stevie were in a deuce-and-a-half, the cold biting through their coats. Luke huddled under a blanket pulled up to his chin, his teeth chattering.

A loud bang jolted the truck to a stop. "Sounds like a flat tire," Brock announced, jumping out. After a quick inspection, he added, "And the axle's damaged."

They set to work, struggling with frozen bolts. Corporal Rodney Jenkins, a troop mechanic, joined them, his toolbox clanking. "Step aside, boys. I got this."

The mechanic applied oil and loosened the bolts, but the repair took time. Stevie kept watch, his hand on his pistol, as the fog muffled every sound. Suddenly, the rumble of engines, German engines, echoed in the woods. "Take cover!" Stevie shouted.

Hoping the Germans would assume the vehicle had been abandoned, the men dove into ditches, weapons ready, the fog hiding them. The German patrol passed at a safe distance. If there was any question about where they were and what the level of danger was, it had just been answered. Soon, the convoy resumed its journey.

The division's movement from England to Belgium had proven a test of endurance: the muddy fields of the Cotswolds, the rough seas of the Channel, the frozen tents at Red Horse, and the foggy roads to the *Schnee Eifel*. As they moved deeper into the Ardennes Forest, everyone knew the training was over. This was the real thing. *They had arrived at the battleground, which, in the next few days, would prove to be anything but safe.*

Twenty-Nine

The division had rolled in under a dark December sky. They were now tasked with taking over the positions, pillboxes, and foxholes being vacated by the 2nd Division along the snow-dusted ridges of the *Schnee Eifel*. Luke adjusted the backpack that carried his SCR-300 radio, the straps pinching his shoulders. After shifting the nearly forty-pound pack to a more secure position, he began to walk, his steps bogged down by the muddy slush.

The Siegfried Line loomed ahead; a German defensive position constructed in the 1930s along Germany's four-hundred-mile western border that ran from the Netherlands to Switzerland. The line consisted of thousands of bunkers, tank traps, and pillboxes, but it was most recognized by the multitude of concrete anti-tank barriers that looked like dragon's teeth.

"Let's go!" snapped Sergeant Getty, hefting a crate of small-round ammunition. Luke struggled to keep up, burdened by the heavy pack. Around him, the men of the 423rd Regiment worked intensely, their faces a mix of nervous excitement and exhaustion. Brock was relieved to find Luke. "Here we are, buddy. The big show."

Nearby, Stevie adjusted the 30-06 caliber Springfield sniper rifle, scanning the tree line through the Redfield scope mounted above the rifle's barrel. The three friends, inseparable since childhood, were now charged with holding a critical stretch of the VIII Army Corps' front. *Few, from generals to privates, realized how difficult this task would prove to be.*

Their mission was clear: replace the 2nd Infantry Division, a battle-hardened outfit that had been holding the Siegfried Line for months. The order that had been delivered to Major General Alan Jones was specific: every foxhole, every machine gun nest, was to be swapped out precisely.

A grizzled sergeant from the 2nd Division, his face carved with the lines of previous battles, approached Luke's squad. "You're the replacements, huh?" he said, his voice gravelly. He eyed his pristine uniform and untested gear with a smirk. "Hope you brought your diapers, kid."

Luke squared his shoulders. "We're ready, sir."

"Ready? You greenhorns wouldn't last a day where we're going. This here's a rest camp, quietest spot on the line. We made it all pretty for you. Don't mess it up."

The disdain was palpable. The 2nd Division had seen action from Normandy to the *Hürtgen* Forest. To them, the 106th was a division of boys playing soldier, fresh-faced recruits who hadn't discharged a single shot under fire. As the veterans prepared to pull out for their next fight, they handed over positions with a mix of relief and contempt, convinced the newcomers wouldn't measure up in battle conditions.

Within a few hours, it became evident to Luke that the process of replacing the 2nd Division was a muddled mess, but there was little he could do. He was just a lowly PFC following orders.

Getting his bearings and acclimating to the freezing weather, he followed a 2nd Division sergeant to a shallow foxhole, its edges crumbling under the weight of fresh snow. "This is you," the veteran said, kicking a rusted M1 Garand leaning against the wall. "Radio operator, right? Set up here. I wouldn't expect much activity in this area."

Luke frowned. "This cover's pretty thin, and the rifle..."

"Good enough for us," the sergeant cut in, already turning away. "You're just holding the line. We need the good stuff for the real fight."

Down the ridge, Brock wrestled with a waterlogged .30-caliber machine gun, its barrel caked in mud. A corporal from the 2nd Division stood over him, arms crossed. "That's your baby now, big guy. Keep it dry, or it'll jam faster than you can blink."

Brock wiped sweat from his brow. "Looks like it's been here since '42."

The corporal shrugged. "Works fine. You probably won't use it anyway."

Stevie climbed into a perch, an unstable platform wedged between two Eifel pines. Taking his newer scoped-in sniper rifle from him, a surly corporal named Hartnell swapped it for his weather-beaten Springfield. "Scope's off by a hair," he said, "but don't matter. Krauts won't be coming this way. I'll put this new rifle of yours to good use where I'm going."

Stevie tested the weight of the older Springfield, his jaw tight. "This thing's a relic."

Hartnell grinned. "You'll get used to it... or you won't."

All along the line, the 106th inherited a hodgepodge of worn-out gear and poorly maintained positions. The veterans had convinced the untested recruits to take the castoffs, arguing that the 2nd Division needed the newer weapons and equipment for their offensive. "You're just resting here," they said, over and over.

When the divisional exchange was complete, the 106th was stretched thin; twenty-two miles of front for a division meant to cover five, with the 423rd Regiment reduced to less than 2,800 men. Overextended, there were significant gaps between foxholes—foxholes dug by the Germans in 1940—meaning the Germans now knew their exact locations.

Luke knelt in his foxhole, his fingers fumbling in the cold, the snow clinging to his gloves. Corporal Diaz appeared, offering a hand. "Need help, amigo?"

"Thanks," he muttered, securing the antenna to the SCR-300. He connected the radio's battery and waited for the tubes to warm. Static crackled through the headset as he tuned the radio dial to the predetermined frequency. "Pierce, Seventh Platoon, radio check."

"Copy, Pierce," came the reply. "Status?"

"Quiet so far. Radio's up and running."

"Roger. Copy. Report anything odd."

"Good job, soldier," said Diaz, moving to the next foxhole.

Luke signed off, wrapping the battery in his wool blanket to fend off the cold. Communication was their link to the division. Just as Sergeant O'Malley had promised back at Fort Monmouth, Luke was now the voice of the platoon.

The next few days blurred into a tense routine. The forest seemed too still; the enemy was there, but invisible beyond the tree line. On the evening of 13 December, Luke stood watch. His teeth were clenched against the biting cold when a low rumble rolled through the night; steady, mechanical, not thunder. He keyed the microphone on the SCR-300. "Pierce, Seventh Platoon. Hearing engines east of the line."

"Copy," the messenger at the company headquarters responded. "Noted. Stay sharp."

He reported what he'd heard to Second Lieutenant Dobkins, the platoon officer, a stiff 'by the book' leader. "Engines, huh? Could be anything. Log it, Pierce."

"I believe they were vehicles, sir."

"Noted," replied the young officer.

The veterans of the 2nd Division had dropped hints, casual, almost mocking. "Krauts have been quiet lately," one said as he packed his kit. "Too quiet, maybe." "Spread too thin." "Yeah, you guys are asking for it," said another before climbing into a deuce-and-a-half. He'd overheard the comments, their words troubling.

By the 14th, the mood had shifted. The soldiers rigged pine branches over their foxholes to give some relief from the freezing wind and frequent snow flurries. The Hanford boys huddled around a small fire, sharing a can of beans. "Miss home yet?" Brock asked, his voice soft.

Luke nodded. "Katie's Dutch lettuce. Your mom's pecan pie."

A low rumble cut through their reminiscing, close, unmistakable. His stomach dropped. "That's not thunder."

Brock squinted into the dark. "Tanks?"

He scrambled to his radio. "Pierce, Seventh Platoon. Engines again. Louder. Possibly tanks."

"Copy. Stand by."

The campfire died down, and Brock and Stevie returned to their posts. Luke settled into his foxhole, staring at the stars through bare branches. The silence returned, heavier now, pressing against his chest. The 2nd Division had called this a rest camp, but something was coming, something big. For now, he waited, the weight of the unknown suffocating him. *This was no rest camp. It was a trap, and he and the rest of the 106th were the bait.*

He huddled deeper into his foxhole, clutching the radio for warmth. The forest grew quiet again, but the memory of those engine sounds lingered.

Something was building beyond the trees, a storm gathering strength before breaking upon them.

Footsteps crunched through the snow as he peered over the rim of the foxhole. A regimental runner moved between the trees, scanning foxholes. "Looking for Lieutenant Dobkins," he called softly.

Luke pointed toward the command post. "The pillbox under the tallest pine."

The messenger nodded and continued. Luke saw him duck into Dobkins' position. Something in the runner's urgency piqued his curiosity. He moved out of the foxhole and moved near to the pillbox, pretending to gather more branches for cover.

"Message from Regiment, sir," the messenger was saying. "Concerning PFC Steven Cower."

Luke froze. *Stevie?* He inched closer.

"PFC Cower has been reassigned to the 87th Infantry Division," the messenger continued. "General Patton's Third Army urgently requires soldiers with sniper qualifications."

The lieutenant's voice carried in the still air. "When does PFC Cower need to leave my command?"

"On the twenty-first, sir. One week from now. A transport will pick him up at Company headquarters and take him to his new assignment. You have him until then. Fortunately, not much action here from what I hear."

Dobkins ignored the messenger's last comment. Snipers were an essential part of an infantry company. He didn't like the idea of further depleting an already short-handed division, spread along twenty-two miles of German front.

Luke's chest tightened. In one week, the three friends from Hanford, California, would be split up. With all they'd been through, it didn't seem possible. He returned to his foxhole, his mind racing. The news would also hit Brock hard.

Journal Entry: *December 14, 1944 - I hear enemy vehicles every night. Headquarters says I'm hearing things. Others hear the same things. HQ says we're green and scared. I know what I hear. Bad news. Stevie's being transferred to Patton's command. Guess the three of us won't be together for Christmas after all.*

Thirty

By 15 December, the Ardennes Forest was a frozen wasteland, its Eifel pines cloaked in a blanket of freshly fallen snow. Luke nestled in his foxhole, the SCR-300's static breaking the eerie silence. The cold was relentless; his fingers felt numb as he adjusted the antenna wire. Snowflakes clung to his jacket, and his breath was a testament to the subzero climate that threatened both soldiers and their weapons.

He checked the BA-80 battery. The nine-pound power source was already sluggish, its life sapped by the persistent subfreezing temperatures. With only one backup, he wrapped it in his thin wool blanket, praying it would hold out. The SCR-300 was I Company's connection to the officers at headquarters. Luke waited ten minutes as the vacuum tubes warmed up, then rotated the butterfly switch on the handset to test the signal. "Pierce, I Company, Seventh Platoon. Radio check."

The response crackled and snapped, faint but unmistakable. "Copy, Pierce. All quiet there?"

"Affirmative. No activity." His voice was steady, but something seemed amiss. The forest was too still, the silence too heavy. Positioned on a salient, they were vulnerable to encirclement, a fact that troubled him despite the assurances that the area they were in was a "rest camp."

The 2nd Division had left behind subpar weapons: rusted rifles, mud-caked machine guns, and misaligned scopes. They had convinced the soldiers of the 106th to accept them since they were assuming a "safe" area. Some of the equipment was barely functional, and the foxholes they inherited were shallow, poorly maintained, waterlogged pits. The 423rd Regiment, already under strength, with its 2nd Battalion held in reserve, was at limited capacity, given the wide swath they were protecting, making their position precarious. The veterans' assurances of a quiet front rang hollow, and Luke couldn't shake the feeling that they'd been set up to fail.

His foxhole was a cramped, muddy refuge. He adjusted the squelch on the SCR-300 to reduce the constant static, thankful for the automatic frequency control that fine-tuned incoming signals. The radio was designed to be user-friendly, vital if he were incapacitated, but he pushed the thought away. He had to stay sharp, for himself and his fellow soldiers, who, like him, were cold and nervous, each with their own uneasiness.

A few hundred yards away, Stevie perched in a tree stand, his Springfield rifle resting across his lap. The older model, a hand-me-down from the 2nd Division, was a far cry from the precision weapons he'd trained with. Its scope was misaligned, the barrel speckled with rust, but it was all he had. At least he'd be getting a better weapon when he transferred to the 87th Infantry Division in a week, a change he was still wrestling with. He shivered in the cold; his breath was visible as he scanned the forest through the scope. The overcast sky dulled the light, making every shadow a potential threat.

He had been on the tree stand since dawn; his sniper's eye keen for any sign of movement. He'd gotten word about his transfer when he had taken a short break earlier to grab some coffee from the HQ pillbox. He wasn't sure if Luke or Brock knew. As soon as the opportunity presented itself, he would let them know.

The dense woods offered perfect cover for an enemy, and the rustling of the wind through the pines played tricks on his ears. He'd heard the same rumble Luke had, a low growl that set his nerves on edge. But when he reported it to his platoon leader, Second Lieutenant Dobkins, he got the same response: "Wind. Let it go. Don't spook the men."

He shifted, trying to ease the ache in his legs. The cold was worse up here in the tree, the icy wind penetrating his uniform. He thought of Luke, struggling with the radio, and Brock, probably fidgeting in his foxhole, itching for a fight. They'd done so much together. Now, they were scattered across this frozen ridge, waiting for an enemy that he sensed was gathering on the other side. A week from now, he'd be gone, no longer a part of the Hanford trio.

A flash of movement caught his eye, a shadow shifting between the trees. He froze, his finger hovering over the trigger. It was just a branch swaying in the wind, and he let out a breath. He was edgy. The forest was playing tricks on him, fueled by the unease that had settled over the platoon. He climbed down, his legs stiff and his hands numb, and joined Luke in his cramped foxhole, thankful for the warmth emitted by his friend and the platoon's radio.

"Anything?" Luke asked, his voice low as he handed him a tin of cold rations.

He shook his head. "Nothing. Just trees and snow. This rifle's a piece of junk, though. If something happens, I'm not sure it'll fire straight."

Luke nodded, his rifle no better. "They keep saying it's a rest camp."

He chuckled. "Yeah, and I'm General Eisenhower. Something's out there. I can feel it."

They ate in silence, the only sound the crunch of their food and the faint hum of the radio.

Brock appeared at the shared trench, his burly frame filling the foxhole entrance. His face was flushed from the cold, but his grin was as wide as ever. "How's it going, radio man?" he asked, his voice booming despite the need for quiet.

Luke smiled, grateful to see his friend. "Same as always. Quiet. Too quiet. Well, at least till you got here."

Stevie laughed, then stood and said he was going back to his foxhole to try to get some sleep, but before he left, he had some news he needed to share. Brock stared up at him, confusion on his face. Luke knew what was coming, but he did his best not to reveal it.

"I'm being transferred to General Patton's 87th Infantry Division. Seems they need snipers more than the 106th."

"When?" Luke asked, trying his best to feign surprise as if he were hearing the news for the first time.

"One week. They're picking me up on the twenty-first. A week from today. So, we got another six days together, boys."

Brock was speechless. With all they had been through together, in Hanford, Camp Roberts, and Camp Atterbury. "Why do they need you?" he asked after a brief moment of silence.

"Like they're gonna tell me. Remember what Sergeant Miller said when we first enlisted, 'It's the army.' It's incredible that we've been together this long. And remember, the war's going to be over in a few weeks. I'll bet I won't fire a single round. You guys either."

Luke watched as Stevie mouthed the words that none of the three believed were true. The reports of an end of the war by New Year's Eve, less than three weeks away, were a pipe dream. *The Germans were up to something, and it sure as hell wasn't surrender.*

"Well, I'm gonna go sack out," Stevie said, not wanting to say more, "Dawn comes early."

Once he left, Brock settled in near Luke. "Stevie's the lucky one. At least he's gonna see some activity. I'm going stir-crazy. Nothing to do but stare at the snow and listen to the wind. I didn't come all this way to freeze to death."

Luke rolled his eyes. "Be careful what you wish for. This place gives me the creeps."

Brock laughed, but there was an edge to it. "Creeps or not, I'm ready for some action. Let's see what these Krauts are made of."

"You're crazy, you know that?"

"Crazy like a fox," Brock replied, grinning. But beneath the bravado, Luke saw the same unease that worried them all. They were spread too thin, their lines were too long, and their equipment was subpar. And the forest was way too quiet. "Think I'll try and get some shuteye," Brock said, climbing out of the foxhole.

Luke, Stevie, and Brock, connected by their Hanford roots, had faced the cold, the boredom, and the growing unease, knowing they were in it together. Luke's radio, Stevie's rifle, and Brock's warrior spirit were their weapons against the gathering storm. And now they were losing Stevie. *What else would they lose? The next seventy-two hours would provide the answer in ways none of them could have imagined.*

Around 2100, a low rumble broke the silence, like distant thunder rolling through the forest. He froze. The heavy air muffled the sound, but it was unmistakable: vehicles—enemy vehicles. He grabbed the handset, his voice urgent. "Pierce, Seventh Platoon, I Company. Hearing engines east of the line, possibly trucks or tanks."

"Copy, Pierce. Probably just the wind in the trees. It's breezy tonight. Keep monitoring."

His jaw tightened. *What the hell*? He'd heard wind before, and this wasn't it. The sound faded, but the unease lingered, his stomach churning, his ears alert. He glanced at the forest, the snow-covered pines a wall of shadows. The clouds had grounded Allied aircraft during the daylight hours, leaving the division blind to whatever was massing across the line in the dark. Luke reported the noise again at 2130, and again at 2300, each time met with the same response: "Just natural sounds. Stay vigilant."

A few minutes later, a sharp crack snapped, a branch breaking underfoot, deliberate. His heart raced as he peered over the foxhole, his rifle at the ready. It was probably nothing, but he reported it anyway. "Pierce, Seventh Platoon. Heard a loud snap, possible enemy movement."

"Copy. Probably wildlife. Keep your eyes open."

He cursed under his breath. *Wildlife? In this cold, what animal would that be?* But he knew better than to contest the response. The officers, lulled by the 2nd Division's assurances that the *Schnee Eifel* was a quiet zone, weren't listening. The 106th was considered a green division, untested and unproven in combat, and the higher-ups seemed willing to ignore their concerns, dismissing them as nerves on edge.

As midnight approached, Luke lay in his foxhole, staring at the stars peeking through gaps in the clouds, the SCR-300's backpack his pillow. He remembered the story Moses Weisbaum had told him about Jacob, who wrestled with God, and how God had changed his name from Jacob to Israel. *I wonder what it would be like to wrestle with God?* Like Jacob in the story, Luke felt entirely alone. The forest was still, too still. His mind wandered to Shaina, recalling the last time they were together. Her loved called him from within the forest. *Luke, come home to me, my love. I'm here waiting for you*. He closed his eyes and thought of pressing her to his chest.

He was comforted by the vision of her being drawn into his arms, yet the thought that never seemed far removed troubled him afresh; the nagging idea that he was a coward, hiding who he was, the son of a Jewish mother, and engaged to a Jewish girl.

A distant rumble broke his reverie, louder than before, unmistakable—engines, many of them, moving in the darkness. Luke's heart pounded as he grabbed the handset. "Pierce, Seventh Platoon. Engines again, closer, definitely movement. East of the line."

The response from Dobkins was distinctly different from previous replies, "Copy, Pierce. We're aware. Stand by."

His frustration boiled over. *Stand by? For what?* "Something's coming," he said without keying the radio.

The sounds grew closer, a low growl that vibrated through the ground. He kept the SCR-300 on, listening for any orders or signs that higher command understood the gravity of the situation. The overcast skies had hidden the German buildup; tanks, infantry, artillery, all massing for an offensive that would shatter the "ghost front." The 423rd and 422nd Regiments, positioned on a vulnerable salient, were sitting ducks, their lines too thin to hold against what was building.

As the night wore on, He checked the radio every few minutes, ensuring the tubes were warm and the signal clear. The battery was fading, but it would have to do. The forest remained still, but it was a lie. A tempest was coming, and when it broke, it would be unlike anything they had ever faced. The 106th Infantry Division, inexperienced and unproven, was about to enter its darkest hour. The Germans were ready to unleash one of the most significant conflicts in the history of warfare—the Battle of the Bulge—featuring over a million combatants.

Thirty-One

At 0525 on 16 December, Luke crouched in his foxhole, sleepless, his entire body shaking from the wintry cold. The earth beyond his position lay covered in an eight-inch-thick blanket of snow, sustained by the subzero temperature.

The SCR-300 radio beside him emitted a soft hum, its vacuum tubes glowing faintly after warming up. The moonlit sky cast an ashen hue across the thick forest. The cloud cover blocked Allied planes from reconnoitering the region, the division unaware of the enemy gathering just out of sight. He glanced at his watch, then checked the battery, which was still functioning despite the frigid conditions. He repositioned the handset, turning the butterfly switch to verify the connection to company headquarters.

"Pierce, 7th Platoon. Radio check," he reported, his voice unwavering despite his increasing unease.

"Copy, Pierce. Things quiet there?" the response came back.

"Affirmative," Luke answered, the silence foreshadowing an impending danger.

Five minutes later, the forest erupted in chaos. A deafening roar of German artillery, 81mm mortars, 105mm howitzers, and massive 420mm railway guns, shattered the dawn. Shells screamed overhead, exploding, creating geysers of snow, earth, and splintered pine. The foxhole shook, dirt mixing with snow as he grabbed the handset. "Pierce to HQ! Heavy artillery fire! Request immediate support!" The response was faint, drowned in static: "Copy, Pierce. Hold position. Help is en route."

His heart pounded. The 106th was isolated, its lines too thin to withstand the determined German assault. He gazed out of the foxhole and saw flashes of orange and white as shells tore through the forest. The barrage was relentless, targeting command posts, supply dumps, and communication lines. The Germans' *Wacht am Rhein*, Adolf Hitler's audacious plan to split the Allied armies and seize the port of Antwerp, had begun, exploiting the overcast skies and the Allies' mistaken belief that the *Wehrmacht* was too weak to launch a major offensive. Conceived by Hitler himself after surviving an assassination attempt in July, despite the skepticism from many of Hitler's top generals, the plan of attack was being executed with ruthless precision by the German 5th Panzer Army.

He ducked as a shell exploded nearby, showering the forest floor with frozen dirt. The SCR-300's signal blinked, static overwhelming the line to the company headquarters. "Pierce to HQ! German infantry and tanks advancing! Need reinforcements!" he shouted, adjusting the squelch knob to reduce noise. The response was garbled: "Hold... position... support... coming..."

His training at Fort Monmouth had prepared him for technical challenges, but not for this. If true, then the plan found on a captured German officer a week earlier was unfolding, and the radio disruption of Operation *Grief* was working flawlessly. The rugged terrain already limited the SCR-300's five-mile range, and the cold was draining the BA-80 battery faster than expected. Now he was having to deal with electromagnetic jamming.

He swapped to his backup battery, changed frequencies, and tried the portable Morse code keyer to increase the distance of his transmission, all without success. The radio's Automatic Frequency Control struggled to lock onto a signal, and his hands shook as he recalibrated the ticklish radio, knowing communication was critical. A nearby explosion rocked the foxhole, and he ducked, grabbing the crumpled grid map. "423rd, I Company! Enemy tanks at grid... two eight four by...three nine two! Infantry in strength! Holding, but need support now!"

The radio went silent, the battery too weak to heat the tubes. He slammed his fist against the foxhole wall, frustration boiling over.

Private Leonard Brown crouched beside him, rifle trembling in his hands. "What's happening, Pierce? Are we gonna die out here?" His voice cracked, his eyes wide with fear.

"Stay calm, Lenny," Luke answered, forcing steadiness into his tone. "We're holding. Keep your rifle ready." He grabbed his own M1 Garand, its barrel cold. A German soldier in white camouflage broke through the tree line fifty yards away, wielding an MP40 submachine gun. He fired, the .30-06 round dropping the man in a spray of crimson. He looked at Brown, "We fight, we live."

Sergeant Matt Whitfield, a grizzled veteran from the 2nd Infantry Division who had stayed to help transition the green troops, appeared at the foxhole's rim. His face was smeared with dirt, his Browning Automatic Rifle (BAR) slung over his shoulder. "Pierce, we're moving to that pillbox!" he barked, pointing to a concrete bunker thirty yards away. "It's our best chance. Private Brown, cover us!"

Luke grabbed the radio, slinging it over his back as he and Whitfield crawled through the snow, bullets kicking up white plumes around them. Brown fired his M1, his shots wild, but sufficient enough to keep the Germans at bay. They reached the pillbox, its walls scarred by shrapnel, and quickly set up inside. He reconnected the SCR-300, praying the battery could still produce sufficient voltage. "Pierce to HQ! We're in a pillbox, grid two eight five by three eight one! Heavy enemy fire!" Static was the only reply. He cursed, suspecting the German jamming was intensifying.

The pillbox was 30 feet by 40 feet, with half of the structure underground for protection and concealment. Made of reinforced concrete, the structure was designed to hold 9 or 10 soldiers. The front wall had two embrasures, narrow openings for machine guns or anti-tank weapons. Whitfield knew that the pillbox could withstand direct hits from field artillery without collapsing.

The sergeant scanned the forest through one of the embrasures. "Panzer IVs out there, and a Tiger II. Our 57mm guns are useless against that armor. We need to hold as long as possible." He handed Luke a BAR from a fallen soldier. "You know how to use this?"

"Yeah, Sarge," he replied, gripping the BAR's wooden forearm beneath the lengthy barrel. Its twenty-round magazine of .30-06 rounds could tear through infantry at close range. With the stock of the Browning tucked tight to his side, Luke experienced a renewed surge of resolve.

Brock fought from a shallow ditch, his burly frame pressed against the frozen earth. The artillery barrage had obliterated his foxhole, and he had grabbed a Thompson submachine gun with a fifty-round drum magazine from a fallen soldier when his M1 ran dry. The sub-machine gun's .45 ACP rounds roared, cutting down an entire squad of German infantry trying to flank his position. "Come on, you bastards!" he shouted, his voice raw with adrenaline. This was what he'd craved since enlisting eighteen months earlier, a chance to prove himself under fire.

A German soldier charged with a bayonet fixed to his Mauser Kar98k rifle. Brock sidestepped, slamming the Thompson's butt into the man's helmet, knocking him out cold. The act was brutal, leaving Brock's hands shaking, but he pushed forward, driven by a mix of fear and fury. The platoon, led by Second Lieutenant Dobkins, was struggling to hold a ridge overlooking a narrow road that was the key access to St. Vith, a small town that served as a road and rail hub, which was central to the German surprise offensive. The location allowed access through the Losheim Gap, making it a prime target for German forces pushing toward Antwerp. Holding St. Vith would disrupt the enemy's advance, altering the course of the battle.

"Fall back to the ridge!" the lieutenant shouted, his voice straining over the chatter of a German MG42 machine gun one hundred yards away. Its 7.92mm rounds tore through the trees, pinning down the squad. Brock spotted the enemy machine-gunner and dashed to a fallen log, firing the Thompson in short bursts. The machine-gunner fell, but another took his place, the MG42's twelve-hundred-rounds-per-minute, relentless.

PFC Neil Jackson, who had joined Brock's squad after losing contact with his own, handled a 57mm anti-tank gun nearby. "It's no use!" he yelled, as a round bounced off a Panzer IV's sloped frontal armor. "We need something bigger!"

Brock went to the platoon's ammo cache in a foxhole nearby and grabbed a bazooka, its 2.36-inch round sufficient for the task. "I'll take care of it," he growled, loading the weapon. He aimed at the Panzer IV, less than a hundred yards away, and fired. The rocket struck the tank's track, disabling it in a shower of sparks. The crew bailed out, only to be cut down by Private Hank Monroe's .30-caliber M1919 machine gun from a nearby mound. Another Panzer IV rolled forward, its 75mm gun blasting a crater where Jackson's position had been. Brock dove for cover, his ears ringing from the explosion.

Sergeant Whitfield rallied the squad. "We hold this ridge! No retreat!" But the Germans were determined, their infantry supported by a second Tiger II tank, its 88mm gun a death sentence for anything or anyone in its path. Brock found an abandoned German MG42, the ammo belt still half-full, then positioned the recovered gun's bipod on a boulder. The weapon's rapid-fire tore through a wave of advancing infantry, but too soon the belt ran out of ammo. "Damn it!" he cursed, grabbing the Thompson again. He fought with reckless courage, his broad-shouldered frame an easy target, but his fighting spirit unbreakable, even as the German pincer movement tightened around the two isolated regiments.

To the north, Stevie lay prone on a makeshift platform in a pine tree, hidden by its branches, his Springfield M1903 sniper rifle trained on the battlefield below.

He had re-sighted the scope on the rusted castoff from the 2nd Division, and it was now exact and accurate. That, combined with Stevie's training, made him deadly. At nineteen, his subdued demeanor amplified his lethal capacity.

Minutes after the artillery barrage had relaxed, he spotted German infantry moving through the trees, their white camouflage blending seamlessly with the snow. Behind them, Panzer IVs rumbled forward, their tracks noisily crunching the frozen ground.

He exhaled slowly, his breath a faint mist, and fired. The .30-06 round struck a German officer in the chest, dropping him instantly. He worked the bolt, targeting a machine-gunner setting up an MG42: another round, another kill. Two more followed, each shot precise, disrupting the German advance. But the enemy spotted his muzzle flash, and an MG42's 7.92mm rounds tore through the branches, knocking Stevie out of the tree, the Springfield dislodged from his hand. He hit the snow hard, pain shooting through his ankle, but he grabbed the rifle and dashed, limping, to a shallow ditch fifty yards away.

Bullets whizzed past, kicking up snow. He dropped into the ditch, setting up his rifle again. Through the scope, he saw a Panzer IV commander exposed above the hatch. The shot was clean, the man collapsing, but the tank's coaxial machine gun roared to life, spraying rounds near the ditch. Once the tank's fire subsided, he crawled to a new spot, his pulse steady despite the chaos. He suspected the division's lines were crumbling, the Germans cutting off escape routes. I Company's resistance was fierce, but the lack of resupply—no ammunition had arrived in days—meant every shot had to count.

He linked up with a small group led by Corporal Albert Kitzler, a German-American soldier who had joined the division to fight the Nazis. Kitzler, fluent in German, had overheard enemy radio chatter before the attack, warning of a major offensive, but his report, like other reports from the 'green' troops, was carelessly dismissed. Now, he fought with a BAR, its heavy fire covering Stevie as he picked off another enemy soldier trying to set up a mortar. "Good shot, Cower!" Kitzler shouted, his accent thick with urgency, "Keep 'em pinned!"

Stevie acknowledged the comment, then fired again, dropping a German soldier carrying a *Panzerfaust* anti-tank weapon, but the enemy's numbers kept increasing, their tanks unstoppable.

By late afternoon, the battle had turned into a nightmare. The Germans, led by the 5th Panzer Army's 18th *Volksgrenadier* Division and 116th Panzer Division, pressed their advantage, their infantry supported by Panzer IVs, Tiger IIs, and trailer-mounted 88mm guns. The 106th's lines buckled, foxholes were overrun, and casualties were mounting.

I Company fought fiercely, their M1 Garands, BARs, and Thompsons barking in defiance, but ammunition was low, and no food had arrived in days. The 424th Regiment, positioned further back, was also under pressure and unable to reinforce the two overwhelmed forward regiments.

The Germans' goal was clear: seize St. Vith by 18 December, split the American and British armies, and open a path to Antwerp. Hitler believed that launching *Wacht am Rhein* would deliver a severe blow, disrupting the Allies and compelling them to return to the negotiating table. His strategy involved seizing the crucial port city, which was vital to the supply chain of the British and Canadian forces. By cutting off these supplies, he aimed to destabilize the Allied front, inflict a decisive defeat—primarily on the American troops—and pressure the Western powers into peace talks. This, he hoped, would free up Germany to shift its full military effort to confronting the Soviet forces on the Eastern Front.

Sergeant Whitfield, in the pillbox with Luke, Private Brown, and two other soldiers, manned the Thompson, its magazine emptying quickly as he cut down a group of three Germans who decided to storm the bunker. Luke fired the BAR, his hands freezing but his aim true, while Brown, hiding in the pines near the pillbox, lobbed M1A1 grenades, their 15-yard blast radius scattering the enemy.

"Keep firing!" the sergeant shouted. "We hold this position or we're done!"

A Panzer IV rolled into view, its 75mm gun swiveling toward the pillbox. Luke's heart sank; the division's 57mm anti-tank gun, positioned a hundred yards away, was useless against the tank's heavy armor. "Get down!" Whitfield yelled as the tank fired, the shell blasting a chunk of concrete from the pillbox's wall. The shockwave knocked him to the ground. Luke dragged him back to cover, blood trickling from a cut on the sergeant's forehead.

"You okay, Sarge?" he asked, his voice hoarse.

"Yeah," Whitfield gasped, retrieving the Thompson. He fired at a group of Germans using the tank for cover, dropping two before the magazine ran out. Private Brown tossed him another magazine, his face pale but determined. "We're running low," he said. "Maybe ten mags left."

Brock, on the ridge, was part of a makeshift unit led by Lieutenant Dobkins. They'd captured a German *Sonderkraftfahrzeug 251* half-track, purposely crashing it, and using its wreckage to block the road in an attempt to slow the German advance. But the Germans were relentless. He managed to secure a second MG42 from the half-track, its 7.92mm rounds tearing through infantry until its ammo belt was depleted. He switched back to his Thompson, his bulk an easy target as he stood to fire.

"Get down!" Dobkins shouted, but Brock was in his element, his courage bordering on recklessness. A German grenade landed nearby, and he dove, the explosion peppering his leg with shrapnel. Private Baker dragged him to cover, wrapping a bandage around the wound.

"You're crazy, man," the private said, shaking his head.

"I'm alive," he grunted, forcing a smile. "That's all that matters."

Stevie, now with Kitzler's group, held a new defensive line near a ruined farmhouse. He perched his Springfield on a stone wall, picking off a German mortar team before they could fire their deadly 8 cm *Granatwerfer 34*. Kitzler's BAR provided covering fire, but their ammunition was dwindling. "We can't hold much longer," Kitzler said, his voice grim. "They're everywhere."

Stevie agreed, his nerves beginning to crack under the strain. He thought of Luke's radio, hoping it was still working, and Brock's swagger, hoping it wouldn't get him killed. Half of the 106th Infantry Division, formed less than two years earlier, was now fighting for its survival. The Germans' pincer movement was nearly complete, severing the 422nd and 423rd Regiments from the rest of the division, isolating six thousand men.

As dusk fell, the fighting slowed, both sides exhausted. The forest was a graveyard of shattered trees, wrecked vehicles, and blood-soaked bodies, the snow streaked red and black. Luke, Brock, and Stevie regrouped in a foxhole near the pillbox, their faces smeared with dirt and blood, their eyes hollow and haunted. The Germans had pulled back to regroup, but their encirclement was almost complete. The two front-line regiments, the 422nd and the 423rd, had no food, little ammunition, and no communication with divisional headquarters. The silence was oppressive, broken only by the groans of the wounded and the rumble of German tanks repositioning for the next morning's assault.

Luke tried his radio one last time, the backup battery struggling to hold a charge. The signal cleared for a moment. "Pierce to HQ! We're surrounded! Need immediate assistance!" The response was faint: "Hold on, Pierce. We're trying to reach you."

But he was beginning to believe that the situation was hopeless. From brief messages he heard when the SCR-300 was not disrupted by German interference, he learned that the 424th Regiment was too far back to help and that the 14th Cavalry Group was under siege.

Sergeant Whitfield joined them, the Thompson slung over his shoulder. "You boys did well," he said, his voice weary. "Your efforts today proved your worth. You held."

Brock, his leg bandaged, but his spirit unbroken, lit a cigarette, inhaling deeply, his first cigarette in more than twelve hours.

"We gave 'em hell, Sarge. But they're coming back."

Stevie, cleaning his Springfield, nodded. "About a dozen kills today. Could've been more if this rifle wasn't junk." His calm exterior hid the exhaustion threatening to overwhelm him.

With the SCR-300 now out of service, Luke felt the weight of the radio's failure. "No word from HQ. We're on our own."

Brown, sitting nearby, clutched his Garand. "What happens tomorrow?" he asked.

The sergeant's face hardened. "We fight. That's all we can do."

The five men shared a canteen of water, all wishing additional rations had made it through. The forest was quiet, but it was a lie. The enemy was out there, their tanks and infantry poised to strike again. The day had been one of survival against impossible odds, but they had survived; most of them, anyway.

Luke, Brock, and Stevie steeled themselves against the dark, preparing for another day, unaware that within a few days, their regiment would face surrender, and one of the three would be dead.

Thirty-Two

Overnight, the *Schnee Eifel* had evolved into a frozen cemetery. At 0430, Luke crouched in the damaged pillbox, exhausted, but unable to sleep. The 423rd Regiment, along with the 422nd and the two support units, the 589th and 590th Field Artillery Battalions, were surrounded by the German 5th Panzer Army near Schönberg, Belgium.

The heavy cloud cover continued to ground Allied aircraft, and the cold temperatures numbed fingers and drained morale. Luke's SCR-300 radio, both batteries dead, was out of action.

With no resupply of food, ammunition, or medical supplies, and no dry clothing to replace their soaked uniforms, I Company was on the brink of collapse.

Wacht am Rhein had shattered the American generals' illusions of a "rest camp." The forward regiments, the 422nd and the 423rd, were now cut off from the rest of the division, their bunkers and foxholes battered.

Sure that they would not be getting replacement batteries, Luke returned to the inoperable SCR-300. He had fought to keep the radio operating amidst jamming from Operation *Grief*, but now destroying it was tactically prudent. He smashed the tubes and cut the wires, damaging it permanently to prevent German use. He now relied solely on the Handie-Talkie. Its limited range kept him in touch with I Company's remnant, but the regimental HQ was unreachable. His squad was down to two .30 caliber magazines and no grenades.

He had fought to keep his radio operating amid jamming from Operation *Grief*, but now, with the SCR-300 useless, he was relying on an SCR-536 Handie-Talkie with a range of less than a mile.

Sergeant Whitfield sat with his back resting against a pine tree, his Thompson submachine gun cradled in his arms. "Any word from HQ, Pierce?" he asked, his voice gravelly.

"Nothing," he said, shaking his head. "The SCR-300's shot. I'm on the Handie-Talkie now, but the range is not beyond the platoon."

Whitfield nodded, resigned to their plight. "Then we hold with what we've got. Ammo's low, no food, no medical supplies. Damn well could use some replenishment."

At 0600, the Germans renewed their assault, a roar of artillery—105 mm howitzers, and 88mm guns—shattering the dawn. Panzer IVs and Panthers rolled through the snow, their 75mm guns blasting foxholes into craters. German infantry in white camouflage followed, wielding MP40 submachine guns and Mauser rifles. The 106th's 57mm anti-tank guns were useless against the German armor, and the 589th and 590th Field Artillery Battalions, also encircled, had exhausted their more powerful 105mm howitzer rounds.

The pillbox Luke shared with Whitfield, Turner, Nelson, Brown, and Adams was now a cracked fortress under siege. As the enemy advanced, Turner fired his Garand, dropping a German soldier 50 yards out with a .30-06 round. Nelson manned a BAR, its magazine emptying in bursts that scattered an advancing German squad. Brown lobbed grenades, their blasts forcing the Germans to take cover. Adams clutched an M1, his hands shaking but his aim steady.

"Keep firing!" Whitfield shouted, his Thompson cutting down an enemy soldier trying to get behind them. Luke grabbed his M1, firing at a soldier wielding an MP40, the recoil jarring his frozen shoulder. A Panzer IV's 75mm gun fired, blasting a chunk of concrete from the pillbox. The shockwave knocked Luke to his knees, dirt raining down on him.

Nelson dragged him back, blood trickling from a cut on his forehead. "You okay, Pierce?" he shouted.

"Yeah," he grunted, suggesting he was not seriously injured, grabbing the BAR as Nelson reloaded. "We're down to three mags," Brown, now inside the pillbox, said, his voice wavering. "One grenade left."

Across the salient, the 422nd Regiment attempted a withdrawal toward Schönberg, hoping to break through the German encirclement. For a while, their maneuver looked like it would succeed as they pushed back a *Volksgrenadier* squad with concentrated BAR and M1919 machine gun fire. But the Germans, reinforced by a second *Volksgrenadier* Division, the 18th, closed the gap, their Panzer IVs cutting off the American retreat. The regiment remained trapped, their failure evidence that the 106th was losing the battle.

Two hundred yards south, Brock fought from behind the wrecked German half-track they had commandeered the day before. He was bloodied from yesterday's shrapnel wound, but his warrior spirit remained strong. His squad, led by Lieutenant Dobkins, was down to five men: Dobkins, PFC Neil Jackson, Private Kenneth Baker, PFC Robby Lewis, and himself.

"Hold the line!" Dobkins shouted, his M1 carbine spitting .30-caliber rounds. The ridge overlooked the critical road to St. Vith. They couldn't let it fall. A Panther tank rolled into view, its 75mm gun swiveling. He grabbed a bazooka, effective the day before, its rocket heavy in his hands. "Cover me!" he yelled, relocating to a better angle. Jackson and Lewis fired their rifles, keeping the infantry at bay. He aimed at the Panther, firing a rocket that ignited the fuel tank in a fireball.

"Nice shot, Brockman!" the lieutenant shouted, but the celebration was short-lived. A Tiger II's 88mm gun blasted the ridge, killing Private Baker instantly. He dove for cover, bullets hammering the snow. A German soldier charged with a bayonet-fixed Mauser, and he tussled with him, finally driving his combat knife into the man's chest. The act left him shaking, his leg wound throbbing.

A few minutes later, an artillery shell exploded nearby, shrapnel tearing into his side. He collapsed, blood soaking his uniform. Stevie, scanning the area with his rifle's scope, saw him lying on the ground, his uniform stained with blood. "Brock!" he shouted, abandoning his position and sprinting through the snow, dodging enemy fire. "Medic!" he yelled as he reached his lifelong friend. Then, helped by PFC Jackson, they dragged him to an empty foxhole.

Corporal Carl Auckland, the company medic, arrived within minutes, his medical bag nearly empty. He assessed Brock's wounds, his face grim. "It's bad. Shrapnel's deep, and he's losing blood fast. Without supplies, I can't do much. You need to keep pressure on that wound."

He administered a morphine syrette, handing Stevie two more. "Wait as long as you can between doses. I'll try to get back, but there are so many wounded, most are pretty serious." He stood, exhaustion etched in his eyes, shaking his head with sympathy, then left to tend others. Stevie stayed with Brock, holding his hand as the big man, his closest friend since childhood, moaned in pain. "Hang on, buddy," he implored.

Luke received the message via the Handie-Talkie. "Private Tim Brockman is down. Injuries are serious. Auckland says he might not make it."

His heart sank. "I'll try to get to your location," he responded, anxious to get to his friend. He relayed the news to Sergeant Whitfield, who cursed under his breath. "We're losing too many. Hold the line, Pierce."

The soldiers of the 423rd did all they could to hang on, but the Germans continued closing in. Despite the dire situation, the remnant of I Company fought on with what they had. A German squad, overconfident and advancing without tank support, was met by Nelson's BAR, combined with Turner's precise Garand shots. "Got 'em!" Nelson shouted, a rare grin breaking through his exhaustion. Luke fired his M1, dropping a soldier carrying an MP40, and Brown's last grenade scattered a mortar team. The skirmish brought the exhausted men a brief respite, an act of their defiance despite the overwhelming odds against them.

The victory was fleeting. The Germans, reinforced by the 116th Panzer Division, pressed harder, their Panzer IVs blasting foxholes into rubble. The 589th Field Artillery, surrounded along with the two infantry regiments, had no shells left, their 105mm howitzers now silent. The 422nd's withdrawal attempt had failed, their lines collapsing under the German onslaught. Regimental orders were sketchy, relayed by runners or limited-range Handie-Talkies. A sense of hopelessness settled over the men of the 423rd. Soldiers drifted from their positions, some wounded, others lost in the bedlam.

Luke, his SCR-536 crackling with platoon chatter, heard fragments of despair: "No ammo... tanks everywhere... where's our cover?" He tried to rally Turner and Adams. "We're still here," he said, his voice firm. "We fight for each other." But his words seemed hollow; the weight of Brock's injury was his primary concern.

When the day's action slowed, He went to Stevie and Brock. With the loss of blood, Brock was delirious, his wound infected, his face pale. Stevie had given him the second dose of morphine, leaving only one syrette. "Luke... Stevie..." Brock mumbled, his voice weak. "Tulare... fishing... in the lake..." His words were unsettling, memories of home twisted by pain.

Luke knelt beside him. "You're a hero, Tim Brockman. We'll get back to Hanford, and we'll go fishing every day. Just like before, the three of us."

Stevie's eyes were red, his calm facade now shattered. "He's not gonna make it, Luke. Not without help."

Luke nodded, tears welling. His words vacant.

Brock's breathing grew shallow. "Tell... Ma... I fought..." he whispered through dry lips, then went still. Stevie clutched his hand, sobbing. Luke stared, numb, as their lifelong friend slipped away. War had claimed another victim, but this one was personal. This one paralyzed his soul, haunted by Willie Jensen's prophetic words, "Most heroes come home in caskets."

As the sun set on 18 December, the 422nd and 423rd Regiments were a shadow of what they were just two days earlier. The Germans, relentless, had tightened their encirclement, their tanks and infantry poised to crush the last pockets of resistance.

Turner, Nelson, and Adams were nearby, their faces gaunt, their weapons silent. Medic Carl Auckland, his shoulder wound bandaged, sat with them, his medical bag empty. "Too many gone," he whispered, exhausted.

Sergeant Whitfield, arm wounded, his Thompson empty, tried to buoy the few gathered, "We did our best," he said, his voice hollow. "That's all we could do."

Luke and Stevie huddled without conversation in the foxhole, oblivious to the cold, both devastated by the death of their friend. Brock was the one who should have survived, based on his confidence and sheer physical presence. The only consoling thought Luke could muster was Brock's repeated declaration that he was created to be a soldier, a warrior. He reasoned that dying on the battlefield was what Brock would have chosen ...but not at nineteen years old, his whole life ahead of him. He closed his eyes, but sleep proved elusive, his spirit drained. *How much longer could they hold on?*

Thirty-Three

At 0215 on 19 December, a runner staggered through the snow, his breath labored in the subzero darkness, the regimental headquarters his destination. As it had over the past four days, the overcast sky choked off Allied air support, leaving the weary soldiers stranded, with little hope and no supplies. Both regiments and the two supporting artillery battalions were surrounded. Three days of relentless combat had stripped them bare; no food, no ammunition, no medical supplies.

The runner reached the headquarters and requested that the regimental commander be awakened. Colonel Charles C. Cavender, commander of the 423rd, came out of his quarters to meet the messenger who thrust a folded paper into his hands. Cavender scanned the order from the 106th Division Commander, Major General Alan W. Jones: "Break out west along the Bleialf-Schönberg-St. Vith Road. Clear the area of Germans. The 422nd, under Colonel George L. Descheneaux, will follow."

Cavender ordered a meeting with his staff at 0500. When the staff was gathered, he informed them of the message he had received from divisional headquarters. He then announced, "Gentlemen, we move at 0900. Get the men ready."

The 106th Infantry Division was now a shadow of its former self; its salient had become a death trap. The 2nd Infantry Division's promise of a "rest camp" had become a cruel joke, shattered by the German *Wacht am Rhein* offensive. Without food or ammo, they would attempt a breakout.

Luke crouched in a foxhole that had survived three days of German bombs and rockets, the SCR-536 tight against his ear. He pressed the radio's push-to-talk switch and announced, "Pierce. Squad Seven. Radio check." The only response was static. He waited thirty seconds, then retransmitted with the same result.

Sergeant Whitfield heard him attempting to make contact and came to the rim of the foxhole. Standing over him, he cautioned, "Pierce, keep that radio alive. We need every word you can catch."

"Yes, Sarge," he replied, keying the Handie-Talkie. "Pierce, Seventh Platoon. Radio check." This time, there was a response, "Roger Pierce. I copy. Stand by for a message from the regimental commander."

"Roger. Standing by."

The soldier at the other end of the radio, a voice Luke did not recognize, announced, "All troops with the 423rd Regiment will break out at 0900. Copy?"

"Roger. Confirming breakout at 0900."

Whitfield overheard the transmission and moved into action, moving from foxhole to foxhole to inform the men of the impending move. The news quickly rippled through the platoon. Private Nelson, remarkably calm, responded to the order, "Finally, we're getting out of this hellhole. I've had enough of being frozen."

"You think it's that easy? The Krauts have us boxed in. We're going on a suicide run," said Private Brown.

Sergeant Whitfield's glare silenced them. "Stow it, both of you. We've got orders, and we're following them. End of story."

After listening to Brown and Nelson's concerns, Luke cleared his head. *I must stay alert and in the moment.* The regiment was fractured, surrounded, and on the verge of capitulation.

Six of the men gathered at the pillbox, or what was left of it. Over the past two days, it had served as platoon headquarters. Now, under constant bombardment, it had been reduced to a single wall. PFC Jackson voiced his concern. "I keep thinking about my farm," he said, his voice low.

Though he had hesitated, Luke found himself responding. "Yeah, I promised my fiancé we'd be together for New Year's. Now, I'm not even sure I'll see her again."

Whitfield's hand rested on Luke's shoulder, firm and steady. "We'll make it, Pierce."

Private Adams contributed, his voice shaky but hopeful. "Maybe this breakout's our ticket home. One last push."

"Don't jinx it," Nelson shot back, his eyes darting to the trees. "Lots of Krauts waiting out there, and they ain't in a giving mood."

Luke's thoughts churned. He imagined a letter to Shaina, words he'd never wanted to write: *Dear Shaina, if you're reading this, I didn't make it. Please know that I fought for us, for our future.* He shook it off, forcing his focus back to the radio.

At 0830, Colonel Cavender briefed the platoon leaders, his words clipped and concise. "We've got one shot. The 18th Volksgrenadiers and the *Führer Begleit* Brigade are out there—panther tanks, cannons, infantry, the works. We hit hard. We move fast, or we're done."

Sergeant Whitfield relayed it to the men, his face grim. "You heard the colonel. Pack up, check your weapons. We're getting out of here."

Lewis fumbled with his BAR, "Sarge, you think we've got a chance?"

Whitfield's jaw tightened. "We've got what we've got, Lewis. Make it count."

Luke heard Nelson complaining to Brown, "We may as well be prisoners. With no ammo, we're dead men walking."

"Shut up, Nelson," Brown hissed, his voice cracking. "I'd rather die fighting than rot here."

Luke felt the tension, his body tight, struggling to move. He thought of Brock, killed the day before, his friend gone forever. They'd promised to stick together, "The Hanford Boys"; Luke, Stevie, Brock. Now they were two.

At 0900, the 423rd began the move, the 422nd trailing behind. The march was a relentless slog through the pine-choked forest, with knee-deep snow in places. Luke trudged beside Stevie, Nelson, and Brown, their Garands slung low, ammo down to almost nothing. The 589th and 590th Field Artillery, with no shells left, joined the march, their crews wielding M1 carbines like infantrymen.

Nelson spoke up again, "Maybe we'll make it, but I wouldn't bet on it."

"Shut up, Kenny," Brown growled.

Whitfield ended the chatter. "Eyes on the road."

The forest was silent, the Germans invisible. Hope surfaced, fragile but heartening. Then, at 0945, hellfire rained down. German artillery, 81mm mortars, 105mm howitzers, 88mm guns, and a storm of *Nebelwerfer* rockets, "screaming meemies," identified by their shrill, high-pitched wailing sound, landed, spraying snow and broken tree limbs in vast swaths. Luke dove behind a tree, his radio held tightly in his hand. "Pierce to platoon! Heavy artillery fire!" he yelled, but static consumed his words.

Assault and flak guns on German half-tracks roared to life, shredding the lines. He saw an entire K Company squad vanish in a single blast.

"Keep moving!" Whitfield bellowed, his Thompson spitting rounds at the nearly invisible white-clad figures.

Brown was hit, his leg torn off by a shell. Luke crawled through the snow, his heart racing. "Medic! Medic!" he yelled, his voice unstable. He reached him, fumbling to apply a tourniquet, but Brown's eyes were fading. "Tell my mother... I love her," he gasped, then went limp.

"Damn it!" he roared, slamming his fist into the snow. He keyed the radio, "Pierce to platoon! Brown's dead! We need support!" Again, there was only a static response. Anger overwhelming him, he keyed the radio three more times without success, then, with all the force he could muster, threw it against a rock, breaking its casing and exposing its inner workings, the platoon's voice now silent.

The barrage was relentless. Turner, fifty yards north, shouted, "They're cutting us to pieces."

Luke saw Auckland darting between the wounded, his injured shoulder ignored, his hands slick with blood, his face a mask of despair.

Nelson dragged himself over, his helmet dented by a German round. "We're done! This ain't a breakout, it's a slaughter!"

"We're not finished," Luke snapped, "We've got to keep going."

"For what?" Nelson spat, his eyes wild. "Brock's dead. Brown's gone. How many more?"

He had no answer; the yearning to live, to see Shaina, and to build a life together was the only thing pushing him forward.

By mid-morning, the 423rd neared the *Schönberg* bridge, the *Our* River a dark ribbon below. They charged, desperate to seize it, but the 18th *Volks-*

grenadiers were dug in. Panzer IVs and StuG IIIs assault guns rumbled forward, their 75mm guns carving larger openings in the regiment. Whitfield continued giving orders, directing their M1s against the advancing German infantry.

Lewis fired his BAR, the 20-round magazine spent in a flash. "They're everywhere!" he yelled, reloading as an MG42 machine gun raked the ground near him.

Stevie, three hundred yards off, steadied his Springfield. He fired, dropping a German radioman. "For Brock," he muttered, his voice thick with grief.

Whitfield rallied them. "We take that bridge or we're finished!" But a group of Panthers closed in, their guns blasting a nearby foxhole, killing three. Luke ducked, shrapnel pinging his helmet. "We can't hold!" Nelson shouted, his M1 Garand empty.

Whitfield faced off with a regimental Lieutenant he did not recognize. "We can't hold without artillery," the Lieutenant said, his voice weak. "We need to fall back."

"Orders are to take the bridge," Whitfield shot back. "We try or we die."

"I'd rather die fighting than surrender," Adams growled.

PFC Lewis, his hands shaking, countered, "And leave your family with nothing? Living's braver."

Luke listened, his gut churning. He thought of Brock. "We're not giving up," he said, more to himself than them, "Not yet."

Turner chimed in, his face pale. "Sarge, what's the point? We're surrounded, outgunned. Nobody's coming."

Whitfield's eyes blazed. "The point is we're still here, Turner. Shut up and fight."

The argument ended when a StuG III's shell exploded nearby, showering them with icy mud. Luke saw Adams slump, clutching his side, blood seeping through his fingers. "I'm fine," he lied, his voice frail, "Keep going."

Amid the bedlam, I Company did not give up. Stevie spotted a German mortar team two hundred yards out, his Springfield barking twice. The gunner and loader dropped, the 81mm gun silent. "Got 'em!" he called. Nelson and Lewis, with a single Thompson between them, ambushed a *Volksgrenadier* squad, the gun's chatter shredding the Germans. "Take that, you bastards!" Lewis shouted, his voice breaking.

It didn't last. Panthers flanked them, their crossfire lethal. A StuG III obliterated a machine gun nest, its crew gone in an instant. The 422nd's earlier retreat had collapsed, and there were no reinforcements. Whitfield's platoon held a ridge, repelling an enemy squad with M1 and BAR fire. "We're still here!" Whitfield roared, his Thompson firing in short bursts, an attempt to conserve ammo.

But the ammo dwindled, and the Germans pressed harder. A private bolted, sprinting across the snow. An MG42 caught him, his body crumpling. Luke stared, "No way out," he said, the words numbing.

Nelson grabbed his arm. "You see that? We're next!"

"We hold," Luke said, "for Brock, ...for Brown, ...for Adams."

"For what?" Nelson yelled, rage consuming him. "They're gone, and we're as good as dead ourselves!"

Luke shoved him off. "Then we die fighting!"

By afternoon, the breakout was wrecked. They'd gained three miles the day before, but now, pinned near Schönberg, they were finished. Luke's arm bled from shrapnel that cut through his light coat, the pain a dull pounding, but he continued firing his M1 until it clicked empty.

At 1400, Colonels Descheneaux and Cavender, the commanders of the 422nd and 423rd Regiments, met in a ruined bunker. “Charles, we’re done,” Descheneaux said, his voice flat. “No ammo, no artillery, no way out.”

Cavender nodded, eyes locked on Descheneaux, his expression stoic. “We can’t let them be butchered. We must surrender.” The two made it official.

The order was passed through the ranks of the weary, tattered soldiers, but it hit like a gut punch. “Destroy your weapons!” Whitfield barked. Luke smashed his M1, bending the barrel. Stevie snapped his Springfield’s bolt, “If we just had a little more ammo,” he choked out.

Nelson stared, his voice questioning. “Surrender? After all this?”

“It’s over,” Whitfield said, his tone subdued. “No choice.”

Turner kicked a rock, “I didn’t sign up for this. We headed to a POW camp? I’d rather be dead.”

Luke thought of the life slipping away, then checked his attitude. “I’m not dead yet,” he whispered. “I’ll live. For Brock, for Katie, ...for Shaina.” Deep in his gut, Luke longed to believe the words he had dared to voice.

Thirty-Four

At 1600 hours on December 19, 1944, Luke stood in a frozen clearing, his M1 Garand bent at his feet. The 423rd Regiment, alongside the 422nd and the 589th and 590th Field Artillery Battalions, had fought for three and a half days, but now they were finished; starving, sleepless, and out of ammunition. Encircled by the German 5th Panzer Army, their breakout attempt collapsed under a storm of infantry and tanks. Colonel Cavender's order was repeated through the ranks: "Surrender. Lay down your arms."

Luke's stomach twisted. Shaina's face, her dark eyes, her promise to wait in New Jersey, flashed in his mind.

Stevie, his Springfield sniper rifle broken, stared at the pile of weapons. "Brock would've hated this," he muttered, his voice raw from grief over their friend's death.

Private Nelson, just eighteen, fought back tears. "I just wanna go home," he sighed.

PFC Turner spat, his eyes blazing. "The people back home, they'll think we're cowards. We should've fought to the last."

"Enough," Whitfield growled. "There's no honor in dying for nothing."

The Germans emerged with Mausers leveled. An officer, his English difficult to understand, ordered, "Line up! You will be searched!" The prisoners shuffled into rows, hands raised, as guards tore through their pockets. Luke's watch was ripped from his wrist. He lunged forward. "That's mine!"

A guard's rifle butt slammed into his shoulder, knocking him to his knees. "*Schweigen!*" the guard snarled. Luke bit back a curse, pain flaring.

Stevie's family photo, tucked in his shirt, was yanked out and tossed into the snow. He dove for it, but a guard kicked it away. "No!" he shouted, his voice breaking. The guard raised his rifle, and Stevie froze, hands up.

Robby's cigarettes vanished into a German's pocket. He stared, eyes cold, as the soldier lit one and exhaled a cloud. Turner's pocketknife was snatched. "That's my granddad's!" he yelled, earning a rifle butt to the gut. He doubled over, gasping.

The Germans stripped some prisoners of their coats or their boots, leaving them in thin wool uniforms. Luke shivered, his breath a light vapor. Stevie's teeth chattered, his jacket gone. Whitfield, also coatless, stood tall, hiding his pain.

Torn undershirts tied to sticks, more gray than white, rose above the American lines, a signal of surrender. Luke's face burned with shame. He'd trained at Fort Monmouth and learned to keep the SCR-536 alive in any condition, but it lay smashed somewhere in the snow. He thought of his lifelong friend, Brock, lying dead on the battlefield. "We failed you," he whispered.

Stevie's eyes were dull, fixed on the snow. "Brock would've fought on," he said, voice low.

"Then he'd be wrong," Whitfield cut in. "We fought three days with nothing. You think he'd want us all dead?"

Turner muttered; his voice venomous. "We're prisoners because of those damn generals. Where are they? Probably back safe behind the lines, eating a nice warm dinner."

The German officer scanned the mass of American soldiers, now a defeated army.

"You will march to Gerolstein," he said. "Obey, or face consequences."

A German guard pointed at Luke, Stevie, Turner, and Nelson. "You four, carry him!" he gestured to a stretcher holding a wounded German soldier, his leg bloody, his foot gone. The man groaned, eyes half-open, as they lifted the litter. The weight was crushing, the snow deep, and each step was a fight for survival. Luke's arms screamed, his shoulder throbbing from the earlier blow.

"Why us?" Nelson complained. "We're half-dead already."

"Keep moving," Stevie whispered, his grip repeatedly slipping on the icy handles. "They'll shoot us if we stop."

The injured German moaned louder, his weight shifting. Luke's boots sank, snow soaking his socks.

Hours dragged on. Turner stumbled, nearly dropping the stretcher. "I can't," he gasped.

"You can," Whitfield said, marching nearby. "Think of your family."

Nelson mumbled, "This is their war, not ours. Why are we saving their guy?"

"Shut up," Luke snapped, his voice sharp. "We're alive. Don't get us killed with your mouth."

They reached the bunker at dusk, a concrete hulk scarred by shellfire. A German medic showed them where to place the wounded man, nodding in agreement. "*Dankeschön.*" Luke's arms trembled as they shuffled back to the other prisoners, legs almost giving out, his breath shallow.

The prisoners formed columns, ragged lines stretching through the forest. Guards, some with Mausers, some with snarling German Shepherds and Doberman Pinschers on leashes, shouted orders in German. Many, like Stevie, had no coat; their wool uniforms were no match for the subzero cold. His lips were blue, his hands tucked under his armpits. Whitfield marched ahead, his voice steady, "Keep together, boys. We're not done."

The terrain was brutal: steep ridges, icy slopes, and valleys with snowdrifts up to their knees. Luke's legs burned, and he fought not to collapse. A prisoner ahead stumbled, and a guard's rifle butt cracked against his skull. The man fell, blood staining the snow. Whitfield lunged forward. The guard swung, catching Whitfield's jaw. He staggered, blood dripping. Luke grabbed him, holding him up. "You okay, Sarge?" he asked, his voice tight.

"I'm okay," Whitfield grunted, spitting blood. "Let's keep moving."

They passed a village, its houses dark, with locals peering from the windows. A boy threw a stone, hitting a prisoner in the back. The guards laughed. A woman, standing close, slipped a crust of bread to a soldier, but a guard knocked it away, shouting at the woman, "*Verboten!*" Luke's stomach growled; they had been three days without nourishment.

At a clearing, the Germans halted the column. "Names, ranks, serial numbers!" an officer demanded. When it was his turn, Luke complied, his voice flat.

"More!" the officer barked. "Unit strength, positions!" "Juden?"

"Pierce, Luke, PFC, 39421436."

The officer glared at him but dismissed him with a command: "Next!"

Turner was next, but he hesitated, his jaw set.

"Name, rank, serial number!"

"Go to hell," Turner spat.

A guard's rifle butt slammed into his ribs, dropping him to his knees. Another blow split his lip. Luke started to charge forward, but Whitfield grabbed him. "Don't, Pierce. You'll make it worse."

The German sneered. "You will not move until you talk." The prisoners stood for almost an hour, snow building on their shoulders. Luke's toes went numb. Frostbite was a real threat. Robby swayed, his face pale. "I can't feel my feet," he whispered.

"If you get a chance, rub them," Stevie said, his own hands shaking. "Keep the blood moving."

The Germans ordered the prisoners, tired, weak, and hungry, to resume walking.

Whitfield's voice was low. "They're breaking the Geneva Convention. Supposed to give us shelter, food, clothes."

"Like they care," Turner muttered, blood drying on his chin.

As evening approached, Gerolstein's lights appeared. The town was filled with German troops, trucks rumbling past. The prisoners, over two thousand strong, shuffled into a barbed-wire enclosure near the railway station. Boxcars loomed nearby, their wooden sides scarred, doors open to reveal black voids. Luke's gut twisted at the sight.

They were given biscuits and a sliver of cheese, not enough to dull the hunger. Luke chewed slowly, "Tastes like ash."

Stevie stared at his portion, eyes distant. "Brock would've eaten this in one bite. Wouldn't have bothered to chew." He said, voice cracking.

Luke smiled, his chapped lips stinging, glad Stevie had not lost his humor. But despair clawed at him. He thought of Katie, her strength keeping their father's anger at bay, his Jewish identity still a secret. "I should've told you," he whispered to himself, imagining Brock receiving his confession.

They huddled against the fence, snow falling gently. Other POWs from other divisions joined them. A soldier from the 28th Division, his face haggard, said, “Got nabbed near St. Vith. You?”

“Same,” he offered, suddenly realizing that something was wrong. A young German guard's eyes were locked on him, his glare penetrating. *Why is he staring at me?*

Thirty-Five

The captured soldiers were relieved that the grueling two-day hike through the snow was finally over. The toll of the march on the men was catastrophic. Several had died, falling victim to the harsh freezing weather or enemy brutality, left to die on the side of the road. The railway platform at Gerolstein signified that they were being moved to a prison camp deep in German territory.

German Shepherds, growling with sharp teeth bared, were restrained by guards with batons, some of them eager, looking for even the slightest infraction to release the dogs on the hapless captives. An occasional thump of a rifle butt against human flesh could be heard as guards removed jewelry, cigarettes, and other valuables not already taken.

It was at that moment when the young German guard, Dieter Zobel, fixed his eyes on Luke, sizing him up; *same dark wavy hair, same jawline.* But it was more than that. When Luke steadied a frail prisoner named Graham, pulling him up with a firm, protective hand, Dieter's gut twisted. *Exact grip, firm and determined, just like the boy's grip of his mother's hand in the train yard, just before they ran away.*

In Dieter's fractured, resentful mind, Luke *was* that boy, ...or close enough. The resemblance, the gesture, it was no coincidence. This wasn't just about the Reich anymore; it was about Werner, about avenging his death. His antisemitism had a face now, and it was Luke's. He'd make him suffer, break him, and prove that justice still existed. Like a predator marking prey, he tracked Luke through the crowd of prisoners.

Sensing trouble, Luke avoided his gaze as the sound of the guard's boots grew louder, his path, straight to him.

His companions fell silent as the tall, muscular German stood among them; the barrel of his *Karabiner* gripped tight in gloved hands. Though approximately the same age as Luke, his face carried the hard edge of someone who'd enjoyed cruelty.

The young German's single word cut through the winter air, "Name?"

Luke straightened his back, reciting the response they'd all been trained to give. "Pierce, Lucas, serial number 39421436."

The guard's eyes narrowed, his gaze dissecting his features with disturbing intensity. "Pierce. What nationality is that?" His English was surprisingly fluent, each word precise. Luke blinked, caught off guard by both the question and the guard's command of English.

"Pierce, Lucas. Serial number 39421436," he repeated, his voice steadier than he felt.

Dieter leaned closer, his breath pungent with the odor of *Mettwurst*, sausage made from minced pork, garlic, and alcohol. Something in his eyes sparked recognition in Luke, a hatred that seemed personal, targeted. "You look like a Jew. I know who you are. You killed my brother, and before I'm done, you will admit it," he snarled. "Is Pierce a Jewish name?" The other prisoners around Luke tensed, sensing the danger.

"Pierce, Lucas. Serial number 3942... "

The rifle butt flashed upward without warning, pain exploding across his chin as the wooden stock connected with brutal force. The world tilted sideways, his vision blurred, and sounds muffled as he collapsed.

Through the haze, he glimpsed the guard as he turned away, satisfaction etched across the young German's face. His gait revealed a pronounced limp as he stalked off, his left leg stiff and unbending.

"My God," Stevie said, dropping beside Luke. "You, okay? Hey, look at me."

With the help of another soldier, Stevie lifted him to a sitting position. Whitfield's face came into view, concerned eyes examining the wound.

"Hold still," the sergeant said, tearing a strip from his already torn undershirt. He pressed it against his jaw where blood trickled down, freezing almost immediately in the bitter cold.

"What the hell was that about?" Robby asked, keeping an eye out for the guard's return.

Luke winced as Whitfield dabbed at the wound. "Don't know," he replied, an acute pain shooting through his jaw. "Never seen him before, I swear."

"He targeted you specifically," the sergeant muttered. "The way he looked at you. It was like he recognized you."

Blood soaked through the makeshift bandage. His head throbbed, the pain radiating in waves. A whistle shrieked across the yard. Guards began shouting orders, pushing prisoners toward the waiting boxcars. The moment of relative quiet ended as madness erupted around them.

"Can you stand?" Whitfield asked, gripping Luke's arm.

He nodded, allowing himself to be pulled upright. The world spun, and he thought he was going to vomit, his empty stomach settling after a few seconds. "I'm okay."

"Stay close to me," PFC Turner said. "That bastard's watching you. I can feel it."

As they shuffled toward the trains, he sensed the same guard's eyes on him again, tracking him through the crowd. Something about the hatred in that gaze was personal, as though they'd met before. He sensed that the secret that he had struggled to keep hidden for so long was now out in the open without a word being spoken. The thought was terrifying.

Dieter eyed him, smiling as he thought of the punishment he would dispense when they arrived at the prison camp. As he surveyed Luke, he fought back against the memory of his brother, his lifeless head against the train track. *I haven't forgotten, Werner. I will make that Jew who killed you regret what he did.* A cynical grin broke across his face.

His head throbbing, caked blood on his chin, Luke stood shivering, his wool uniform offering little resistance to the cold. Between the pain and the chill, he sensed his determination slipping away. Around him, the remnant of I Company—Stevie, Whitfield, Lewis, and Turner—stood in a ragged line, an attempt to remain a unit, their faces gaunt from nearly five days without food. The regiment's surrender two days earlier had shattered them. They were no longer fighting German soldiers. They were no longer fighting German soldiers. Now, their fight was against hunger and discouragement, a battle to stay alive.

Guards, Mausers slung over their shoulders, barked orders. "*Schnell*! Into the cars!" The wooden boxcars, wooden, deteriorated, and filthy, were marked "*Forty hommes, eight chevaux*" (Forty men, eight horses). Designed to hold forty, as many as seventy men were being crammed into each boxcar, not enough space for all of them to sit.

"Keep moving, Luke," Whitfield urged, his voice hoarse but firm.

Inside, the boxcar was a black void, lit only by a single small window at the rear. Guards shoved them in, pressed so tight Luke had difficulty breathing. The door slammed shut with a heavy metallic clank, eerily similar to the sound of a prison cell closing. The air was stagnant, the stench of bodies crammed like sardines in a tin. He wedged himself against a wall, his jaw a steady throb.

The young German guard, the one who dealt Luke the rifle's blow, appeared at the door, his English sharp. "No Jews on this car. If you're Jewish, get off now!"

He stood at the doorway, glancing at the men pressed against one another, his eyes again landing on Luke, who looked down, saying nothing. After a minute, with no one moving toward the sliding door, he slammed the door shut. In the locked-in boxcar, Luke hoped that would be the last he would see of the guard, still uncertain why he had been targeted. Once again, his secret was preserved, but it was a snare that continued to haunt his conscience, sure now that at least one German guard knew the truth.

The train lurched, wheels screeching. He braced himself, his legs already aching. "Four or five days to *Mühlberg*," a guard had said, "*Stammlager* IV-B." He didn't know for sure what awaited them, but if the railcar was any indication, the worst still lay ahead.

Stevie, sandwiched between Luke and a soldier he didn't recognize, stood, staring into space. Today was the day he was supposed to be transferred to Patton's 87th Infantry Division. Instead, he was now crammed in a stench-filled boxcar with seventy captives, heading to a prison camp.

The train's rhythm was a relentless clack, jarring Luke's bones. He stood, pressed against Stevie, their shoulders touching in the crush. The air was stifling, despite the cold seeping through cracks. Men groaned, some praying, others cursing. They took turns sitting, with room for only 9 or 10 at a time. Again, hunger gnawed at his gut. Five days without a proper meal left him woozy and unsteady.

His bladder ached, but there was no toilet. Someone passed a helmet toward the back, its contents sloshing. “Up to the window,” a voice called. He took it, grimacing, and stretched toward the high opening. His fingers brushed the icy frame, and the helmet slipped, spilling urine onto his boots and the men nearby.

“Damn it,” a soldier shouted, "you got piss all over me!" He shoved Luke’s leg with his shoulder.

“Sorry,” Luke said, his face burning.

Night fell, and the boxcar became a black pit. The stench grew worse, a mingling of waste and unwashed bodies. He tried to doze, his head nodding against the soldier next to him, but sleep was impossible with the continual clacking and steady vibration of the train’s steel wheels grinding against iron rails.

The linked boxcars stopped abruptly, jolting him and sending a new wave of pain as his face banged the boxcar’s wall. Within minutes of their stopping, guards began banging rifle butts on the car’s sides, shouting, “No sleeping!” The torment was repeated every two hours, a calculated annoyance to keep them exhausted.

“Why’re they doing this?” Robby asked, staring into space, his voice shaky.

“To break us,” Whitfield said, his jaw clenched. “Makes us easier to control. Don’t let ‘em.”

Luke’s mind drifted to Shaina, one of only two people who knew his secret. *But if the limping guard knew, how many others?* He pushed the thought down. *I’ll deal with it later.* The same thing he always said.

The second day brought new terror. The train halted mid-morning, nearby explosions shaking the boxcars. Luke tensed. Allied bombers were targeting German railways. They most likely didn't know Americans were on board. The Germans hadn't bothered to mark the tops of the boxcars.

"What's that?" Robby asked, his eyes wide.

"Allied bombers," Whitfield said, his voice low. "I recognize the sound of the Pratt & Whitney engines. Stay calm."

"Calm?" Turner snapped. "Our own guys are trying to kill us!"

"Shut up," Stevie growled.

The bomb blasts grew closer, shaking the boxcar more violently. Men pressed tighter. The guards outside shouted, their voices tense. "*Ruhe*! Quiet!" They were scared, too, Luke realized. If the Allied bombers hit their target, the Germans would die along with the Americans.

The bombing stopped, and before the train resumed its movement, a loaf of bread and a block of Limburger cheese were passed around; one bite of each per man. Luke chewed slowly, the odor rank, the taste dry, the only thing he had eaten for several days.

"I can't do this," Robby said, his voice breaking. "It's almost Christmas. I want to go home like they promised."

"You'll get home," Whitfield said, gripping his shoulder. "Hold on."

By the third day, the boxcar was a cesspool. The stench of waste was unbearable, helmets overflowing before they could be emptied. Luke's throat was raw, his lips chapped from dehydration. He stood, swaying, his back screaming from the constant pressure.

A soldier from the 422nd, a Private named Wicker, began pounding the wall and screaming, "I can't take it! Let me out!" His fists bloodied, his sobs reverberating. Another soldier grabbed him, pinning his arms. "Stop it! You'll get us all killed."

Robby, curled against the wall, pleaded, "I don't wanna die here."

"You won't," Stevie said, his voice firm despite his exhaustion. "We're tougher than this."

Luke wanted to believe it, but despair clawed at him too. He thought of Brock, gone forever. *Gone where? Was death the end? Where was God?* He thought of Moses Weisbaum and the hundreds of questions he would ask him if he ever got back to Hanford.

He seriously considered confessing his Jewish heritage to Stevie, but fear held him back. *Why put both of them at risk?*

The train stopped again, and the guards resumed their persecution, banging on the car and shouting. "No sleeping!" The noise was relentless, shredding the captive's nerves.

Luke gazed at the men crammed together. These were his brothers. His eyes burned, his body begging for rest, the young German guard keeping him alert. Stripped of their warm clothing, with little to eat, and in offensive conditions, all they had was one another.

Thirty-Six

The train's brakes screeched, a sound that unnerved Luke following four days of suffering in the dark, cramped boxcar. *Raus! Schnell! Aus machen!* The German shouted, his Mauser pointed at Stevie's head, finger pressed against the trigger. Luke stepped onto the snow-covered platform, squinting out the blinding sunlight, his legs trembling from standing almost the entire time. Around him, the remnants of their platoon spilled out, eyes sunken, faces gaunt from hunger and exhaustion.

The hellhole that would be their home for the next five months sprawled before them, a fortress of barbed wire and wooden barracks, its guard towers bristling with MG42 machine guns. At the entrance, twelve feet in the air, supported by eight massive pillars, a wooden beam carried the carved letters: *M. STAMMLAGER IV B.*

Intended primarily for Polish prisoners, the prison camp had become a frenzied mix of cultures and languages: English, French, Polish, Italian, and Russian. Overriding the fusion of languages was the recurrent shouting of German commands.

"This place sounds like the tower of Babel," Stevie joked, low enough that the guards could not hear. Luke grinned, the facial expression bringing a sharp pain to his bruised jaw. It was the first time he had smiled in days, and it felt good despite the tenderness.

Luke looked around the camp, his eyes acclimating to the light. In addition to the double barbed wires around the perimeter, he noticed a second wire stretched twenty yards inside the outer wires. In a few days, he would witness firsthand that the area between the inner and outer wires was strictly forbidden when he saw a delirious Soviet prisoner, just two steps over the inner wire, mowed down by machine gun fire.

A short distance off, he heard the sound of barking Alsatian dogs, a noise he and the other POWs would come to dread.

Guards in gray uniforms shouted orders in harsh German, sorting the Americans with callous efficiency, their rifle butts prodding those they judged moving too slowly. The new arrivals swelled the camp's already strained capacity, forcing men to crowd together in snaking lines that seemed to stretch for miles.

The exhausted group was marched into a small compound. The floor was stained with the residue of the thousands that had been herded through previously. A Russian prisoner wielded shears that buzzed through their hair in swift, mechanical swoops, his face blank. Within ten minutes, the seven comrades of I Company stood hairless, their shorn locks piled in heaps. They were shoved outside and pushed to the next building, where pools of standing water were at the base of the walls.

"Line up! Strip!" yelled a guard, his voice slicing through the winter chill. "Put your clothes into the baskets!"

Another sentry forced the prisoners into a large shower area where the stench of disinfectant burned their nostrils. Luke peeled off his uniform, the cold biting his exposed skin. Hot water blasted from the shower heads, scalding their naked flesh. The guard motioned with his hand, indicating they should scrub themselves despite the absence of soap. As each man emerged, dripping and shivering as soon as the hot water ceased. They were forced to stand spread-eagled while a Russian prisoner extended a pole with a rag dripping with disinfectant, swiping it under their arms and across their groins. Luke recoiled, letting out a muffled gasp as the antiseptic seared his skin.

Still naked, the prisoners were shuffled into a space not much larger than a closet, where a German doctor plunged a needle into their arms without a word of explanation.

"What's this for?" Sergeant Whitfield asked.

"*Schweigen!*" the guard snapped, shoving him forward.

The baskets, containing their damp uniforms, which had been hastily washed and rinsed, were brought to the men, who eagerly dressed. Heads shaved, showered, disinfected, and clothed, they were each registered and given a metal tag, an *Erkennungsmarken,* similar in shape and size to the dog tags the army issued. The pressed-metal plates bore only the words "Stalag IVB" and the prisoner's ID number. A perforation down the center allowed the tag to be broken in two if the prisoner died; one half was kept with the body, and the other half was used to notify German authorities of the death. Luke studied the zinc plate stamped with the number 714662, the six-digit number a cold replacement for his name.

He clutched the cold metal tag, fingers numb. He'd heard whispers that Jewish prisoners were required to have an "H" on their tags, a letter that could mean death. He couldn't let that happen; he had too much to live for. So, despite the guilt and shame, he continued to hide his heritage.

Whitfield, his jaw set, said, "Keep it together. Let's focus on staying alive."

Robby Lewis wrapped his arms around his chest, a feeble attempt to warm up. In the shower, he'd noticed the frostbite beginning to blacken the tips of his toes. He wondered for how long?

"*Bewegen!*" a guard shouted, prodding them with his rifle. They were shuffled down a dirt road in the center of the camp, leading to the endless rows of barracks on either side.

The same young German who had harassed Luke when they were being loaded into the boxcars in Gerolstein stepped forward, his familiar English accent sharp. "You," he said, pointing at him. "This way."

He flinched, sensing renewed danger. The guard's eyes were cold, his limp pronounced, a clipboard clutched in his gloved hand. "Why me?" he asked, voice steady despite his growing angst.

"Orders," Dieter Zobel grinned, his tone final. He gestured to a nearby barracks, Block Fourteen.

Stevie glared at the guard, grabbing for his friend's arm. "Where you taking him?"

Zobel raised his Mauser. "Back in line, or you'll join him."

Whitfield pulled him away, his voice low. "Don't, Stevie, we'll get him back."

Dieter's gaze lingered, as if he saw through Luke's lies about his heritage. There was no doubt, he was the same young German guard from Gerolstein, the one who'd pressed him about being Jewish, then hit him in the jaw with the butt of his rifle. *Why me?*

The next morning, Luke, separated from the men of I Company , was taken to the processing shed, a wooden structure with several rooms reserved for medical exams and prisoner interrogations. The atmosphere was a mixture of shouts and shoves, slapping and striking prisoners who didn't respond to orders screamed in a language they didn't understand.

He stood rigid in his place, his uniform, once a source of pride, now hung loosely from his frame, tattered and faded after weeks of exposure to the subzero weather.

The exam was a farce, nothing more than a token ritual. White-coated doctors, their faces impassive, barely glanced at frostbitten feet or acknowledged the hacking coughs that echoed throughout the shed. One doctor waved men past after the briefest of glances, writing hasty notes that could mean life or death with flippant disinterest. Dysentery and pneumonia were spreading through the ranks of prisoners. The stench of sickness and desperation—now swelled by the newly arrived Americans—permeated every inch of the camp.

A guard with a pockmarked face and dead eyes led him to a small room at the end of a narrow corridor. The space was claustrophobic, its walls bare except for a single faded notice in German, a solitary chair positioned in the center. An officer sat behind a desk, his uniform neat despite the squalor surrounding him. His eyes, cold and calculating, scanned a ledger filled with the names of prisoners.

"Name, rank, serial number," he demanded, his English brief and precise.

"Pierce, Luke, PFC, 39421436," Luke said, revealing nothing beyond the required basics.

The officer's pen scratched against paper as he made his notation. Without looking up, he asked, "Nationality?" His pen remained poised, waiting to categorize him, to place him in some clearly defined box.

His throat tightened. The rumors had circulated among the men during their long march to the camp, answering Jewish could mark him for worse treatment, segregation, and possibly death. "English," he replied, eyes fixed on the floor, studying the scuffed boots of the officer, unwilling to meet the man's penetrating gaze.

The officer's eyes narrowed; suspicion was written across his features. "English?" he questioned, his tone suggesting he found this answer suspect.

"Yes, sir," he said, sweat beading on his forehead.

The German studied him for a moment, his expression unreadable, before scribbling something in his ledger. Then he gestured him out with a dismissive wave of his wrist, already looking past Luke to the next prisoner. Luke sighed with relief as he stepped outside, but the fear lingered. *Had he dodged a bullet, or just delayed the inevitable?* He hadn't lied; his father, he believed, was English. Still, the half-truth, denying his mother's heritage, plagued him as he rejoined the shuffling mass of prisoners.

In the muddy yard, the guards corralled them into the barracks like sheep, shouting and striking those who moved too slowly. He saw his comrades from I Company and went toward them, hoping the guards would not notice him so he could rejoin them in Block Twelve.

From out of the shadows, Dieter reappeared, intercepting him. "Block Fourteen," he said, his voice cold as ice. "Move!"

"Why him?" Whitfield demanded, stepping forward, his calm demeanor cracking under the strain of seeing their group split in two. Though exhausted and malnourished, his protective instinct flared, his hands balled into fists at his sides.

Dieter's rifle snapped up, the barrel pointing at the sergeant's chest. "Obey, or you all will suffer, you first," he warned, his finger hovering near the trigger. Whitfield retreated a single step, never taking his eye off the guard.

Luke caught Stevie's eye across the short distance, now insurmountable. In that silent exchange was a plea, a promise, and the shared understanding of men who had faced death together. Stevie tensed as he managed a knowing wink toward him, his face revealing concern for the threat to his friend.

"I'll be okay," Luke mouthed, trying to project a confidence he struggled to muster. As he turned and followed the guard, the gap between him and his friends widened, quashing any hope that they would continue together on the harsh journey that had led to this desolate German prison camp.

Block Fourteen was a grim mirror of the other blocks; cramped, filthy, the wooden walls damp with mold, creating a perpetual chill. He had never felt so alone. A few dim bulbs swung gently from the ceiling, casting eerie silhouettes across the weathered planks. He climbed to a top bunk, the straw mattress thin and lumpy beneath his palms, its surface worn smooth by nameless bodies before him. While the top bunk required climbing on tired legs, he was thankful that Auckland had told him it provided more headroom, that heat rises, and, most importantly, that no bodily fluids from sick men in bunks above him would fall on him while he slept.

Coughs echoed through the barracks, a chorus of suffering as men tossed in restless sleep, their dreams troubled. The barracks mainly housed Soviets, their faces hollow and eyes sunken into dark sockets, along with a few British. No longer with his brothers from I Company, Luke was adrift in a sea of strangers, cut off from the men with whom he'd fought beside.

He lay staring at the ceiling, counting the knots in the wooden beams to distract himself from the hunger in his stomach. The young German guard's face was now burned into his mind. That distinctive limp, that cold stare that seemed to penetrate through flesh and bone, it was the same guard from Gerolstein, he was sure now. The realization sent a shiver down his spine. *Why him? Of all the guards in all the camps, why did this one haunt his steps? How did he know Luke's heritage, or was he guessing? Had something in his manner or speech given him away?*

The thought twisted in his gut, fear mingling with guilt. He'd hidden his Jewish roots from Stevie, whose friendship had helped him get through basic training; from Whitfield, who'd saved his life at Schönberg; from Brock, his lifelong friend now dead on the battlefield; from everyone except Shaina and Katie. His secret was a necessary deception in a world gone mad with hatred toward Jews.

About midnight, the door creaked on rusty hinges, the sound resembling a wounded animal's cry, and an older guard, near sixty, entered the barracks. He moved to wherever there was loud coughing, giving out small packages of sulfa to the ailing men, or to nearby bunkmates to administer.

Luke watched with admiration as the German, whom he later learned was Oskar Schottin, moved quickly and silently, treating almost a dozen men. Then, as quietly as he had entered, he was gone. He realized that the guard was risking his own life to help the sick and dying prisoners. *Why would a German guard take such a risk?*

Thirty-Seven

Days turned to weeks. On day twenty-one of their captivity, the guards roused the prisoners for roll call at 0600. Luke stood in the snow, his fingers beyond numb, his clothing soaked through from night sweat and the damp straw that served as his bed. The threadbare uniform clung to his skin, each gust of wind cutting through to his bones.

His condition reflected the thousands of Americans added to the rolls of the already overcrowded population, now numbering more than thirty thousand, their faces pale and hollowed from hunger, confident postures bent by despair and uncertainty.

His daily meal consisted of a bowl of watery turnip soup, more like dishwater than broth, accompanied by a crust of stale, moldy black bread, baked weeks earlier. He chewed the bland food slowly, trying to make the meager portion last. He fought the urge to gulp it down, knowing that would only leave his stomach aching for more.

He gazed across the yard, toward Block Twelve, and saw several of his friends, even at a distance, recognizing that they had changed. Stevie's face, now wrinkled and creased, made him look much older. Whitfield stood beside him, shoulders squared despite everything, encouraging Robby to stand straight as if they were still at basic training. Auckland, whose medical supplies had been confiscated, looked defeated, his hands, trained to give aid and comfort, hanging useless at his sides. Jerry and Neil huddled together for warmth; their appearance distant.

He wanted to join them, to draw strength from their collective resilience, but Block Fourteen, separated by less than fifty yards, was a world away. The camp's strict segregation kept him isolated from the only familiar faces in this nightmare. He stood alone, Dieter Zobel's shadow looming large in his mind, a presence that had haunted him since first encountering him at the train station in Gerolstein, a month earlier. He appeared during roll call as he always did, moving with surprising speed despite his disability; his clipboard was ever-present, a symbol of the meticulous German record-keeping that documented their suffering. "Pierce," he called.

Luke stepped forward. "Yes, sir," he responded, forcing his body to remain steady and refusing to show fear.

The guard's eyes, pale and calculating, bored into him like drills determined to find weakness. "You'll work in the kitchen tomorrow. Be ready." The words were delivered without emotion, a simple statement of fact that could mean anything.

He nodded, the movement sending pain through his stiff neck, but the order felt like a trap being set. Questions raced through his mind, unanswerable and dangerous. *Why the kitchen? Why me?* He returned to his line with a new level of uncertainty about what the next day would bring.

That afternoon, he was called to a small office near the camp's edge. Dieter sat behind a desk, his Mauser propped against the wall, the rifle's barrel shining dully in the dim winter light. The room was sparse, consisting only of a desk, two chairs, and a gray metal filing cabinet with peeling paint. A single window, yellowed by seasons of rain and snow, revealed the barbed-wire perimeter beyond.

"Sit here, my friend," he said, his English precise.

He sat on the rickety wooden chair. "Pierce, Luke, PFC, 39421436.

"That's not what I want. I already know that. No, what I want to know is what religion do you practice? Who is your rabbi?" he pressed, smirking, his pen tapping against the ledger spread before him.

"None," he said, his voice steady but his hands clenching into fists, not caring if the German saw the gesture.

Dieter leaned forward, his smile cold, eyes narrowing with predatory interest. "I don't believe you. In the Hitler Youth, we were shown many pictures of Jews to help us identify them and remove them from our streets. We studied the nose, the eyes, and the hair in great detail. You look like them." He paused, studying Luke's face with clinical detachment. "I have time, months, maybe years. I'll find out, Pierce."

"I'm telling the truth," Luke replied, meeting the young guard's gaze, while fighting to harness the anger building inside him.

"We'll see," Dieter said, "We Aryans can smell impurity in our midst, and you stink like a Jew." He waited a moment, then waved him out with a dismissive shake of his wrist, the gesture more threatening than a shout.

He walked back to Block Fourteen, weak from fever, and with a growing concern. The guard's interest wasn't random; he knew something was amiss. Luke's secret, buried deep for survival's sake, was a ticking time bomb that could detonate at any time. In Hanford, it meant jokes and slurs. Here, it could be a death sentence.

Back at the barracks, he squirmed on his straw bed, freezing one moment, sweating the next. His elbow knocked against the bony shoulder of another prisoner, who muttered something incomprehensible. The stacked beds squeaked continually, a constant annoyance with a little more than twelve inches between bunks. Lice scurried over his body as he shifted on the straw mattress, leaving trails of angry red welts that he fought not to scratch. The corner latrines had overflowed again, the putrid odor seeping into everything: their clothes, their skin, their breath. Across the room, a man retched, the fifth case of dysentery this week.

His eyes, glassy from sickness, remained fixed on the ceiling as coughing and whimpering echoed through the barracks. Searchlight beams swept across the grimy windows, momentarily illuminating the emaciated faces surrounding him.

A little after midnight, the weathered door to block twelve creaked open, and Oskar Schottin stepped inside. As before, he went to the inmates who most needed medicine, distributing small packets of life-saving medicine to each. Luke hacked loudly several times. Oskar moved toward him, quick but alert. When he reached Luke's bed and saw his condition, he offered him a small packet, which Luke gladly accepted, his hand quivering. "What you do in secret is seen by God," Luke whispered, drawing on something Moses had told him. His voice was weak and unsteady, uncertain if the guard understood.

Oskar looked at him, reflecting on Luke's words. "*Danke*, that is kind of you," he replied. After a brief pause, he took Luke's right hand, cold and sweaty, between both of his own, acknowledging their connection. "I know you are Pierce. I am Oskar Schottin. Be careful, Zobel has it in for you. He knows you are Jewish," he said, slowly releasing Luke's hand.

Luke nodded in agreement. It was the first time since crossing the Atlantic that he had not denied his Jewish roots. Something deep inside him convinced him that he could trust the German. "Thank you, Oskar. I will be cautious."

The old guard held his gaze for a moment, his eyes bright with compassion, then said, "I must go." He turned and left the barracks as quickly as he had entered. Luke watched until the door closed behind him, the human bond stronger than any military uniform. Weak, he swallowed the sulfa and resolved to fight, to live.

The searchlight passed, throwing him back into reality, alone in the dark.

The six men of I Company huddled in the far corner of Block Twelve, voices whispered. Whitfield's gaunt face was illuminated by the weak moonlight filtering through the small, cracked window. The former sergeant had lost twenty pounds but none of his authority.

"Luke's in trouble," Whitfield said, his voice hoarse from the constant cold. "That limping bastard's got it in for him."

Stevie nodded, "I saw him during roll call. He was barely able to stand, worse than yesterday." He glanced around the circle of haggard faces. "That damn guard, Zobel, keeps harassing him."

"It's more than random harassment," Auckland added, the medic's clinical eye missing nothing despite his deteriorating condition. "He views Luke differently, like he's hunting."

Lewis leaned in, shivering in his thin, shabby uniform. "But why Luke?

Whitfield shook his head. "Doesn't matter why. What matters is getting him back here, where we can watch his back."

“And bring him back to health,” added Auckland.

"How can we get him back here?" Jackson asked. "They've got the blocks segregated tighter than Fort Knox."

Lewis, the youngest among them, had been silent until now. "What about the work details? Kitchen duty rotates between blocks."

Stevie snapped his fingers. "That's perfect! If he's strong enough, Block Fourteen has kitchen duty tomorrow."

"That's our opening," Whitfield said, energy returning to his voice. "We need someone on that detail."

Auckland raised his hand. "I can fake a medical emergency. The guards hate disease; they'll want me out of there fast."

"Good," Whitfield said. "But we need more. A distraction so large that they'll reassign prisoners."

Jackson's eyes lit up. "What if we create a situation where they need extra hands? Something urgent but not suspicious."

"The garbage pit behind the kitchen," Lewis suggested. "If it collapsed or overflowed somehow..."

"And they'd need extra men to clean it up," Stevie finished, a trace of his old smile returning.

Whitfield considered this. "I can talk to Kitzler in Block Eight. He's been here longest, knows which guards take bribes."

"Bribes with what?" Lewis asked. "We've got nothing."

"Cigarettes," Stevie said, pulling three from inside his boot. "Got these yesterday, won those playing cards with some Brits."

Whitfield agreed. "Kitzler might know which guard supervises reassignments. One cigarette could buy us information, another might buy action."

"Once we're all there," Auckland continued, "I'll create a medical situation, something contagious. They'll want to isolate the infected together."

"And we make sure he's part of that group," Stevie said.

"It's risky," Whitfield admitted. "If they catch on..."

"If we do nothing, Zobel will break him," Lewis said. "You've seen how he badgers him."

"Like he knows something about Luke we don't," Jackson added.

An uncomfortable silence fell over the group. "Tomorrow then," Whitfield declared. "Stevie, get those cigarettes to Kitzler at first light. Auckland, be ready with your medical emergency. The rest of you, be prepared to move fast when the opportunity comes."

The men placed their hands together in the center of their circle, a gesture reminiscent of their days as soldiers rather than prisoners.

"For Luke," Stevie said.

"For all of us," Whitfield corrected. "We're getting out of this hellhole as one, or not at all."

As they went back to their bunks, Stevie gazed through the window toward Block Fourteen, where his friend currently fought the battle alone. "Hang on, buddy," he murmured. "The cavalry's on the way."

Thirty-Eight

At dawn, Stevie threaded his way through the crowd of prisoners gathering for roll call, three precious cigarettes concealed in the lining of his borrowed jacket. His eyes looked nervously between the guards as he made his way toward Block Eight, where he'd been told he could find Kitzler. The man's reputation for knowing the inner workings of the camp had spread throughout the compound. Stevie was nervous, but his mind was focused entirely on the task at hand, a mission that could mean life or death for his friend.

The prisoners around him shuffled forward with downcast eyes, their starved bodies moving in unison, void of emotion. Some coughed weakly, their lungs rattling from disease and malnutrition. The mass of unwashed bodies and festering wounds mingled, creating a repulsive odor. He kept his head down, but his eyes alert, as he navigated through the mass of humanity, careful not to draw attention from the watchtowers where Germans were continually scanning for anything unusual.

Gravel crunched beneath his feet as he maneuvered between rows of prisoners. The camp was coming alive—another day of suffering. Guards shouted orders, dogs barked, and the clang of gates opening and closing echoed through the air. His stomach twisted with familiar hunger pangs, having learned to ignore the hollow ache that was never satisfied. His body, once athletic enough to keep pace with Luke and Brock during their carefree days in Hanford, was now weak and sore.

As he passed the edge of Block Six, he noticed a Soviet prisoner being beaten by a guard for stepping out of line. The man's face was a mask of terror as he cowered beneath the raised baton. He quickened his pace, knowing that slowing to watch the incident could make him the next target. *Every interaction in Stalag IV-B was a calculated risk.*

A sentry turned suddenly in his direction, and he froze. The guard's eyes swept over him, then moved on to other prisoners, settling on a prisoner who had fallen from exhaustion. He exhaled slowly, forcing his trembling legs forward. He fingered the cigarettes, heavy in his jacket, each one representing a favor if used correctly. He'd been lucky to win them, the Brits somehow failing to realize he'd changed the rules midway through a hand of poker. He promised himself he would make it right with them after he rescued his friend.

"Which guard handles the work reassignments?" he asked in a hushed tone when he reached Kitzler, glancing over his shoulder to ensure he wasn't being observed. Kitzler's weathered face remained impassive as his calculating gaze fixed on the slight bulge in Stevie's coat pocket. His skin was like tanned leather, deep lines revealing a life of hardship before the war. A jagged scar ran halfway down his forearm. Stevie was curious about the story behind the wound, but decided not to ask.

"Schmidt. The one with the crooked nose," Kitzler responded, pausing to run his tongue over cracked lips, craving moisture. His eyes, sunken, retained a sharp intelligence that had kept him alive when many others had perished. "But he's Zobel's lap dog. They're inseparable, especially when it comes to torture. It's a game with them. Whatever Zobel wants, Schmidt delivers. And believe me, what Zobel wants is never good for us. They target the weakest."

Stevie recoiled at the mention of Zobel's name. The young guard's reputation for cruelty was becoming known throughout the camp. The prisoners saw that he was increasingly cruel to the captured Soviets, taking advantage of the fact that the Geneva Convention had not been agreed to between the Germans and the Soviets. Dieter Zobel embodied everything the prisoners feared; the product of the Hitler Youth program's indoctrination of Aryan superiority was now a merciless enforcer; against the Soviets, against suspected Jews, ...against Luke Pierce.

Memories of Dieter's previous "inspections" flashed through his mind, the calculated way he'd select men for punishment, how he'd circle like a vulture. Just last week, he'd ordered a prisoner, faint from dysentery, to stand at attention for hours in the freezing rain until the man had collapsed. He then beat the man with a baton until he didn't move, then left him for dead.

He withdrew one cigarette and handed it to Kitzler. Tobacco was more valuable than gold within the barbed wire confines. The paper was lightly yellowed, the tobacco inside offering a few moments of pleasure. "Can you get us transferred to kitchen duty? It's important." His voice carried an urgency that conveyed just how desperate their situation had become. Luke needed that transfer, needed access to the extra scraps of food that might help him regain his strength.

"Two more cigarettes," Kitzler demanded, his calloused fingers already striking the match he kept hidden in the seam of his trousers, the tiny flame cupped against the wind. The glow illuminated the hollows beneath his cheekbones, casting eerie lines across his hardened face. Stevie handed him the other two cigarettes and shook his hand, sealing the deal. He then walked, head down, back to Block Twelve.

The next morning, he and Whitfield executed their plan with military precision. The uproar at the garbage pit drew guards away exactly as planned. Auckland created the diversion, clutching his stomach and collapsing, his face writhing with pain. The commotion provided just enough cover for them to infiltrate Block Fourteen. When they found Luke, he was barely conscious, his skin burning with fever.

"Damn," Whitfield whispered, kneeling beside Luke's bunk. "He's worse than I thought."

They carried him between them, his body light, back to Block Twelve, where they had prepared a space for him. The medic's hands moved with efficiency, checking his pulse and pupils while the others formed a protective circle.

"Dehydration, malnutrition, possibly pneumonia starting in the left lung," Auckland said, pressing his ear to Luke's chest. "We need to get fluids in him and bring down that fever."

Dieter paced his office, his limp more pronounced when he was agitated, as he was now. The leather of his boot creaked with each step, a sound that had come to signal danger to prisoners within earshot.

"Explain to me, Schmidt," he said, his voice threatening, "how my responsibility, the Jew, Pierce, was transferred from Block Fourteen without my authorization."

Schmidt stood at attention, sweat beading on his forehead despite the cold. "There was confusion during the morning count. The prisoner was ill..."

"I don't care if he was dying!" He slammed his fist on the desk, sending papers scattering. "He was mine to deal with."

The door opened, and *Hauptmann* Rolf Weber entered without knocking. Dieter straightened immediately, his face transforming from rage to military discipline.

"Dietrich Zobel," Weber said, his voice carrying the aristocratic tone of old Prussian military families. "I've received reports of your... special interest in certain prisoners."

His jaw tightened. "Yes, I'm ensuring discipline, Herr Weber."

Weber circled the desk, noting the papers strewn on the floor. He opened the file he had carried in with him, examining it with deliberate slowness. "Americans are valuable assets, Zobel. Berlin has plans for prisoner exchanges. They must remain... functional."

"Of course, *Hauptmann*."

"I understand your frustration with your current assignment," he continued. "A man of your talents, trained for *Unternehmen Greif*, now reduced to guarding prisoners." He closed the file with a snap. "But these are your orders. All American prisoners are to be maintained in working condition. Is that clear?"

"*Jawohl*, Herr Weber," he replied, his face a mask of compliance.

After Weber left, he remained motionless, staring at the wall where a portrait of the *Führer* hung.

"Schmidt," he said, his voice flat.

"*Ja*, Dietrich?"

"Double the work detail for Block Twelve tomorrow. I want them working from dawn to dusk, no breaks. Let them carry fifty-pound bags of coal, and reduce their rations by half."

If he couldn't single out Luke Pierce, he would make all of them suffer, especially his friends who had intervened. Time was on his side. The war might be turning against Germany, but here, in this isolated corner of hell, he still ruled.

For three days, the captives from I Company took turns watching Luke, sacrificing their meager rations to feed him broth smuggled from the kitchen. Auckland had traded his father's gold wedding band, the one possession he'd managed to hide from the Germans, for a bottle of sulfa powder from a Polish doctor in Block Nine.

Luke struggled to focus on his surroundings, unaware that his friends had moved him back to Block Twelve. Still feverish, he pulled the thin gray woolen blanket around his torso one moment, then flung it to the end of the bed the next. He wanted to pray, trying to remember what Moses Weisbaum had taught him, a verse from Psalm 91. He grabbed at words like "shadow," "Almighty," and "safe," but, in his weakened condition, he was unable to form a meaningful sentence from them. Desperate, he whispered, "God, help me," as his body, wet from fever, shook.

On the fourth night, his fever broke. His eyes, though sunken in their sockets, focused on the faces around him. "You guys look terrible," he said, his voice low and raspy.

Stevie laughed; a sound so foreign in the barracks that several prisoners turned to stare. "Says the guy who's been sleeping for days while we did all his work."

Over the next two weeks, Luke's recovery continued under Auckland's vigilant care. He regained enough strength to sit up, then stand, then walk short distances inside the barracks. "I don't know how to thank you," he said one evening as they sat on his bunk, his voice still weak but growing stronger each day.

Whitfield shook his head. "We're brothers. Brock would've done the same."

The mention of his fallen friend brought a moment of silence, broken by the sound of guards changing shifts outside.

"Tell me about Shaina again," Stevie said, not wanting to think about his fallen friend. "The part where she threw the bread at the rude customer."

Luke smiled, the memory warming him more than any blanket could. "It wasn't bread. It was a slice of banana cream pie, right in his face."

Their laughter was an act of defiance, and it felt good. It reminded them they were still alive.

By mid-February, Luke had regained enough strength to join the others for roll call. Standing in the predawn darkness, he sensed Dieter's eyes burning into him from across the yard.

"Don't look at him," Whitfield murmured. "That's what he wants."

He looked down at the muddy ground, but he could feel the hatred on the back of his neck, radiating from the German guard. Something personal burned in his gaze, something far larger than the usual contempt the guards showed their prisoners.

"He knows," Luke whispered to Stevie later as they chipped frozen earth in the work yard, their fingers numb despite the rags wrapped around them. "About my mother."

Stevie shook his head, confused. "What are you saying?"

He panicked, realizing how close he had just come to sharing the secret kept hidden until now. *I must be more careful.* "I just meant that the

Germans are so focused on fathers. Always talking about the *Führer* and the Fatherland, they ignore their mothers."

The answer made no sense, but Stevie didn't pursue the conversation, noticing that Dieter was again looking in their direction. He bumped his shoulder, a motion that he understood meant to pick up the bags of coal at their feet and move toward the next barrack.

For the next few days, he kept vigil, watching for Dieter and trying to find out why he had singled him out. The way he scrutinized him seemed targeted, personal, as if Luke represented something the German personally despised.

The next day, the scene repeated, the guard limping toward him, his baton slapping against his thigh. The prisoners around Luke worked faster, heads down, trying to become invisible.

Dieter stopped in front of him, close enough that he could whiff the schnapps on his breath. "Working hard, Pierce?"

"Yes, sir," he replied, keeping his eyes lowered.

"Your friends went to great trouble to save you," he said. "It would be a shame if their efforts were wasted."

Luke said nothing, focusing on the shovel in his hands, on the frozen dirt, on anything but the cold eyes studying him.

"I'm a patient man," he continued, his voice dropping to a near whisper. "And unlike you, I'm not going anywhere, Jew."

He moved on, but the chill of his words remained. Luke glanced at Stevie, whose face had gone pale.

"We stick together," Stevie said firmly. "All of us. That's how we made it this far."

Luke nodded, his stomach tightening. He recognized the look in the German's eyes. It was the same look his father had when he was drunk and raging about Jews and foreigners; hatred so deep it transcended reason, and took no orders.

For now, he had his friends, Auckland's medical knowledge, and his growing strength. But as the winter deepened around them, he knew Zobel was watching, waiting for an opportunity. The German had found his target, and he understood with certainty that this was a vendetta that would only end when one of them was broken... or dead.

Thirty-Nine

Late February brought no relief to the men imprisoned in Stalag IV-B. If anything, the winter had worsened, shrouding the camp in a bone-chilling grip. Luke huddled on his bunk in Block Twelve, wrapped in the threadbare blanket that was no match against the cold.

Following an evening meal of tepid turnip soup and stale black bread, Whitfield rallied the remnant of I Company near his bed for a conversation he said was meaningful. The men, macerated and weary after almost two months of captivity, sat huddled together on nearby beds, thankful for the warmth generated by the crowded bodies.

He was standing next to a new prisoner that none of the men recognized. "Guys, I want you to meet Corporal Brent Young from General Patton's 80th Infantry Division." He paused and scanned the assembled crowd before continuing. "Corporal Young was captured in January near Bastogne and was just transferred to IV-B. He would like to share with you what he learned about your efforts at the *Schnee Eifel* back in December. Corporal." Whitfield clapped Young on the shoulder, then extended his arm toward the men, a gesture that encouraged him to share.

"On behalf of those who successfully defeated the Germans at Bastogne, I just want to say, thank you. Your efforts during those first three and a half days of the enemy's offensive were instrumental in later victories. We know that you were spread too thin and overwhelmed, but I want you to know that you are all considered heroes by the men with whom I served in the 80th." He paused long enough to make eye contact with each of the men gathered.

"Your stubborn resistance delayed the Germans from reaching St. Vith by the deadline they had established. We learned that the port at Antwerp was their goal. They needed to take St. Vith by the evening of 17 December. You men, you heroes, delayed them by four days. They did not reach their objective until the twenty-first. This gave us time to reinforce the First Army from the north and Patton's Third Army from the south." Again, he acknowledged each man, all of them hanging on his every word.

"Before I was captured on 18 January, a foolish blunder on my part, we were well on the way to victory. I can't be positive, but I believe that victory was secured within a week. When this is over, you, the men of the 106th, will be known and acknowledged for your valor in helping to defeat the Germans. Thank you, men. You are not forgotten. History will note your bravery." The corporal then reached out and shook every man's hand, pausing to look each one in the eye.

The gathered men of I Company looked at one another, their faces transformed by Young's report. Despite their gaunt cheeks and hollow eyes, a spark had returned, something Luke hadn't seen since before their capture.

"Four days," Whitfield repeated, his voice stronger than it had been in weeks. "We earned Patton and his men four days."

Stevie squared his shoulders despite his weakened frame. "Brock would've loved to hear that report. He worried we weren't doing enough. Thank you, corporal."

"We held the line. When they told us to dig in, we dug in. When they told us to fight, we fought," Whitfield summarized.

Robby Lewis, who hadn't spoken much since capture, looked up. "You think the folks back home know what we did?"

"They will," Auckland said. "When we get back, we'll make sure they know."

The men nodded in agreement. Their sacrifice hadn't been meaningless. Every night in a frozen foxhole, every desperate stand against Panzers, every fallen friend, it had all mattered.

Luke thought of Brock's final moments, how he'd asked if he'd fought well. Now he knew the answer.

"We weren't just green troops," Turner said, his usual cynicism absent. "We were the wall that slowed the Krauts down."

A murmur of agreement passed through the group. Even though they were now prisoners, they had accomplished something vital, and they were not forgotten.

“Gentlemen,” Whitfield said, his voice dropping to avoid guard attention, “the Germans might have robbed us of our freedom, ignored our health, and stolen our possessions, but they can never take away our achievement. I’ve never been prouder to serve with any group of men.”

Ignoring the threat of the guards, the men broke into applause; for Young, for Sergeant Whitfield, and most, for themselves. They understood the importance of not being forgotten.

Luke glanced around at these soldiers who'd become brothers. They might be prisoners now, but they were still soldiers of the 106th Infantry Division, men who'd changed the course of the war.

As curfew approached and the rejuvenated men returned to their bunks, he mulled over the report Young had shared. Despite his perpetual hunger and the persistent cold, there was a warmth inside. Whatever came next—Dieter's harassment, dwindling rations, or bitter winter nights—they would find the strength to endure it. They would accomplish the mission they were given. In December, the mission had been to hold the Germans for as long as possible. Now, the mission was to survive.

When he was certain that the guards were gone, Luke pulled out the pencil stub and the sheet of paper Oskar had dropped on his bunk. He needed to finish the letter to Shaina and then figure out how to get it past Dieter.

My Dearest Shaina,

I pray you receive this letter. If you do, then you know I am alive. Life here is a constant battle with hunger and cold. We sleep on boards with thin straw mattresses. My feet ache constantly, but I rest when I can. The guards watch us like shadows, and I do my best to keep out of sight. We share what little we have, but it is never enough. When I think of you, I find the strength to survive. Please don't lose faith in me. We have a life to build when this nightmare is over. Your hope carries me through.

Love,

Luke

A few days later, Luke huddled against the back wall of the supply shed, breath forming small clouds in the frigid air. The rendezvous with Oskar was risky; if Zobel discovered them, they'd both face severe consequences. But desperation drove Luke to take the chance.

The door creaked open, and he tensed until, in the dim light, he confirmed it was the older guard. The German glanced over his shoulder before slipping inside.

"You should not be here, *Junge*," he whispered, his accent thick. "Zobel has eyes everywhere."

"I know," Luke said, pulling two folded papers from inside his threadbare shirt. "I need to get these out."

Oskar's lined face softened as he took the letters. One addressed to Shaina in New Jersey, the other to Katie in Hanford.

"Zobel searches mail from Block Twelve now," Oskar said, tucking the letters into his coat. "But I have a friend in Mühlberg who posts letters when he goes to Dresden."

He nodded gratefully. "Thank you, friend. I know what I'm asking you is dangerous."

The old guard waved away his concern. "Danger is nothing new in Germany these days." Convinced Dieter was nowhere near, he settled onto an upturned bucket, knees cracking. "My wife worries, but I tell her, what more can they do to an old man? I shouldn't even be here."

The guard pulled a small package from his pocket, unwrapped a piece of dark bread, and offered half to Luke. "From home. Real bread, not the..." he searched for the word, "... garbage they feed you prisoners." He smiled, then added, "Ours is not much better."

Luke accepted it, fighting to keep from devouring it ravenously, then was surprised when Oskar offered a brief prayer of thanks.

"Why help me, Oskar?" Luke asked, looking at the elder German with a new level of respect. "If Zobel found out."

Oskar's eyes clouded. "I had a son... Fritz. He was a good boy before Hitler Youth." He tapped his temple. "They filled his head with nonsense. Taught him to hate his own *vater* and *mutter* when we spoke against the *Führer*."

Luke chewed slowly, savoring both the bread and the connection with Oskar, a connection that transcended opposing military uniforms.

"Fritz joined the *Wehrmacht* at eighteen. So proud in his uniform." The German's voice cracked. "Last year, they sent him to *Ostfront* ...the Eastern Front. The freezing weather took him. Not a bullet, *kälte*. Cold."

"I'm sorry," Luke said.

"When I see Zobel, I see what my son became. What they did to our children." Oskar's weathered hands trembled. "They turned our boys into monsters. Hitler Youth taught them to hate, to see others as *Untermenschen,* less than human, specifically the Jews, blaming them for everything wrong in Germany."

Luke thought of his father with the same deep hatred, blaming the Jews for everything wrong in America. And here was this German soldier, older than his father, risking his life for an enemy prisoner.

"You remind me of Moses," Luke said.

"The one who led the Hebrews out of Egypt?"

"No, no," Luke smiled. "Moses Weisbaum."

"Moses Weisbaum?" Oskar's eyebrows raised.

"A man back home. He owns the hardware store where I used to work. Jewish man. He..." Luke hesitated, then decided to trust the old German completely. "He treated me like a son when my father couldn't. Especially after I learned my mother was Jewish."

Oskar's eyes widened. "So Zobel is right about you?"

Luke nodded. "Yes, my mother's name was Matya Spielmann. She died when I was very young. I only found out about my Jewish heritage last year."

"*Mein Gott,*" Oskar whispered. "If Zobel discovers proof..."

"I know," Luke said, his voice flat. "That's why these letters matter. If something happens to me, I want them to know I didn't betray their trust."

Oskar placed a hand on Luke's leg. "I will make sure they receive your words. I promise."

"How did you avoid becoming like the others?" Luke asked. "So many Germans seem to believe in Hitler, especially the young ones."

He sighed heavily. "I am old enough to remember Germany before Hitler, before the Nazis. I fought in the Great War, the first one. I saw what nationalism did then. When it started again..." He shook his head. "Some of us were too old to be fooled twice."

A distant shout made them both freeze.

He broke off the commentary. "You must go. Roll call soon."

Luke stood, brushing crumbs from his uniform. "Oskar, one more question. Why did you agree to be a guard? You don't seem to believe in any of this."

"They changed the age of service last October; sixteen to sixty. I had no choice." He shrugged. "Better here than Berlin. Maybe I can do some small good things, even in this bad place."

Like Moses Weisbaum explaining why he stayed in Hanford despite the prejudice, Luke thought, *doing small good things in bad places.*

"One minute apart," Oskar instructed. "You first, then me."

Luke moved toward the door, then turned back. "The letter to Shaina, my fiancée, tells her I'm alive. The one to Katie asks her to tell Moses I remember what he taught me about the Jewish faith."

Oskar nodded, not fully understanding, but committed to the assignment.

He slipped out, making his way back to Block Twelve. The morning chill was piercing, but the bread in his stomach and Oskar's kindness warmed him.

In the distance, he saw Dieter limping across the yard, scanning the compound like a hawk seeking its morning meal. He ducked his head and quickened his pace. The letters were now safe with Oskar. Whatever happened next, Katie and Shaina would know he hadn't given up, that he was still alive.

As he reached the barracks, he glanced back to see Oskar emerge from the shed, resuming his patrol as if nothing had happened. The old guard caught his eye, giving a slight nod before turning away.

He slipped into Block Twelve and moved toward his bunk, trying to appear casual.

"*Achtung*!" The command sliced through the barracks.

Dieter stood in the doorway, his uniform pressed despite the early hour, his eyes cold as they swept across the room. Two guards flanked him, rifles ready.

"Inspection," he announced, his voice carrying a dangerous edge. "Everyone, stand at attention beside your bunks."

The prisoners scrambled to comply. Luke caught Stevie's questioning glance from across the room. He gave an imperceptible bow of his head; no time to explain his early morning absence.

Whitfield, always the sergeant, even in captivity, straightened his spine as the guard limped past. The German's gaze lingered on each man, assessing, searching.

"Turn out your pockets," Zobel ordered. "All contents on your bunks."

Luke's stomach tightened. He had nothing incriminating; Oskar now had his letters, but Dieter's intensity suggested he knew something.

The officer moved through the barracks, upending thin mattresses, checking beneath bunks, rifling through the few possessions the prisoners had managed to keep. Unlike other inspections, he didn't bother restoring anything to its place, leaving a path of chaos in his wake.

"What's he looking for?" Robby whispered to Luke.

"Quiet!" Schmidt barked, the guard's eyes darting nervously.

Luke remained silent; watching Dieter's deliberate progress through the line of prisoners. This wasn't routine; this was personal. The guard's limp seemed more pronounced, his knuckles tight around his baton.

When he reached Luke's bunk, he paused. His eyes met Luke's, a flash of hatred so pure it felt like a physical blow.

"Pierce," he said, the name sounding like something foul in his mouth. "You've been busy at night, I hear."

Luke maintained his gaze straight ahead.

"Schmidt tells me you've been writing." He began a meticulous examination of his bunk, his movements unhurried, almost theatrical. "Perhaps planning something? A little... escape?"

"No, sir." He kept his voice steady despite the cold sweat forming on his back.

The German lifted his thin blanket, checking the seams. Finding nothing, his frustration grew visible. He turned to Luke, his face inches away.

"Take off your shirt."

The barracks fell silent. Even the guards looked uncomfortable.

"Now!" His voice cracked like a whip.

Luke unbuttoned his shirt. The shirt had lost most of its original color; the olive drab cotton faded to a pale, tired green. He handed the shirt to Dieter, the cold air hitting his emaciated chest. Dieter snatched the garment and examined it with methodical precision. His fingers found the slight thickness in the hem where Luke had sewn in Shaina's photograph.

A smile spread across his face as he worked his finger into the stitching, tearing it open. The small photograph, Luke's most precious possession, fell into his palm.

"What have we here?" Dieter held it up to the light. Shaina's face, with her dark eyes and gentle smile, looked back at him. "Your woman, *ja*?"

Luke stood silent and motionless; his jaw clenched so tight it ached.

To his surprise, Dieter extended his hand and offered the picture. "Here, this is yours."

Luke hesitated, then took it, his fingers brushing against the guard's gloved hand.

"Get dressed," Dieter ordered. "Then come outside. Just you."

He turned and limped out, Schmidt and the other guard following.

Luke pulled his shirt back on, shooting a worried glance at the sergeant.

"Be careful," Whitfield murmured.

The early morning air cut through his thin clothing. Dieter stood by a small metal barrel where a fire burned, its heat offering meager warmth to the guards during their shifts. Other prisoners observed from a distance.

"Come here, Pierce," he called, his voice almost friendly.

Luke approached as Dieter's hand moved to his holster, slowly drawing his Luger.

"Hold out the photograph of the Jew woman."

His fingers tightened around Shaina's picture. "Sir?"

"The photograph," he ordered as he raised the pistol, pointing it at Luke's temple. "Hold it out."

Luke extended his hand, Shaina's face turned upward.

"Now drop it in the fire."

His heart lurched, fingers trembling. "No."

"Burn it, Jew!" Dieter hissed, pressing the gun's cold barrel against Luke's temple.

He remained frozen, unwilling to destroy this last connection to the woman he loved.

The pistol swung down suddenly, cracking against Luke's knuckles. Pain shot up his arm, but somehow his fingers still clutched the photograph.

"Do it, coward!" Dieter's face contorted with rage. "Do it now!"

Tears formed in Luke's eyes, not from the pain, but from the knowledge that this small victory would cost him dearly. Across the yard, he saw Oskar watching, the old guard's face a mask of helpless sympathy.

With one final glance at Shaina's face, he dropped the photo into the flames. It curled instantly, her smile blackening, her eyes disappearing in the flame.

Dieter holstered the Luger, then pulled the baton from his belt, swinging it with all the force he could muster, striking Luke on the neck, sending him sprawling onto the frozen ground. The assembled prisoners and guards watched in silence as he lay there, his last tangible connection to home reduced to ashes.

The hateful German crouched beside him, his voice low enough that only Luke could hear.

"You have a future, I don't," he said, his gaze moving from Luke's legs to his own damaged limb. "When this war ends, you go home to your woman, your family. But me?" He tapped his crippled leg.

His neck throbbing, Luke looked up and saw something beyond hatred in Dieter's eyes. *Envy?* Perhaps, or the bitterness of a man who had lost his soul.

As he limped away, Luke remained on the ground, the last fragments of Shaina's photograph reduced to floating embers. He closed his eyes and reconstructed her face in his mind, the curve of her smile, the determination in her eyes, the Star of David hanging from her neck.

The heartless German could harass, even kill him, but he could never take the memory of Shaina from him.

"I'm not defeated," Luke vowed, as he rose from the icy ground.

Forty

February turned to March, and with it came a subtle shift in the camp's dynamics. Luke noticed it first during roll call; Dieter's piercing gaze didn't seek him out with the same intensity. The guard's attention had drifted elsewhere, to the far end of Block Twelve, where the Soviet captives stood in ragged formation.

"They have it worse than we do," Whitfield murmured as he saw a Soviet prisoner collapse, only to be clubbed by a guard, no more than sixteen, until the man somehow found the strength to stand again.

Unlike the Americans and British prisoners, the Soviets received no Red Cross packages. Their rations were half those of other prisoners, and their work details were more difficult. The Germans claimed that the Geneva Convention did not apply to the Soviets because the Soviets, unlike the other Allied nations, had not ratified the 1929 agreement. As a result, the Germans did not feel obligated to the requirements.

"He's going to kill them all," Stevie said as they shuffled back into the barracks after another Soviet prisoner had been beaten senseless for having a button missing from his tattered uniform.

Luke watched helplessly. His suffering seemed insignificant compared to the cruelty being inflicted on the Soviets. At night, he heard their weakened coughs from the other end of the barracks, the sounds growing fainter as pneumonia claimed more victims.

"We should do something," he said one evening, sitting on his bunk beside Stevie.

"Like what?" Robby asked. "We scarcely have enough food ourselves."

Auckland shook his head. "I've tried to treat them when I can, but without medicine..." His voice trailed off; the medic's frustration obvious to the others.

The next day, Luke witnessed Oskar Schottin slip extra bread to a severely emaciated Soviet prisoner during kitchen duty. The older guard's kindness was a poignant act of defiance against the camp's brutality. *Small good things in bad places.*

Later, as prisoners hauled fifty-pound sacks of coal, Dieter appeared, limping between the work groups. He stopped near a Soviet prisoner who had paused to catch his breath.

"Work faster, Soviet pig!" he said, raising his baton.

"He cannot work faster," Oskar intervened, stepping between them. "He is sick. Let me take him back to the barracks."

Dieter's face contorted with rage. "You dare interfere, old man?"

The young guard swung his baton at Oskar's shoulder, but the older man sidestepped with surprising agility. The younger man, thrown off balance by his damaged leg, stumbled forward, falling.

A ripple of suppressed laughter spread through the prisoners. His face flushed crimson as he regained his footing.

"You think this is funny?" he shouted, glaring at the onlookers. "Double work detail for everyone!"

That evening, while he was distributing soup in the mess hall, Luke saw Oskar. "Thank you for what you did today," Luke whispered.

"Small things," Oskar replied with a shrug. "It's all we can do sometimes."

From across the room, he saw that Zobel's eyes were on them, watching their interaction with calculated interest.

"Be careful," Luke warned. "He's watching us."

The older guard nodded. "I know. He thinks we are... how you say... conspiring?"

Later, Dieter questioned Schmidt about Oskar's duties and movements.

"That old man is not loyal to the Fatherland. He and the American seem too friendly. I want to know what they're doing."

"Perhaps nothing, Dietrich," Schmidt suggested.

"Nobody does anything in this camp," he snapped. "Watch them both whenever they're together."

That night, Luke lay awake thinking of the Soviets dying slowly at the other end of the building, of Oskar's risking everything to help prisoners, and of Dieter's growing suspicion. The hateful German guard might have shifted his focus from Luke to the weaker prisoners, but something told him this was simply the calm before the storm.

Luke sat on his bunk, legs crossed, as the men of I Company huddled around him. The early March evening brought a reprieve from the day's labor, and with it, a moment for the prisoners to gather and share what little they had.

"I'm telling you, the Soviets are fifty miles from Berlin," Lewis insisted, his hollow cheeks flushed with excitement. "New guy in Block Eight swears his lieutenant heard it before they were captured."

Turner shook his head. "That's horseshit. The British guy who came in yesterday said the Germans have pushed the Allies back, and now we're losing ground."

Luke watched his friends argue, their faces drawn, but their eyes still intense.

"We need facts, not rumors," Whitfield said, his authoritative voice cutting through the debate. "Every new batch of prisoners brings more gossip, but few facts."

Luke cleared his throat. "There's a way we could know for sure."

The men turned to him, curiosity etched on their faces.

"Back at Fort Monmouth, I heard about something a prisoner built in an Italian prison camp last year. A radio. Simple, but effective enough to pick up the BBC broadcast in German if the signal is strong.

“If that’s true, we could get Kitzler to translate. Probably cost us a few cigarettes,” Stevie said.

"A radio?" Lewis scoffed. "With what? They search everything."

"It's called a foxhole radio," Luke explained, keeping his voice low. "It doesn’t need batteries or tubes. Just basic components we could find or trade for around the camp."

Stevie leaned forward. "What would we need?"

Luke counted off slowly on his fingers, "A razor blade, ...some wire, ...a pencil lead, ...a safety pin, ...a toilet paper tube, ...and a ceramic earpiece, which we could get from a broken headphone."

"That's it?" Jackson asked.

"That's it. The razor blade and pencil lead create a crude detector. The safety pin and cardboard tube make a tuning coil. With the earpiece and a decent long wire antenna, we could pick up any strong radio signals." The men nodded, though none of them had any idea what a detector was.

Whitfield's eyes narrowed. "And the guards wouldn't find it?"

Luke looked at Whitfield with admiration. The sergeant had kept the remnant from I Company strong over the past three months. He did not want to let him down. "Yeah, Sarge, it's small. We could hide it, take it apart when it's not in use."

The men exchanged glances, a spark of hope in their eyes for the first time in weeks.

"I've got a razor blade," Auckland offered. "They let me keep one for medical purposes."

"I've seen broken headphones in the garbage behind the administration building," Stevie added.

"We need to be careful. Collect the items slowly, nothing suspicious. If Zobel catches on..."

He did not need to finish the sentence. They all knew what would happen.

"It's worth the risk," Whitfield decided. "There are prisoners here who are giving up hope, and without hope, some are dying. We need to know what's really happening out there, not just the latest scuttlebutt."

Turner, who had been skeptical moments before, now looked animated. "If the Soviets are close, or the Americans are pushing through the Rhin e..."

"Then we might have a real hope of getting out of here alive," Luke finished.

They heard footsteps just outside the barracks. The men dispersed, returning to their bunks as a guard passed by the window.

Later, as darkness settled over the camp, he stared at the ceiling, cataloging their needs. The radio wouldn't be built in a day, but having a plan and a purpose beyond mere survival made a difference. *Purpose delivered hope.*

"You think it'll work?" Stevie queried from the adjacent bunk.

"It will," Luke replied, conviction in his voice. "And when it does, we'll know exactly when help is coming."

He closed his eyes, picturing the pieces assembled. Somewhere beyond the barbed wire and guard towers, armies were moving, battles were being waged. The war continued without them, but if he could build a radio, they would no longer be cut off from the truth of its progress.

For the first time since their capture, he experienced the antidote to despair: purpose.

The components for the foxhole radio began appearing over the next week: a safety pin first, a cardboard tube next, and then a pencil lead. He kept them hidden beneath a loose floorboard under Stevie's bunk, wrapped in a scrap of cloth. Each new piece brought them closer to connection with the outside world.

In mid-March, a Red Cross shipment arrived, the first in two months. The guards distributed the packages with their usual contempt. Luke received cigarettes, chocolate, powdered milk, and canned meat; treasures more valuable than money in the camp's economy.

Three days later, he traded four cigarettes with a British prisoner from Block Nine for something he valued more than food: a small bound book with blank pages.

The cover read, *YMCA Wartime Log.* "It came in some of the packages," the Brit explained. "Not much use to me. I can't draw for toffee, but I surely can smoke."

Luke caressed the book, remembering his journal in Hanford, and Mrs. Dugan's encouragement to write something every day. He'd passed that journal to Katie before departing for boot camp. Then came the new journal acquired after his enlistment. It included entries from Camp Roberts,

Camp Atterbury, and, most importantly, entries made at Fort Monmouth, including those about Shaina Levine. He'd kept writing during the voyage on the *Queen Elizabeth*, but the journal was in his duffel bag that never reached the front-line regiments when they relieved the Second Division at the *Schnee Eifel*. This new logbook offered an opportunity to capture his thoughts, document the camp's events, and perhaps recreate, from memory, the entries lost during his time in England and France. That night, he made his first entry.

Journal Entry: *March 15, 1945 - I hear distant explosions. Soviet artillery? The guards seem nervous. Something is changing. I must be careful with the radio components and this log. If the guards find either. Did Shaina receive my letter? When I think of her, I feel the urge to get up and walk past the guards, into the forest, on to the seashore, and across the ocean, right into her arms. For now, best to stay put and alert.*

Forty-One

Luke returned from work detail to find Oskar waiting near Block Twelve, his face betraying nothing as he pressed an envelope into Luke's palm during roll call.

"From home," he said, his voice weak in the wind. "I found it in Zobel's office under some files. I think it's been there a while. He'll figure out it's gone. Be careful."

He shook Oskar's hand, squeezing hard to convey his respect for the man, then concealed the letter in his shirt. He waited until after lights out, when the barracks settled into the familiar hum of coughs, snores, and whispered conversations. In the darkness, he crept to the narrow space between empty bunks where moonlight filtered through a small window. His fingers trembled as he unfolded the paper, recognizing Katie's neat handwriting immediately.

January 13, 1945

Dear Luke,

Every night I pray my letters reach you. Two days ago, we received a telegram that you were reported missing in action in Germany since December 21. There were no other details, and we haven't heard anything since. I've never seen Dad so shaken. I'm not sure what his sadness means. He seems lost. Maybe he's changing. Too soon to tell. Since the telegram, the house is different. Almost no rants or racial slurs. Odd, but the silence is worse. It's like waiting for a storm that never comes.

Something happened after Dad spoke with Mr. Jensen, Willie's father, a few weeks ago. He came home and sat at the kitchen table for more than an hour, just staring into space. When I asked what was wrong, he started talking about Mom. He called her Matya. He told me everything, at least from his point of view.

"Everything?" Luke whispered into the darkness, skeptical.

He said that Mom received a letter from her parents in Austria in 1927. That has to be the very same letter we found, Luke. After reading the letter many times, Mom told Dad she had to go and help her parents. Her parents were being shunned with no way out. Mom felt she had to do whatever she could, maybe bring them back to America. Dad begged her not to go alone, but she insisted. She promised to return within two months.

But she never came back. No letters. No telegrams. Nothing.

He paused, trying to organize his jumbled thoughts. His Dad had never said that she died, only that she was gone. He and Katie just assumed that meant she was dead. And his mother hadn't abandoned them. She had gone to Austria to help her parents. He had many unresolved questions as he continued reading.

Dad waited a year, hoping. He said it was the worst year of his life, that he loved Matya with all his heart. He contacted everyone he could. Then he lost hope and started drinking to help him cope. Within the next two years, he lost his job, and it was then that he decided to move to Hanford. He said that as you grew older, every time he saw you, he remembered her, and it hurt too much. At first, he blamed her Jewish parents for writing to her. Before long, he was accusing all Jews. His hatred expanded to anyone who looked different or anyone he could blame for his troubles. He said if it weren't for me, he would have given up completely. I guess I didn't remind him of what he had lost. I don't think he realizes how much pressure that put on me, or how unfair that was to you.

Luke put the letter down, needing time to consider all that he was learning for the first time. His mind drifted from his father to Moses Weisbaum. How did he say it? "When hatred clutches a man, that man cannot find peace," Moses said it was an old Buddhist saying. So, if he could believe what Katie was saying, his father had loved his mother deeply, so profoundly that he couldn't handle it when she was no longer there. It also meant that Matya was courageous. He thought of Shaina and how she had defied her parents to come and meet him in Indianapolis before he deployed.

Luke fought to organize his thoughts. *Our mother had to choose between her children and her parents. She planned to return within two months, but she was never heard from again. Was she alive? And what about her parents, my grandparents? And what about Dad? Had he actually changed?* He had so many questions, and he would think of many more. He resolved that a single letter was not going to move him to forgive and forget how his father had treated him. For now, at least, he had a glimpse into the reasons for the way his father had acted.

Luke froze. He heard the door to the barracks open, and a guard poked his head in, looked around, but did not enter. He waited a minute, then resumed reading, straining to put the pieces together.

Luke, I know this doesn't excuse how he treated you, but after the telegram came, something broke in him. He sat on your bed, holding parts of the broken radio you had left in the box in the closet. He told me he was sorry. I can't tell you what to do, but I wanted you to know the truth.

He shook his head, trying to clear the web of tangled thoughts, his mind racing.

I've been meeting with Moses at the store every few weeks. He's teaching me about our Jewish heritage, our mother's faith. It's like filling a void that I didn't know was there. He talks about you constantly, as if you were his son. He jokes that when you come home, if you go back to work at the hardware store, he'll change the name to Weisbaum & Son. He laughs, but I think he's serious. He told me to remind you that you are safe in the shadow of the Almighty. He said you would understand. I hope so. It seemed important to him.

He brushed away a tear that rested on his cheek. Katie, his dad, and Moses, all tied together in a web of love, hate, prejudice, faith, and secrets. He wasn't sure he could untangle it all.

Shaina and I communicate often. She's remarkable. So strong in her faith. I phoned her after we received the telegram. It was hard to tell her the news, but she took it well. She said she knows you're coming home to us. She said God told her. I pray she is right. Know this, Luke, my dearest brother, we will never give up hope.

Love, Katie

He closed his eyes. *He who dwells in the shelter of the Most High will rest in the shadow of the Almighty*. He remembered the way Moses explained the verse, without preaching or pushing him to agree. "People hear the word shadow and they think of darkness, of hiding, of fear. But in the Jewish tradition, the shadow is a place of protection." And the part that he was still struggling to understand, "The shadow is not just about safety, it's about mystery. You don't always know what's in the shadow."

He folded the paper carefully, Katie's words racing through his mind; his father, sober and quiet; Moses, voicing divine protection; Katie and Shaina, forming a bond of faith and family.

He smiled. *Home still existed. And they were waiting.*

And then it hit him. Oskar said that he had removed Katie's letter from Dieter's desk. Based on the letter's date, the vengeful German had likely known that Luke was Jewish since January. Dieter had continually harassed him, trying to get him to admit his heritage, but could not admit he had stolen and hidden Luke's mail; the riddle now solved.

He slipped from his hiding place and retrieved his logbook from beneath the floorboard. By the same thin moonlight, he added a new entry.

Journal Entry: *March 20, 1945. Letter from Katie today. Written over two months ago. They know I'm missing. I hope they know I'm not dead. Dieter knows I am Jewish. He stole Katie's letter. Dad is changing? Katie and Shaina write to each other. Home seems possible again. The foxhole radio is almost complete. Just need a long wire antenna.*

Oskar Schottin sauntered through the camp's muddy grounds, his aging eyes scanning the debris near the administration building. He'd been assigned to oversee the clearing of trash, a menial task for an older guard, but today the assignment proved auspicious. Nestled among discarded papers and broken furniture, he saw a broken table fan, sure to contain an electric motor.

Luke had trusted the old guard with his plans for a radio. This motor contained exactly what the American needed, copper wire. Anything he could do to help end this war and get him out of this hellhole, back home and to his wife, was worth the risk. He could never get back Fritz, but he could help the young American who reminded him of his son get home.

Oskar glanced around, confirmed no one was watching, and slipped the small fan motor into his pocket.

"Just trash," he muttered to himself, continuing his patrol with feigned indifference.

Behind a nearby supply shed, Dieter stood motionless, watching Oskar's every move. The older guard's furtive glances and sudden pocket-stuffing aroused his suspicion. He couldn't see what the old guard had taken, but the secretive manner told him enough. He'd long suspected him of sympathizing with prisoners; now he had proof.

Oskar moved with deliberate casualness, visiting Block Nine first, then Block Ten, checking trash cans and speaking briefly with the guards whenever he found garbage on the ground. To anyone watching, he appeared to be performing routine trash inspections. But Dieter knew better. He followed at a distance, hidden from the older guard's view.

After forty minutes of patrolling, Oskar approached Block Twelve. Dieter's eyes narrowed. The door creaked open. The guard moved through the barracks, stopping at a trash can near Robby Lewis's bunk.

"Lewis," he said loud enough for others to hear. "Why is there trash outside the can?"

As he leaned down, pretending to inspect the floor for more loose waste, Oskar pressed the small motor into Lewis's palm. "Wire," he whispered. "For Luke."

Robby's fingers closed around the motor just as the barracks door opened. Dieter stood in the entrance, his cold eyes sweeping the room before locking onto Oskar and Lewis.

"What did you give him?" he demanded, striding forward, his limp more pronounced in his haste.

The old guard straightened; his expression impassive. "Extra bread."

Robby, thinking quickly, made exaggerated chewing motions, carefully tossing the motor to the back of his mattress, hoping it landed out of view.

"Bread?" Dieter's voice dripped with skepticism. He grabbed Oskar's collar and twisted it tight. "Show me your pockets."

"Empty now," he replied calmly, turning his pockets inside out. "I gave him the last piece."

Outraged, he turned to Robby. "Show me!"

Robby complied, opening wide, his mouth empty. "Swallowed it, sir. Thank you."

A ripple of nervous laughter moved through the barracks. Dieter's face darkened as he scanned the area around Robby's bunk. The motor lay hidden in the shadow of the crumpled blanket.

"So," Zobel said, turning back to Oskar, "you steal bread from the kitchen to feed prisoners?" His voice rose. "You betray Germany to coddle our enemies?"

"It was stale," Oskar replied. "Going to be thrown..."

The crack of Dieter's baton against Oskar's forehead echoed through the barracks. Blood splattered across Robby's blanket as the older man crumpled, his body hitting the floor with a sickening thud. A collective gasp blanketed the room. “He should not have moved,” Dieter said nervously. “I... I was aiming for his shoulder.”

Luke lunged forward, blind rage obliterating reason. Months of hunger, humiliation, and the young German's unceasing hatred crystallized into raw fury. His hands reached for the young guard’s throat.

Sergeant Whitfield's arms locked around him from behind, yanking him backward. "Not now,” he hissed in his ear, his grip iron-tight. "You'll die for nothing."

Luke struggled against the sergeant's restraint, watching blood pool beneath Oskar's head. The old guard's eyes glazed, fixed on the ceiling, his final act of kindness costing him his life.

Dieter lowered the baton, looking down at Oskar's body with detached interest. Blood had spattered his uniform, but he made no move to remove it.

"Take him to the infirmary," he ordered, gesturing to two nearby prisoners. "Or bury him. I don't care." He turned his cold gaze to the men watching, "This is what happens to those who forget to obey orders, ...prisoner or guard."

Luke shook with rage as Whitfield continued to hold him back. Dieter's eyes met Luke's, and something, perhaps an admission of how far he'd gone, passed between them. In that moment, he realized Luke Pierce would not hesitate to kill him.

"You," he said, looking directly at Luke, "remember this when you think of defying me."

He pivoted and walked out, his familiar limp more pronounced, leaving Oskar's blood to soak into the floorboard.

Whitfield released Luke only when the young guard was well away from the block. Luke collapsed onto his knees beside Oskar's body, tears streaming down his face.

"He killed him," he sobbed. "Just... just killed him."

"For a piece of bread," Robby added, his voice perking up as he retrieved the motor from his blanket. "Or for this."

He took the motor, feeling its weight, the last act of compassion from the one German who'd shown kindness in the often brutal, sadistic prison camp. The copper wire produced a dull glow in the barracks' dim light. At less than a pound, it represented both hope and devastating loss.

"Oskar knew what he was doing," Whitfield said, kneeling beside Luke. "He made his choice."

"He didn't deserve this," Luke replied, his voice breaking.

As prisoners carried Oskar's body away, Luke clutched the small motor. The rage inside him burned white-hot, threatening to consume everything: his hope, his humanity, his future with Shaina. He'd witnessed too much death: Brock in the Ardennes, others beaten and left for dead on the march, the boxcars, and now Oskar, murdered for no reason.

"I could have killed him," he said, his voice shaking. "Should have."

"And then what?" Whitfield asked. "You'd be dead, too. What good would that do Shaina? Or any of us?"

Luke looked down at the motor in his hands, the copper wire a key to completing the foxhole radio, their connection to the outside world. Oskar had given his life to bring them this chance.

"We finish the radio," he said, his voice steadying. "We hear what's happening beyond these walls. We survive." He looked up at his friends, wiping away the dried tears, determination replacing wrath. "We survive and we tell the world what happened here."

That evening, as darkness fell over the camp, Dieter avoided Block Twelve. The guards whispered that he'd been dressed down by *Hauptmann* Weber over Oskar's death. Nothing official happened, and the young German's abuse shifted from the Americans to the Soviets.

Later, Luke began carefully unwinding the copper wire from the motor, each turn a silent tribute to Oskar Schottin. The old guard's final gift would help connect them to the world beyond the barbed wire fences. He understood that this was the most expensive wire he had ever handled, the wire's length not measured in feet or inches, but in blood.

"Thank you," he whispered to the darkness. "You did not die in vain, my friend. I will always remember what you said, 'Small good things in bad places.' I promise, I will never let them forget your sacrifice."

In the days following the murder, Dieter's focus intensified. The Soviets, surviving on half-rations and denied Red Cross packages, became the continual target for his unchecked cruelty.

Luke watched from the work area as Dieter forced a group of emaciated Soviets to stand in the April rain for hours. One man, little more than skin stretched over bones, collapsed face-first into the mud. Instead of allowing medical attention, he ordered the man to crawl on his belly back to the barracks, prodding him with his boot when he moved too slowly.

"The Geneva Convention doesn't apply to Bolshevik animals," he announced, making sure the American prisoners could hear. His eyes drifted toward Block Twelve, his glare daring Luke or the others to intervene.

"He crossed a line with Oskar," Whitfield muttered to Luke. "Weber must have reprimanded him pretty harshly. Now he's taking it out on the weaker ones, the ones who can't fight back."

Luke nodded, the shovel in his hands suddenly feeling heavier. "When you hate that much, eventually you even hate yourself." Even as he said the words, he immediately thought of his father and the revelations in Katie's letter.

Schmidt, Dieter's loyal subordinate, stood nearby with his hand resting on his holster, watching the Americans with suspicious eyes. Since Oskar's death, the remaining guards, mostly teenagers trained in the Hitler Youth program themselves, had closed ranks around Dieter. Their faces showed the same mindless belief in Aryan superiority, drilled into them since childhood.

"Break time's over!" Schmidt barked in broken English. "Back to work!"

That evening in Block Twelve, the remnant of I Company gathered around Luke's nearly completed foxhole radio. The copper wire from the fan motor had been tightly wound around the toilet paper tube, forming the coil he needed.

"Any news about when the Allies might reach us?" Robby asked, his once-round face now gaunt from months of starvation.

Stevie shook his head. "Just rumors. Some say the Soviets are fifty miles away. Others claim the Americans have already taken Berlin."

"It's all bull crap," Turner spat. "We've been hearing the same rumors for weeks."

The monotony of imprisonment had become almost as unbearable as the hunger. Days melded together in an endless cycle of roll calls, watery turnip soup, and backbreaking labor. The initial solidarity among prisoners had begun to unravel under the weight of prolonged captivity. Petty arguments erupted over crumbs of bread or extra minutes near the heat of the burn barrel. *How long could they hold on?*

Luke connected the final wires to the makeshift earpiece, a ceramic cup with a small wire coil inside. "We'll know the truth soon enough," he said, fingers crossed.

After fifteen minutes of trying, there was nothing but some faint static. He realized he would need a longer antenna, elevated above the ground. Somehow, he needed the antenna to reach the peak of the barracks roof. The gathered prisoners were disappointed as he disassembled the foxhole radio, useless until he could get an effective antenna.

The next morning, Dieter arrived at roll call with a fresh batch of Soviet prisoners, their hollow eyes and shuffling gaits suggesting they'd been marched for days without adequate food or rest.

"New workers," he announced, smirking at the line of prisoners from Block Twelve. "These Soviet pigs will show you how real men work."

One Soviet, taller than the others, made eye contact with Luke. Something in his gaze, a quiet dignity despite the circumstances, reminded him of Oskar.

Throughout the day, Luke watched as Dieter singled out this particular prisoner, forcing him to carry impossibly heavy loads without rest. When the man stumbled, he struck him across the back with his baton, drawing blood through the thin fabric of his uniform.

"Stop looking, Luke," Whitfield warned. "You'll only make it worse for him."

"How much longer can this go on?" Luke asked, his voice muffled by the sound of shovels straining against the embedded coal.

"Until the war ends or we die," Stevie replied, humorless. "Whichever comes first."

Journal Entry: *April 15, 1945 - Dieter grows more desperate as rumors of Allied advances spread. The Soviets suffer most. Has to do with the Geneva Convention. I saw a man beaten until he couldn't stand, all because he looked a guard in the eye. The foxhole radio is finished, but couldn't get a strong signal. Tomorrow, we'll try to connect a better antenna. The men are desperate to hear something, anything, from the outside world.*

Forty-Two

"He knows," Whitfield murmured, his voice low as he worked beside Luke, careful to keep his head down. "Look at him. He's like a cornered animal. The Soviets must be closer than we thought."

Luke followed Whitfield's gaze across the muddy yard, taking care not to be obvious. Dieter's once-immaculate uniform was no longer snug, revealing the toll that dwindling rations had taken, even on the guards. Luke glanced toward the eastern horizon, where the sound of competing artillery rumbled. The German guard's limp seemed more pronounced today, his gloved hand wrapped around his baton as he thumped it against his right leg.

"Yeah, makes him more dangerous," Luke replied, driving his shovel into the damp earth with renewed effort. He could feel the blisters on his palms reopening, small stabs of pain that he'd come to ignore over the months of captivity. "Like wild animals, desperate men do desperate things."

Across the yard, Dieter shouted at a Soviet prisoner who had paused to catch his breath. The man, the same one Dieter had harassed days before, received a vicious blow to his kidneys that sent him sprawling face-first into the mud. For a moment, Luke thought he might not rise again. When another Soviet prisoner attempted to help him up, extending a thin hand to his comrade, Dieter struck him too, the baton delivering a bone-breaking blow to the man's forearm.

"Faster! All of you!" he screamed, his voice cracking with a fury that bordered on hysteria. Spittle flew wildly from his mouth as he continued his tirade, "The Reich demands your labor! Germany will prevail! Work or die where you stand!"

Schmidt and the younger guards, eager to prove their loyalty, followed his example, increasing their brutality toward the weakest Soviet prisoners. They moved through the work detail with calculated cruelty, striking at random to keep everyone in a perpetual state of terror. One prisoner, a man who had been coughing blood for days, collapsed onto his knees and didn't move again. The guards demanded that other prisoners drag his body aside, leaving a dark smear in the mud, then ordered the work to continue as if nothing unusual had occurred.

"He's losing control," Stevie said, his hollow cheeks flushed with anger. His once-bright eyes burned with intensity as the scene unfolded. "He sees the war's ending. They all do. Look at how they're trying to squeeze out the last drops of pain and suffering from the weak and helpless ones."

Luke nodded, scanning the perimeter where other guards stood watch, their nervous energy obvious even from a distance. "Which means we need that radio working tonight. If the Soviets are as close as we think, we have to know when to make our move and stop this madness." He drove his shovel into the ground with renewed determination, his mind racing with possibilities and dangers that lay ahead.

Dusk began to settle over Stalag IV-B, the sky gradually changing from blue to gray. Stevie crouched near the eastern corner of Block Twelve, a thin length of wire coiled in his left hand and a small rock tied to its end. Luke kept watch while Whitfield distracted the nearest guard with questions about the evening meal.

"Third time's a charm," he muttered, winding up for another throw after two failed attempts. His arm trembled with the effort, but he was resolved to succeed. The rock arced through the fading light, trailing the precious copper wire behind it. It cleared the edge of the roof and caught on a protruding vent. He tugged gently to test it, then nodded to Luke.

"Got it. But we'll need to get it down before the guards see it."

Luke glanced toward the guard towers. "Agreed. Tonight's our only chance. If they spot that wire, we're dead."

They moved inside with rehearsed casualness, their shuffling matching the other prisoners' exhausted movements. No one moved quickly in Stalag IV-B anymore. There wasn't energy for it, and any movement out of the ordinary attracted attention, which could mean death. In the dim barracks, Turner stood by the door, his gaunt face revealing nothing as he kept watch.

Luke knelt beside a loose floorboard near his bunk, prying it up. Beneath it lay their collection of contraband; the components of the foxhole radio, gathered over weeks through trades, theft, and the final gift from Oskar.

"Hand me the razor blade and the pencil lead," he whispered to Stevie, who passed them with shaky hands.

He connected the copper wire from Oskar's motor to the razor blade, then wound it around the pencil lead to create a crude detector. The toilet paper tube formed the coil, with the safety pin serving as a contact point. Every component represented a risk someone had taken.

Around them, Whitfield had organized a perimeter of men playing cards, telling stories, and pretending to engage in normal evening activities. Their bodies created a human shield around Luke's work, their voices calibrated to mask the sounds of the radio's assembly.

"If this works," Stevie said, "we'll know if the rumors are true."

Luke nodded, making a final adjustment to the wire. "For Oskar," he murmured, connecting the antenna wire that stretched to the roof.

He pressed the ceramic earpiece, salvaged from a broken field telephone, to his ear and began the delicate process of searching for a signal. His fingers made tiny adjustments to the contact point, probing for a voice in the static.

At first, there was nothing but hiss and crackle. Luke's heart sank. Then... a single voice, faint but unmistakable, speaking English with a British accent. He pressed the earpiece harder against his ear, straining to catch every word. He was confident it was a BBC broadcast. He knew the BBC had been adding broadcast locations throughout the war, now, even in the heart of Germany.

"The Allied forces have established bridgeheads across the Rhine at multiple points," the announcer stated with measured confidence. *"American and British troops continue their advance into the German heartland, while Soviet forces are now less than twenty miles from Berlin."*

His eyes widened. He passed the earpiece to Stevie, whose face transformed into a broad smile as he listened.

"My God," Stevie proclaimed, handing it to Whitfield. "It's almost over."

The news traveled through their circle in hushed whispers. The Soviets were coming. Freedom was no longer a distant dream, but an approaching reality.

"Someone's coming," Turner called from his position by the door.

In a few moments, Luke had disassembled the radio. His fingers worked with practiced speed, disconnecting wires, removing the components from the small board, wrapping them in a cloth, and dropping them into the hidden chamber beneath the floorboard. The antenna wire was pulled down and coiled beneath his thin blanket just as the barracks door creaked open. A young guard peered inside, his eyes suspicious, but his inspection cursory. Seeing nothing but weak and tired prisoners preparing for sleep, he moved on to the next block.

Whitfield went through the barracks afterward, spreading the news in hushed tones. Men who had been lying listless on their bunks sat up, eyes brightening with something that had been absent for months. *Hope.* Conversations broke out in corners, plans whispered between friends.

Luke sat on his bunk, running his fingers over the copper wire from Oskar's motor. The old guard's face flashed in his memory; his quiet defiance, his small kindnesses, his final sacrifice. He would live to tell that story. He would make it home to Shaina, to Katie, to a world where men like Dietrich Zobel couldn't abuse others without consequence. He hated the young German guard and all he represented, his never-ending rants, claiming to be of superior pure Aryan blood. He thought about his father and what hate had done to him, worried at what he had become during their confinement. *What do I do with this hate building in me? Am I just like my father?* He pushed the thought aside. For the first time in months, freedom seemed within reach, not just a wish to keep hopelessness at bay. "Soon," he whispered to himself, "Soon."

Forty-Three

For the next three days, whispers of liberation raced through the camp like electricity. Luke noticed the prisoners standing straighter, despite their hollow eyes and protruding ribs. Even the weakest men found reserves of strength, hope renewed, freedom possibly just days away.

The guards sensed it too. Patrols became erratic, as the Germans constantly looked eastward, where the sound of Soviet artillery grew louder each day. Some guards vanished overnight. Others clung to their routines, as if the familiar patterns could hold back the inevitable.

Dieter, though, became progressively more menacing. Luke viewed him from the corner of his eye during morning roll call, the guard's cheeks sunken, eyes feverish, an internal battle of rage and fear. The swagger, developed over a decade in Hitler Youth, remained, but desperation now overshadowed confidence.

"He knows it's ending," Stevie said. "You can see it in his face."

Luke nodded, keeping his head down. "That makes him more dangerous, not less."

That afternoon, the group of Soviet prisoners that had arrived a few weeks earlier once again gained Dieter's attention. They were in worse condition than any prisoners Luke had seen in Stalag IV-B. They were little more than walking skeletons with vacant eyes. All except one.

Dieter noticed him too. The guard's eyes narrowed as he stalked over, circling the prisoner like a vulture, just as he had done with Luke at the Gerolstein rail station.

"*Du*," he barked in German, "Name?"

The prisoner looked straight ahead. "Pavel Nikitin."

Zobel struck him across the face with his gloved hand. "Eyes down when speaking to me!"

The Soviet prisoner's gaze lowered, but Luke saw the difference in his stance; compliance, not submission; bending, not breaking.

All afternoon, the German targeted his latest victim. He assigned him the heaviest rocks, denied him water, and struck him at the slightest infraction. The prisoner absorbed the punishment in silence.

As the sun began to set, he ordered Nikitin to carry a boulder that far exceeded his capability. When he staggered, Dieter struck him behind the knees.

"Weak Soviet pig!" he shouted. "Get up!"

What happened next stunned the prisoners watching. As Nikitin rose to his knees, his hand shot out, grabbing the German's damaged leg. With a single, powerful twist, he toppled the guard.

The yard froze. For one breathless moment, no one moved. No other German guards were near to see the skirmish.

Dieter's face twisted with rage and pain as he scrambled for his sidearm. But before he could draw it, three other Soviet prisoners surged forward, pinning him down. One wrenched the Luger from his holster and handed it to Nikitin, while another pressed a hand over the despised German's mouth.

Nikitin stood, pistol in hand, ordering Dieter to his feet. The other Soviets forced him up.

Luke recognized that the tables had turned. All of the anger and grief of the past four months surged inside him, his tormentor now in the clutches of the abused, the ones Dieter had tortured on a whim, smiling. He deserved to die, and now was the time. He decided to act, sprinting toward the Soviets.

Four of them had surrounded the German, with Nikitin pointing the pistol at the guard's head. Their faces were masks of pure loathing, months of suffering and humiliation distilled into this single moment.

"Wait!" Luke shouted, pushing his way into the group.

The Soviets stared, confusion flashing in their eyes. Nikitin's finger remained on the trigger, his gaze cold, determined.

Luke raised his hand in a halting motion, his look pleading. "Please," he said, hoping at least one of the Soviets understood English. "Don't do it. Not like this."

Nikitin's eyes narrowed. He understood.

"Yes, he deserves to die," Luke said, voice trembling but strong. "I know he deserves it. God knows he's earned it. But not like this."

Behind him, Dieter trembled. Luke could feel the man's fear radiating like heat. The guard who had tormented him for months, who had murdered Oskar, who had burned Shaina's photograph while laughing, now cowered.

"If you kill him," Luke said, meeting Nikitin's gaze, "if you let your hatred decide, we become no better than them." He gestured at the guard towers, the barracks, the barbed wire fences, everything the Nazis had built. "This place exists because of hatred. Because people decided others were less than human: Gypsies, Jews, Soviets."

Nikitin spoke to the others in Russian. One spat on the ground, gesturing disdainfully at the German guard.

"I know what he's done," Luke pressed. "I know what all of them have done. But our liberators are near, Soviets like you. Let justice prevail, not vengeance."

He turned, looking at Dieter for the first time. The German's face was ashen, sweat beading on his brow. His eyes darted between Luke and the Soviets, calculating.

"He will pay," Luke said, turning back to the Russian. "They all will. But we cannot become what we hate."

Nikitin translated. The Soviets argued, gesturing angrily. One mimed a hanging. Another tapped his head where Oskar had been struck.

"This man," Nikitin said in halting English, "he kill many. Why you protect?"

Luke took a deep breath. The question pierced him. *Why was he protecting Dietrich Zobel?* He stared at the sadistic German who had made his life hell, who had targeted him for his Jewish heritage, and who had murdered a kind man who tried to help. Every instinct inside him screamed for revenge.

But something much deeper spoke louder.

"I'm not protecting him," he said calmly. "I'm protecting us. What makes us different?" He gestured toward Dieter. "He chose hatred. We must choose something better."

Nikitin studied him for a long moment. The yard was silent, every eye watching.

"You are Jew. I see it. Like my friend in Minsk."

Luke stiffened but didn't deny it. "Yes, my mother was Jewish. He tilted his head toward Dieter, "That's why he targeted me."

The Russian's eyes widened. He spoke again to his comrades, his voice softer now. The Soviet prisoner's expressions shifted from rage to something more complex.

"You have more reason to kill him," Nikitin said, offering Luke the firearm.

Luke declined the Luger. "Maybe I do, but I won't. If I kill him in revenge, he wins."

There was a long silence. Luke remained fixed, every muscle taut. Behind him, Dieter stirred nervously.

At last, Nikitin lowered the pistol. "You are right," he said. "We are not them. Never them."

The others protested, but he silenced them with a single word. "*Nyet.*" Reluctantly, they released the German, stepping back.

Then Nikitin did the unthinkable. He reversed the pistol, holding it with the handle extended to Dieter.

"Take," he said.

Time stopped. Dieter stared at the offered weapon, stunned. His hand trembled as he reached for the Luger from the Soviet, then straightened. Some of his old arrogance returned as he felt the weight and security of the weapon. He raised it, pointing first at Nikitin, then at Luke.

“You think this makes you better? Your mercy is weakness.”

Luke met his gaze. “I'm a Jew, and I am no less or greater than anyone here. And you, Dietrich Zobel, are certainly no better than any man here. You have hated me for no reason except for the Nazi lies you were fed as a child. You fight for a cause that is crumbling.”

“You know nothing of my sacrifices! My brother's death,” Dieter raged, but something in him wavered. For an instant, Luke saw past the German's uniform, past the Hitler Youth indoctrination, to the broken man beneath.

Dieter's finger tensed on the trigger. Luke didn't flinch.

From across the yard, the camp commander shouted, "Zobel!"

Dieter jerked, saw the commander, and quickly holstered the weapon. Without a word, he turned and limped away, his shoulders hunched, defeat written in his gait.

The Soviets watched him go, their expressions a mixture of disbelief and revulsion.

Nikitin turned to Luke. "You have courage," he said. "More than him."

Luke took a deep breath, the pent-up tension draining from his body. He thought of Matya, Shaina, Katie, Brock, Oskar, Stevie, and Moses Weisbaum, the people who mattered in his life. The past four months had been dark, very dark, but he realized he'd never been alone. He remembered Oskar's words in the supply shed: "We must guard against becoming what we fight against."

Standing in the dirt yard of the prison camp, freedom just days away, he finally understood. Victory wasn't defeating the enemy, whether that enemy was an abusive father, a hate-filled German guard, or the entire Third Reich. True victory was refusing to let hatred forge good men into the men they fought against.

Journal Entry: *April 20, 1945 – I'm Jewish. I'm a proud Jew. No more secrets. Now, I can tell my story without fear. The whole story. These pages hold my pain, my fears, and my dreams. The words I've scribbled, often in darkness, are silent witnesses that the stars still shine, even in the shadows.*

Forty-Four

For the next two days, an uneasy calm settled over the camp. The guards moved through the camp indifferently, completely ignoring prisoners who, before, they had scrutinized like hawks. Prisoners now talked openly, no longer needing to whisper. They made a game of counting the growing number of empty guard towers.

"Guard in tower three's gone," someone shouted. "That makes five."

Less concerned about the consequences, but still cautious, Luke tuned the foxhole radio with painstaking precision, his fingers working the delicate components they'd scavenged and assembled. The men of I Company huddled in a tight circle to hear the latest BBC reports. Faint transmissions described Soviet forces plowing relentlessly from the east. At the same time, American and British troops pushed from the west, embarking on a race to Berlin, which was nearly surrounded and caught in a tightening vise. Hitler's thousand-year Reich, built on hatred and bravado, was collapsing.

"Won't be long," Whitfield said, his voice steady. He had survived too much to risk hope carelessly. "Another week at most. Possibly less if they keep running."

Stevie grinned. Eyes sunken from months of near-starvation, he still managed his characteristic sarcasm: "Think they'll just open the gates and run? Maybe leave us a nice note saying 'Sorry for the inconvenience, help yourselves to whatever's left in the kitchen'?" Luke laughed, along with all the men from I Company.

"Yeah, some will run," Luke said, thinking of the younger guards, boys really, who recoiled at every distant rumble. "They know what happens to the losers. A few might fight to the end. The true believers." He adjusted the radio's connection, careful not to lose the signal he'd found.

"And Zobel?" Turner asked, his fingers tracing the scar along his jaw where Dieter had struck him with a rifle butt months earlier. "What about that bastard?"

Luke didn't answer immediately. He'd seen Dieter earlier that day, limping, not strutting, across the yard. The guard's transformation was striking, unsettling in its completeness. His eyes, once burning with ferocity, were now hollow. His swagger, the physical manifestation of his cruelty, was abandoned; his movements were now cautious and uncertain, baton gone. The twenty-year-old Nazi guard who had terrorized the prisoners for months, drawing strength from their suffering, was experiencing his entire superior worldview collapsing around him.

"He's broken," Luke said, "But that doesn't make him less dangerous. "A dying snake, even one that's dead, can still deliver venom."

The next morning, Luke spotted Dieter standing alone by the camp's eastern fence, staring at the horizon, waiting for something. When their eyes met across the yard, he saw something he'd never expected: uncertainty and fear. The German looked away, barking half-hearted orders at nearby prisoners before limping toward the administration building. His voice lacked its former authority, his commands delivered without conviction.

"He knows what's coming," Whitfield observed.

Luke nodded. "The Soviets will want revenge. Especially for what he did to their people."

"Can't say I'd blame them," the sergeant replied.

Throughout the day, Dieter went through the motions of his duties—counting inmates at roll call, assigning light work details, patrolling the perimeter—but the cruel edge was gone. He no longer punished minor infractions. He had become a ghost of his former self.

The prisoners still gave him a wide berth. No one met his gaze or engaged with him. When he approached, conversations died. The Soviets viewed him with cold, calculating eyes, their hatred deep. Given the opportunity, they still might kill him.

Luke saw him pause outside Block Twelve, his hand moving to the door's handle, then dropping away. For a moment, it seemed he might speak, might ask for something; understanding, or even help. But pride kept him silent, and he limped away without a word.

"He's looking for allies," Stevie observed later. "He knows the Soviets will kill him if they get the chance. He would already be dead, if not for you, Luke."

"He's not our problem," Turner interrupted. "After what he did to Oskar, let the Soviets have him."

Luke said nothing, but once again, he remembered Oskar's words about doing small good things in bad places. He wondered what the kind guard would say now, with liberation so close, vengeance at hand. Somehow, he was sure Oskar would choose mercy, not for Dieter's sake, but for theirs.

On 23 April 1945, Stalag IV-B awoke to rumbling that grew steadily louder. It was the same sound they had heard at 0530 on 16 December; the unmistakable sound of tanks. But this time, they were not enemy tanks. By mid-morning, the remaining German guards had gathered in the administration building, their faces drawn with fear.

"It's happening," Stevie said, gripping Luke's arm. "They're coming."

The prisoners gathered in small groups, looking eastward, inside the single barbed wire that previously would have meant certain death. No one tried to stop them. The camp's everyday routines had been abandoned: there was no roll call, no work details, and no guards patrolling the perimeter.

Shortly after noon, the first Soviet vehicles appeared, grinding toward the camp. Luke watched from the front of Block Twelve. After months of captivity, starvation, and abuse, freedom was now at their doorstep.

"Look," Whitfield said, pointing toward the administration building.

A white flag had appeared, hanging from an upstairs window. Moments later, the main gates swung open, and the camp commander and a handful of guards, including Dietrich Zobel, emerged, hands raised in surrender.

The Soviet forces approached, tanks positioned at strategic points around the perimeter, while infantry advanced through the gates. An officer stepped forward to meet the Germans, his voice carrying across the yard as he demanded an immediate and unconditional surrender.

The camp commandant met him, unholstering his pistol and offering it, grip-first. The guards followed suit, voluntarily disarming themselves.

Luke scanned the assembled Germans, spotting Dieter standing apart from the others. The former adversary looked small, his arrogance utterly deflated.

As the Soviets took control of the camp, prisoners began to emerge from their barracks, moving cautiously at first, then with growing confidence.

The Soviet soldiers were greeted by the prisoners, especially the Soviet prisoners, as liberators, with cheers and embraces.

Luke, Whitfield, and Stevie moved together toward the main gate, drawn by a commotion. They saw the Soviets secure the guards, binding their hands and forming them into a line for transport. When they reached Zobel, something changed. Pavel Nikitin appeared suddenly, pointing and speaking Russian to the officer in charge. Other Soviet prisoners joined him, their voices rising in accusation, their gestures animated.

"They're telling them about him," Stevie said. "About what he did."

Luke nodded in agreement, watching as the Soviet officer's expression darkened. The officer barked an order, and two soldiers grabbed Dieter roughly, pulling him away from the other Germans.

"Should we say something?" Stevie asked, looking uncertainly at Luke and Whitfield.

Whitfield shook his head. "What would we add? That he was cruel to us, too? The Soviets suffered the worst at his hands. They have plenty of evidence of his cruelty."

"Sarge is right," Luke said. "What he did to the Soviets is enough. We don't need to add our two cents."

They watched as Dieter was led away, his head bowed. For a moment, he looked up, his gaze sweeping across the yard until he found Luke. Something passed between them, not understanding or forgiveness. *Recognition?* Then he was gone, pushed into a waiting truck with the other Germans.

"You think they'll execute him?" Stevie asked.

"Probably not," Whitfield replied. "The Soviets will want information, and then he'll probably face trial."

Luke felt an emptiness where disdain for the German had long lived. "He won't be free for many years, if ever. He imprisoned himself... shackled by hate. Maybe one day he'll find that God's mercy can break his chains."

As the truck carrying the Germans pulled away, he felt the weight lift from his shoulders. The man who had tormented him, who had killed Oskar Schottin, and who had brutalized countless others, was now powerless. "It's over," he sighed.

Whitfield clapped a hand on his shoulder. "Not quite. We still need to get home."

His thoughts turned to Shaina, waiting in New Jersey, and Katie, waiting in Hanford. Soon, he could move forward with the life he'd put on hold to fight this war.

A Soviet liberator approached, offering cigarettes and chocolate from a canvas bag. The man's smile was genuine, his eyes kind, despite the weariness etched on his face. Luke thought of Oskar.

"Thank you, Luke said, "You do good things in a bad place."

The kind Soviet had no idea what Luke meant, but he smiled, moving on to other prisoners with his bag of delights.

As the day wore on, Luke assisted Soviet medical teams in tending to the sickest prisoners, while other healthy prisoners helped distribute food and supplies. The camp that had been their prison was transformed before his eyes. In the barracks, he removed his boots, then picked up the right boot. He took the foxhole radio's razor blade and carefully cut the seam of the boot's tongue. Smiling, he removed the locket Shaina had given him on the final day they were together. He held it up to the light. Like his faith, it no longer required hiding.

That night, sitting outside Block Twelve under a dark sky filled with stars, Luke wrote in his journal.

Journal Entry: *April 23, 1945 - We are free. The Soviets arrived today. Dieter Zobel has been taken away to face justice. I thought I would feel triumph when they cuffed him. I felt relief. It's over. We survived. Soon we'll be going home. I think of Brock often. I'm glad he didn't experience Stalag IV-B. I think of Oskar, too, and so many others who didn't make it. Their stories deserve to be told. That will be my life's purpose when I return. Tell the stories so that they are never forgotten.*

The next morning, Luke woke to the unfamiliar sound of Soviet voices outside Block Twelve. For a moment, he thought he was dreaming, the absence of German commands and whistles surreal after months of captivity.

A Soviet officer gathered the former prisoners in the yard, standing atop a wooden crate as an interpreter translated his words. The man introduced himself as General Konstantin Novikov, his uniform adorned with medals that shone brightly in the sun.

"You are no longer under German control," the interpreter relayed. "The fascists have been removed."

A cheer rose from the assembled men, then quieted when the general raised his hand.

"However, according to the Yalta Agreement signed in February, prisoners cannot be released until diplomatic arrangements are made. You will remain here under Soviet protection."

A collective sigh rippled through the men. Luke exchanged glances with Whitfield, whose expression remained neutral.

"What's he saying?" Stevie questioned. "We're still prisoners?"

"Not prisoners," Whitfield responded. "Just not free to leave yet."

The general continued, explaining that they would receive food, medical attention, and protection while diplomatic channels worked to arrange their return home. The process, he warned, could take several weeks.

As the men went back to their barracks, Whitfield gathered the remnant from I Company.

"This isn't ideal," he admitted, "but it's better than before. The war's still going on out there. Maybe it's safer here until things are settled for good."

Luke thought of Nelson and Lewis, too sick to leave their beds to hear the general's announcement. Nelson's dysentery had worsened in the last few weeks, and Lewis' frostbitten feet had developed a dangerous infection that Auckland had been fighting with limited supplies.

"Some of our guys wouldn't be able to make it home right now anyway," Luke said. "It's better we stay here with them."

The men established new routines. Soviet medics visited Block Twelve each morning, examining the sickest men. They provided sulfa drugs for Lewis's infection and a tonic for Nelson's dysentery. The medicine was basic but effective, and within a week, both men improved.

"You're lucky," a Soviet doctor told Auckland in broken English. "Many camps, guards kill sick ones before we arrive."

Auckland looked at the doctor and shook his head, "Believe me, we've had more than our share of dying."

April turned into May, and still they waited. Some men grew restless, arguing that they should attempt to leave on their own, but Whitfield counseled patience.

"The fighting's still going on," he reminded them. "And we don't know the territory. Better to wait for official transport."

Luke spent his days helping Auckland tend to the recovering men. Nelson's condition steadily improved; his sunken cheeks filled out as he ate more food. Lewis's infection retreated, though Auckland warned he might always walk with a slight limp.

"Maybe I'll become a prison guard. You know, like Dieter Zobel," he joked. Nobody laughed.

On 8 May, the Soviets brought a *Volksempfänger*, the German people's radio, to the yard and gathered all the prisoners. The scene reminded Luke of the Emerson 502 at Weisbaum's, where customers gathered around the radio to hear the latest war news back in 1942, a lifetime ago. The crackling announcement confirmed what many had suspected: Germany had surrendered. The war in Europe was over.

The celebration was subdued; the men were too weak and too traumatized to engage in wild jubilation. Luke felt something loosen in his chest, a knot of tension he'd carried since that first artillery barrage in the Ardennes Forest.

"We made it," Stevie said, his voice thick with emotion. "We made it."

"Not all of us," Luke replied.

The first week of June brought the news they'd been waiting for. American transport had been arranged. They would be going home.

On their final morning at Stalag IV-B, Luke gathered with the surviving men of I Company: Whitfield, Stevie, Auckland, Turner, Nelson, and Lewis. They stood together in the yard where they had endured countless roll calls, where they had been humiliated and starved, and where they had seen fellow soldiers weaken and die.

Whitfield looked at each man in turn. "Whatever happens next, remember what we survived here. Remember what we learned about each other, ...and about ourselves."

Luke smiled, thinking of Oskar's sacrifice and all the many acts of courage and kindness that had sustained them through their darkest days. He thought of the foxhole radio that had given them hope, of the journal where he'd begun recording their ordeal.

"We should go," Auckland said, gesturing toward the gates where trucks waited.

As they walked from Block Twelve for the final time, Luke had a strange mix of emotions; relief, certainly, but also a solemn recognition of what they had endured together. They had entered this place as prisoners and were leaving as survivors, carrying wounds, both visible and invisible.

For the men of I Company, the war was over. It was time to go home.

Epilogue

Tuesday, September 18, 1945

The morning dawned clear and bright over Hanford, California. Luke stood at the window of his childhood bedroom, Tippy at his feet, refusing to let him out of his sight. The war was now over everywhere; Japan's unconditional surrender sixteen days earlier made it official.

A knock at the door interrupted his thoughts.

"Come in," he called.

Katie entered, dressed in her maid-of-honor's gown—a simple blue dress that matched her eyes. "Look at you," she said, smiling. "My little brother, all grown up." She crossed the room and straightened his tie. "Shaina's parents just arrived. Her mother's already crying."

"And Dad?"

"Not yet," she shrugged. "But he said he might come. A Jewish wedding ceremony might be too much to ask at this point."

He smiled, unsurprised. His father had been making an effort to bridge the chasm between them. The fact that he'd considered attending the Jewish wedding ceremony at all represented progress, unimaginable before the war.

"Are you nervous?" she asked.

"About marrying Shaina? No," he smiled. "That's the one thing I'm certain about."

"You deserve this happiness, Luke. After everything..."

"We all do," he said, thinking of those who hadn't returned from the battlefield, who would never have the chance he now had to marry and raise a family. "Brock should be here."

She squeezed his arm. "He is, in his way."

Both heard the sound of the front door opening, followed by familiar voices, Stevie's laugh, then Matt Whitfield's deeper tones.

"Your groomsmen await," she said. "I'll go check on Shaina."

As she turned to leave, he caught her hand. "Katie? Thank you. For everything. For keeping Mom's memory alive, for taking risks with Dad, for discovering the truth."

She blinked back sudden tears. "We did it together. We always do."

After she left, he took one last look around the room. The Zenith radio Moses had given him sat on his dresser, alongside his Red Cross YMCA journal and a photograph of I Company taken at Camp Atterbury, many of the boys in the photo now casualties of the war.

Stevie and Matt waited in the living room, both in dark suits with white carnations in their lapels. Carl Auckland stood by the fireplace, examining the family photographs, now including the photo Katie had found, restoring Matya to her rightful place.

"There he is," Stevie said, grinning as Luke entered the living room. "The man of the hour."

Matt crossed the room and clasped Luke's shoulder. "Ready for the big day, soldier?"

"As ready as I'll ever be," he replied.

The men laughed, the sound warm and genuine in the morning light. There was an ease between them that could only come from shared hardship, a bond born of survival.

"Mrs. Dugan stopped by earlier," Stevie said. "She's determined to get your journals published."

"She believes the world needs to know what happened," Luke replied. "I agree, and not just the battles, but the quiet moments. The waiting. The heroes we lost."

"And the heroes we found," Matt added. "Like Oskar Schottin."

Luke paused, remembering the guard who had risked everything, who paid the ultimate price, the man who did small good things. "Especially Oskar."

"Speaking of finding people," Stevie said, his expression turning bashful. "Katie and I have a date this weekend."

Luke raised an eyebrow. "Is that so?"

"Don't give me that look," Stevie protested. "I've had my eye on your sister since our sophomore year."

"I know," Luke said, smiling. "Everyone knew... except Katie."

"She knows now," he replied, brimming with confidence gained in battle. Stevie Cower, the awkward teen who'd boarded the bus to Camp Roberts two years before, had returned a man who knew his worth.

"Brock would approve," Luke said.

They drove to the Civic Auditorium in Stevie's Chevrolet, a gift from his parents on his return. The streets were a blur of memorable storefronts and trees clothed in multicolored autumn leaves. The town looked much as it had when Luke left, but he saw it differently now, appreciating its quiet beauty, its familiarity, in ways he couldn't have before.

The auditorium had been decorated with white flowers and blue ribbons. Outside, people gathered in small groups; neighbors, former classmates, and fellow veterans, some in uniform. He recognized Brock's parents standing near the entrance, their faces solemn.

As he approached them, Mrs. Brockman reached out and took Luke's hands in hers. "We're so glad for you," she said, her voice steady despite the grief that was mirrored in her eyes. "Tim would have wanted to see this day."

"He should be here, standing beside me," he replied.

Mr. Brockman, standing beside his wife, agreed. "We know. But hearing about how brave he was, how he never lost his spirit, even at the end, that helps." Luke nodded, then hugged Brock's father, holding him close. Both men fought back tears. The moment required no more words.

Inside, the auditorium filled quickly. Luke stood at the front with Rabbi Ezra Cohen, who had traveled from Fresno at Moses Weisbaum's request. When he saw the elderly rabbi, he remembered that it was the same man who had visited Weisbaum's back in early 1943 and had given him, at the time, what had seemed like a senseless riddle: "The path is dark, but the stars still shine." Now, he understood, and he was pleased that such a wise man was officiating his wedding.

Moses Weisbaum sat in the front row, beaming with pride. It would have been easy to mistake him for the father of the groom.

The *klezmorim*, with their violin, clarinet, and viola, began to play *kallah's bageyn*, the bride's song as Shaina appeared, radiant in a simple white gown, her dark hair pinned back with small white flowers. She carried a bouquet of red roses. Her father, a stocky man with the same warm brown eyes as his daughter, held her arm in his as they walked down the center aisle.

Luke's breath caught at the sight of her. After months of separation, the uncertainty of his imprisonment, and the joyful reunion upon his return, this moment was nothing short of a miracle.

Rabbi Cohen welcomed the guests and spoke about the significance of marriage in Jewish tradition, particularly during times of renewal after great suffering. "Today we gather not just to celebrate the union of Lucas and Shaina, but to honor survival, renewal, and hope. Many of our young men went to war. Not all returned. Today, we celebrate not just love, but sacrifice."

Luke lowered the veil over Shaina's face, as she circled him seven times, representing the creation of a new family. The rabbi recited blessings over a cup of wine, which both Luke and Shaina sipped from, explaining that it symbolized their shared life.

When it came time for the exchange of rings, Luke's hands quivered. Shaina steadied them with her own as he placed the simple gold band on her finger. "*Harei at mekudeshet li*," he recited, Hebrew words he'd rehearsed numerous times over the past few weeks. "Behold, you are consecrated to me with this ring according to the laws of Moses and Israel."

After seven blessings, Rabbi Cohen wrapped them both in his prayer shawl, creating a moment of private communion amidst the public ceremony. "Remember this moment," he whispered to them. "In difficult times, return to it."

The ceremony concluded with Luke breaking a glass wrapped in cloth with the heel of his foot. The sharp crack was followed by shouts of "*mazel tov*" as the guests erupted in applause.

For the remainder of the day, the room was filled with celebration. Katie laughed at something Stevie said, their hands intertwined. The nine-month age difference that had seemed an impossible chasm in high school had vanished in the wake of war. He had returned from Europe a different man, and she had noticed the change immediately. Luke eyed them with a smile, more thankful than ever for his loving sister and his devoted friend.

Carl Auckland approached with two glasses of champagne and handed one to him. "To survival," he toasted.

"And to those who didn't make it," Luke added.

Matt Whitfield joined them, raising his glass. "To the path ahead."

Shaina joined them, slipping her hand into Luke's, her touch sending chills down his back. "What are we toasting to?" she asked.

Luke glanced around at the faces of those who had helped shape his journey: Katie, who had kept their mother's memory alive; Moses, who had guided him with wisdom; Matt, Carl, and Stevie, who had helped keep him alive through combat and imprisonment; and Mrs. Dugan, who had helped him find his voice.

"To coming home," he said, lifting his glass. "And to new beginnings."

As the glasses clinked together, he experienced a feeling of completion. The war had stolen much from him, but it had also uncovered truths he would never have discovered otherwise: about claiming his heritage without shame, how to act with courage, even when circumstances were overwhelming, and that the world was filled with the potential for kindness, but also for cruelty. Every person was free to choose which of these they would pursue.

A few minutes later, Moses Weisbaum appeared at Luke's side, his eyes twinkling. "*Der yung-er iz gevorn a mentsh,* the young one has become a man." Luke looked at the wise old sage whose insights had carried him through times of confusion, with endearing admiration. "Mr. Weisbaum, I mean Moses, you have been like a father to me. I can never repay you for the wisdom you have given me. When I was on the battlefield, and later, in the German prison camp, your words gave me hope when I wanted to give up."

"No, my son," Moses said, holding Luke's gaze, "You are kind, but it is not my wisdom. It is God's wisdom that sustained you." He smiled, then added, "Well, my prayers may have helped a little."

Luke chuckled, then drew the older man to his chest and kissed him on the forehead.

Luke concluded that the day was a complete success except for the one thing that remained unresolved, reconciliation with his father. They were closer, but the gap still existed. He dismissed the concern, choosing to focus on the joy of his wedding day, despite his father's decision not to attend.

A little while later, Stevie told Katie that he needed to speak with Luke and asked if she would join them. The three moved to a quiet corner of the hall. Luke saw that Stevie was nervous, and encouraged him to share whatever was bothering him.

Stevie, hesitant, looked at Luke, "Your father was here earlier, before the ceremony, but he couldn't bring himself to come in. It was tough seeing him so unsettled. He asked me for a favor."

"Yeah?" Luke said, confused.

"He asked me to give you the gift from him. He asked that you open it privately, apart from the other wedding gifts, and in the presence of Katie. It's on the table with the other presents. It's the one wrapped in plain brown paper. Not very fancy, huh?" The three laughed, then walked to the table.

Luke gestured for Shaina to join them. He and Shaina were one now. He didn't want any secrets between them. He'd had enough of keeping secrets.

Together, they unwrapped the gift. Luke froze, alarming Shaina, who didn't understand his reaction. With the paper removed, a brand-new RCA Model 143 radio was revealed, its walnut cabinet buffed to a brilliant shine. Luke stood motionless, staring at the radio.

Katie broke the silence, "I think ...I think it's his way of saying he's sorry, Luke."

"I wish he would just say the words, but for now, this will do." Luke turned his head away from the others, not wanting them to see the tears he was struggling to hold back. He would have liked to hug his father, to tell him he loved him and that he was forgiven, but for now, that would have to wait.

Later, as the celebration continued, Luke and Shaina stepped outside into the warm September evening. The sky above Hanford was clear, stars emerging one by one as dusk gave way to night.

"What are you thinking about?" she asked, her head resting against his shoulder.

He considered the question. He thought about the teenager who had swept the floor at Weisbaum's Hardware, listening to war news and fearing the draft. He thought about the soldier who had huddled in a frozen foxhole, the prisoner who had endured Zobel's hatred, and the man who had finally come to grips with his heritage.

"I'm thinking about stories," he said. "The ones we tell others, the ones others tell us, and most importantly, the ones we tell ourselves."

"And which story are you thinking about now?" she asked.

Luke looked down at her, at the Star of David shining in the starlight, identical to the one Katie now wore in honor of their mother.

"That even in the darkest times, there are always stars to guide us home," he said. "And that home isn't simply a place. It's the people who stand by you, no matter what."

She smiled and reached up to touch his face. "That's a good story."

"It's our story now," he said, and bent to kiss her beneath the canopy of stars.

In the distance, music played and laughter rose from the reception. Tomorrow would bring its challenges: a college degree to earn, a new home to build, and a life to create together. But tonight, in this moment of perfect peace, Luke and Shaina Pierce were precisely where they belonged.

Author's Note

Besides honoring the brave men of the 106th Infantry Division, the "Golden Lions," *Shadows Beneath the Stars* carries a personal significance. My father, PFC Mason L. Lane, served in the 106th Infantry Division, 423rd Regiment, Company I. The fictional Luke Pierce's military ID number, 39421436, is actually my father's ID, issued in 1943.

It has been my goal to be as historically accurate as possible, particularly regarding the events of 16-19 December 1944. As relayed by the fictional character Brent Young, history records that the efforts of the 106th Infantry Division were vital in delaying the Germans' goal of taking St. Vith by 17 December. Without their efforts, the outcome of the Battle of the Bulge might have been dramatically different.

Like Luke, my father was captured, marched through freezing snow, loaded into a cramped boxcar, and imprisoned in Stalag IV-B until he was liberated in April 1945. For his service, my father received several awards, including the Purple Heart for wounds received near Radscheid in the *Schnee Eifel*. Like Stevie Cower in the novel, my father was an expert marksman.

In 1985, Congress established the Prisoner of War Medal, which my father received in early 1986. It was one of his proudest moments. He passed away in 1990 at age 65. It is my sincere hope that this, my debut novel, serves as a worthy tribute to his memory and service .

FOR FURTHER READING

If you enjoyed *Shadows Beneath the Stars*, you might also appreciate these works of nonfiction that provide essential history, firsthand accounts, and deeper context than a fictional novel allows:

Warriors of the 106th – *Martin King, Ken Johnson, Michael Collins*
A vivid chronicle that follows the men of the 106th Infantry Division into the chaos of the Battle of the Bulge, sharing soldiers' stories of heroism, sacrifice, and survival, even as POWs.

St. Vith: Lion in the Way: 106th Infantry Division in World War II – *R. Ernest Dupuy*
A classic account focused on the pivotal battle for St. Vith, the experiences of the 106th Infantry Division, and the events that led to mass capture and imprisonment.

Survival at Stalag IVB – *Tony Vercoe*
Rich with firsthand POW testimonies, this book offers a compassionate sobering view into life, resilience, and loss within Stalag IV-B.

Boys, Just Boys: Stories from the 106th – *Brian Welke*
Drawing from personal memoirs and letters, Welke's work captures the unvarnished experiences of young soldiers thrust into Europe's deadliest winter and, for many, POW camps.

Made in the USA
Coppell, TX
18 January 2026